Terror in Paris

(a novel)

Dave Admire

Three Towers Press
Milwaukee, Wisconsin

Published by
Three Towers Press
An imprint of HenschelHAUS Publishing, Inc.
www.HenschelHAUSbooks.com

HenschelHAUS titles may be purchased in bulk for educational,
business, fundraising, or promotional use. For information,
please email info@henschelhausbooks.com

Hardcover ISBN: 978159598-485-2
Paperback ISBN: 978159598-486-9
E-ISBN: 978159598-487-6
Library of Congress Control Number: 2016951841

Publisher's Cataloging-In-Publication Data
(Prepared by The Donohue Group, Inc.)
Names: Admire, Dave.
Title: Terror in Paris : a novel / Dave Admire.
Description: Milwaukee, Wisconsin : Three Towers Press, an imprint of
    HenschelHAUS Publishing, Inc., [2016]
Identifiers: LCCN 2016951841 | ISBN 978-1-59598-485-2 (hardcover) |
    ISBN 978-1-59598-486-9 (paperback) | ISBN 978-1-59598-487-6 (ebook)
Subjects: LCSH: Foreign study--Fiction. | College students--Fiction. |
    Terrorism--France--Paris--Fiction. | Suspense fiction. | Paris (France)--Fiction.
Classification: LCC PS3611.D58 T47 2016 | DDC 813.6--dc23

Cover design by Ryan Allen, Big R Design.com

Printed in the United States of America or other location.

This book is dedicated to my wife, Sharyl.
It is only because of her unending love and constant support
that this book has become a reality.

Chapter 1

The room was dark and to some, forbidding. Samir lay in his bed, not asleep yet not awake. A few minutes passed. He slowly opened his eyes and glanced around the room. It was simple and somewhat stark. No photos or pictures hung on the wall. The only furniture consisted of his bed, a nightstand, an old sofa, a small desk and chair. This room, which he rented, reminded him of every other place he had stayed since leaving home. He took comfort in the sameness of the places he had stayed.

Samir was used to simple things and found it difficult to understand why so many people needed so many useless objects. More specifically, he found the Americans' need to possess things as indicative of the corrupt nature of their values. It was bad enough that they did this among themselves, but now, they were bringing this moral decay to millions of Muslims around the world.

He rose, walked to the bathroom and glanced at the old mirror hanging from the wall. Samir smiled, as he always did, when he saw his reflection. The image that stared back at him was not what he imagined he looked like. He wondered if other people had similar reactions. His face was thin, as was his physique. He really should eat more, he thought, but there were just too many things to do.

Samir looked down at the sink. The white porcelain reminded him of the porcelain bowls he used at home as a child. He remembered his childhood with fondness. His life was not unlike other children in his village; however, his dreams were greater than most. Samir's dream had always been to be a doctor. He had seen too many children suffer from the lack of medical care. Even as a child, he knew that he could make a difference for his people. Samir had a vision far beyond his friends and was not content to simply follow the life of most of the people in his village. He would make a difference.

His parents knew that he was unique. Not only in his abilities and intelligence, but also that he had a unique quality of leadership. Even as a child playing in the street, other children flocked to him and followed him as he led them in their playtime. Leadership came easily to him. In fact, he never really thought about the qualities of leadership. Leading others was simply so easy for him that there was no need to even think about it. His mother encouraged his dreams of becoming a doctor when she told him he could help so many. His father rarely spoke to him, but Samir felt his approval with his father's simple smile at his accomplishments.

His dream died an uncertain death one hot afternoon. The young man was sitting in front of the mosque when the imam, his religious leader, approached and sat next to him. The older man, slight of stature, spoke softly to him. He talked to Samir of Allah and the peace of Allah. It did not seem odd to Samir that the peace of Allah required the taking of innocent lives. He asked the imam whether he should feel guilty if he should cause the death of someone. The imam explained that the lives of infidels simply did not matter to Allah. This had satisfied Samir's curiosity.

The imam departed and the process of Samir's movement to radical Islam had begun. He felt the passion begin to burn within him, a fervor he had not experienced before. He would meet with the imam many times after that. His faith grew stronger; his passion for Allah knew no bounds and his life changed.

When his mother and father realized the conversion going on within him, they tried to steer Samir in a different direction. He resisted their actions and understood that they were not totally committed to Allah, as he was. He and his parents drifted slowly apart. In fact, they saw the anger in his eyes when they tried to talk with him. Eventually, that anger turned to pity and it was not long before he left his family home. Once gone, he did not talk to them again.

Samir still felt a great fondness and affection for the imam, even though the man had been killed several years before. While it was unclear who brought about his death, Samir knew that the great Satan had a hand in it.

He glanced back into the mirror and observed the steeliness in his eyes. This was his time and this was his place to make a difference and he would, all for the glory of Allah.

He removed his clothes and walked to the shower. Samir turned the cold water tap on but did not touch the hot water tap. Stepping into the shower, he was assaulted by an ice-cold rain. He used this time and manner of showering to harden his body and his mind. When both were cleansed, Samir stepped out of the shower and dried off. He then spread his prayer rug on the floor facing Mecca. He knelt and began his morning prayers. This lifted his spirit and hardened his soul.

He rose and sat on his bed for a few moments. Following his prayers, Samir always started his day by contemplating what he was trying to accomplish. He had come to Paris with a desire to teach these nonbelievers that their way of life was a blasphemy to Allah. Samir would rather have gone to the United States, but it would have been more difficult to complete the operation he had developed. Samir knew there was still much to be done before Allah would be pleased. But his will would be done.

After dressing, he took his fruit and yogurt to the desk upon which his laptop sat. He ate slowly, thinking of what needed to be done that day. The yogurt was sweet and the fruit refreshing. Samir flipped opened his laptop, typed in his password and began his day.

Chapter 2

I glanced out the window of the Boeing 767 and saw we were a few feet above the runway. Seconds later, I was greeted with a slight bump as the plane touched down. It had been a long flight and everyone was glad we had finally arrived. Seated next to me were my two close friends, Mac and Ty. Mac was across the aisle, and Ty just beyond in the window seat.

The two men were very much alike and yet very different from me. As former police officers, their view of the criminal justice system focused on capturing and punishing the perceived bad guy. I, on the other hand, as a lawyer, viewed the protection of individual rights as paramount. Not only did I like them, I also admired and respected them. Mac and Ty, like myself, enjoyed working with students. It was always fun when you saw the light go on in the eyes of students when they finally understood a difficult concept.

Prior to teaching at the university, the three of us had spent our time trying to keep young people out of trouble. Now, we were helping young people who wanted to make something of themselves. It was quite a difference and made life much easier and more enjoyable for us.

Tyler Smith was a new hire to the Criminal Justice Department at our university. On his first day at the office, he made it clear that he was to be called Ty. He had retired from the Metro Police Department in Las Vegas after serving 22 years. Ty had traveled around the planet for the last 48 years and had grown into his stocky five-foot-ten frame. His hair was prematurely gray and of medium length, typical of a retired police officer. He was quick to laugh at himself and his eyes sparkled when he did so. He had done very well in his inaugural year at the university. Students flocked to his classes as he enthralled them with stories of his activities as a police officer—some real and some imagined. It was clear he was going to be a student favorite.

Robert MacDonald went by the name of "Mac." He was 55 and carried his 185 pounds on a tall, lean body. Mac had been with the department for several years. He too had served more than 20 years in police operations. His hair was white and he joked that he wasn't sure whether that had been caused by his wife or his job. Mac had grown tired of teaching and would be retiring from academia to spend more time on his ranch. This trip would be his last study abroad excursion.

Of course, both Ty and I would miss Mac, but he would really be missed by the students he taught. Through his experiences, he was able to bring to life the dry material contained in textbooks. Mac also liked to have fun with the students and surprise them whenever he could.

As the plane slowly taxied to the terminal, Mac leaned over to me. "Are we there yet, Daddy?"

My friends call me DJ, which I much prefer to my full name and which I try to avoid using. As Chair of the Criminal Justice Department, I was the nominal leader of this trip abroad to study the French criminal justice system. The three of us had worked well together preparing this program. Then again, we always seemed to collaborate easily on any project we took on.

Our personalities seemed to mesh well and I could not recall any serious conflict between us. So when I looked at Mac, I knew it would be taken in fun when I answered, "If you keep it up, I will have to send you home to your mother."

Ty, who had been listening to this conversation, spoke before Mac could reply. "I thought his mom threw him out years ago."

"I believe you're absolutely correct, Ty. In fact, as I understand it, she tried that more than once," I added with a grin.

Mac frowned at me and then answered Ty. "At least I had a mom. I heard you grew up in the woods and were raised by a mama skunk. But she said you smelled too bad and sent you to the city. Now all of the civilized people have to deal with you."

Ty chuckled once more and shook his head, "I give up."

"Oh, come on, Tyler boy, don't give up so easily."

"Mac, I'm not giving up. Because it's just so damned easy, I feel ashamed taking advantage of you. Besides that, I promised your mom I would take care of you. You know, you being the old man you are."

As the plane came to a stop, I unbuckled my belt and stood up. I looked toward the back of the plane and saw that our twenty students were in the process of opening the overhead bins to get their carry-on luggage. We had quite a group on this trip. Almost equally split between males and females, they included freshmen through seniors. As they worked their way toward the exit door, Mac, who was behind me, whispered, "Hurry up, I have to go potty."

Ty heard the comment and laughed. "Someone should check to see if his seat is wet."

I responded, "It wouldn't surprise me one bit. You know, Ty, Mac told me he was bringing along some Depends, those adult diapers. However, I think he is too old to remember to use them."

Mac looked at both of us, rolled his eyes and chuckled, "I'm the only one who has anything remotely resembling an appropriate sense of humor. I think you both need to be spanked just like the children you are." With that, we exited the plane at the Charles de Gaulle airport outside of Paris.

The students followed us through the terminal and passed through the long immigration lines. Then we all headed for baggage claim. Derek, a senior who had previously served in the military, approached us. He was a tall, buff 22-year-old with an easy-going manner. The students all liked him; they knew he was the one they could turn to for assistance. As he came forward, it was clear from the expression on his face that he was concerned about something.

Derek looked at each of us. In a low voice, he asked, "Did you see the army guys carrying those automatic weapons? What's that all about?"

I looked at him and smiled. "They take their security very seriously here."

"Are they expecting any problems?"

"Nothing out of the ordinary. They're just more open about the need for security here in France than in the U.S."

Mac took over. "They believe that this show of force has a deterrent effect on those who might wish to cause problems. Don't worry about it. You should be more worried about the young French women you'll be meeting here in Paris."

Ty placed his hand on Derek's shoulder and whispered. "Please leave some of them for the other guys."

"Too bad you guys are too old to enjoy the finer things of Paris."

With that, all of us started laughing. Derek turned red when Sheila, an attractive young freshman, came up and asked what the joke was about. The three of us looked at Derek, waiting for his reply.

Mac clapped Derek on the shoulder. "Well, Derek, Sheila asked you a question."

Derek turned on his heels and walked to the baggage carousel. We started laughing again and Derek, with his back to us, raised his middle finger. I looked at Sheila, "Ask Derek about it later. I'm sure he'll explain it to you."

Sheila tossed her shoulder-length blonde hair and turned to go back to the other students. We couldn't help but admire her lean, toned figure as she strode through the airport.

It didn't take too long for all of us to gather our baggage, pass through customs, and walk into the terminal. Standing there, holding a sign with our group's name on it, was a lovely young French woman—Sophie, our guide in Paris. She showed us to the bus, where we loaded our bags and headed into downtown Paris amidst a flurry of taxis, passenger cars, and other buses.

Chapter 3

The man in the doorway was tall and thin. He looked each way to see if he was being observed and saw nothing. Opening the door into a darkened hallway, he heard nothing unusual. He climbed the stairs slowly, concentrating on the sounds coming from the doors above him. The man was ready to bolt back to the street if any unexpected sound came his way. He reached the second floor and stood before apartment 207. He knocked lightly on the door, and a muffled voice from inside asked, "Who is it?"

The man outside simply said, "Samir." Slowly the door opened to reveal a short, stocky man whose face was dominated by a full black beard. Samir entered the apartment and saw two other men seated at a table covered with papers.

Salah, who had let him in, was an old friend who had been with him for many years. Samir and Salah had lived in the same village in Saudi Arabia as children. While Samir stood six foot three, tall for a Saudi, Salah was barely five foot ten. Though he was short of stature, Salah's strong voice commanded the respect of the other men in the room. He had a small scar above his right eye, which he had received while fighting in Afghanistan and was lucky that the shrapnel had not pierced his dark, black eyes. Salah was the only person Samir trusted with his life. They worked together like a well-oiled machine.

Respectfully, Kamil and Ahmed rose from the table and came to greet Samir. Their handshakes were firm like the purpose of their spirit. Both were critical cogs in his organization. Kamil's responsibility was to obtain and facilitate the collection of armaments and explosives. These typically came to him from sources outside of Paris.

At the age of thirty, Kamil looked like a typical Saudi—dark, shiny hair cut short, deep serious eyes, and a slender, muscular frame. He had a quick temper that did not take well to teasing. He had already been through a lot in his short life.

Ahmed, on the other hand, directed the recruitment and training of holy warriors needed to carry out their operations. Several years younger than Kamil, Ahmed was also tall for a Saudi and sported a thick, curly, black beard. His mind was as quick as the smile that came easily to his face. One had the sense that he was far older than his years.

Looking at Salah, Samir asked, "Have there been any security issues?"

"None."

"Have you seen any strange individuals in the neighborhood or vehicles we should be concerned about? As you know, the French are getting better at counter-terrorism measures."

"Ahmed has several men in the apartment down the street who are keeping constant watch on our apartment and surroundings. They've reported nothing unusual."

Samir glanced at Ahmed. "We're too close to our operational date to have some young man drift off to sleep during his watch and miss something. I want you to double the lookouts and make sure you instill in them the importance of their job."

Ahmed nodded, "I am confident they are properly motivated, but I will revisit this issue with all of them."

Samir walked to the window and opened the blinds an inch or two, gazing at the street below, but saw nothing that concerned him. He stayed at the window several moments and let his experienced eye continue to watch as the people and vehicles moved below him. He knew that this time held the greatest danger for his group and his operation. A potential discovery of this location by the French security forces could occur from the slightest misstep by any one of them.

Then Samir's eyes were drawn to an individual standing before a shop window. It appeared that the man wanted others to believe he was interested in the dresses in the window. A flicker of concern crossed Samir's face as he watched this man. Within a minute, however, a young woman crossed the street and stood next to the man. He pointed at the dress, she nodded, and they entered the store. Samir smiled to himself as he realized how suspicious he had become of normal, everyday life.

He turned and walked to the table to join the other three. "Are we ready? Tell me what is left to be done."

Salah turned toward Samir. "As you know, we have planned a coordinated attack on many targets, which required specialized training for the men involved. Ahmed has been in charge of training our warriors to complete the various missions. Ahmed, why don't you brief Samir on the state of our training and recruitment?"

Ahmed walked over to the table to pick up some papers he had been working on. "As of this moment, we have sufficient manpower to complete our operation. Our people have been coming into this country over the last year or so. As I got to know them, I was able to determine which part of the operation each individual would be best suited for. Once that was completed, I was able to organize training for everyone. This has taken the better part of a year because I had to work with either groups or individuals, depending on their target. We had to make sure they were completely familiar with Paris."

Samir nodded, encouraging Ahmed to continue his briefing.

"Each of the groups has completed run-throughs of their operation. I should tell you, part of the training for everyone has been the necessary religious indoctrination. Sometimes, as you can imagine, a person who is going to martyr himself during an attack has second thoughts. I spent a lot of time with these individuals, trying to make sure that their dedication to complete their mission was not interrupted by any doubts. I think that all of them are ready."

Ahmed looked down at the paperwork in his hands. "We do not have, as yet, all the necessary weapons or explosives required to complete the job. Kamil has assured me that all necessary armaments should be ready by tonight. That being the case, we can go at almost any time."

Samir watched Ahmed closely as he gave his report. "Ahmed, I know we have discussed this before, but security among your warriors must be maintained at all cost. Should just one of our fighters brag about his future operation, we all might be arrested or killed. I want you to go back to each one of them once again and review our security requirements. We cannot emphasize enough that no one can do anything that would bring the French down on us. Will you make sure you do that?"

"Yes, I will. I want you to know that I emphasize security every time I talk with someone. But I will once again reinforce those concerns to all of them."

"Good. We are counting on you. Kamil, what is your report?"

The older man cleared his throat nervously. "We have over a period of time delivered the automatic weapons to each group that needs them. We are short a few rifles. They should be arriving shortly with the rest of the explosives we need. My best guess is that those remaining items should be available for distribution in the next couple of days. I will work with Ahmed to make sure we distribute everything as required.

He continued. "As to security, we also have to take great care as we bring these weapons and explosives into the country. Once inside France, we have to make sure we can get them transported to Paris without disruption. If they stop one of our trucks and find out what it is carrying, the authorities will be alerted and we could potentially be in danger. I have drummed into my people the importance of not being discovered. With the grace of Allah, we will be ready shortly."

"Are you concerned that the French may be focusing on our operation?" Samir asked.

"No. I've heard nothing on the street that would lead me to that conclusion. I'm just saying, we need to be very careful as we complete the transport of weapons."

Samir appeared to be satisfied with what each man had reported. He once again walked over to the window and peered out. Samir saw nothing of concern and returned to the three men. "It seems to me that each of you have completed or will have completed your work shortly. I believe we are set to do Allah's work."

In response, Salah asked, "Has a day been set yet?"

Samir smiled and said, "Very soon."

Chapter 4

Our tour bus had traveled the freeway from Charles de Gaulle and was now winding its way through the streets of Paris. The students stared out the windows, excitedly pointing out sites they had read about or had seen on TV. Ty had traveled overseas previously, but this was his first trip to Paris.

Maneuvering through the narrow streets for what seemed like hours, given our jet lag and eagerness to explore the city, the bus pulled up in front of a small hotel. The driver stopped, blocking the roadway, and announced that we had reached our destination.

Sophie stood up. She was around 25, a bit taller and certainly more slender than me. I admired the way she carried herself with an elegance only Parisian women seem to possess. Her wavy, dark brown hair flowed below her shoulders and the little make-up she wore highlighted her natural beauty and lovely, high cheekbones.

With her delightful French accent and perfect English, Sophie reminded the students that they might not be able to check in due to the early hour. We followed her into the hotel and watched her talk with the receptionist. Soon, she turned and announced that some rooms were ready and others would not be vacated and cleaned until 2:00 p.m.

Sophie informed everyone that in twenty minutes, she would give us her orientation about the city. Those students who were able to check in had a few minutes to go to their rooms before meeting the group back in the surprisingly spacious lobby.

I was one of the lucky ones whose room was ready. I looked at Mac and Ty, who had not been so fortunate. "Now, children, sit down and wait until Dad gets back." I had already turned to head to my room, but I could almost hear their eyes roll in their heads.

Sophie's orientation was brief and to the point. She handed out Metro passes, tickets to the subway, and maps of the city. She told the students that she would see them at 6 o'clock in the evening and the next morning at 9 o'clock. Then she reminded the students that France used the 24-hour clock, but to make it easier for them, she would be using the 12-hour clock. When she spoke, Sophie occasionally brushed away a curly wisp of hair that fell across her eyes with a slender, manicured hand. I heard one of our male students sigh.

Then I rose and spoke to the students. "You have the remainder of the day free. I know that some of you are tired and may want to nap at some point. I suggest that you try not to so that you can adjust to the time change more quickly. Remember, we are meeting back here at 6 o'clock sharp for the welcoming dinner."

After I was done, Mac stood and looked at the group. He began, "Remember the rules we have discussed more than once. Obey the laws of this country and don't be stupid. Do not wander off on your own and travel in groups of at least two. While we don't expect anything to happen, it is important that you use your common sense in any large city. If you run into any trouble, you have our cell phone numbers. Just call. Any questions?" No one raised a hand. "Good, we want you to have fun here, but don't screw up."

Ty piped up. "If you can't follow the rules, I suggest you post bail before you leave. Remember, we did not bring any extra cash for that purpose. More importantly, any cash we do have, we intend to use to enjoy the local food and wine."

"If any of you would like to come with us at any time, you're welcome to do so. But we probably won't be as much fun as your fellow students," I added.

Beside me, I heard Derek talking to Jared, who was sitting next to him. "If we go with the profs, I bet we would hear a hell of a lot of outrageous stories, and who knows, they might even be true."

Jared, a senior like Derek, responded with a broad smile that warmed his freckled face. He had been a wrestler in high school and his short, thick body had maintained its musculature. He was shorter than his friend, and they seemed to get along well. Jared's almost flame-red hair could be spotted easily in any crowd.

Jared chuckled. "Yeah, I bet if we bought them a couple of beers, the stories would even be better. You know, I've been in class with Ty and Mac and they don't hold back when they have a story to tell."

"DJ's different, though. He has that lawyer's face that doesn't let you know whether he is joking or telling the truth. A couple of times, he's given me that look. You know what I mean? He looks over his glasses and I always wonder what's coming next. First time I had him in class, he was intimidating as hell. Damned lawyers can do that to you, don't you know?"

"Yes, I do. Maybe during this trip, we'll see what these guys are really made of."

A few minutes later, the room emptied and Mac, Ty and I were left alone.

"Well, fearless leader," Ty said, looking at me. "What shall we do now? Personally, I would like to try out an outdoor café for a cup of coffee. Do either of you have any suggestions?"

Mac stepped forward. "Sounds good to me. Let's get something to eat. I'm starving."

I approach them both. "I like Ty's idea, and I could use something to eat, too. Ty?"

"Let's go see what we can find."

We stepped outside into a day full of sunshine. There was little pedestrian traffic near our hotel and we ambled down the cobblestone street unhindered. At the corner, we saw a promising café. I looked questioningly at the other two and they both nodded.

We found a table with three chairs that were unoccupied. I ordered a café crème and Ty ordered the same. Mac looked at us with disgust and ordered espresso. He smiled, "I thought I was traveling with men, but I guess not."

Ty leaned forward, "Real men don't have to make statements by drinking that crap."

Mac laughed, "Real men don't make excuses!"

"Have you always been full of shit?"

"Actually, no, I've had to work up to it."

"Well, you certainly have been successful."

I enjoyed their repartee. "I hate to break up your bonding session, but we have matters to work out. First, the important ones. What shall we do until dinner?"

Before I could say another word, I was interrupted by Mac.

"You realize you're taking away our bonding time?"

Ty nodded his agreement. "We're just starting to get close."

I looked at Ty. "I'm really disappointed in you. I didn't realize that you're even more full of shit than he is."

"Thank you, Daddy."

I knew this was a discussion I would not win. "Are you guys ready to order some food?"

When the waiter came by, we each ordered croissants filled with ham and cheese.

Taking an enormous bite, Mac wiped the crumbs off his beard. "Damn, these Frenchmen know how to make croissants. I don't think I've ever tasted anything quite so good."

I was still enjoying my coffee. I had finished my croissant and was considering ordering another. "Do you guys want to order anything else?" Both Ty and Mac indicated they were good. "Okay, any suggestions for the day from the children's section?"

Ty was ready to move on. "How about we go see Notre Dame?"

"That's probably a pretty good idea. I understand Mac has a lot to confess."

We signaled the waiter for the bill and paid. Mac slapped the table and stood up. "I have a lot I could confess, but I choose not to since I have the right to remain silent, asshole."

We all had a good laugh and set off for the closest Metro station.

Chapter 5

Pierre Belcher, who was nearing 60, was a very worried man. His forehead was furrowed deeply from the stress that came with his job. He was the director of counter-terrorism for the French government. It was his responsibility to keep France safe from terrorism—from outside and from within. He had held his position for almost two years now. So far, there had been no successful terrorist attacks on his watch. However, he knew that a terrorist only needed to be successful once out of a hundred attempts to be deemed a success. Pierre also knew that he would be branded a failure if any terrorist attack was not intercepted and prevented.

He did not fear for his reputation, but he was deeply concerned about his country. To stop a planned terrorist attack, one needed very good intelligence, government agencies that worked together, and a fair amount of luck. Preparation could take care of the first two, but good fortune seemed to come at the whim of the wind. He did not agree with the notion that you made your own luck. Too often, he had seen that they discovered a potential attack, not as a result of their hard work, but just dumb luck.

During the past month, his intelligence officers had not discovered any potential dangerous activity. Usually, there would be odds and ends of information, either of potential attacks or the entry of potential terrorists onto French soil. In fact, the last report of any significance was in early April and that turned out to be a false alarm. Belcher liked that intelligence had found nothing, but the fact that they may have missed something worried him a great deal. On one hand, a real threat might be looming. On the other, they may be looking for something that simply did not exist. In any event, these times laid heavy upon his heart.

There was a light knocking on his door. He looked up. "Enter."

Claude Trion and Mael Couseau walked into his office. Both held deputy directorships in his organization. Claude was a short man, impeccably dressed in a light gray suit. His cropped auburn hair showed no gray, though his face reflected the stress of the times. Contrary to Pierre, the stress radiated in his eyes.

Claude had just turned 49 and had spent most of his adult life in the intelligence arena. He had served in the field when he was younger, but now, and for the past several years, he was in administration. The focus of his responsibilities was to evaluate, predict and respond to foreign terrorist threats. In doing this, he worked closely with Interpol and his compatriots in other countries.

Mael, on the other hand, was a large man of six foot four. He was approximately 250 pounds of solid muscle, which came from a regular workout schedule. His face maintained a seriousness that caused others to pause. He had served France both overseas and in country. Until six months ago, he had worked the streets of France, especially Paris. In doing so, he went where others hesitated. He had a talent for changing his appearance, which made him successful, where others failed.

To Pierre, Mael seemed frustrated and bored in his current position. He seemed to want to go back to where the action was. However, Pierre had impressed upon him the need for his expertise in his current position and especially in assisting him. At the age of 52, Mael would be considered by most to be too old to be a field operative. However, anyone who had gone up against him, even recently, would acknowledge that he was not a man to be trifled with. Pierre had heard one agent indicate that he would not like to run into him in a dark alley. From his perspective, Pierre knew he would not want to be on Mael's bad side even in broad daylight, surrounded by a well-armed security squad.

Pierre smiled at each man in turn. "Gentlemen, come in and be seated. We have much to talk about. Claude, what news do you have for me?"

In his well-educated Parisian accent, Claude updated the others. "Nothing earth-shaking really. The Americans shared information which indicates there may be more trouble in Yemen. That's nothing really new. Closer to home, we're still getting reports of potential attacks in Algeria and Tunisia. I have discussed them with the appropriate people in those countries and, I believe, they are taking them seriously."

"Do we know who's behind those potential attacks? Are they the people we have watched previously or are there new groups in the game?" Pierre asked.

"It appears that they are the same players we have dealt with before. We continue to try to infiltrate those groups but have not been successful as yet. As you know, Pierre, terrorists are becoming wiser with experience. One advantage we have is that it is much easier to obtain electronic surveillance on suspects in both of those countries than it is in France. I can't imagine operating in the United States with all the restrictions placed upon security officials by their courts."

Mael said, "Thank God for little favors."

With a nod from Pierre, Claude went on. "We are hearing rumblings about a large transfer of weapons, specifically small arms and RPGs. None of our sources have been able to confirm where the transfer originates or ends. While this in and of itself is not unusual, I am concerned because where those go, explosives seem to follow. We have passed these reports on to the U.S. and

United Kingdom to see if they have any information that may be of assistance."

Looking at his colleagues, Claude said, "We've not detected anything unusual about shipments coming into the country. We continue to do spot inspections of containers and other smaller ships, but nothing has turned up yet. We've also been watching cargo aircraft with the same result."

"Mael, what do you have to report?" Pierre turned to the large man.

"There are no specific indications that anything is afoot. The Americans informed us yesterday that there's been no change in the chatter they are hearing from the groups they're following. The Americans believe that when the chatter increases, an attack is imminent. I also happen to believe that when the chatter goes quiet, we need to be very watchful. If I were a terrorist, the closer I got to a planned attack, the more I would insist that electronic communications cease. Our informants report nothing unusual either. The various police agencies have not contacted me with any concerns. There have been no unusual arrests of Muslims, which might be indicative of problems. In sum, nothing seems to be brewing. My plan is to keep pressure on the entire department to make sure we miss nothing."

Pierre looked at each man in turn. "It seems too good to be true. But I'm having trouble sleeping. Something's there. I feel it in my gut. It is like an American movie I saw once. An American cowboy said he knew Indians were nearby. The reason he knew—his head itched. My head isn't itching, but it's damned close. I don't know. Maybe in a month, we will all laugh about this."

Mael replied, "I hope so." He usually chuckled at his boss' penchant for referring to American movies. He knew Pierre particularly liked American westerns. But today, his concerns were not about Indians, but rather about radical Muslims who desired to

destroy his country. Mael also felt uneasy about the lack of actionable intelligence. His work on the streets had given him a good sixth
sense about what was going on. While he felt uneasy, there was
nothing he could point to that would cause him concern. Maybe that
was the problem—his gut told him he should be concerned. He just
did not know what his concern should be about.

Claude interjected, "I agree with you, Director. I'm afraid we are
missing something. Let's hope we all are being oversensitive."

Pierre rose and walked his men to the door. "Keep looking until
we find something. They must be out there." As they left, he closed
his door and returned to his desk. He looked at the clock on the
wall. It read 0830. The day had barely begun.

Chapter 6

I t was a nondescript building, chosen for that very reason. When Kamil began looking for a delivery point, he wanted something that did not draw attention to either the building or its occupants. The building itself was a dull white, streaked with dirt. It was located in a suburb of Paris in an area of many unnoticeable warehouses. There were few windows and those that existed were covered, barring anyone from looking in and discovering the activities being carried on inside.

Kamil fumbled for his keys, found them, and inserted the appropriate key into the lock. When they rented this building, the door had a lock. His first action was to replace it so only he, Salah and Samir had keys for the door. Prior to entering the warehouse, Kamil glanced to his left and right to see if anyone was looking at them. He saw nothing out of the ordinary. He pushed the steel door open and entered quietly. He took his time and looked around the warehouse to see if he could determine if anything had changed since he last left.

Salah entered behind him and asked, "Is there a problem?"

"Nothing that I can see. We will do a sweep later to ensure that no bugs have been planted. It shouldn't be a problem, though. We have yet to use this building for anything. It is not unusual for these buildings to be rented and not used for a period of time. We shut down our last warehouse a day ago. As planned, we've used our warehouses in a rotating manner as a security measure. No one warehouse is used for any length of time."

"When do we expect our last shipment?" Salah asked.

"This evening. I've chosen five men to assist me in the unloading of the trucks."

"How many trucks are coming?"

"We're expecting five tonight," Kamil said.

"As I understand, there will be no more trucks arriving after tonight?"

Kamil nodded. "That's correct. These vehicles will bring the last of the needed armaments. As with the previous warehouses, this warehouse will be cleaned out. We hope to leave no trace of what occurred here. Following that, we will allow the leases to expire and inform the owners that we do not need to extend them."

"I'm concerned that this sudden burst of activity might draw attention to this location," Salah said.

"That's always a possibility; however, our trucks will have the signage of a furniture company located in Marseille. The story will be that we are a distribution center for that company. The company does not exist except for a small office in Marseille that we set up. Our people will be manning the phones to respond to any questions about the shipments here." Kamil switched on the lights and continued his inspection.

Salah watched Kamil go about his business as he strolled through the warehouse. He and Samir had made a wise choice in placing Kamil in charge of this portion of their operation. His countenance rarely changed and it was difficult to determine what he was thinking. But Kamil's face radiated a deadly seriousness that promised a quick response should he believe his orders were not carried out to the letter.

Salah had known Kamil for several years now. The younger man had always been a serious individual, but very inexperienced in the tradecraft of terror. However, his knowledge seemed to grow by leaps and bounds as he proceeded from one operation to another.

Salah had initially questioned Kamil's dedication and belief in their purpose. He wondered whether the other man had the guts to make the hard decisions required in their operations. That concern evaporated when he observed Kamil take the life of the man who was thought to be an informant. Even so, Salah had assigned a man to watch Kamil over a six-month period. The man's report solidified in Salah's mind the trustworthiness of Kamil.

"How long do you think that the unloading process will take?" Salah now asked.

Kamil was quick to respond. "The first truck scheduled to arrive is also bringing two forklifts. We shall load all the cartons on pallets and unload them with the forklifts. Running in tandem, they should be able to unload each truck within 30 minutes. If we run into any trouble, I will have extra bodies to assist. I am confident we can get this done on time as scheduled. The bigger issue will be delivering the arms and explosives to the various groups."

"Samir is making arrangements for as much security as possible when the material is transferred. If one of those transfers is discovered, it could endanger our whole operation. If you have any concerns when the transfers are being made, you should contact Samir immediately. Any questions, Kamil?"

"No, I think we've prepared as best we can. If Allah shines his face on us, we will bring much joy to him." A brief look of satisfaction drifted across Kamil's lean face.

As they were walking back toward the door, Kamil stopped and suddenly put his index finger to his lips. He slowly withdrew the Glock hidden under his shirt. He walked to the nearest window, pulled back the covering and looked out. Standing near the door was a young, dark-skinned man. He seemed to be nervous as he glanced up and down the street.

Kamil strode quickly toward the door and motioned for Salah to stand behind him. Slowly the door opened and the young man walked in. Kamil grabbed the young man's collar and jerked him to the floor. He placed the barrel of the semi-automatic pistol squarely against the man's forehead. Kamil could see the terror in the man's eyes. "Who are you and what you doing here?"

The young man stammered, unable to say anything. He was clearly stunned at the change of events. He had wet himself as was evidenced by the darkness at the front of his jeans. He seemed to be on the verge of crying.

Kamil's eyes were dark and merciless. "I'm going to ask you one more time. Who are you and what you doing here? I'm not going to give you another chance to answer."

The young man's voice squeaked as he tried to speak. He swallowed audibly and finally was able to state, "Antoine. I wanted to see what was in here."

"You mean you wanted to see what was in here so you could take it?"

"No, sir, I assure you that was not the case," the young man stammered unconvincingly.

"Why do you lie to me? Never mind. It doesn't matter." Kamil glanced at Salah and saw him nod slightly. With that, Kamil took the young man into the bathroom where any sound would be lessened.

The man's voice quavered as he asked, "You're not going to hurt me, are you? I did nothing wrong. I just want to go home. Please, I just want to go home."

Grabbing the young man from behind, Kamil said, "You should ask Allah for forgiveness." Before the young man could reply, Kamil used the training he had been given in Afghanistan to break the man's neck.

He lowered the body gently to the floor. He walked out of the bathroom, looked at Salah and shrugged. "Wrong place, wrong time. The body will be removed this evening."

He and Salah then turned and walked toward the door. They did not say another word about the young man as they locked the door and walked off.

Chapter 7

As we sat in the hotel lobby waiting for the dinner hour to roll around, the students' stories began to come out.

Natalie, a somewhat plump sophomore, who, while not unattractive, seemed plain by Parisian standards. Her light brown hair was pulled into a tight ponytail, and she wore glasses that to me, seemed a bit large for her face. Sitting down next to Derek, her face lit up, eyes sparkling with youthful energy, Natalie began her story. "We had so much fun. We went to that street with all the very high-end stores. The street with the funny-sounding name." She looked at Sarah, who was sitting across from her. "What's the name of that street?"

Sarah, a more worldly junior, looked at Natalie with mild amusement. "*Champs Elysees.* Don't you know anything, Natalie? I mean, it is probably the most famous street in the world."

"Whatever! It's not like I've been here before. As if you're a world traveler."

"No, but I do read," Sarah retorted, shaking her short auburn curls and her green eyes flashing. "I actually read about Paris before we left. Not only does it have great shopping, but the museums are supposed to be amazing as well."

"Anyway, Derek, we saw the new Paris fashions. They are so cool. You don't see anything like that back home."

Derek smiled at her. "I did not see the fashions that you did, but I did see the Parisian women wearing them. Oh, my God! These women have their own style. I saw more incredibly beautiful women this afternoon than I have in the last year. They all seem to wear very nice outfits. Even the women going to the store, pushing strollers, were dressed fashionably. And they certainly don't wear sweats."

He gave Natalie a what-the-hell-is-wrong-with-you kind of smile as she tried to hide her sweatpants with her coat. "I'm not saying there's anything wrong with sweats, but there's something very right in how the Parisian women dress."

Natalie smirked, "What would your girlfriend say if I told her about your comments, Derek?"

"She would probably kick me in the balls. However, that doesn't change the facts as I stated them. Have you noticed, there are no overweight men or women in this town? You know that's part of their style. They have terrific figures, which they obviously take great pride in. And another thing, they like to flirt. I mean, they understand there's a reason why there are differences between men and women. I think that's been lost in the U.S."

"Derek, you're such a sexist," Natalie frowned at him.

"Why, just because I talk about what I observed with Parisian women? You're excited about the Paris fashions. I'm excited about the Paris fashions as worn by Parisian women. No, that's not entirely right. I'm just excited about Parisian women. What's wrong with that?"

"You're hopeless," Natalie replied.

Derek just grinned, his straight, white teeth gleaming. "I hope I die with the same smile I have on my face and for the same reason. You know, American women can learn from these Parisian women. I think America would benefit from less unisex and more appreciation of the differences in sexes. I bet you don't see a lot of sexual harassment suits here. In fact, I read a story once about a French president. He got in a car accident in the early morning hours after he left his mistress. Because he had a mistress, his poll numbers went up. Can you imagine what would happen if that were the American president? Sometimes, I think Americans are just prudes."

Dressed in a dark blue silk blouse and designer jeans, Sophie walked in and proceeded to count the number of people present. "No stragglers, that's great. Let's head for dinner."

Derek raised his eyebrows toward Natalie and Sarah, bowing his head slightly in Sophie's direction. "Case in point."

As the students walked out of the hotel to follow Sophie down the street, Ty and I closed up the rear.

Ty began, "I'm glad Sophie arrived when she did. Otherwise, we might have had a fight on our hands. Did you notice that Derek and Natalie's conversation was being followed by most of the other students? I have to agree with Derek though; these Parisian women are amazing. Do you think our students will have a problem with that?"

I grinned at him. "Probably, because of the way guys are responding to what they see. There are very few heavy people in Paris, contrary to the United States, where overweight people seem to be everywhere. What scares the girls is that the guys wonder why American women can't be like these Parisian women. Females wonder how the Parisians can hold their figures without starving. What the students don't realize is that the French walk everywhere. However, Americans drive their cars across the street to go to the store. Starting tomorrow, they will get a sense of what walking in Paris is like. If they're smart, they will understand why the Parisian women are as they are," I said from my soapbox.

"It will be interesting to see if this conversation continues at the restaurant. Maybe it would be a good idea to lead the conversation back to this issue. It could be another learning experience. What do you think, DJ?"

"I think that's a great idea. As long as you're the one to do so, Ty."

"Coward."

"No, just smart," I responded with a chuckle.

The group seemed to slow down as we entered the restaurant. Mac, Ty, and I had decided previously that we would not sit together but rather spread ourselves among the students. That way we'd be as able to assist as many of them as we could with any questions they might have about the food and other things.

While sitting back and watching people is expected in Paris, listening to the students as they talked about their escapades that afternoon made all of us smile a bit.

Mike was our computer nerd. He was tall, gawky and awkward, blue eyes hidden behind black horn-rimmed glasses, which he kept pushing up on his beaky nose. He sat across the table and described his group's visit to the Louvre. They were overwhelmed by how large it really was and stunned at how small the Mona Lisa was. He explained how he had watched a group of Parisian students sitting on the floor drawing. He was amazed when he realized that the students were copying the Master's work while looking at the original piece of art. In the U.S., students can only look at books containing pictures of the art. The more he spoke, the more it became evident that his appreciation for the cultural riches found in the Paris' museums had grown immensely.

Natalie was closer to Ty than she was to me when she spoke to Becky. "Did you hear what Derek was saying back at the hotel?"

"You mean about the women of France and how beautiful they are?" Becky raised her carefully plucked eyebrows. Becky was our fashion queen, always immaculately groomed and dressed. Unlike most of the students, who had traveled with backpacks, she brought with her two enormous suitcases, as well as a huge make-up bag. She was known for spending an inordinate amount of time in front of the mirror, making sure every one of her golden hairs was in place.

"Yes, exactly about that," Natalie nodded her head, which set her brown curls bouncing. "I think he's such a sexist. I think it just shows how far ahead we are of the French. Derek would probably love living here."

Becky, who also had a great sense of humor, started laughing. "Knowing Derek, I think you're right. I wonder what the other guys think." She saw that Jason was listening to their conversation. "Jason, what do you think?

"Honestly, I'm not sure," Jason said, leaning back in his chair. "If I agree with Derek, you'll probably tell all the women back home and I won't be able to get a date for the next year. If I agree with you, there's probably no way I'll be able to go out with one of these beautiful French women. Therefore, taking everything into consideration, I agree with Derek wholeheartedly." Everyone sitting around them started laughing.

Natalie pointed her finger at him. "You mean to tell me you agree with that sexist?" Jason grinned at her and nodded his agreement. "You are such an asshole, Jason. I wonder why I was ever was attracted to you."

"You told me it was because of my blue eyes. What's the difference between that and my being attracted to a beautiful Parisian woman? I mean I think the differences in the sexes should be celebrated. If you weren't such a girl, you would understand."

"I can't believe you, Jason. How could you possibly say that?" Natalie blurted, outraged.

"Well, it's better than what a friend of mine said. After breaking up with his girlfriend, he told her that if it wasn't for sex, he'd probably be gay."

Everyone, including Natalie, started laughing then.

Jason continued. "He said that's because women are a pain in the ass."

The argument stopped as the waiters approached the table with loaded trays. "Saved by the food!" I thought with a smile.

The first course was a salmon paté. Some students tasted it immediately. Others seemed to believe the gray and pink paté needed to be poked and touched because of its unfamiliarity. But soon enough, everyone had tasted it. Somewhere down the table, a young woman's voice whined, "I wonder if there is a McDonald's nearby. This is just too strange for me."

I heard laughter coming from my right. It seemed that something had struck Ty's funny bone. Whatever it was had tears coming from his eyes. I looked at him, "What's so hilarious?"

Ty wiped his eyes and took a couple of deep breaths before he could answer. He looked across the table at Jared, who was turning bright red. "He's killing me. Jared, tell them what you told me."

"No, this doesn't need to go any further."

"I'm sorry, but this is just too good. I asked Jared if he knew any French. He said that he didn't, but that it couldn't be that hard. When I asked him what he meant, he said, 'Haven't you noticed that all of the children speak French. So it can't be that difficult.'"

Ty had trouble getting that last part out since he was laughing again. "But I have to give him an A for being so observant." He wiped his eyes once again as his laughter continued.

Jared looked at him, "You know that's not what I meant, Professor."

Ty was holding his sides as he tried to control his laughter. "What else could it mean?"

By this time, the entire table was enjoying this discussion. Jared smiled wickedly. "You know payback is hell. Your time will come."

"I'm sure you will do something. The only question I have is whether or not you will say it in French. I mean, if the French kids can speak French so easily, I'm sure you'll pick it up without a problem."

The entire table started laughing far too loud for the restaurant, and even Jared broke down and joined in.

After the hilarity passed, I glanced over at Rick, who was seated across the table to my left. He was a very quiet and shy student, longish brown hair constantly flopping in his eyes. He was going to be a sophomore in the fall, and had a conservative freshness about him. Rick didn't speak much and I noticed he had some difficulty in talking with the women in our group. Rick was also very bright, which appealed to those of equal intelligence.

At the moment, he was talking quietly to Dana, a nursing student, who was listening intently. Dana was a cute, perky blonde with a ready smile who exuded competence in everything she did.

Covertly, I listened to their conversation, hoping he would be able to make a connection. It was clear to me that Dana was attracted to him. I hoped he would close the deal and have her join him for the evening. However, Rick seemed to have run out of conversation topics. Dana wasn't going to be put off, and she invited him to go find a dance club with her. Peering out from beneath his hair, Rick smiled and quickly agreed.

Mac, our beer connoisseur, was enjoying his second beer. He saw me looking at him and raised his glass. "Cheers, my friend."

I raised my glass of wine. "May your eyes stay clear, your walk remain steady and your glass remain full."

"Where the hell did that come from?" Mac grinned.

"I haven't a clue. I just made it up."

"Not bad from the wine drinker, I guess," he countered.

* * * * *

When we left the restaurant a short time later, the students gathered on the sidewalk to decide what they were going to do for the rest of the evening. Some of them were going to the Eiffel Tower and other famous monuments. Others were tired and wanted to return to the hotel to get some sleep. A few more wanted to party and decided to go look for some dance clubs.

While they were getting ready to venture out, Ty, Mac, and I turned to head back to the hotel. Mac spun around and faced the students. "Above all, please be safe."

The three of us watched them walk off in their respective directions to enjoy Paris. The few who were returning to the hotel left us standing there. I looked at my two compatriots. "Well, gentlemen—and I use that term loosely—what is your pleasure for the rest of the evening?"

Ty answered first. "Well, I sure as hell don't want to go to a dance club, and my feet are too tired to walk around a museum. I think what I would like to do is go have another drink in one of these great outdoor cafés. We can watch the people walk by and make up stories about them."

Mac looked at me and jerked his thumb toward Ty. "He must be one of the most boring people I know. However, I'm tired and my feet hurt too, so I agree with him."

I put my hands on my hips and stared at both of them. "I'm so disappointed in both of you. You have no interest in seeing the great monuments of Paris. You have no desire to dance the night away. I'm almost ready to say that I'm sorry to be here with you. But my feet hurt, too, so let's find a place to have a drink and then turn in for the night."

They both responded at once. "Asshole!"

Chapter 8

The ship appeared to be old and rusty. It did not have the well-run or well-cared for look like that of the other ships in the harbor. She sailed under the Liberian flag, which had many advantages in that there was little regulation by the Liberian government. The current name listed on her stern read *Janae*. Given her history, this was only one of the many names she had sailed under. The *Janae* had had many owners, and the current owner obviously was not concerned about maintenance. The ship had not been painted for some time and there was rust that had not been dealt with. The ship looked like it was being run as hard as possible until it would slowly sink beneath the sea.

Standing on the bridge, the captain gazed at the harbor before him. They had entered the harbor the night before and had been informed where to drop anchor prior to being assigned a berthing space. Captain Awadi had taken command of the vessel in March. He had a long history of sailing the Mediterranean, which made his captaincy seem appropriate.

The years at sea were etched on his weather-beaten face and had hardened him both physically and mentally. Awadi had specifically kept his face clear of facial hair, as he did not want to give anyone cause for concern given his Arabic heritage. In these difficult times, it did not pay to draw attention to one's ethnic background.

The sun seemed to hang in the sky. He knew that customs officials would be visiting his vessel shortly. Even as the thought passed through his mind, he observed the government boat heading toward his command. While outwardly he seemed to bear no concern, his stomach tightened as he saw them approach the *Janae*.

Awadi had deliberately dressed casually for this encounter, wearing khaki slacks and a light blue polo shirt, rather than a uniform. He decided not to meet the three customs officials at the gangway, but rather have the man in charge brought directly to the bridge. He saw the head official, who was slightly overweight and about 45 years of age, climb the stairs toward the bridge. The first mate, who had met the uniformed men at the gangway, opened the door to the bridge. The captain approached the official with his hand extended and said," Welcome to the *Janae*, I am Captain Awadi."

"I am Marcel Jourdan, the official assigned to your vessel. I want to welcome you to France and wish you a pleasant and profitable stay. I do not expect our business here to take long. I will be reviewing your paperwork and two associates are inspecting your cargo holds as we speak."

"I'm happy to see you have assistance in inspecting our cargo. You have no idea how many ports have only one person assigned to each vessel. That makes for a long process in accomplishing your job. I have everything I believe you will need laid out on the chart table. If it is not there, please request it and I will make sure you get it."

Jourdan replied with a nod, "Thank you, Captain. Your cooperation is much appreciated."

Just as they were finishing up the paperwork, Jourdan's associates entered the bridge. In low voices, they informed Jourdan that all seemed in compliance below. Picking up the papers from the chart table, Jourdan shook Awadi's hand, "Thanks for your cooperation. Everything seems in order. Until next time."

"Do you have any idea when we will be assigned a berth?" Awadi responded.

"While I'm not privy to that information, I would expect it will be within a few short hours."

Awadi watched Jourdan and his colleagues walk down the gangplank onto the much smaller boat, which shipped off immediately. He was not surprised that nothing had been found. What they had below decks was appropriate cargo. The items that Jourdan was looking for had been offloaded earlier the previous evening to a small schooner, which had met them some 40 kilometers offshore. He could now go about his honest business, which was not nearly as financially worthwhile as the transactions he had completed the previous evening.

Chapter 9

Mike, Jackie, and Melanie left the restaurant and headed for the Luxembourg RER station. They boarded the train to the Denfert Rochereau station. After getting off the train, they took Line 6 to Bir-Hakeim, their final stop. When they emerged at sidewalk level and exited the station, they were able to see the Eiffel Tower. Mike exclaimed, "Wow, absolutely amazing." It was impossible for him to take his eyes off the world-famous structure.

Jackie stood there speechless, which was something new for her. Tonight, the blouse she was wearing perfectly matched her light brown hair, as did her lip gloss. She was a bit overweight, which she disguised well beneath appropriate attire. Very rarely at a loss for words, Jackie was on track to become a lawyer.

A head shorter than Jackie, Melanie, chocolate-brown eyes sparkling in her tanned face, simply said, "Awesome. I need to ride to the top. Are you with me?"

Mike grinned at her. "No, we just came here to look at it. Of course, we're going to the top. What planet have you been living on?"

"Shut up. Let's go." Jackie started striding toward the iconic monument.

With that, they headed for the shortest line that sold tickets. The first elevator they rode up was very crowded. They seemed to be crunched together. Melanie was obviously in some discomfort. It was written across her face, with her nose crunched up and her brow furrowed. As they exited, Melanie stated, "Did you smell that body odor? Don't these people know what a bath is? I almost threw up on the guy in front of me, and that would've improved his smell."

Mike gently took her elbow and looked down at Melanie. "Don't worry about it and quit complaining. I think it's just a cultural difference. Let's get to the top." With that, Mike headed for the next elevator. The second ride up was not complicated by malodorous smells.

The three friends walked to the guardrail and glanced out over the panorama of Paris below them. It was dark now and the lights of the city sparkled as it welcomed these visitors. They slowly walked around, taking in the sights from each vantage point. Jackie and Melanie had been talking continuously as they identified each site below them.

Mike, on the other hand, remained quiet. After half an hour at the top of the Tower, Mike suggested it was time to go.

"Why are you in such a hurry?" asked Melanie. "This may be the only time we are here."

Jackie asked, "What's the problem, Mike? It's not like we have anything else to do. I've always wanted to be here. Let's stay for a while." With that, Jackie looked at Melanie, who nodded her approval.

Mike responded, ever the geek. "I can feel the Tower sway in the wind. It's making me very uneasy. Can't you feel that movement? My stomach seems to be rolling. I'm going to head down." He looked at his friends and asked, "Have you ever thought about what it would take to topple this Tower? It's a long way down. I wonder if you would be dead before you hit the ground."

With that, the lanky young man turned and headed for the elevator. He was smiling to himself because he knew he had hit a sore point with Jackie. On the flight over, she had told him she had a fear of heights. He was sure his comments would cause her some concern. He also knew that it would irritate the hell out of Melanie, which was fun for him to do. Who said computer nerds didn't have a sense of humor?

"You're such a killjoy." Melanie was not happy with his comments. She turned toward Jackie, only to see her friend following Mike to the elevator. "Where are you going?"

"I'm going with him. It is a long way down and I can feel the swaying, too."

"Damn babies!" Melanie sulked, but then turned to follow them down. Now that her attention had been drawn to it, she could feel the swaying as well.

As the three friends entered the elevator, Jackie asked, "Hey, what are you guys doing after this?"

Melanie responded first. "I'm meeting up with Becky. We're just going to hang out, I think. Maybe walk around. Would you like to go with us?"

Jackie shook her head, feeling the speed of the descending elevator through her feet. "No, but thanks for the offer. I think I'm just going to go back to the hotel and get some rest. I'm still a little jet-lagged. How about you, Mike?"

"I'm meeting Derek at a club we heard about. Should be fun."

Chapter 10

Rizwan wanted to be on the road. He did not care for the loading process that was scheduled at this rocky beach. It would be very easy for someone to stumble upon them as they unloaded the schooner. He could see the schooner was anchored only 50 meters off the beach.

Rizwan had watched the schooner as it approached the anchoring point earlier that afternoon. He had stayed hidden behind the bushes and observed. His truck was parked among some trees 100 meters away. It appeared that the schooner was like any other vacationing sailboat. Both men and women lay on the deck sunning themselves. He had wondered whether this was the correct boat or not.

He was a short man, but what he lacked in height, he made up for in muscle. His biceps were hard and his hands huge and calloused as a result of the physical work he did for a living. His large chest fell to a 32-inch waist. As a trucker, he understood that his body could not continue this type of work forever. However, right now, he enjoyed the physicality of his job.

While he did not have movie-star looks, his body seemed to attract a sufficient number of women, and a sly grin came across his face as he thought of the young blonde he had met the night before. She had entertained him in a way that he liked and he had returned the favor. Perhaps he would see her again on a future trip. The mere thought of that gave him pause to smile.

As the sun set, the people on the schooner seemed to change before him. Gone were the swimsuits and bikinis, to be replaced by jeans and T-shirts. It was apparent that the fun-in-the-sun times were changing to a work-in-the-evening event. As darkness fell, veiled lights appeared on the boat.

He watched as two large rubber rafts were inflated. Two men, one tall and one short, climbed into the first raft and paddled toward the beach. The ocean was like glass and caused no problems for the pair as they headed for shore. Once they arrived, they pulled the raft onto the beach and waited. Rizwan heard them speaking in low tones.

From his hiding place, he could barely make out the two men as they stood there. He watched each of them walk in opposite directions on the beach. It appeared they were looking to see if there were unexpected visitors. Finding none, they once again came together.

The first man faced inland and in a low voice called, "Rizwan? Are you there?"

It had been previously agreed that everyone would speak French. They didn't want to raise any concerns if someone heard Arabic being spoken.

Rizwan waited for the code words to be uttered.

The man continued, "Paris is waiting."

That was the message he had been waiting for. Rizwan slowly stood and walked toward the two men. "Paris is waiting for me."

The code having been completed, the parties approached each other. They did not exchange names; it was safer that way. Rizwan looked at the two men and announced, "The truck is close by. I can bring it very close to the beach. How many loads will it take to bring everything here?"

The tall man responded, "It will take many loads. We have two rafts and more people to load and unload the cargo. I expect we can have it completed within five to six hours."

"The road is approximately 60 meters from here. It would be helpful if we could station someone there who could warn us of potential traffic or other problems. Do you have someone available?"

"Yes, one of the women can handle that. I suggest that we start immediately. We will return to the boat and load both rafts. Please get the truck down here as soon as you can."

"I will. See you shortly." With that, Rizwan made his way back to the truck. He had carefully reviewed how to approach the beach from where he had parked the truck. He knew it would be tricky given the size of the trailer he was pulling, but he was confident he would have no problems.

He climbed up into the cab, started the engine and proceeded forward. When he crossed the path he intended to take, he shifted into reverse and began backing up slowly. Even though the night was pitch black, the taillights provided sufficient illumination for him to successfully complete this task. He stopped approximately five meters from the water's edge, engaged the parking brake and turned off the engine. Rizwan climbed down from the cab and walked to the back of the truck. It was positioned exactly as he wanted. He smiled at his accomplishment, realizing that backing an 18-meter trailer in this manner required no small amount of skill.

He heard the oars splashing in the water and turned toward the sea. He saw the first raft approaching the beach. It was approximately three meters long and one and a half meters wide. There were four men, two on each side, using their oars to push the raft forward. When they reached the beach, they hopped out and pulled the raft onto the sand.

Without speaking, the men began hauling the boxes from the raft to the trailer. When all the boxes had been unloaded, two men jumped into the raft and began their journey back to the schooner. The two remaining men jumped into the trailer and began moving the boxes to the front.

Within a few minutes, the second raft appeared. Four men and one woman were paddling. When it reached the beach, the woman, dressed in all-black clothing, came forward and indicated that she would be the lookout. Rizwan motioned for her to follow him.

They clambered slowly through the scrub brush and low trees, which blocked a view of the beach from the road. Within a few minutes, they arrived at the road and Rizwan pointed out a hiding place to the woman in black.

"You have a good view from here in both directions. I've been here for a while and there's been very little traffic. It's not necessary for you to do anything but observe traffic on the road unless someone stops. At that time, come and inform us immediately. Make sure they don't see you. Any questions?"

Seeing her shake her head, he turned and walked back to the beach. When he arrived, the second raft was returning to the schooner and he could see the first raft approaching the beach. This process continued on for several hours and finished at 0300.

When the last raft had been unloaded, the tall man said, "This is it. There's nothing left to bring. We are ready to get out of here. I want to be far away when dawn arrives. Where is the woman?"

"I will bring her to you. It will just be a few minutes." Rizwan turned and hurried toward the road. He found the woman standing under a tree near where he left her. "Has there been any traffic?"

The woman shook her head no.

"We are done. I will take you back to the beach."

When they arrived, Rizwan shook the tall man's hand. "May the peace of Allah be with you." The man nodded, stepped into the raft, and faded into the night.

Rizwan climbed into the cab and slowly drove the truck to the road. He saw no evidence of traffic in either direction. He turned on his headlights and drove forward, heading in the direction that would lead him to Paris. He could feel the weight of his cargo as he shifted through the gears. Now his task was to have an uneventful ride to Paris and unload his cargo at the warehouse. He had discussed his route with Salah and they had decided that he would not take the highway but rather travel on back roads.

The trip was uneventful until he was on a lonely stretch of road between two villages. He saw the lights of the police vehicle flashing behind him. He pulled over to the side of the road. Rizwan opened the door and stepped down. He saw an officer getting out of his vehicle and walk toward Rizwan.

"Do you know why I stopped you?"

"I have no idea. What's the problem?"

"I find it unusual that you are traveling on this road rather than using the highway. Why is that?"

"I'm following the route my boss gave me. He is an asshole. He always gives me the slow routes and then writes me up for being late."

The officer eyed him closely. This did not feel right. "Open the back. I want to see what you're carrying. If there's nothing unusual, you'll be on your way in a minute."

"Okay." Rizwan complied, opened the door of the trailer and stepped back. The officer approached the back of the truck and left Rizwan behind him. That was a deadly mistake. Rizwan pulled out the silenced Glock, pointed it at the back the officer's head, and pulled the trigger. The officer dropped silently to the ground.

Rizwan fired another round into the officer's head. He dragged the officer 20 meters into the trees before running back and driving the officer's car into the trees as well. He returned to the road, looked each way and saw no traffic.

Sweating and with his heart pounding, Rizwan climbed into the cab and drove off.

France had suffered its first non-civilian casualty.

Chapter 11

After dinner, a group of students had gone to a dance club. Jared sat in the booth watching the people gyrate on the crowded dance floor. The music, overseen by a DJ, was pounding in his ears. The club they were in was small but lively. The music selection met the patron's needs, as evidenced by the pulsating bodies on the dance floor. Sheila was sitting next to him, watching him watch everyone else. They had come to this club with four other students.

Jason and Rondell were standing at the bar talking with two French girls. Rondell was too busy and too enthralled with the French woman he was speaking with to notice what Jason was up to. He was lost in the eyes of the lovely French woman standing before him.

Rondell was a good-looking, athletic African American in his early twenties who easily drew the attention of the girls. He had a quick smile that matched his keen sense of humor. However, he also had a tendency to push too hard too quickly, which seemed to put people off, especially females. Jared had talked to him about this and hoped that their conversation would have some effect on Rondell.

As Jared watched, he noticed that Rondell was talking less and listening more. Jared's advice to his friend had been to talk less about himself and find out more about the women he approached. One of the girls leaned over and whispered into Rondell's ear. This brought a smile to Rondell's café-au-lait face and the two moved toward the dance floor. Jason looked at Jared, nodded toward Rondell, and gave a thumbs up.

Renee and Jen had been sitting at the table a few minutes earlier when two Australian guys came to the table to talk with them. The young women were won over by the Aussie accent and the handsome young men. It wasn't long before they joined the two men on the dance floor, swaying to the beat of the music. It was obvious that Paris agreed with them.

Despite all that was going on around them, Jared noticed that it seemed that Sheila had taken quite a fancy to him. He felt as if she was hanging on his every word. Each time he looked at the lovely blonde sitting next to him, those deep blue eyes of hers smiled back at him. He had somewhat of a girlfriend back at school, but was not sure whether they were in a committed relationship or not. They had never really ever talked about it. He knew he enjoyed being with Sheila, who had a sweetness about her he had not found in anyone else.

With a gentle gesture, Sheila reached over to brush Jared's red hair back on his forehead and with an inviting smile, said, "I think it's time you and I dance." She rose from her seat, walked in front of him, and held out an open hand. Her sassy smile was hard to say no to. Jared returned her smile, took her hand and kissed it like he imagined a Frenchman would.

They walked hand in hand to the dance floor. Soon the music had enveloped them with the energy of its beat. Jared only had eyes for Sheila as she danced in her own sexy way. She raised her hands over her head, which had the effect of lifting her ample breasts. And as she watched him watch her, she knew an exciting evening awaited her.

* * * * *

Not far from the dance club, Melanie and Becky were sitting on the grass of a nearby park. Seated with them was Ali, who currently lived in Paris. He had dark Arabic coloring, which was set off by his glossy black hair. He had seen Melanie and Becky sitting on the grass and decided to approach them. At first, they were taken aback by being approached by a complete stranger, but were quickly charmed by his dancing eyes and quick smile.

After a short few minutes of conversation, they invited him to sit and join them. The girls were intoxicated by his exotic accent and the sensual quality of his voice.

He inquired about how they had come to be in the park and in Paris. Becky gushed. "We are on a study-abroad trip. I think Paris is so cool. I love sitting here in the park watching the city. Why are you here?"

"I was walking through the park when I saw you. I hope you don't take this wrong, but both of you are so beautiful. I could not live with myself if I passed you by."

Becky positively glowed. "I bet you say that to all the girls."

"Only those who are truly beautiful. You Americans have something that the French women not only don't have, but do not understand. Their beauty is so contrived and yours is so natural."

His body slowly moved downward until he was lying on his back, facing the star-studded sky. He made a sweeping motion toward the heavens. "You see the beauty of the stars? That is so natural. Angels reside there and sometimes they come to earth — like you."

Unseen by the other two, Melanie rolled her eyes. As a senior, she had spent time in Las Vegas clubs and on the beaches of Fort Lauderdale on school breaks. She had flirted with a lot of guys; this young man was the smoothest yet, but still way too obvious. Becky, on the other hand, was rather new to the game.

A chuckle rose within Melanie as she watched Becky's reactions. The younger woman seemed to be too enthralled by it all.

Melanie remained quiet, waiting to watch how it played out. At his urgings, Becky also lay back on the grass. Not to be outdone, Melanie joined her. They talked for several minutes more about the differences in French and American women.

Ali turned on his side, his elbow on the ground, and placed his head in his hand. He looked at Becky and Melanie with a mischievous grin and said, "You know, I've never kissed an American woman. I think I would like to kiss both of you."

Becky seemed excited at the prospect, while Melanie just thought it might be fun. Since he was now between the two of them, he turned toward Becky and slowly brought his lips to hers. He raised his head and gazed into her eyes as she giggled. He kissed her again, more deeply, and was rewarded as her arm went up around his neck.

Ali then pulled back and said, "I think it's Melanie's turn," eliciting a pout on Becky's face.

He rolled over and looked at Melanie. She smiled, looked into his eyes, and said, "I haven't got all night." Recognizing the experience of Melanie over Becky, Ali began kissing her aggressively. She returned his affections, but when his hand moved about her body, she sat up, and said, "I think that's enough for tonight." She stood and the others joined her.

Ali, recognizing that his chances with Melanie had slipped away, once again took Becky's hand in his own and kissed it. Becky giggled. He looked at her and announced, "I think you should come with me into the trees over there. I think we'll discover some magic. The magic of an angel." He again brought her hand to his lips.

Before Becky could respond, Melanie pulled her away and said, "I'm sorry, but we have to meet our friends in a few minutes."

Becky jerked her arm back and said, "Melanie, I think it would be fun."

"It might be fun, but it also might be deadly. We don't know who he is."

Reluctantly, Becky started to walk with Melanie toward the well-lit street. She looked back at Ali, smiled and waved. As they reached the street, she looked at Melanie and said, "I can't believe it. I kissed a French boy!" A delighted giggle bubbled up.

* * * * *

It was approaching 2 a.m. Mike and Derek walked out of yet another nightclub. It was time to return to their hotel. They hustled down the stairs to the Metro stop, only to discover that the famed Paris subway had stopped running. They returned to the street and looked for a taxi.

While Mike looked up and down the street for an available cab, he said, "Well, Buddy, I think we're walking back to the hotel tonight. We might as well get started."

Derek responded, "I told you we should have left an hour ago. I hope that girl you were dancing with was worth it."

"She was, thank you very much."

And they walked off.

Chapter 12

Paris was enjoying a quiet and uneventful morning. The sun was interrupted by large, fluffy clouds that drifted by. Luxembourg Park was filled with families and lovers. Some people walked along the gravel paths, while others lay in the grass enjoying the fine weather. Fathers helped their children sail their boats in the manmade pond. One couple, oblivious to those around them, was enjoying soft kisses. It was simply a lovely day to be in Paris.

While Parisians and tourists went about their business of living in and visiting Paris, something was soon to draw Samir's attention outside the apartment where he and Salah were working.

The phone rang.

"Hello?" Samir answered cautiously.

One of the lookouts across the street was on the line. He spoke quickly in a hushed voice. "I have some news. I was walking back from lunch and looking at magazines at the newsstand. A man inside the open newsstand was talking to the owner. He was asking questions about the people in your apartment building. I did not think much of it until he asked if there were new Muslims in this area."

At that point, Samir's ears perked up and he listened intently. The man on the other end of the line paused for a moment.

Samir said, "Go on."

"The man indicated to the operator of the newsstand that he was willing to pay for good information. The operator inquired about the type of information he was looking for. The man said he was trying to make sure no one was present in the area who might cause problems. He continued by telling the newsstand operator that the government was concerned about potential terrorist attacks. It was obvious he was some kind of government agent."

"Did the operator of the newsstand provide any additional information?" Samir asked, his stomach clenching slightly.

"None that I heard," the caller said.

"Where is the man now?"

"He is in the café across the street from your apartment and has been there for about 20 minutes. If you look out your window, you will see him in the second row of tables on the sidewalk."

Samir walked to the window, pulled the shade back an inch or so, and glanced at the café across the street. "I see three men at three different tables. Which one are you talking about?"

"From your position, the one on the left. He is wearing jeans with a white shirt. He has black hair and is wearing wraparound sunglasses. Do you see him now?"

Samir could see the man clearly. "I have him. We'll take care of it from here. We'll talk later."

For the next 20 minutes, Samir observed the man closely. A cup of espresso stood on the round table in front of him as he watched the people who walked by. This in and of itself is not unusual in Paris, where people watching is the number-one sport.

It was easy to tell, however, that he was not simply a Parisian enjoying an afternoon drink. The man did not watch the various women who walked by, a favorite occupation of Parisian men. His attention was directed at young men of Middle Eastern appearance. Samir could tell that this individual seemed to be cataloging the men walking by. He wondered if the man had a hidden camera to record the passersby.

Salah, who had joined him a few minutes earlier at the window, stepped back and said, "I don't like the looks of this. Do you think he is looking for us? Or is it simply some kind of preventive work?"

"I don't think it matters at this point. He has become an instant danger to us. Now the question is, how do we respond? Do you have any suggestions, Salah?"

For the next several minutes, the two men discussed multiple options. Each ended with the removal of the government agent sitting below their window at the café. After they agreed upon a course of action, Salah went to locate Yussof.

Samir left the apartment and walked down the stairs to the basement. A small room, about four meters square, was located there. Its only furnishings were a small metal table bolted to the floor and a chair. He sat down to wait.

Salah found Yussof in his room. Salah told Yussof he had an important job for him, then explained what was needed.

Yussof was a small, thin man. The clothes he wore were somewhat shabby and hung on his slender frame. As instructed, Yussof walked across the street toward the café. He approached the man who was still sitting at the table. The man eyed him carefully as he approached. Yussof, with a nervous look about him, spoke in a low voice. "The man at the newsstand said you were willing to pay for information. Is that correct?"

"Perhaps. Why do you ask?"

"I need some money and may have some information that could be valuable to you."

"What makes you think it is valuable?" the man in the jeans asked.

"It is about some new men who moved into the neighborhood."

"Sit down. Let's talk," the man said.

"No. These men look very dangerous and I am taking a chance just talking to you here. How much money are we talking about?"

"That depends on the information you have, but I will make it worth your while. Let's go someplace where we can talk in private."

"Where would you like to go?"

"There's a quiet park down the street, approximately two blocks from here. We can meet there."

"No, I don't feel safe in a place that is open to the public. If these people are who I think they are, I would be in severe danger."

The man in the jeans looked at the man closely. He almost looked like a homeless man, a haunted expression etched on his gaunt face. To the man's eyes, it seemed that the small Arab had clothed himself at a thrift shop. His pants were baggy and his shirt hung from his bony shoulders.

The man had to make a decision on how to proceed.

Yussof realized that the next few minutes would determine whether he could lure the agent to the small room where Samir waited.

In a low voice, Yussof said, "I heard one of the men state to one of his friends that the attack would be happening soon. I was going up the stairs to my girlfriend's apartment. As I passed by the door, that is what I heard. I did not hang around because I didn't want to get involved. I can tell you about those men. That should be worth a lot of money."

As the man looked at Yussof, he could see real fear in the smaller man's eyes. He was clearly afraid of being involved, but the money was obviously enticing.

"I think we can make this very worth your while. Where would you like to go so that we can talk?"

"I have a room in the basement of the apartment building across the street. I don't think anybody would expect anything there. I would have to go first. We could not go together. There are stairs down to the basement. My apartment is number 03. I will go there now and wait for half an hour for you to come. If you decide not to come, please forget that this conversation ever took place."

With that, Yussof crossed the street and entered the apartment building.

The man, whose name was René Bastine, watched the small man leave and enter the building. He knew that this information probably meant nothing other than a simple attempt to obtain money. However, if there was anything to this man's information, it could be critical. He looked up and down the street and gazed at the buildings around him, but nothing seemed out of place. He rose, crossed the street, and entered the apartment building.

A few feet in front of him, he saw the stairs that led to the basement. He walked slowly down the stairs, listening for anything out of the ordinary. He heard nothing. In the dim light, he saw a small hallway with several doors on each side. It appeared that each of the doors entered not into an apartment, but rather, into individual rooms. He could not tell what type of rooms they were.

As the man walked down the hallway, he soon came to room 03. He stood, listened at the door, and heard music coming from within. He knocked softly and waited for a reply. The door opened about two inches; Yussof peered through the slit. He turned back into the apartment and muttered, "Please come in."

René looked behind him. His right hand rested in the small of his back, where his revolver was hidden. He pushed open the door and took two steps into the room. Suddenly, he felt a sharp pain in the right side of his neck. He turned and saw a man smiling at him, holding a hypodermic needle. Before he could say anything, the room went black.

* * * * *

René was not sure how long he had been out when he finally opened his eyes. He tried to move but could not. He was sitting in a chair. A table stood in front of him. His arms and legs were bound to the chair. Across the table stood Samir, with Salah behind him.

As Samir watched René shake off the effects of the drug, he noticed that the man seemed more curious than afraid. This was strange given the circumstances he found himself in. Samir simply stared at the man for a two long minutes.

Then he smiled at René and in perfect, though accented French, said. "My friend, I hear you've been asking a lot of questions. Not only that, I hear you are willing to pay for good information. What kind of information are you looking for?

René decided to be aggressive. "Who are you and why are you doing this to me? You can't just go around grabbing people. It's against the law, or don't you know that?"

"I don't know whether you are brave or just stupid. I am asking the questions, not you. I suggest you get rid of this act and answer me when I ask a question."

"You can't do..."

With unexpected swiftness, Samir crushed his fist into René's face. "You need to understand that I'm not going to waste my time with you. Answer my questions!"

René realized his time had come. He had served his country well and would continue to do so. He said nothing and smiled at Samir, tasting blood in his mouth where his lip had been mashed.

Samir looked at the man. "Have it your way. You know, we have ways to make you talk. Every man has a breaking point, and we will find yours. Unless you tell me what we want to know, yours will be a long and painful death, and in the end, we will still have the information we want." He waited for a response from the man, but received none. "It is your choice."

Samir turned to Salah. "It's your turn."

Then Samir walked out the door and closed it behind him.

Salah walked to the front of the man. "You know, I dislike this part of my job. But only you can avoid what is to come by telling us what we want to know. This is your last chance before I have to begin my work."

René remained silent and just looked at him. Salah walked to the closet and removed a small box from the shelf. He returned to the table and placed the box upon it. "Well, my friend, this small box contains the tools of my trade. You know, the Americans use waterboarding and it is truly very effective. However, for me, it is not as much fun and someone has to clean up the water. I want you to look around the room. If you haven't noticed yet, it is heavily insulated so your screams will not be heard."

Salah opened the box and perused the items within it. He chose a small instrument that resembled a Phillips-head screwdriver. The end, however, was much sharper. "For torture to be truly effective, it is important that the subject not know what is coming next. Now, I could blindfold you, but you might be able to see anyway. So I'm going to use this instrument to blind you. I'm going to heat it up and then insert it into your eye. I'm sorry to tell you that it is very painful, but also very effective."

While René watched, Salah placed a small candle on the table and lit it. He then motioned for Yussof to come forward to assist him. Yussof came up behind René and grabbed his head to hold it still. René struggled as much as he could. He watched Salah hold the instrument in the flame of the candle and then come toward him. He heard himself scream. "No, no! Please don't do this!"

Salah pulled back and brought his face directly in front of René's eyes. "Are you going to answer my questions or not?"

Though Salah saw fear in René's eyes, he also saw the resolve to not give away information. "So be it." He brought the instrument up to René's right eye and slowly inserted it. The resulting scream was animal-like in its intensity. He withdrew the instrument and slowly inserted it into René's other eye. He was greeted with another unholy scream.

Salah worked on René for another hour before he broke. The man answered every question Salah asked. He stood behind René, who was whimpering in pain. Salah removed the pistol from his jacket. For privacy, it had a silencer attached to it.

"You have one minute to make peace with your God."

Before René could say a word, the pistol fired and the bullet entered René's head. He was no more.

Salah placed the barrel against the back of René's neck and fired once again. He looked at Yussof. "Get rid of him tonight in the usual manner."

With that, Salah walked out the door.

Chapter 13

It was late in the day and Pierre was ready to go home. In a few short hours, he would be attending a reception at the American Embassy. He did not necessarily enjoy these gatherings, but sometimes, they were valuable for the information he obtained. He locked his important files in the safe behind his desk. Pierre rose and walked to the door to get his jacket.

Just then, there was a sharp knock and the door opened. With a determined step, Mael Couseau entered.

Without any pretense of respect to the office or the man, he began. "We may have a problem."

Pierre looked at him, walked back to his desk and sat down. "What is it?"

"It may be nothing, but I don't think so. We have two instances where government officers or agents have been killed or are missing. Incidents we can't explain."

"What do you mean?"

"A police officer on a small road south of Lyon radioed his dispatcher that he had stopped a semi-truck. The officer indicated that it appeared unusual for that type of truck to be on that road. After 15 minutes, the dispatcher tried to contact the officer and was unsuccessful. She sent another officer to investigate. He was unable to find anything. They tried to contact the officer for several hours, but were unsuccessful. In a subsequent search this morning, they found the officer's car parked off the road hidden by trees. They found his body a short distance away. He had been shot in the back of the head."

"Have they developed any other information or leads?" Pierre felt his stomach lurch with the bad news.

"None. The truck seems to have disappeared into thin air."

"Did the officer give any description of the truck other than it was a semi?"

"No. They are grasping at straws here. There is no reason we can find that would cause the murder of this officer. What concerns me, however, is that this truck could be moving weapons from the south of France to the north. With all the trucks we have in France hauling material, it is like looking for a needle in a haystack. I have ordered that all trucks stopping at weigh stations be searched," Mael stated in his gravelly voice.

"I'm not sure there's anything else we can do. Did you have something else?"

"Yes, this is more disturbing. One of our agents is missing."

"What do you mean, missing?"

"He was assigned to develop informants in areas of high Muslim population here in Paris. He normally checks in every two to three hours. Yesterday, he checked in at around 1000, but we've heard nothing since. I've called his home and his wife said she had not seen him since yesterday. She wasn't concerned because it was not unusual for him to be gone for several days at a time."

"Do you know in what area he was working yesterday?" Pierre asked.

"He was in the 17th Arrondissement. That's the closest we can get."

"Have you sent other agents into the area?"

"Yes, but they have turned up nothing. You know how it is in those Muslim areas. They are very suspicious of any government activity that questions what they're doing. If he ran into problems, we may never find out what happened."

Pierre stood up and paced back and forth lost in thought. He pondered the ramifications of this information. Could they be linked? Or were these simply two separate, unrelated incidences? He looked at Mael. "Do you believe there is some connection between these two events?"

"I can't say for sure, but we should operate assuming that there is. If they are connected, then we have a problem without any knowledge of what it might be. If we believe these are separate occurrences, we may miss something without even knowing it."

Pierre could see the concern on Mael's face. There was something he wasn't telling him. "What else is on your mind?"

"I received a report from Marseille this morning. It seemed to be very innocuous. Someone up the coast complained to the local police establishment that people were trespassing on his property. The officer in charge did not think much of it, but to satisfy the person, he sent another officer out to investigate. When the officer arrived, he could see truck tracks going from the road down to the beach. A separate track goes from the beach to the road heading north. The second set of tracks dug deeper into the field. The officer speculated that something had been loaded onto the truck, which accounted for the deeper tracks."

Mael stopped for a moment to gauge Pierre's reaction, then continued.

"Upon receipt of that information, I had one of our agents in Marseilles check it out. He confirmed the information developed by the local officer. He also talked with residents of the various houses along the beach. One person indicated he had seen a vessel anchored a short distance off the beach where the tracks were located. He said it was some kind of sailboat. He also indicated it was not unusual to see that type of vessel in the bay. In sum, he wasn't concerned about it."

"Pierre, again, this may be nothing. What bothers me, however, is that a vessel may have offloaded cargo onto the beach and into the truck. If that's the case, I can only suspect that it is some kind of arms shipment. Why else would they do that rather than unloading at a marina? It may be possible that this is connected with the officer's murder further north."

"What steps do you think we should take to address this, Mael?" Pierre queried.

"I sent some forensics experts to the beach to see if they can determine the type of vehicle that was parked there. Maybe the tires will tell us something. I'm afraid something is afoot."

"The Indians are near. My head is beginning to itch. Mael, keep me informed of what you find out."

Mael left the room. Pierre continued to pace back and forth, trying to bring the parts of this puzzle together. Unfortunately, he simply did not have all the pieces to make sense of what was going on, but something was going on. Of that, he was sure. He reached for the phone, called his wife, and informed her he had to work late. He hoped that time was not running out.

Chapter 14

I watched Sophie as she walked ahead, leading our full group to the Jean Moulin Museum. She had a quiet beauty about her and carried herself with an air of confidence. Again, she was dressed in snug blue jeans and a white silk blouse open at the neck. Her dark hair fell easily upon her shoulders.

Sophie's most amazing feature was her eyes, which are hard to describe other than they looked like crystals. I had asked her about them the evening before and she shared that they likely originated in Brittany. The only people she had known with similar eyes had all come from that part of France. When talking with her, it was difficult not to look at, and be amazed, by those eyes.

Natalie and Sheila were walking in front of Mac and me. Their conversation was loud enough for me to hear, but Sophie did not seem aware of what they were saying.

Natalie said, "She is truly beautiful. I would have to say that she embodies all the best qualities of French women. Her face never seems stressed and always wears a smile. Her eyes invite you in for conversation. She makes you feel like the most important person in her life."

Sheila nodded, "And look how she dresses, casual yet elegant. I mean, she is just wearing jeans and a silk blouse. I assure you those would not look the same on me. The open neck on her blouse falls in such a way that it is sensuous and provocative, yet conservative. And look at her shoes, simple, yet beautiful. I asked her about the clothes she buys, and you know what she told me? She said she doesn't have a lot of clothes, but what she does have is of high quality. She tries to buy things that are interchangeable so that she can have several different looks."

"It's not just what she buys, it's how she wears them. I don't understand it. I can wear the same outfit and it's totally different. What's that all about?"

Mike, who was behind them, interrupted their conversation. "You're starting to see what I noticed on our first day here. Can you explain how she does it?"

Sheila glanced at him and shook her head. "I haven't a clue."

As that conversation came to an end, Sophie opened the door to the museum and entered. We followed her into the small reception area. Sophie was speaking in rapid French with the receptionist, who picked up the phone and made a short call.

A moment later, a middle-aged woman appeared and announced that she would be our guide through the museum. Having been here before, I wasn't sure the guide was necessary.

The Jean Moulin Museum was comprised of a series of exhibits on one floor. Glass cases contained uniforms, newspapers and written explanations of the life and times of Jean Moulin, a dedicated French Resistance leader during World War II. The students seemed interested at first, but then became restless and bored. We spent about 45 minutes touring the area before we were led out the door and into another door to the General LeClerc museum. The General had been a famous fighter during the same war. Many of the male students found this more interesting than the story of Jean Moulin.

As I sat near the front door waiting for the students to satisfy their curiosity, Mac walked up and joined me on the bench. Since I'd seen both museums on a previous visit to Paris, I wanted to get his take on including these institutions in our study-abroad program. "What do you think?"

"The two museums are very different. The Jean Moulin is a story of one incredibly brave man. Makes you wonder about those times. Some of the French were collaborators while others risked everything as members of the resistance. General LeClerc and the soldiers who fought with the free French army had to have a different type of courage. The same type of courage that soldiers in all armies are expected to exhibit. But when you're in the Resistance, alone, and trying to make a difference for your country, that takes a special person. You know there were many women in the Resistance as well. If these people were caught, they were tortured and killed. I wonder if I would have the courage to do it."

"I hear ya. Do you think the students understand why we brought them here?" I asked.

"I'm not sure. We should ask them during our down time."

"I have something that might bring all of this home for them," I said, ready to launch into my new idea.

Just then, the students converged on us, ready to leave. We walked a short distance away and I had them gather around. "We've added an additional stop for this morning. You will follow us. Sophie, you won't need to go with us since this is not part of the tour. Since we have a free afternoon, we'll see you in the morning. Thanks as always for your help."

As Sophie walked off, we headed for the nearest Metro station. Thirty minutes later, we exited at the Cité Metro stop. We walked as a group toward Notre Dame. The students who had visited previously were urging the remaining students to see it. As we approached the grand cathedral, we walked down the path to the right. Soon, we were at the memorial for those French men and women who had been deported during the Second World War.

We stopped before the gate. "This is a memorial for many French men and women who died after the Germans transported them out of Paris. As such, it is almost a holy place and you should act accordingly," I said.

Only small groups were allowed to enter at any one time. The students walked down the stairs into the memorial, followed by Mac and Ty. Since I had been in the memorial before, I waited outside for them to return. When they had finished, all the students had somber looks on their faces. After that, I led them to a grassy area and asked them to sit down. "What did you think of this?"

Jared responded first. "This memorial really brings the war home to me. The iron bars and candle, wow, I'm really kind of shaken."

Natalie raised her hand. "The simplicity of the memorial added to the effect it had on me. It's hard to imagine that people can be ripped out of their everyday lives and shipped off. It makes me thankful that the United States has never been occupied. I can't even imagine what that would be like."

Mac interrupted, "Can you relate this place back to Jean Moulin?"

Mike stood up. "It seems clear that he risked his life by being in the Resistance. You see your fellow citizens being arrested and sent God knows where, and you don't know if you will be next to go. I'm sure some people thought it was safer not to risk being involved with the Resistance. Frankly, I'm not sure what I would've done. But this sure makes you think."

Ty nodded at Mike. "That's why we brought you here. It's important that we think of these things."

The mood was quiet as we sat there, each of us pondering our own thoughts. For a while, the students engaged in quiet conversation with each other. Even though they had a free afternoon, this experience had caused them to pause. They realized that some of the issues they thought were important in their lives were small in comparison to what they had just experienced.

As their conversations came to a close, I rose and faced them. "This is the end of the organized activities for today. You can now explore the cultural riches of the city or you can go to a bar and meet new friends. Whichever you choose, please be safe. Mac, Ty and I are going to the Marché aux Puces. It is a flea market. If anyone wants to join us, you can."

It was obvious that no one wanted to be with us since no one took up our invitation. "Well, guys, I guess no one wants to hang with the old folks."

Ty placed his hand on my shoulder, "Lead on, fearless leader."

Mac, standing next to him, smiled at me, "We will follow you anywhere."

"One of these days, I will lead you to a place where you will be sorry."

"I can't wait," Ty laughed.

"Are we there yet, Daddy?" Mac's eyes twinkled. And we left.

Chapter 15

They drove to a small farmhouse not far from Paris, which had been rented several months before. Samir had decided that he, Salah, Kamil, and Ahmed should come to this location for their final meeting. Since the agent had been killed, Samir had been concerned that his apartment had been compromised.

The farmhouse had only three rooms: a bedroom, a bathroom and a combined kitchen and living room. Rustic and old, it was situated in the middle of three acres. The nearest other structure was a home about 500 meters to the south.

Because the farmhouse had been swept for bugs the day before, Samir knew that no one would be listening to their conversations. Even so, the cameras they had installed were being monitored by one of the Ahmed's men in the bedroom. They had arrived in two different cars so as not to raise suspicion among the local residents.

Samir opened the meeting. "Are we ready?"

Ahmed responded first. "We have sufficient men to accomplish the missions you planned. Each man has been trained to fulfill his individual assigned task. Most of our recruits have gone through training camps in Afghanistan, so we did not have to redo that training. I have discussed with each man his responsibilities. I've also had a minimum of two run-throughs of his specific job with each man. All of them were satisfied that they could accomplish what they've been given to do. They are, however, becoming somewhat anxious to begin. They are concerned, as we all are, that our plans may be discovered. They do not want to end up in a French prison for nothing."

Samir looked at Kamil. "Are we lacking any arms or supplies?"

"Since we added the final project, I would like to have more ammunition available. However, it should be sufficient. The explosives in their various forms are ready. The only matter to be completed is the fertilizer/oil mixture, which should be finished today. We've been gathering the fertilizer in small increments over the past several months, and the oil was not difficult to obtain. We have, however, waited until today to mix them appropriately.

With more confidence in his voice than he felt, Kamil went on, "The trucks that will be carrying the explosives will arrive early this evening at the warehouse. They should be totally prepared for use by midnight. I'm confident they will be ready."

Samir nodded for Kamil to continue.

"We're still in the process of transferring the weapons and explosives to those who need them. We're taking great care not to draw attention to this task. As we discussed, this is the area in which we are most vulnerable. Barring unforeseen circumstances, we should have confirmation by this evening that everything has been delivered."

"Have we met our communication needs?" Samir asked.

Knowing the critical importance of this matter, Salah had taken care of it himself. "I have purchased in excess of 100 throw-away cell phones. Ahmed and I delivered each one. It was an opportunity for me not only to explain the communication protocol, but also to judge the dedication of those selected. I went over the codes with each one several times to make sure he understood how we were going to proceed. Each individual has been briefed where and exactly when he needs to be once the date has been set. I've completed a dry run to determine if we can communicate in the timeframe we want to. It appears that we can do so with some time to spare."

"Samir, once you've made a decision on the date, we will send each person a coded text message informing him of the date," Salah concluded.

Then Samir asked, "How will it be coded?"

"It will say, for example: 'Ariel's birthday party is now set for the tenth. Each man has been told that the actual date is five days before the date stated, so, in this instance, the actual date would be the fifth. We intend to send that text out the day before the actual operation. That will limit the time that the government has to respond."

Salah continued, "It is expected that each individual on the day of the operation will be where he needs to be as we discussed. The final communication will simply be a text reading "Go." At that point, the operation will proceed as planned. We have told the men that, if their part does not involve their death, they should, after they have completed their job, go about their normal lives. We will contact them at a later date."

Samir thought about what he had heard. "Are you convinced that each man can count the days backward appropriately? I mean, what if they potentially miss a day one way or the other."

Salah responded, "It certainly is possible. However, I reviewed with each individual how this works. I've gone so far as to provide multiple examples and had each man solve it for me. I also gave each man a number to reach me if he had any questions at all. I think we need to trust that it will work. I'm not sure what else we could do."

"Okay, we'll have to make that work. We can deal with it if someone doesn't complete his job on the day in question. What we can't afford is to have anyone complete his task one day early. That would put the government on notice and make our remaining attacks immensely more difficult."

"Very true. But I've also informed each one of them that the operation would not take place on the day he received the text; the earliest date would be the following day."

Samir nodded his approval. "That's an added protection that makes me feel better." He had been leaning against the wall as the conversation took place. Now he walked forward and sat on the sofa. "Let's review the plan. I want to make sure that none of us have any concerns. If so, I want you to bring them up now so that we can discuss them and make appropriate changes if necessary." The others nodded their agreement.

"First, the initial steps are scheduled to begin at 1000. Is there any reason you know why we should not keep that time?"

Kamil looked at Samir. "I see no reason to change. As we discussed many times, we should get the maximum benefit for what we have planned at that time of day. If no one has a different view, I think we should proceed as planned."

Salah and Ahmed nodded their agreement. Samir could see in their eyes the excitement they felt for the upcoming attack. "The second phase, the car bombs, is scheduled to begin at 1035. Any reason we should change that?"

Salah shook his head and added, "We also have bombs set to explode at irregular intervals throughout the day. Those cars are all in place now, and, as you know, they will be set off remotely by cell phone. One of our men has a schedule for these car bombs. He will make the call to each car as set forth in the schedule."

"How long do you think it will take before the government deploys its security forces and the military?"

"That's hard to determine. It's obvious the police will respond initially, and until it is clear that they are unable to contain the violence, I do not expect the army will be brought out. But that's only speculation on my part. We have no idea what their contingency plans are."

Salah looked at the other men. "Have any of you learned anything different?"

There was no response.

Salah continued, "I think we have to play that by ear."

Samir seemed satisfied. "What time do you suggest we initiate the final part of our plan?" As the others pondered the question, the man monitoring the cameras walked in and asked Samir to join him. Samir walked into the bedroom and the man pointed at one screen. He could see a car driving up their driveway and coming to a stop.

Samir returned to the living room and closed the door to the bedroom. "Someone is coming and will be at the door momentarily. Let's proceed as planned." Kamil got up, opened the refrigerator and gave each one of them a beer.

There was a sharp knock on the door. Samir walked to the door and opened it. On the porch was an old man with white hair, gnarled hands and the look of a lifelong farmer.

Samir smiled, and said in his perfect, disarming French, "*Bon jour*, can I help you?"

The man peered closely at Samir and glanced over Samir's shoulder into the living room. He said, "I live in the house over there," as he pointed to the west. "There hasn't been much activity in this house for some time until I saw your cars arrive this morning. I came over to check things out. We tend to watch out for each other in this community."

Samir held the door open and invited the man in. "And I'm glad you do. We just came for a little downtime. We work in Paris."

The man saw the other three men seated around the room, each of them holding a beer in his hand. He looked at Samir, curiosity sparkling in his eyes. "Are you Muslims? If so, I didn't think you drank alcohol."

"Yes, we are Muslims," Samir answered. "And you're correct, sir, good Muslims are not supposed to drink alcohol. That's why we come here to relax and not to be spied upon by those more religious than us. Would you like to join us in a beer?"

"Don't mind if I do," the old man said, a smile crossing his face.

Ahmed rose, went to the refrigerator and brought a beer to the man. He gestured for the old farmer to sit down with them.

For the next half hour, the men discussed farming in this part of France. As the conversation slowed, the man rose and stated, "Maybe the next time you're here for some downtime, you can come to my place and enjoy some wine. My son is a vintner and makes wonderful wine."

Samir rose and shook the man's hand. "That sounds like a lot of fun. We plan to return in about two weeks. Would that work?"

The man smiled. "I'll make it work." He shook hands with the others and walked out the door. He had no idea how close death had come to him.

Kamil walked to the window and watch the man's vehicle drive down the road. "Samir, it only takes one suspicious man to ruin this operation. When are we going to do this?"

Samir hesitated for a few brief moments. "Tomorrow, unless someone has an objection." No one raised their hand and he saw the excitement build in them once again. "Then the decision has been made. Make your calls and may Allah be with us."

Chapter 16

Our Metro ride to the Marché aux Puces continued until it reached the Porte de Clignancourt stop, which was the last on the subway line. As a result, all the passengers, including our group, exited the train and walked toward the stairs that would take us to the street. As we poured out onto the sidewalk, the sun seemed very bright compared to the lights of the station. I pointed in the direction we would take.

"This is the way to the flea market. We have a couple blocks to go. Before we get there, there are some open-air stalls you may want to wander through," I told Mac and Ty. "If you find something you want, remember to negotiate the price. Only Americans pay the asking price. A couple years ago, I bought a nice leather jacket for half the price they were asking."

We three oldsters strolled along slowly, watching the activity about us. Various street sellers approached us with cheap knockoff Rolexes, new phones and about anything else they expected they could sell. This area was rather seedy, dirty and full of pickpockets. Both Ty and Mac were alert.

Mac elbowed me, "You notice something about these guys?" Before I could respond, he stated, "They are all Middle Eastern. Why do you think that is?"

I had noticed that before on my trips to the market. "I can't tell you. It's been like this since the first time I came."

Ty broke in. "There's something odd going on. Maybe it's because I haven't been here before, but these guys seem to be acting odd. I've been among street sellers before, but I'm not getting the same vibe here."

I started watching the vendors more closely. I could not see what he was talking about, but then again, I was not a trained police officer. Experienced cops see things the rest of us miss.

As the three of us meandered down the street, Mac spoke up. "I think I see it now. Did you notice how they come up, smile, and offer you their wares? When we say no, their smile remains as they walk away. I've been among street sellers, too; they typically frown at you or say something to encourage you to buy. These guys keep that funny smile on their faces like they know something we don't. It's not only strange, it's a little freaky. It's almost like we could get mugged or something."

Ty continued watching as the various sellers approached us and left. "Mac, you're absolutely right. They are different in the way they're relating to potential buyers. What is that about? It's a little strange."

I had been watching the vendors, listening to their conversations. I still didn't see it. "You guys are too damn suspicious and you're making me uncomfortable."

Mac nudged Ty and nodded toward me. "Dumb lawyers." With that, we entered the flea market. The market spread out over a large area with only two main exits. Narrow passages snaked around the market. On either side of the passageway were rooms of various size with roll-up doors that opened into the shops. Some vendors were selling exotic spices, others clothing, handmade toys and carvings, and beautifully embroidered scarves and dresses. Other vendors sold old farm utensils, paintings, or furniture. Tourists and Parisians alike threaded their way through the market, which was filled with the exotic odors of meals being consumed.

My friends and I spent almost three hours wandering through the various narrow alleys of the market. We heard experienced buyers haggling for more favorable transactions. At some shops, we stopped to examine items that held some interest. In the end, we left without purchasing anything.

As Mac, Ty and I walked back to the metro, we passed through the throng of street sellers again. No one said anything.

Mac nudged me. "Did you see it this time?"

"No, you guys are nuts."

"Really dumb lawyer!"

We finally reached the Metro station, walked down the stairs, and waited for the next train. I had been thinking about our conversation about the street sellers. "Hey, were you serious about those guys trying to sell us stuff on the street? Or are you simply giving me a bad time? The reason I ask is because I really saw nothing I would consider out of the ordinary."

Mac seemed to wonder what was wrong with me. "You're being serious, aren't you? I thought you were joking. It's hard to explain, DJ. Ty and I have worked the streets for so long that we can sense when something is not right."

"I'm well aware of that, but we're in a different country that has its own culture. Couldn't it simply be that?"

"Of course it could. However, people are the same all over the world. I think that's where Ty and I are coming from. Ty, what do you think?"

"I agree with you. Could it be something different? Yes, it could, but it doesn't feel right. I could spend all night trying to explain it to you, but I couldn't. It's something in my gut that has developed during my time as a police officer."

"Well, if both of you feel this way, can you give me an idea of what you think you're seeing? Surely, something stands out to you."

Mac replied, "The fact that Ty and I feel something is amiss does not mean we know what it is. We've also admitted that it may be nothing. When this happens to us, we just become more alert and try to determine if there is anything there that can help us understand what's going on."

I saw Ty nodding as Mac spoke. "Okay, if you see anything else, let me know so I can begin to understand how you two see things. Or maybe I should say, don't see things. It's all very interesting to me."

We rode the subway to the Cité stop. I had told them of a great restaurant on Île Saint-Louis. They both indicated that it sounded like a great place to eat before returning to our hotel. We walked past Notre Dame and crossed over the bridge before walking down the small road that ran the length of the island. I pointed out our destination on the left. We entered the Auberge de la Reine Blanche, a small restaurant that could seat only 20 or 30 people.

A maître d' showed us to a small table and with typical French aplomb and provided us with menus. Having been there before, I chose the steak with burning thyme, as did Ty. Mac chose the filet. We agreed to share a bottle of Bordeaux. We started with a light aperitif, Kir Royale. As we waited for our food to come, I asked my friends how they thought this trip was going.

Mac shook his head, "I'm a little surprised at how quickly the students adjusted to the cultural differences they were experiencing. I've had more trouble at that than they have, but I'm getting better at it. It is still difficult not to compare Paris to the U.S. For the most part, the students have been totally engaged in our various activities. They're certainly having fun at night."

"Hey, I just go with the flow," responded Ty. "I think it's great. I love the outdoor cafés. People watching is a kick in the ass. I'm not worried about the kids. They seem to be making smart decisions and not getting themselves into trouble. It will be fun to read their journals when we get back. That should make for some interesting reading. I want to read Derek's to see how he did with the women."

"I understand," said Mac, "but I think Melanie's might be the best of all." We all nodded our heads and laughed. Melanie had more real-world experience than the rest of the young women put together. Furthermore, she was not shy in sharing her experiences.

The food arrived soon enough and we enjoyed the way the meal was prepared and tasted. When the waiter returned to our table and asked whether we would like dessert, I suggested to the other two that we decline. I told them I had another treat for them. We paid our bill and left the restaurant.

Each of us had a warm glow from the Bordeaux and were in no hurry to rush anywhere. We headed toward Notre Dame in a slow walk. Just before we were to cross the bridge to the Île de la Cité, I turned left.

At Le Flore en l'île, we found some seats outside and sat down. The waiter, clad in the traditional white shirt and black trousers, as well as a bored expression, brought us menus. I told Mac and Ty they would not be disappointed with the hot chocolate. I ordered mine and Ty concurred. Mac, however, decided to be different. He knew what he wanted but didn't know what it was on the menu. So he led the waiter back into the restaurant and pointed to what he wanted on the dessert cart. Within minutes, he returned and joined us at the table.

I looked at him. "Well, what did you order?"

Mac leaned forward, smiled and said, "I don't know what it is, but it looks good. The waiter told me I had ordered the best of the best of the best. It was an apple pie kind of thing."

"Yeah, and he probably convinced you to pay twice the asking price." Ty nodded his agreement.

"Now I'm with the dumb lawyer and a dumb cop."

When we finished, I signaled for the check. The waiter approached and handed it to Mac. Ty and I rose to leave and Mac stated, "Hey, we are splitting this."

I started laughing and looked at Mac. "Since you are the best the best of the best, I'm sure the waiter expects you to take care of it." As Ty and I walked away, Mac was muttering under his breath and threatening us with bodily harm.

Chapter 17

Malik turned the corner and saw the mosque in front of him. He was not always a faithful attendee at prayer services, but he felt the need to go right now. One hour ago, he had received the text he was told would be coming. It surprised him because it was so soon. He had checked and double-checked the dates until he was sure that tomorrow was the day they had been waiting for. He paused for a moment to observe the street in front of him. There were a few men and a lesser number of women walking toward the mosque. He took a deep breath to calm his nerves, and continued on.

As he approached the entrance to the mosque, he saw Jawad, a man he had spoken with many times before. Occasionally, after their daily prayer, they would stop at a nearby café to enjoy an espresso together. Jawad waved at him as he approached. He smiled and returned Jawad's greeting. He grasped his friend's hand. "May the peace of Allah be with you."

"And with you, my friend. How is your day going?" Jawad asked.

"It is quite good. I am at peace. And you? What is happening in your life?" Malik asked in return.

"It is much the same as every other day. You wake up, you pray, you eat, you pray, and at some point you fall asleep. My wife tells me that I am a good provider. I try my best, but I'm not sure it's enough. We seem to live week to week, but we're better off than many others. Have you found work yet?"

"No, but I have several things that may be promising. You're lucky to have a job in these times. I will find one, I'm sure. It's just a matter of time. I try not to get discouraged, but it is difficult. There are many others like me in the city. Sometimes I feel shut out by the Parisians who control everything. I just wish the opportunities for us were better than they are."

Jawad watched his friend and did not really discern any discouragement in his face. It seemed to be more of an acceptance of his place. He tried to lighten his friend's mood by asking, "Have you met any women worthy of you?"

Malik could not help but laugh. "Only those dogs you've attempted set me up with. Why don't you find me someone who would fit my needs?"

Jawad joined him in laughter. "I suppose you'll want a woman with big breasts and who speaks very little? I will do my best."

Jawad realized that he and Malik could pass as brothers. They both were of average height, with black hair and while he was 27, Malik was 24. More importantly, a bond had developed between them in the last several months. From their shared time in the mosque and through their social time together, they had become close. It was almost like Jawad was Malik's older brother, to whom he could turn for advice.

Malik pointed toward the mosque. "Are you going in?

"No, I'm just leaving. I had some private time with the imam, which was very helpful to me."

"All right, I will see you soon." He started to turn away, stopped and looked back at Jawad. "Perhaps that may not be true. I think I will soon meet my 72 virgins. If so, I will only see you again in another world."

Jawad saw the change come over Malik. He had not heard the younger man speak like this before. "What do you mean, Malik? I do not understand."

"My time has come. I cannot tell you anything further. By tomorrow, you will comprehend. The peace of Allah be with you." Without another word, Malik turned and entered the mosque.

Jawad hurried away. After he turned the corner, he looked around and saw no one else of the Muslim faith near him. He pulled out his phone and entered the number only he knew. He waited a few seconds before the phone was answered. "My friend, we need to meet immediately. Can you come to the café?"

"Yes, I'll be there in 15 minutes." With that, Jawad pressed the END button.

Jawad walked to the metro, whose entrance was a short distance away. He got off at the second stop and took the escalator to the street. One block away was a small café that seemed empty of customers. As he approached the café, he saw that no one was seated outside. Jawad sat down at the table farthest from the door. That would make this conversation easier, for he wanted no one else to hear.

Within five minutes, he saw the man approach from the opposite direction. He did not rise, but merely motioned to the chair next to him. The man sat down and said nothing. Jawad had known this man for 15 years. While Jawad appeared to be Middle Eastern and spoke perfect Arabic, he was not. He was a French national who had worked undercover in service to his country for many years.

He looked at his friend. "Mael, I believe I have stumbled onto something very serious. One of the men at the mosque whom I have come to know talked to me today. His name is Malik. Toward the end of our discussion, just as we were about to leave, he said he would see me soon. Then he changed and said perhaps not—he thought he would be meeting his 72 virgins, and if so, he would see me in another world. I inquired what he meant but he would only say that by tomorrow, I would understand. I have no indication that he is involved in any terrorist group. However, he has been unemployed for some time. I hope I'm not overreacting, but you know, I would not contact you directly unless I thought it was important."

Mael understood exactly what Jawad meant. The young man was not one to fluster easily, but it was apparent that he considered the conversation with Malik to be very serious. There was no reason for Mael to doubt his friend's conclusions. The question that now presented itself was what, if any, action should be taken. "Do you think we should take him into custody and interrogate him?"

"That is not my call. However, if you're asking my opinion, it may be the only safe thing to do. If it is nothing, you can release him as if it were a simple investigation. But if it is something more, not acting may have dire consequences. You know, sometimes terrorists may not look like terrorists, but simply appear to be one of us. "

"I agree. How will I know who he is?"

"I've got a picture on my phone that I took of both of us some time ago. I'll send it to you right now."

"Do you know where he is now?"

"He is in the mosque praying. You should be able to contact him when he leaves."

"I'm going to arrange it now. I will be in touch and let you know what I find out." With that, Mael rose and signaled down the street. In a moment, a shiny black Peugeot pulled up. Mael got in and was gone.

Jawad was deeply troubled as he watched his friend drive off. He was certain he had done the right thing, but if it was a misunderstanding, Malik was in for a difficult time.

Chapter 18

Malik had entered the mosque with the intent of staying for an extended period of time. His prayers had come easily, however, and a deep peace had descended upon him. His spirit was full once again. Malik took comfort in the fact that he did not feel nervous at all and was filled with the warmth of Allah. He did not need to talk with the imam. Deep within his soul, he knew he was sure of his purpose and was filled with a firm determination.

After tomorrow, Malik knew he would never have to go searching for a job again. He detested having to be submissive to potential employers. He would no longer have to smile at them when it was clear they regarded him as a nobody. He would no longer have to live in a shabby apartment he could barely afford or have to worry about finding a woman to share his life.

After tomorrow, none of these worldly concerns would have a place in his life. As he looked back upon his situation, he realized how difficult a struggle his life in Paris had become. After tomorrow, he would be looked up to and his name would be spoken with reverence.

As a result, he left the mosque early. The sun shone upon his face. It was clearly a sign that Allah was pleased. Malik had some time to pass before he needed to go to his assigned location for the attack. He entered a small café facing the mosque, and chose a table near the window. When the waiter arrived, he ordered an espresso. As he sipped the drink, it seemed that all was right with his world.

Suddenly, he saw two cars pull to the curb in front of the mosque. Two men got out of each vehicle. They were wearing dark suits, which set them apart from everyone else. He also saw a police van pull up behind the mosque. Several men got out, each carrying an automatic weapon. They surrounded the mosque but did not enter. This was obviously a police raid of some type. Malik had heard of these happening, but had never seen one occur.

Malik watched with fascination as the faithful began to exit the mosque. The men in dark suits closely watched every male who came out. Each had what appeared to be a photograph in their hand. As the last person left the mosque without being stopped, two of the men in the dark suits conversed for a few moments. One then entered the mosque. A short time later, he returned and shook his head. It was apparent to Malik that whoever they were looking for had not been found.

The man who appeared to be the leader of this operation looked up and down the street. His gaze crossed over the café where Malik sat. Suddenly, it dawned on Malik that he might be the object of their search. He was not sure why that would be the case. He had done nothing illegal or anything that would draw attention to himself. As the man's gaze started to return, Malik stood and began walking to the rear of the cafe.

Mael had looked down the street but then stopped. When his gaze returned to the café, he paused. Something was wrong. Then, he realized there had been a man sitting behind the window watching them. Now he was gone. He needed to check that individual out and started walking quickly toward the door of the café.

Meanwhile, Malik had exited the café through the back door and took off running down the alley. As soon as he reached the corner, he turned and continued running for the metro stop. As he reached its entrance, he looked around and discovered no one was following him. Still, he knew he had to get out of there. He raced down the steps and hopped on the first train that came by. It really didn't matter where it was going as long as it was away from this place.

Malik gazed at the people seated in the train to see if anyone took any notice of him. No one was paying him the slightest attention. His relief was obvious and he took a deep, calming breath. He closed his eyes and let the wheels of the train carry him away.

* * * * *

Mael entered the café and swiftly glanced around. The man he was looking for was not there. He was sure there'd been a man in the window watching what was happening outside He walked up to the waiter and showed him the photograph. "Have you seen this man today?"

The waiter studied the photograph closely. "I think he was sitting right over there." He had pointed to the window that had drawn Mael's interest initially. "I don't know where he has gone. He didn't pay for his espresso either. These foreigners, they care little for our way of life. They have no honor."

Mael was beginning to believe he had missed his man. He looked at the waiter. "Is there another way out?"

The waiter nodded and pointed toward the back door. Mael ran to the door, stepped out and looked both ways, but the alley was empty. He returned to his men. "He was in the café but got away. Let's go to his address and see if we can catch him there." They returned to their cars and sped off.

* * * * *

Malik exited the metro and walked to the nearest taxi stop. Soon a taxi pulled over. He entered and gave the driver the address. It was two blocks from where he wanted to be. After leaving the taxi, he walked slowly to that location and looked around to see if anyone was following him. Seeing nothing, he knocked on the door. It was opened by Kamil, who smiled and let him enter.

Within five minutes of Malik having arrived at his location, Mael and his team pulled up in front of an apartment building. They walked quietly up the stairs to the third floor. There were seven of them, the four men in suits and three officers. When he was ready, Mael gave the signal and the officer using the battering ram he carried knocked the door open. The seven men rushed in with guns drawn. As they swept the apartment, it became clear that no one was there.

Mael wondered where the man was. Unfortunately, they had no other leads to follow.

* * * * *

Arms crossed over his chest, Malik stood watching the activity in the warehouse. Weapons were being cleaned and prepared for use. Several men pried open heavy wooden boxes that appeared to be filled with explosives, then carefully packed their deadly loads into carrying cases of various sizes. Malik could see beads of sweat rolling down their faces. He gave Allah thanks that this work was not his responsibility.

Kamil placed his hand on the younger man's shoulder and smiled. "Your truck will be ready in plenty of time. Go upstairs and rest."

Malik did as he was told, a broad smile crossing his face.

Chapter 19

Despite the thick Paris traffic, It didn't take long for Mael to return to his office. He immediately picked up the phone and dialed. A secretary answered the phone. "This is the director's office. May I help you?"

"It's Mael. Is the director in?"

"Yes, he is. He has just returned from a meeting."

"Please tell him I need to see him immediately. I'm on my way up." Without waiting for a response, he hung up and walked out. He took the stairs two at a time and arrived at Pierre Belcher's office a few moments later.

The secretary nodded toward the director's door. "He's expecting you now."

After thanking her, Mael opened the door and walked in. He saw the director sitting behind his desk. He walked up and sat in the stiff wooden visitor's chair, then looked at Pierre. "We have a problem."

"Please explain."

"One of my agents contacted me earlier today. He wanted to meet as soon as possible. I've known him for many years and he is not one prone to excitability. In essence, one of the men he met while undercover talked with him today. The man said he was going to be with his 72 virgins and would not see my agent until the afterlife. When my man questioned him further, he only said that he would understand tomorrow.

Mael continued. "After discussing this matter with my agent, we decided to bring this individual into custody and determine whether there was an issue or not. We quickly put together a field team, backed up by the police, to check this out. I was informed that he was in the mosque for his daily prayers. We waited outside for him to leave, but did not see him exit the mosque."

Pierre Belcher felt his stomach clench, which it did whenever he sensed trouble. "Please go on, Mael."

"My agent had given me a picture of him so we knew who we were looking for. As I was looking up and down the street, I noticed someone who had been in a café looking at us had suddenly disappeared. I showed the waiter who had been serving him the man's photo and he acknowledged that the man had been there. I checked the alley and the surrounding area. The man was nowhere to be seen."

Pierre raised his hand to interrupt. "As I understand what you've told me, our agent informed you that this individual would be in the mosque. Is that correct?"

"Yes, that is correct."

"I take it there were other people in the mosque at the time. How do we know that he simply did not come out?"

Mael nodded and said, "That was also one of our concerns. I sent one of my men into the mosque to determine if anyone else was there. He did a quick search and found no one. He also talked with the imam, who indicated that everyone had left previously."

"Then how is it you and your men did not see him leave?" Pierre asked.

"I cannot answer that specifically, director. However, he must've left before we arrived. When I saw the individual sitting in the café, he did not seem particularly concerned. Something aroused his suspicion to cause him to leave. Other than the fact that we were obviously looking for someone, I have no other information that would answer the question why he left."

Pierre nodded. "Is it possible he was tipped off?"

Once again, Mael nodded his head. "It certainly is possible. However, if he was concerned about being discovered, why would he remain near the mosque? I would expect him to have left immediately."

"So what's the bottom line on this, Mael?"

"I believe he saw us and took off. I obtained his address prior to arriving at the mosque. We decided to see if we could catch him there. We broke into his apartment, but it was empty. My concern, obviously, is that there may be something planned for tomorrow in which he is a participant. It certainly is possible that is not the case, but the circumstances lead me to believe otherwise."

Pierre stood and paced back and forth. "Could it be possible that he simply wanted to avoid the authorities? Has this guy been on our watch list?"

"No, we have neither had contact with him nor heard of him previously," Mael responded.

"Does your agent have any knowledge of any friends or family he may have?"

"I asked him that same question and he replied in the negative. His only contact with this individual has been at the mosque or sharing an espresso with him after worship. He told me he had no knowledge of any family or friends the man might have. He also indicated the man had been looking for a job, but had been unsuccessful. It seems he had been trying to become employed, but was having a very difficult time.

"What do you suggest we do, Mael?" Pierre inquired of his deputy director.

"I have men watching his apartment, and the mosque is also under surveillance. We are doing a more in-depth review of his background and movements. We don't have much to go on, though. I've also sent copies of his photograph to all police agencies with the instructions that should they see him, they should detain him until our people arrive. I'm afraid that, unless we get a break, we may never find him."

"Okay. Keep me informed."

Mael nodded and left the director's office.

As Pierre paced back and forth in front of the windows, his concern increased. If the man who made those statements had not tried to flee, he would not be so concerned. His officers could have stopped the man and interrogated him to determine what he knew. If they had not gotten satisfactory answers, they would have moved him to a house outside of Paris, where more extensive interrogation techniques could have been used. If he knew that we were on to him, he would go into hiding and it would be very difficult to locate the man.

Pierre stared out the window at his city, wondering if this was truly a matter he should be concerned with. Then, his head began to itch.

Chapter 20

Anna was 13 years old and had just finished seventh grade at her school in Dallas. She was a bright girl who worked hard and excelled in her studies. Her interest in subjects was very eclectic. She loved history, art, and math. Her blonde hair fell below her shoulders and today, it was tied back in a ponytail. She wore no makeup and had clear skin that other teenagers envied. She was dressed in jeans and a bright red and white blouse. Her feet were clad in the latest footwear from Nike.

Her parents always made sure that she was well and stylishly dressed, but it was not really important to her. That was a major difference from other girls her age. She did not seem to take wealth seriously; many of her friends were from families that lived paycheck to paycheck. Furthermore, race played no part in her life for she was truly colorblind. In fact, she once scolded her father when he made a negative statement about Hispanics.

Her mother, Roberta, was next to her in the cab. She was also wearing jeans, paired with a more conservative white blouse. Roberta knew she looked good for a 38-year-old woman. Her hair was sandy blonde and cut short so she didn't have to spend a lot of time getting ready in the morning. She no longer had to prepare herself like she did when she was younger. Roberta had been married to Nick for 18 years now and her life was very comfortable. Nick was the vice president at a local bank and did very well for himself. They had three children now. Anna was the oldest, followed by her brothers, Jack and Jonas.

Anna's relationship with her mother was special. Her mother doted on her like so many mothers do. Even as Anna got older, she loved the time she and her mother spent together. This was one of those times. Since she had turned 10, her mother had, every year, taken her on special trips they planned together. Nick liked the idea and felt that this bond would help them as she entered her teen years. Jack and Jonas had no desire to be involved in these trips as they were heavily involved in sports. So it was always a special time for this mother and daughter.

Last year, Anna and her mother had taken a wonderful two-week trip to Rome and Athens. They had seen the Pope giving his weekly blessing in Rome and walked the Acropolis in Athens. They had stayed in four-star hotels and ate delicious, varied meals. Each day, Anna had written in her journal an account of her day. When she came home, she shared these memories with her friends. Some were jealous, but most loved to hear about places and people that they had not experienced themselves.

This year, Anna and Roberta had chosen Paris as their destination. They had been in Paris for four days and were staying in a small boutique hotel in the Marais. Anna loved to walk with her mother through the Marais because of how exciting and different it was. She believed she could wander the streets in the area and never see everything there was to see.

It had been a very busy time for both of them. They had visited Notre Dame, the Musée d'Orsay and many other large and small museums. Today, their schedule included a visit to the Eiffel Tower and shopping in St. Germain. If they had time, they planned to visit the Pantheon. Her mother could see that Anna was visibly excited as they were dropped off at the Eiffel Tower.

Staring up at the world-renowned tower, Anna told her mother, "I had no idea it was so big. I know it looks big from different parts of the city, but this is just awesome. How could they have possibly built this?"

"I'm not sure, honey. It's amazing considering that it was built in the late 1800s. We'll definitely get a different view of Paris from the top. Do you want to walk around first or go straight up?"

"Let's go up now."

Even though it was only 9:15 in the morning, long lines of tourists stretched from beneath the four legs where the ticket booths were located. Roberta had warned her daughter that they may need patience at this time of year. After five minutes, they were standing before the ticket booth and Roberta purchased the tickets that would allow them to go to the top of the Tower. It took a few minutes before they were able to get on the first elevator.

As the elevator began its trek to the next level, Anna glanced at her mother. "How do they get this to go up at an angle? I've never seen any elevator that didn't go straight up."

Roberta smiled at her daughter's unending inquisitiveness. Anna's curiosity seemed endless. She knew that was one of the reasons Anna did so well in school. She and Nick had many discussions about how to help Anna continue to grow while she still had this wide-eyed innocence about her. "This whole structure is quite an engineering achievement. I could not possibly explain that to you. With your interest in math, perhaps you'll become an engineer."

When they reached the first level, they walked around the perimeter and looked at the city. Once they were satisfied they had seen everything they could, mother and daughter continued their journey to the top in the second elevator. Finally arriving at the top observation deck, they were amazed at how much the view had changed. Even though they were looking at the same vista, they were so high it changed their perspective dramatically.

"Mom, this is really interesting. Not just because we've gone higher, but what we see looks different. I wonder why that is."

Anna continued to explore Paris from above. She knew this would be one of the highlights of her trip. "I will be writing in my journal a lot tonight trying to describe what I am seeing. I'm not sure I can even describe this to my friends. Oh, well, maybe they'll just have to come to Paris and experience it themselves."

Anna and her mother took another walk around the entire observation deck, avoiding the throngs of other tourists. Anna kept trying to identify all the landmarks she recognized. Suddenly, she stopped looking and glanced at her mother. "Can you feel the Tower moving?

"Yes, a bit. It's the wind," answered her mother.

"That is so cool." Anna continued to stand there, trying to determine how much it was swaying.

Chapter 21

Malik heard something that tore him out of his sleep. He looked at his watch and it read 0800. He got up, walked to the bathroom and threw some water on his face. Slowly, he became fully awake. He walked downstairs to see the activity that had woken him. There were many people in the warehouse—some working, some watching.

As he stood at the bottom of the stairs, Kamil came up to him. "Were you able to sleep?"

"Like a baby. Is everything ready to go?"

"Yes. We are ahead of schedule. Everyone who is supposed to be here has arrived. Let's go check your truck out." With that, the two men walked to the back of the warehouse to Malik's truck.

"As you can see, the truck carries the name of the company that services the restaurants. Hopefully, that will cause the security forces to hesitate and give you more time to reach your target. Your truck is ready. The fertilizer/oil mixture is already loaded and the detonator has been installed. The means to trigger the explosion is in the cab. Let me show you."

From either side of the truck, they pulled open the cab doors and Malik could see the setup. Two buttons were installed in the dash. The one on the left was green and the one on the right was red.

Kamil explained, pointing, "The detonator is in place, but it has not been activated. To assure that there is no premature explosion, the detonator has to be armed first by pushing the green button here." Malik nodded.

Kamil continued. "Once that button is pushed, the detonator will be armed. You then have to push the red button to set off the explosion. Are you sure you understand that? Do you have any questions?"

"Yes, it is quite clear to me. I push the green button first, and to detonate, I push the red button."

"Exactly. Now I must ask you a question of faith. Are you sure you can do this?"

"Yes, I am ready."

"Your actions are critically important to us. The target you have been assigned will affect the entire self-image of the French. Once it is gone, the whole world will be able to see and understand our ability to strike anywhere. If there is any concern in your own mind that you cannot push the red button, I need to know now. Some people are not ready to take this step. It takes great courage to fight for Allah in this way. I want you to search your heart very carefully before you answer."

"I understand what you are telling me, my friend. But my heart is good. I'm filled with great peace and I'm looking forward to the journey."

Kamil nodded his approval. "Do you remember your route?"

"Yes, of course. Once we are on Quai Branly, we will take a right on Avenue de Suffren. We then turn left on Avenue Gustave Eiffel. Then we turn left toward the target. Kamil, you need not be concerned. I've not only driven that route many times, I've walked it as well."

"Good, but you understand I cannot leave anything to chance."

"I do understand. I just want you to know that I'm not only ready, but well prepared."

"Yes, I can see that, Malik. Come with me so that I can introduce you to the people who will be working with you."

They carefully closed the doors to the truck and Kamil led him to a table where several people sat. This introduction was necessary since all the parties to this part of the plan had not met until this day. That was the only way to assure the best security.

Addressing the others, Kamil began, "You have already met the people in your operation except for Malik." He pointed to Malik.

"He will be driving the second truck. Malik, this is Hani. He will be driving the lead van. As I've described to you previously, the van will be carrying your security force. The three men with him will be armed and prepared to make sure that you reach your target."

Gesturing to a slender man who carried himself with grim determination, Kamil went on. "This is Azam, the driver of the second truck. Each of you will also have someone who's armed in your vehicle. The guards are eating right now. I will introduce you to them later. In case something happens to you or Azam, they've been instructed on how to arm and detonate the explosive. Remember, the van leads you in, provides protection if necessary and you drive to the target. Once you reach your target, do not delay or hesitate in setting off the explosion. Any delay could result in your not being able to activate the detonator and set off the explosion. Any questions?"

No one asked a question. Kamil looked around at the men. "Each of you has been carefully selected for this mission. We believe that you have the strength of faith and the courage to carry out your responsibilities. I trust you are ready." Kamil peered down at his watch. "It is almost 0900 and the time of your departure is near. May Allah keep you and guide you. You are the most important piece of today's operation. We will strike at the heart of those who oppose us."

Kamil looked at each one of them, smiled, turned and left the warehouse.

Malik was surprised at how fast the time had passed. He walked to his truck and entered the cab. Seated in the passenger seat, holding an AK-47, was the man who was to provide security. Malik nodded to the other. There was no reason to exchange names.

Ahead of them were two other vehicles, the van and the second truck. Malik watched as the men he had just met climbed into their respective vehicles. He saw Kamil in front of the van.

After waiting a moment, Kamil raised his hand and pointed toward the door, which was being opened. Malik turned the key, started the truck and saw the van pull forward to exit the warehouse. The first truck in their group followed the van, and Malik followed it.

Malik had driven this route several times. Despite the early hour, the traffic was moving well with no apparent delays. It would take approximately one hour to reach their target if nothing unusual happened. All three vehicles traveled at the speed limit. It had been drilled into them that to speed on this day invited a police officer to stop them. If that occurred, their whole plan would be at risk.

In due time, they were traveling along the Seine, and soon the small convoy had reached the Quai Branly. Malik realized that his dream had become his reality. The idea of striking a blow for Allah had brought him to this group. In his mind, he had lived this moment many times. There were instances when he wondered whether he would have the courage to cause his own death. Those doubts seemed very far away now. He was prepared to do what Allah had called on him to do.

Soon the convoy turned right on Avenue de Suffren. Moments later, the three vehicles turned left on Avenue Gustave Eiffel, then left again to a tree-lined park that led to the Tower.

Because the signs on their trucks indicated they were food suppliers, it was expected everyone in the French security forces would believe they were bringing goods to the restaurants located here. Up ahead, Malik could see three soldiers carrying automatic weapons raise their hands to stop the van. The van came to a stop a few feet from the soldiers. They had been instructed not to try to bluff their way through. The doors of the van flew open and the three men jumped out. Their automatic rifle fire cut down the soldiers before they could fire a shot.

Malik saw the other truck shoot forward, heading to the left. He pressed the accelerator and drove toward the right. As he was coming toward his target, he heard additional firing behind him and assumed that more security forces were shooting at the three men. He did not let it distract him and continued on. Suddenly, he realized that shells were striking his truck. The man sitting in the passenger seat had been hit and was slumped over. While he was badly frightened, Malik knew he would do his duty. He pulled up beneath the right leg of the Tower nearest the Seine. He looked to his left and saw the other truck had reached its destination. The other driver looked at him and smiled.

Just before more bullets entered the cab of his truck, he reached over and pushed the green button. He muttered, "Allah be praised." Malik then pushed the red button.

The resulting explosions could be heard miles away.

Chapter 22

Anna and Roberta were stunned by the roar from below. They peered over the rail, looking down. What had been a peaceful view of the Seine was now being marred by black smoke that was rising quickly.

Anna, eyes wide with shock, looked at her mother. "Mom, what was that?"

Her mother felt fear clutch at her throat. She did not understand what had occurred so far below. She knew she needed to do something but did not know what. This could actually be nothing. Something burning in the kitchen of one of the restaurants perhaps. Her mind would not let her grasp the enormity of what very probably had happened. Roberta seemed frozen to the floor, unable to move. Her mind was once again disturbed by the scream of her daughter, who was trying to get her attention.

"Mom, do you know what happened? I'm so scared!"

Her daughter's words seemed to bring Roberta out of her inability to move. She looked over the railing once again and saw that the black smoke had risen half the height of the tower. Her mind took her back to the attack on the Twin Towers in 2001. She knew that she and Anna needed to get off of the Eiffel Tower as quickly as possible. After a stunned silence, the crowd of tourists started running and pushing their way toward the elevator.

Roberta grabbed Anna's hand. "I don't know what has happened, but I think we should take the elevator down as far as we can until we know it's safe."

They ran toward the elevator and saw the door closing. There was no need to try to open it since the elevator was stuffed full of people. Roberta could see in the eyes of those people the fear that she felt.

She and Anna ran once again to the railing to see what was happening. She was able to hear the sirens of police vehicles and see their flashing lights as they approached the Tower. Roberta felt some relief as she saw the black smoke start to blow away and dissipate. While she could see the ground now, she could not determine what had happened.

"Look, Anna. The smoke is blowing away. I think we're going to be all right."

"Mom, do you think we should walk down the stairs?"

Before she could answer, a loud, grinding scream of bending metal pierced the air.

Slowly at first and then very quickly, the grinding and crunching of metal became so loud that Roberta could not hear herself think. The Eiffel Tower began its collapse toward the Seine, two of its legs disastrously damaged by the explosions.

As the Tower tilted, both Roberta and Anna were thrown to the floor and began to slide toward the railing. Roberta saw Anna ahead of her, reaching back toward her mother.

The only sound Roberta heard was the voice of her daughter. "Mama!"

Then there was nothing but a stifling fear clutching her heart and the feeling of terror, knowing her life was at its end.

Chapter 23

Ty, Mac and I followed Sophie out of the police museum. The students, talking excitedly, traipsed after us to the sidewalk. This visit, which had begun at 8:30 a.m., was the only event planned for the day. During breakfast, the students had talked about what they could do for the rest of the day.

Several of the students were going to Versailles and were trying to convince the remainder of the students to go with them. However, a number of them did not want to venture out of the city, not yet comfortable taking a train even though they had adjusted to traveling on the metro.

We decided not to try to sway their opinion about traveling to Versailles. Mac, who was listening, smiled at me. "That will be a visit they won't forget. I know I was stunned when I first visited Versailles."

"I think they are..." My statement was cut off by a massive explosion, and then another. We all ducked at the sound. Two students actually fell to the ground. "What the hell was that?" I looked at Ty.

"It sounded like a gas explosion."

Everybody talked excitedly for several minutes. The theories of what happened ran from Ty's gas explosion theory to a terrorist attack.

A look of astonishment crossing his face, Jared pointed in the direction of the Eiffel Tower. "Look at that!"

We all turned. Bubbling up was a black cloud of smoke near the famous landmark.

Mac could not take his eyes off the scene. "That's no gas explosion. This doesn't look good."

As we watched, slowly and inexorably, the Eiffel Tower began to fall away from us. Even as far away as we were, the sound of screeching metal touched our ears.

Jared responded first. "Oh, my God. Oh, my God."

Then we heard the enormous, ear-shattering clamor of the Tower completing its fall.

Melanie had tears streaming down her face. "How many people were there? They must all be dead. Oh, my God. This can't be happening." Everyone stood in stunned silence, trying to take in and understand what they had just seen. Natalie fell to her knees, her body wracked with sobs.

Mac, Ty and I were, for the first time, without words.

Then I said what both Mac and Ty were thinking. "It can only be a terrorist attack." I motioned for them to join me a few feet away from the students. "Now what do we do?" We could hear sirens screaming all over Paris. I looked at Ty first.

"Obviously, we have to stay together. Whatever plans the kids had are no longer in play." I looked at Mac next.

"The city will be going crazy trying to take care of the victims and find the perps. I don't think our students should be out on the streets; there's no telling how the police will respond. Let's head back to the hotel and figure this out."

Both Ty and I nodded our agreement before turning back to the students.

"Listen up. We believe this might be a terrorist attack. All of your plans are now canceled. We will stay together as a group and return to the hotel. We'll be staying there until things sort themselves out. Let's go."

Stunned, Sophie stood there, looking at the smoke, trying to figure out what had just happened in her city. "I must leave you now. You know how to get back to the hotel?"

Ty and Mac had already started off in the direction of the hotel, the students trailing behind wordlessly.

"Yes, go and call us tomorrow, Sophie," I said, squeezing her arm with as much reassurance as I could muster.

Thousands of Parisians must be wondering what happened to their city.

As we moved quickly along the sidewalk to our hotel, the students began speaking in low voices. We passed many people on the sidewalk, some angry, some crying, but most feeling the same helplessness we did. It took us about a half hour to reach our lodgings, the howl of sirens surrounding us.

As we entered the hotel, the receptionist looked at us with tears streaming down her face. "What is happening in my city?"

She walked out the door and looked down the street. Just then, there was another massive explosion. Her body was thrown backwards as if someone had yanked her away like a marionette. The first car bomb had just exploded.

The explosion happened down the street, in front of another business. The force of the blast and its accompanying shrapnel traveled down the sidewalk, but had not struck the building we were in. Many of the students were screaming in terror. They had all dropped to the floor, as had the three of us.

Ty stood up and ran to the door. He looked in the direction of the explosion and saw only a smoking hulk. He turned and ran toward the receptionist. Mac and I followed him out the door.

He was kneeling over the receptionist to see if he could give her any assistance. When I arrived at his side, it was clear that she was dead. She had multiple shrapnel wounds. Her riddled body had suffered massive blood loss, which turned the sidewalk red.

Mac knelt down and tried to find a pulse, though he knew it would not exist. "She's gone."

I returned to the lobby and saw the second receptionist hiding behind the desk. "Call the police and tell them what happened."

She did not move and was obviously terrified. I walked behind the desk, grabbed her by the arms and picked up the slender young woman. She was trembling violently.

"Do you understand what I said?" I asked her.

Her eyes just looked at me with a blank stare. I took her to the telephone and told her to dial the police.

After several tries, the terrified woman dialed the correct number. I took the phone from her.

When someone answered, I said, "Do you speak English?"

"Yes. What is the problem?"

"A car bomb has just gone off near our hotel." I gave the officer the name of the hotel and the address. "At least one person is dead that I know of and I'm not sure if there are any other casualties."

Soon a police car and ambulance arrived. As I walked out of the hotel, I saw Mac talking with the officers, explaining what had happened.

While the building adjacent to where the car had been parked had been severely damaged, a thorough search revealed no further casualties. If our hotel and other buildings nearby had a view of the Eiffel Tower, there might have been more people on the street, gawking at the catastrophe. There could have been far more injuries than our poor receptionist.

The ambulance had taken the dead woman away.

Mac, Ty and I were watching the officers go about their business. The senior officer approached us. "We will be leaving here momentarily."

Before he said anything further, Ty asked, "Who is going to investigate the scene?"

"No one at this time."

"But the scene will be contaminated and evidence will be lost if you don't close it off."

In clear but accented English, the officer went on, "I understand what you're saying. But what you don't understand is that Paris is under attack. This is but one of many car bombs that have exploded already. We have no idea if there are others. We have no idea what else may be coming. It is our job to protect the living. I suggest you and your group stay in the hotel and not venture out. The authorities simply do not know what else might happen." He gave a typical French shrug, turned, got into his car and drove off.

Ty looked at us. "I think that's good advice. What do you guys think?"

I looked at both of them. "You know the emergency plan we drafted as required by the University? It requires us to head to the American Embassy. Should we do that?"

Mac looked back at the smoking car. "I think the question is where will the students be safer. Do we head for the safety of the embassy? Once we were there, I think we would be safe. However, I'm not convinced, given what's going on in the city, that that is the best solution. We do not know how many, if any, car bombs are still out there. I think we should follow the advice of the police officer."

Ty nodded his agreement.

Then I said, "I concur. I'm going to try to contact the university and fill them in on what is happening and what we are going to do."

I took out my cell phone, and dialed the number of our university contact. The automated voice came back indicating that all circuits were busy. "I can't get through. I bet it will be some time before we can make calls. I'm going to try to contact them by email."

Rushing back into the hotel, I went to the computer reserved for guests and typed in the address for our contact. After thinking about it, I copied the president of the university. I explained what had occurred and our decision to stay in the hotel. I explained that we tried to call but that all circuits were busy. I asked them to contact the students' families to let them know their children were safe. Furthermore, I told them I'd be in touch by phone as soon as it was possible. I hit the send button and watched the confirmation come in that the email had gone out appropriately.

Mac and Ty were trying to comfort the students. It was obvious that they were very shaken. As I approached, Sheila stood up. "I tried to contact my folks, but I can't get through. None of us can."

"With what is happening here, I'm not surprised. I can't either. I have, however, just emailed the university and asked them to contact your parents to tell them you're safe. Since it's 11:00 a.m. here, it's seven hours earlier in the States. This email will not be read for several hours. If you hear from your folks, or anyone, please let me know immediately.

I adopted my lecture voice, keeping it steady and calm. "As you know, our emergency plan directs us to go the American Embassy. However, Mac, Ty and I believe that it is safer to remain here at the hotel. It was a recommendation from the police also. So for the time being, let's hunker down and wait this out."

The students nodded their understanding and continued talking among themselves. We three adults walked back outside. There was very little movement on the streets. It was as if everybody had agreed to stay inside and await developments.

Mac spoke first. "Ty and I've been talking about this whole situation. What do we do if any terrorists happened to come by here?"

"Oh, shit, it never occurred to me, but that could be a possibility," I said.

"Well, we'd better get prepared now, just in case."

"What do you suggest, Mac?" I asked.

Ty responded, "We have no weapons with us, but there must be knives and other things downstairs in the kitchen. I'll check that out."

"Let's not tell the students what we are doing. It would just freak them out more than they are now."

Mac smiled at me. "Well, Daddy, what do you want to do now?"

Chapter 24

When Mael arrived at the director's office, there was nothing but absolute chaos within the department. The director's secretary appeared to have been crying and just pointed to Pierre Belcher's office. As he entered, Claude Trion was already there.

Pierre looked at Mael, anguish in his eyes. "What in the hell is this world coming to? It is one thing to kill innocent people, but it is quite another to destroy the historical icon of France. Do you have any information, Mael?"

"This is obviously a coordinated attack. We've lost the Tower. Seven car bombs have exploded, and it's only been 30 minutes since the Tower went down. Both the city and its government are in complete disarray. For that matter, so is your department. If we're going to get to the bottom of this, I suggest you get your department under control and focused on what they need to do. My guess is that when things settle down, heads will roll if for no other reason than to show the people that the government is taking action."

Pierre nodded. "You're absolutely right. I will get on the department as soon as we complete this briefing. It is my belief that my time here is short. I am the obvious target to be dismissed. However, before that happens, we need to find those who did this and either kill them or bring them to justice. At this point in time, I really don't care which of those options occurs."

"Do you want me to fill you in on how it happened, sir?"

"Yes, please."

"From what I've learned, it appears that three vehicles turned off the Avenue Gustave Eiffel toward the Tower. The first vehicle was a van, which was initially stopped by army personnel. Several men jumped out of the van and eliminated the soldiers with automatic rifle fire. Two trucks drove to the two legs of the Tower closest to the Seine. Other security personnel fired on those two trucks, but were unable to stop them before they reached their chosen positions. Following that, the explosives in the trucks were detonated. Our security forces at the Tower killed some of the terrorists. They believe, however, that the van, and anyone remaining in it, escaped. The van was found a few minutes ago on a side street. It was empty, full of bullet holes and there was evidence someone had been wounded inside of it.

Claude remained silent while Mael continued. "The two explosions were massive enough to weaken the two legs of the Tower and the weight of the structure itself and gravity did the rest. My guess is that it was similar to the Twin Towers attacks in New York. It wasn't necessary to destroy the structure, but rather merely throw off its engineering so that it did not have sufficient strength to remain standing.

"As you've both probably seen on TV, the Tower actually fell into the river. All available emergency personnel have converged on the scene. We will not have a count of casualties for some time. It is an absolute jumble of steel that has blocked the Quai Branly next to the river. I'm not sure anyone ever seriously considered that a successful attack on the Tower could occur."

"I have been warning the president for some time that there was insufficient security at the Tower. I'm sure that those warnings will be conveniently forgotten by the powers that be," murmured the director.

"Sir, may I assume that these were in writing and you have kept copies of these warnings?"

"Yes, they were. I have several copies at various locations just in case someone wanted to destroy the ones in my office."

"I'm fully behind you on this, Pierre, and will not hesitate to say so publicly," Mael assured his superior.

Pierre could see that the events of the day had taken a toll on the younger man; his normally neat hair was in disarray from Claude's running his fingers through it in dismay. With a nod of his head, Claude indicated he was in agreement with Mael.

The director peered at Claude, not sure he believed him. He knew it was going to be a time of covering one's own ass. Mael was different, however. He had been in the field too long and knew the importance of loyalty.

"Have we determined the type of explosive that was used, sir?" Claude asked in an effort to show his support.

"Not that I've heard. Emergency personnel are in rescue mode at this time. I assume the police have experts at the scenes who will begin the investigation. But I've not heard for sure. It was clearly a very powerful type of explosive. Until the appropriate chemical tests have been completed, we will not know definitively."

"What do you know about the car bombs?" Mael spoke up.

"At this time, it appears they have been placed randomly around the city. Our concern is that there may be more scheduled to go off at a later time. Given all the cars parked in Paris, it's almost impossible to stop these from detonating. We've explained the situation to the news media and asked them to request that citizens call in if any new, suspicious vehicles are seen in their area. We have heard nothing yet."

"Claude, do you have anything that can shed light on the situation?" the director inquired.

"Nothing at all, sir. We had no indication that this was coming. I've been in contact with our allies and they are as surprised as we are. They pledged to give us whatever help we require. We have increased security at all airports and have also stepped up screening for those trying to leave the country. I guess this will merely cause an irritating delay for passengers. If I were a terrorist involved in this attack, I would simply lay low. It will be very difficult to tie anyone to any specific action," Claude answered.

"Well, Mael, it appears that your agent's concern over the man we missed was real. We should get him back into the mosque to see if he can learn anything."

"I have a call into him and will give him those directions."

Pierre looked at both men. "As you can imagine, the president and other officials have been on the phone to me demanding answers. In fact, I have an emergency meeting with the president and his ministers in two hours. I would like to have something I can tell them about the attacks. If you learn anything at all, let me know immediately. Now, go out there, and find out what the hell's going on."

Chapter 25

The Paris Metro is an amazing mover of people serving approximately 1.5 billion riders every year. The Metro has 16 separate lines and 303 stations. There are various stations within the system at which multiple lines connect to allow people greater flexibility in reaching their destination.

The most important of these connecting stations are Châtelet, Nation, République, Gare du Nord, Gare de L'Est, Opéra, and Saint Lazare. The importance of this system to the people of Paris and its environs cannot be underestimated. While every Parisian understands the key role the metro plays in their lives, Samir and Salah also knew.

The plan Samir had developed required seven men for the Châtelet station. Each man was provided a large suitcase filled with C4 explosives. Each explosive had a simple but effective detonator. The Châtelet station had lines that used it including Metro lines 1, 4, 7 and 11. RER, the train system, lines B and D. Each man had been instructed and trained to enter his assigned station and go to a point nearest where each line entered the tunnel. That would be at the end of where the passengers gathered. The purpose of the explosions was not to kill people, but simply to stop each line from running.

Men were similarly distributed at each of the connecting stations. Because Ahmed had been extremely successful in recruiting volunteers, each Metro line had a minimum of two, and in some instances, three individuals in separate trains. Each man was carrying luggage filled with C4. Samir's instruction to these volunteers was to be at their location by 1115. If they received the message to go at 1120, they were to detonate their explosives at 1130.

Samir realized that he had no control over whether the individuals actually caused the detonation. However, it was hoped, their indoctrination and training would help overcome their natural hesitation to end their lives.

He paced back and forth in the apartment, watching the various newscasts. At 1100, he gave the order to send the go signal. At 1120, every individual had received the signal. At 1130, all but one individual followed his training and initiated the detonation of the C4.

The result was immediate and beyond description. Each train that carried a terrorist exploded with death and destruction. Every explosion was so massive that most of the tunnels in which the trains travelled collapsed. Most of the passengers on trains in which the terrorists detonated their explosives died quickly; those who survived would not be reached by rescuers for many hours or days.

Each connecting station had one or more tunnel entrances. These collapsed, preventing any access to those trapped below ground.

Immediately, the entire Metro system was thrown into utter chaos. Hundreds of people had been injured or killed. Some could be reached and be given aid immediately, while others continued to suffer. These multiple acts of violence overwhelmed the government's ability to respond. Many people were stuck on trains that could not move.

Slowly, but surely, the Metro system was able to empty trains that had not been damaged. Passengers on those trains found themselves in places far from where they needed to be. Lines of the stunned and shocked walked down tracks to the next station. Others, fearful of being on the tracks, waited to be rescued. In some areas, men and women took the lead in helping others. Where leaders did not come forward, people stayed put in a state of panic and fear.

Paris ground to a stop.

Any interruption in the movement of people in a city the size of Paris would cause drastic and irreparable damage. The economy of Paris and of France were in peril. Paris stood on the precipice of economic collapse.

These were facts well known to Samir when he planned his attack on the Metro system.

Chapter 26

Before Mael and Claude could leave the director's office, they each felt more than heard something unusual. Instantaneously, they turned to face the director.

Claude asked, "Did you feel that, sir?"

Pierre stood abruptly and walked to the window. He could see nothing below that told him what was going on. He looked back at the two men standing before him. "I think so. Could it have been an earthquake? That's all we need."

Mael, who had not moved, pulled out his cell phone and dialed a number. He hit the button that allowed the phone to be on speaker. "Jean, I'm in the director's office. We just felt something. Has there been an earthquake?"

"I felt it also. We had no reports either of potential earthquake activity if, in fact, it was an earthquake."

"Okay. Make some calls and find out if earthquake activity has been recorded. If you learn of anything else, call me immediately."

With that, Mael disconnected the call. He turned back and faced Pierre. "I have a bad feeling this may be another attack."

As they waited for more information, they discussed the various possibilities that could present themselves.

The shrill ring of the director's phone interrupted their conversation. In two long steps, the director rushed to his desk and picked up the phone. "Yes?"

The director stood quietly, listening to the caller. Mael and Claude could see a cloud come over his face. Pierre kept listening but said nothing. Finally, after an agonizing several minutes, the director spoke. "Yes, I understand. Please keep me informed."

Pierre slumped in his chair and remained silent for a few seconds. He then looked at both Mael and Claude. "That was no earthquake. What we felt was one of many bombs that went off in the Metro system. The person on the phone was the assistant director of the Metro system. He was asked by his director to contact me. The director was on the phone with the president.

Both Claude and Mael stared at Pierre, disbelief registering on their faces.

The director continued. "He told me they did not have complete information about the damage, but their initial reports indicated that multiple explosions have occurred throughout the system. They're currently attempting to determine the extent of the damage. They are receiving calls from their employees in various parts of the system. What they've been told would lead them to believe that the attacks are centered not only on the Metro stations, but also on some of the other lines. He also told me they are currently in a rescue mode, even as they try to ascertain the scope of the damage."

Claude slid into a chair in front of Pierre's desk, running his fingers through his already tousled brown hair. "My God, if this is true, it is a catastrophe. Paris cannot run without its Metro system intact. The economic impact alone would be enormous. If they have struck some or all of the Metro system, this would indicate an incredibly well-organized attack. How could they have possibly pulled this off without us having heard of it?

"I can't imagine that someone involved in this attack would not have discussed it in some way that would've come back to us. I mean, think about it. They would have to have assembled the necessary arms, ammunition, and explosives. There must have been men trained to carry out the attack on the Tower. They would need people to construct and place bombs in the various cars. They would have to have men available to either plant the explosives in the Metro system or act as suicide bombers. And yet, we heard about none of this. And more importantly, none of these individuals broke security. How could that possibly be?"

Mael sat down in the hard wooden chair next to Claude. "That is a remarkable achievement. It's obvious that these people are well trained, well disciplined and ready to give up their lives. When we face an opponent like that, our job becomes almost impossible to do successfully. Now the question remains, are there more attacks coming? It feels to me that because of the lack of intelligence, we may be forced to just wait to see what happens. With what has occurred so far, it appears that all of the attackers have died, leaving us with no, or at the very least, very little information to go on. At this point, it seems that the most we can hope for is some DNA splattered on the walls. director, if this is not the end of their attacks, we must find some way to act proactively to stop any future terrorism."

Pulling himself together, Pierre spoke up, "But you have just laid out the difficulties we face, since we have no actionable intelligence. How can we act proactively?"

Mael looked back at his superior. "Frankly, I'm not sure. But if we don't figure it out, we merely become spectators watching this event play out. It seems to me that we must get the military involved in this. It is obviously too big for the police themselves. We need to have important places like museums and critical transportation infrastructures protected as soon as possible. We need as many people on the street as we can muster to watch for anyone who might be carrying out these attacks. If we're lucky and can capture one, we may be able to gain some insight as to their future plans."

"But Mael," said Pierre, "I would think that the individuals carrying out the attacks are mere soldiers and not involved in the planning. If their internal security is as good as Claude believes, why would you think we would be able to obtain any actionable intelligence?"

"You may very well be right, but what other choices do we have? Have we picked up any electronic intelligence? Someone has to be communicating with these people. I assume the mode of communication would be cell phones. Do we have any information that would be helpful from our people who monitor these types of communications?"

Claude spoke up. "I'm not aware of any intelligence coming from that source. You understand that much of this type of information is captured by computers and then has to be run through a software program that identifies key words. Only then would a human listen to those intercepts. I will contact our people and see if it is possible to do any real-time listening to try and find the communications coordinating these activities. However, quite honestly, I don't believe there is any way, given the amount of electronic communications that exist today."

The discussion of how to act proactively continued for some time. However, it was obvious to all three men that without actual intelligence of real value, they were probably wasting their time. But each man knew that they had to find some means to discover and head off any new planned attacks. Regardless of how slim their chances of success were, they knew they had to try.

Once again, the ring of the director's phone interrupted them. Pierre answered the phone, knowing the information he was about to receive would not be good. "Hello."

He turned the phone speaker on so the other two men could hear. It was the assistant director of the Metro system once again. "What have you learned since we last talked?"

"What I have to tell you is not good. In fact, what we've learned is catastrophic. First, several of our main stations have been attacked. It appears that the individuals were suicide bombers.

Some placed themselves near the entrance to various tunnels when they set off their explosions. It also appears, and we're not sure of the number, several trains have been attacked. When I say this, I mean that evidently, a suicide bomber rode on each of these trains. When the bombers initiated the explosions, these were powerful enough to not only destroy the train car but to cause, in many instances, the tunnels to collapse."

The three men in the director's office stared at one another in disbelief and horror, all the while trying to put the pieces to this horrific puzzle together as well as they could.

The caller went on. "Also, every line has been attacked at least once, and sometimes twice or more. Our initial estimates indicate that it will take weeks or even months to repair the damage that has been done. Currently, we are trying to rescue those passengers who are still alive. You can imagine, however, that this has strained our human resources to the maximum."

The director responded, "I can't even imagine. Are you receiving assistance from the army or others?"

"That has been requested, but we have not received an answer. Our people involved in the rescue operation are very concerned that there may be delayed explosives placed in the trains. That makes for slow going. What we really need is for these attacks to stop. Do you have any information you can share with me?"

"None at this time. We are as much in the dark as you are. We have every man and woman in our organization scouring the streets looking for answers."

"I wish you luck. If they hit us again, it may take years for us to recover."

Pierre hung up his phone. "Gentlemen, this is the worst setback for France since the Germans attacked us in 1940. Go get your people to shake every tree and look under every rock, and let's find these people who are responsible. France is depending on us."

Chapter 27

Ty and Mac had joined me in my room on the second floor of the hotel. We were watching the newscast on CNN. We sat there for a long time without saying a word. What we were watching was simply too stunning. Finally, I spoke up. "My God, this is unbelievable."

Mac, without taking his eyes from the TV, commented, "Whoever did this had to have spent a long time planning and preparing for it. It is amazingly well coordinated. I am amazed at the amount of explosives that were necessary to carry this off. How could they get into the country undetected? Even more amazing is given how tight French security is, they obviously did not know about this attack."

Previously, the newscast indicated that preliminary tests at the Eiffel Tower showed that the explosives used were the fertilizer/oil mixture, the same used in the Oklahoma City bombing by Timothy McVeigh. "After our experience with McVeigh, you think they would be monitoring the purchase of that type of fertilizer."

Ty shook his head. "That's not necessarily correct. If this has been planned as well as it appears, they may have started purchasing fertilizer some time ago. They may have been buying small amounts that would fly under the official's radar. I'm sure they are looking at suppliers trying to follow the mountain of deliveries that went to someone other than farmers. But I'll tell you one thing, I would not want to be sitting in the chair of whoever is responsible for protecting this country from terrorist attacks. If he or she hasn't been fired yet, I bet it's only a matter of time."

At that point, the news commentator came on and indicated that the death toll from the bombing of the Eiffel Tower had reached 150. He further indicated that several bodies were found floating in the Seine. The television footage that continued to be shown while the commentators talked was quite graphic. They informed the audience several times that this footage was not appropriate for children. It showed the rescue workers moving in among the ruins of the Tower searching for people. Occasionally, a body would be found, placed on a gurney, and taken to an ambulance.

As we continued to watch in horror, the TV showed police boats in the Seine. Occasionally, we'd see divers go over the side and disappear into the water. Once in a while, they would return with a body. The scope of the devastation was such that neither CNN, nor the local French channels, ever returned to their scheduled programming.

Ty remarked, "What is unbelievable to me is not that they were able to bring down the Eiffel Tower, but the scope of the attack on the Metro system. I mean, my God, how many people were required to carry that out? What have they said so far? There's been an explosion in every Metro line and some with more than one. I'm not sure that even now they know the scope of the attack. Can you imagine how long it's going to take to repair that system? Not to mention the number of lives lost and rescuing injured passengers. I mean, they have to clear the wreckage, repair the tunnel, lay new track, and fix the electrical power."

I looked at both of them and shook my head. "Whoever planned this seems to have had every important point covered. They've reported that every Metro stop that connects to other lines has also been damaged. How the hell are people going to move around the city? While the number of deaths seems to be enormous, can you imagine the economic impact this will have not only in Paris, but on the entire country? Even once everyone has settled down some-what, how are people are going to move about the city? You know, when I lived in Seattle, I read a report that the government's greatest concern for the economy of the area was if the two floating bridges were destroyed. They were afraid that the transportation system would collapse and that the effect on the economy would be enough to bring the city to its knees."

Mac interrupted my story abruptly. "DJ, forget Seattle. How can they possibly find the people who did this? This destruction is on such a vast scale, I'm not sure any country would be able to investigate it thoroughly. I mean, could this be the perfect crime simply because the authorities do not have the resources or time to investigate it properly? Perhaps other countries could send investigators to assist the French."

Ty got up and was walking around the room. "Well, that's certainly a valid concern, but are we sure that this attack is over? For crying out loud, if they coordinated this attack this well, is there more to come? I mean, look. First, there was the attack on the Eiffel Tower. Once they had obtained the explosives and loaded them on trucks, it really just took a few people to carry out the attack. What did the TV say? They thought there were two trucks and a van. You have probably two people in each truck and whatever shooters they had in the van. In any event, it had to be less than ten. Once that attack was completed, all the terrorists involved are dead, and there's no means at this time to quickly discover anyone else involved."

He went on, drawing on his criminalist training, "From the news reports, it appears that the attack on the Metro system was well coordinated. Again, everyone involved was killed and there is no quick way to connect these actions to anyone else."

He paced even more vigorously. "For God's sake, if all the terrorists are dead, the only way to identify them would be from any DNA. In a well-planned operation, they certainly would not have been carrying any documents that would identify them. Even if they found parts of any body from which DNA could be extracted, it will still take weeks to identify them. In sum, it seems to me that whoever the leaders of this attack are, they are in no danger of being detected quickly. Given that, it could mean that new attacks have been planned and have not yet been carried out. Think about it, guys. What else could they do?"

Mac continued to ponder this question. From his furrowed brow, I could see that he was lost in thought. He looked at both of us. "Well, let's think about it. They could attack the first responders. That's been a favorite tactic with terrorists. They can attack additional buildings or monuments. However, I would suspect that would be difficult, given the fact that the streets will be congested. They would have to have had their explosives previously planted. They could attack the bridges, which are also crucial to the economy of Paris, as well as the transportation system. I just don't know. It may simply depend on the number of people they have available. Hopefully, most of them have died. Anybody else have any bright ideas? I am still awestruck by the scope of the attacks."

I got up to stretch my legs and back. I walked to the open door and looked out. There were students at various locations in the hallway talking. Some were scared and others excited. I turned back to my two colleagues and said, "Well, it's obvious that our trip here is now over. I don't foresee any way that we could continue given what's going on in the city now." Both men nodded their agreement.

"So the question becomes, what do we do now? I'm sure the airports are a madhouse with people trying to leave. New visitors are arriving every hour who will want to turn around and get out. So, what do we do?"

Mac responded, "Well, it seems to me we have several options. We can stay here for the length of our stay and try to get out on our scheduled flight. We could try to get a train and fly out from a different city or country. Even if we could rent vans, I'm not sure that trying to drive in Paris makes any sense."

Ty nodded. "I haven't heard any reports indicating that the train service has been attacked or disrupted. Of course, that doesn't mean it won't be. I suggest that tomorrow, if things have calmed down, we make reservations for either London or Amsterdam. They would have the most flights to the U.S."

"That's fine," I said sitting down once again. "However, I'll bet that most of the students do not have the funds available to purchase either train tickets or airline tickets. I suppose we could put them on our credit cards. If we can get in touch with the university, I bet that they would put up the cost. In any event, we're talking thousands of dollars. Are you willing to put that on your card or a portion of that on your card?"

I was not surprised to see both of them nod their assent. "Well, I guess we've agreed on our next course of action. We should probably inform the students."

Just then, my cell phone rang. Talk about a surprise. I couldn't imagine that the cell phone system would allow a call to come through. I took the phone out of my pocket, and answered the call. "Hello?"

"Where the hell are you?" a gruff voice stated.

"Who the hell is this?"

"It's the president of your damned university."

"We are at our hotel," I answered as calmly as I could.

"Why haven't you taken the students to the protection of the American Embassy? Just what the hell are you doing not following our plan?"

"Are you serious, Jack?" I was livid. "Do you have any idea what's going on here? Because if we do what you say, it is almost certain that some students will be killed. There are still car bombs going off in the city. I mean, you need to pull your head out of your ass."

"How dare you talk to me like that?"

Mac and Ty were surprised at the vehemence in my voice. Simultaneously, they mouthed, "Who is it?"

I placed my hand over the mouthpiece and said, "The president of the university, Jack Mason." Then I put the phone on speaker. "It is our responsibility to take care of these students. If you had any sense, you would let us do that."

"What I will do is fire your ass. I'll make sure you never work in another university," Jack countered.

"Fine. Do what you want. And when I'm standing before the Board of Regents explaining the danger you are directing us to put the students in, I'm sure they'll find your actions interesting, to say the least. So if you want to fire us, tell me now, and you can take care of the students from there."

There was a long silence on the other end of the phone. I could sense Dr. Mason was trying to get his emotions under control. "Perhaps we should calm down. You have no idea the pressure I'm receiving from the Board of Regents, the Board of Trustees, and the parents of all your students. I'm sorry. Let's start over. What are you planning to do, DJ?"

I explained to him the situation as I knew it. I further explained to him the various options we discussed. Finally I said, "It is our opinion that the best course of action is to wait until we are sure, as best we can be, that no further attacks are coming. What we would like to do is tomorrow or the next day, take a train either to London or Amsterdam. It will be easier, we believe, to fly out of those cities rather than Paris. You have no idea how crazy it is in the city right now. One problem we have, however, is how to pay for the train and airline tickets. Most of the students have tapped out their resources already."

To my astonishment, the president responded immediately. "We will take care of that. In fact, I will see if we can make and pay for the train reservations from here, and also pay for the airline flights. How does that sound?"

"That's great. That solves an important problem for us. Please let us know as soon as you can. If you can't reach me by phone, please try my email. I promise you that we will do everything we can to keep the students safe."

"I know you will." A few seconds later, the call ended.

Mac stated, "What an asshole. Hope he comes through. Let's go tell the students what the plan is."

Chapter 28

The tension in the city hung heavy as people tried to go about their daily business. There was evidence that the army had entered the city to try and prevent further attacks. However, they had no intelligence that would give them any idea where their forces should be located.

In the French president's office, a high-level meeting had just begun. At the head of the long and ornate conference table sat the president, a tall and distinguished gentleman, who had held office for less than a year. To his right sat the prime minister, who appeared to be in his early 50s. In truth, the prime minister was a fit and elegant 65. Both he and the president were speaking to each other in hushed voices.

The president looked up and gazed at the individuals sitting around the table, which included the heads of the ministries of Justice, Finance, Defense, and the Interior, the Mayor of Paris, and at the end of the table was Pierre Belcher, director of French Counterterrorism.

"Ladies and gentlemen," the president began. "It is quite clear to each of you, and in fact to the entire nation, that we are under attack. We've lost a large number of citizens, national treasures and the Paris transportation system. Before we begin discussing how we should proceed, I want to make sure that all of us are on the same page as to what we know about the attacks. The Mayor's office has been responding to these events, and he will give us a brief overview."

With that, the Mayor rose to speak. The lines in his face seemed deeper than yesterday. The stress he was under was obvious to all. He proceeded to describe the attacks on the Eiffel Tower and the various attacks on the Metro system. He explained the actions his office had taken. He stopped and took a deep breath. "We are overwhelmed. As you know, we have planned for emergencies such as these. We were ready for individual terrorist attacks, but this coordinated effort is beyond our resources. I suggest that this is not simply an attack on Paris, but on all of France. As such, the national government should coordinate a response to these outrageous attacks. What I fear most, however, is that the attacks will continue." With that, he sat down.

The prime minister looked at Pierre. "What is your opinion on whether there will be more attacks, Monsieur Belcher?"

Pierre stood. "We have no intelligence to indicate one way or another. We obviously had no information about today's attacks. It's also evident that these were well-planned and coordinated actions. The terrorists were able to maintain operational secrecy. That, in and of itself, is amazing. Given the number of people involved, one would normally expect that operational security would be breached by some individual. We had no hint that this was coming. That being the case, one can presume that there is some probability more attacks will occur. We must be prepared for that. My people are going over everything we have once again. All of our informants on the street are being pushed to gain whatever information they can. Unless we are lucky, we probably will not learn of further planned attacks until they happen."

The prime minister looked up and down the table. "We have had today an extreme failure in our antiterrorist efforts." Then once again looking at Pierre, he asked, "Can you give us any assurance of any kind that our country is safe?

Pierre knew there was no love lost between the prime minister and himself. He believed the prime minister would do or say anything to protect his own political position. This was the initial shot across the bow in determining who would be the scapegoat for today's attacks. The prime minister was trying to set Pierre up to take the fall.

Pierre addressed him directly. "Perhaps today is not the right time to try to place blame, Monsieur Prime Minister. I'm not going to address your continued reduction in my department's efforts to ferret out the enemies of France by reducing our overall funding. Your attempt to direct this department's actions, when you have little experience in this area, has contributed to this intelligence failure. I suggest that this is the time for us to determine what the government's response should be now. There will be plenty of time later for recriminations."

The prime minister turned red, his anger barely in check as Pierre spoke, but before he could respond, Pierre looked directly at the president. "Sir, we have plenty of time in the future to study and determine whose fault, if any, should be addressed. However, you need to decide how we are to proceed from this point on to protect our people."

As the prime minister started to respond, the president shook his head. He looked to the head of the Defense Ministry. "Do you believe we need to bring more army units into the city?"

"Since the mayor has indicated the city resources are over-whelmed, I believe we should deploy some additional troops immediately," the Defense Minister responded.

"To what end? Where would you deploy them? What will be their orders?" the president asked.

"To assist the police in maintaining order. The mere disruption of the transportation system may very well cause chaos when people begin returning home at the end of the day. I propose the

Army would merely be additional assets for the police in that respect. Perhaps, the Army's presence may cause the terrorists to pause before carrying out other attacks. We certainly would be a back-up to the police should they find any terrorists. It appears that most of the attacks have been made by one, or at the most, a few individuals. We must, I suggest, be careful in bringing in the Army if the police believe they have the capabilities to deal with the terrorists. We do not want to give the impression that the terrorists have forced us into becoming a military state."

The president nodded toward the Minister of Finance. "Have you made any initial calculation as to the cost of the damage or its effect on our budget?"

"No, sir. There's been insufficient time to make those calculations. I will let you know as soon as we have done so."

The president continued. "I am afraid that in spite of the terrible human cost we have suffered today, the effect on our economy and our infrastructure will be in the billions of Euros. I want each of the ministries to curtail any unnecessary expenses at this time. We are going to have to find a way to fund the reconstruction of the Metro."

The president paused and looked at each of his advisers around the table. He took a deep breath before speaking. "This is the most serious attack on our Republic since World War II. Our focus must be directed solely at catching these terrorists and protecting our people. No infighting will be tolerated. I'm going to conclude this meeting momentarily. However, we will reconvene at 2100 this evening to assess the situation and decide how we are going to proceed. The Minister of Defense will discuss with the Mayor and police officials the issue of providing troops to assist them."

As the president rose from his chair, several very loud explosions could be heard outside. These were not the simple car bomb explosions that had been going off all day. There was a dash to the windows to see what had occurred. The din of voices rose as each person speculated on what had just happened. The tension in the room climbed as their anger and frustration came out.

The door to the conference room opened and a presidential aide walked quickly to the president's side. He spoke a few minutes and then left. The president pounded his hand on the table.

"I have just been informed that at least four bridges over the Seine have been destroyed."

The room went deathly quiet.

The president continued. "Defense Minister, I want you to immediately deploy troops to the bridges that are still standing. In conjunction with the Mayor, you are to determine what other potential targets exist and deploy troops there. We have merely been reacting to the terrorist's actions, but now we must get ahead of them and be proactive. We will meet again at 2100. Each of you should be prepared to report the actions your departments have taken and what other further recommendations you may have. We are at war. Let the nation be proud of how we conduct ourselves from this moment on."

Chapter 29

"Holy shit!" I just couldn't believe it. We had been watching CNN. Somehow CNN had established a television camera overlooking the city from somewhere near Notre Dame. We watched two bridges explode and fall into the Seine. "My God, what comes next?"

Ty, who was standing near me, looked at Mac. "These people have their shit together. It's one attack after another. Can you imagine what it's like in the French government right now? I'm glad it's their problem and not mine. What the hell are they gonna do?"

I responded first. "How could the terrorists have pulled this off? It's going to take years for France and Paris to recover."

Mac just shook his head. "How can the government possibly determine who did this? It will take years just to process the evidence. Their only hope, in my opinion, is to catch someone involved who spills the beans. This is simply unbelievable. You're right, Ty. These people really do have their shit together."

Just then, Mike and Jared came to my room. Jared looked at me. "What the hell are we going to do? Some of the students are very near losing it. One girl can't stop crying. You do have a plan, don't you? We need to know what you're going to do."

Mike continued, "And we need to know it sooner than later."

I looked at both of them. "Listen, go get everybody and meet us in the lobby, and we will tell you what we're going to do." Mike and Jared quickly left to notify the others. I looked at Ty and Mac. "Any suggestions?"

Mac smiled. "You are our fearless leader. I will follow you into hell."

"And you, my friend, are so full of bullshit."

"And why would you expect anything different?"

Ty, who was chuckling, stated, "I think we should just be honest with them. There's no reason to sugarcoat it. I'm not sure what else we can do. These are good kids. I think we can count on them."

I smiled at Ty. "I agree with you. But what about this dumb shit over here?"

Ty looked at Mac and sighed, "Well, I'm sure he's good for something."

Mac stood and bowed to each of us. "It's about time someone recognized my qualities. If you two bimbos have done enough talking, let's go set the record straight for these kids. They'll be all right." With that, he gave us each the finger and walked out the door laughing. We followed, chuckling as well.

We took the stairs to the lobby and found all the students waiting for us. They were talking in hushed tones among themselves and didn't see us arrive.

Someone in the back said, "Here they are." Soon it was silent. All the students had their eyes on us, waiting and hoping we had the answers for them. I motioned for all of them to sit down. All the chairs and sofas in the lobby were occupied within seconds.

Before I could say anything, Mac stepped forward. "DJ, Ty and I are leaving on a 6:00 p.m. flight tonight. The only flight we could get for you is next week. I'm sure you'll be fine.

The students jumped up as one and started screaming at us.

Mac yelled, "Shut up and sit down. You guys are so dumb. Can't you take a joke?" His smile was so large and his laughter so deep that the students couldn't be mad. In short order, everyone was laughing, including me. The tension had been released.

I looked at their young faces, some still stained with tears. "Okay, here's how we see it. Paris is a very dangerous place right now. You have all seen the pictures on TV. The Eiffel Tower is down. There have been a series of explosions in the Metro, which apparently has paralyzed the transportation in the city. And now, several bridges over the Seine River are down. You've also heard about the random car bomb explosions, like the one just up the street. Our biggest concern is what, if any, attacks, might come next. So, for the time being, we are going to hunker down in this hotel."

Sarah raised her hand and I nodded at her. "We all have a copy of our emergency plan. I assume we are going to follow that and head for the American Embassy. It seems to me that's the safest place to be."

Ty answered her. "That was the first thing we considered. The problem is there are bombs going off randomly throughout the city. We could be walking past one when it went off. We also don't know if the terrorists have planned any other type of attacks. Our view is that the safest course of action is to stay in the hotel until we learn more."

Mac picked up from there. "The other problem we see is that the local police forces are going to be jumpy. We do not want to get into a position where they are unsure of who we are, or what we're doing. The only way to avoid that is to sit tight for a while until the attacks have run their course. We have to be careful not to put ourselves in a position where we are vulnerable. At this point, the only safe place is right here. Does that make sense to you?"

Most of the students nodded after this comment. I looked at Sarah. "We believe that there are two primary issues that confront us. One, how do we keep everyone safe, and two, obviously this study abroad cannot continue given the attacks. I'm sure your parents and friends are concerned about you. I can tell you that the school feels the same way. I have talked with the president and he has agreed to our proposed course of action. And that is, as soon as the danger has subsided, we will take a train either to London or Amsterdam to fly home. The university will pay for the travel arrangements so you don't have to worry about that. "

I looked around the room at their young faces and saw that they were hanging on my every word. *Wouldn't it be great if my students paid this much attention during one of my lectures*, I thought. "When we will go depends on how soon the situation here calms down. Personally, I hope that we can leave in the next day or two. So for now, we all need to sit tight and let the authorities respond to these attacks as they see fit. We should be able to follow most of their actions on CNN. Does anyone have any questions?"

Several of the students raised their hands.

I pointed at Natalie.

"Do you know anything about this attack or situation that you haven't told us?" she asked.

"No. Not at all."

I next pointed to Derek.

"Do you think we're in danger here?" he asked.

"There is no reason to believe we are in any danger at all. It appears that all the attacks are aimed at transportation facilities and the Tower. I've seen nothing that would indicate that individuals are being targeted. Nor is there any evidence that Americans are being targeted. It would seem that while the attacks have caused a large number of casualties, those who were killed or injured, like the receptionist, were simply in the wrong place at the wrong time."

Jason stood and pointed out the windows to the street. "I understand what you're saying. However, we appear to be sitting ducks in this hotel. Have you given any thought as to how we can protect ourselves if something should occur? I think we should do that now rather than wait until it's too late."

Before I could answer, Mac spoke. "We've considered that also. I spoke with the hotel manager about this very issue. He assured me that we were in no danger. He informed me that if we wished, we could go into their kitchen and take any knives they have for our self-protection. I informed him that we would do so. He thought that was quite funny and only asked that we return all the knives when things settle down. In a few minutes, Ty and I will be going down to lower level to check out the breakfast room and kitchen and see what's available, both food-wise and weapon-wise."

I looked around and saw that no one else stood or raised a hand. "That's it for now. I will keep you informed of anything new that we learn. Jason's concern and suggestion that we prepare ourselves are well taken. I suggest you talk among yourselves and discuss any other defensive measures you believe might be appropriate. We will meet again later today to update you on what we have learned."

The students began to wander off, some staying in the lobby and others going to their rooms. I watched Ty and Mac head toward the kitchen. I walked out the door to the sidewalk. I looked both ways and saw nothing of concern. I just hoped that it would stay that way.

Chapter 30

The room was quiet except for the words of the news commentators as they discussed the day's events. Samir was alone in the room, sitting on a sofa facing the TV. He had not moved for some time as he followed the reporting of the attacks he had directed. At various times during the day, he had smiled as each new attack was described. There was no shouting as each success came on the television. Even now, he must maintain security. He could hold the joy he felt tightly within him. His time for celebration would come later, in a place far from here, and to be sure, there was much to celebrate.

He stood and stretched, feeling the tightness in the muscles in his back. He walked around for a few minutes to get the blood moving in his legs. Samir walked to the window and pulled the blinds back just enough to view the street.

Coming down the street nonchalantly was Salah. He stopped occasionally to look in various windows to maintain the charade that he was not a man on a mission. Samir watched him cross the street and approach the door of the building where the apartment was located. Shortly thereafter, there was a light knock on the door. Samir walked to the door, looked through the peephole and opened it enough to allow Salah to step in.

They both embraced and Samir saw the smile that covered Salah's face. "Salah, we've done it. For all the time we have taken to plan this operation, I cannot say that I was sure we would be successful. But we have been." The smile on Samir's face matched Salah's.

"My friend, Allah has smiled upon us this day. And our work is not yet done. I find myself feeling quite excited for the next part of our operation. Do you feel trapped in this apartment?" Salah asked.

"I wish I could just walk down the street and enjoy the fresh air. But, alas, my duties require that I remain here and available to give instructions to our men. Are you hungry?"

"No, Samir, thank you. I had something not too long ago. Have you decided when we will begin the final part of our plan?"

"No, not yet. I'm waiting for more information on the plans of the French. I understand that the Army has brought in troops to protect the remaining bridges and other areas. Have you noticed if the police or the Army are stopping cars or setting up checkpoints?" Samir asked.

"I've seen nothing to that effect. I doubt they could initiate such a plan so quickly. I believe the window to strike is still open. Needless to say, we still have car bombs that are scheduled to go off. That keeps a certain amount of pressure, not only on the populace, but on the government officials who are trying to respond to these attacks."

"I think you're right, Salah. Do you think we should give the order to proceed with our final attacks?" Samir queried.

His friend responded, "Yes, but we must give ourselves sufficient time to notify each of the groups so they are prepared and can begin at the same time. If one group starts too early, it may disrupt the ability of the other groups to attack their targets without opposition. I suggest that we authorize each group to leave and plan to attack their target at 1400, one hour from now. I'm sure that each group is anxiously awaiting your orders. And one hour is sufficient time to get the word out."

"After those groups begin the attack, will we have any men left in reserve?"

"Yes, I have five separate units ready to move to any target we direct them to."

"You have my authorization to initiate the next attacks. May Allah continue to shine his light upon us. I want you and Kamil to join me here so that we can watch the fruition of our plan together."

"As you wish." Salah walked to the door, opened it, turned and smiled at Samir. He held that smile for a few seconds, then turned and walked out the door.

Samir returned to the sofa and sat down. He watched the TV for a few minutes. Nothing new was being reported other than the French response to the numerous casualties. The hospitals were overwhelmed and simply unable to handle all of the casualties. The Metro system had come to a complete stop and the authorities were having difficulty evacuating the riders. In many places, panic had ensued, multiplying the problems for the French transit workers. Samir knew that it was going to take hours, if not days, for the police to remove the dead and rescue those still alive in the Metro trains and tunnels. By the time this was completed, he would be far away from Paris.

CNN switched to a different reporter, who was explaining the world's reaction to the attacks in Paris. Samir chuckled as the reporter detailed the individual nation's response. Each claimed that such terrorist action was immoral and that the perpetrators would be found and dealt with. They pledged their assistance to the French. The problem, Samir knew, was that the authorities had no idea who was behind the attacks. He had decided he would not claim credit for these attacks. In addition, he was sure that others would step into the vacuum and claim credit for his work. That was fine as far as he was concerned, for the more the authorities chased these other groups, the less likely it would be that they would find him.

Samir was different from other terrorist leaders. He did not seek glory, esteem or recognition from external sources. He only cared for what Allah thought. He knew that his glory would come from the simple success of his attacks. Accolades would be given to other groups. His ego could only be satisfied by the approval of Allah. And that made him dangerous. Very dangerous.

Chapter 31

Pierre Belcher felt like an outsider as he sat in the conference room of the police command center. The Minister of Defense sat at the head of the table. He had been appointed by the president to take command of the country's response to the attacks in Paris. To the minister's right sat General Philippe Dugand, whom the minister had selected to command all French armed forces responding to this catastrophe. To the minister's left sat Jean-Paul Foray, the commander of all police forces in Paris. They were examining any and all options available to them. No questions were directed at Pierre. He merely sat and watched.

The minister looked at General Dugand. "At this point, General, where have you assigned your troops?"

The general cleared his throat. "First of all, not all of the troops have arrived. We have skeleton forces at all the major monuments, including Notre Dame, Sainte Chapelle, the Arc de Triumph, and all others of importance to the French people—major museums, churches and other monuments. Unfortunately, we do not, as of yet, have sufficient troops to assure that we can turn away a determined attack. However, troops are arriving by the hour and are being assigned as soon as they reach Paris. Since the major train stations have not been attacked, we have increased security there also. I expect that by tomorrow morning, all necessary forces will be in place."

"Is there anything I can do for you to assist in this process?" the minister inquired.

The burly general shook his head. "No, Minister, it is simply a matter of getting the troops here and having them properly assigned. Everything is going as fast as can reasonably be expected."

The minister turned to Foray. "Jean-Paul, can you bring us up to date on the situation as it exists now?"

Foray reviewed the notes in front of him, as well as his phone. "Well, you know the nature of the attacks that have occurred so far. As far as the Eiffel Tower is concerned, most of the injured have been transported to various hospitals. The search for the dead continues, and for the most part, I expect that all casualties on the ground around the Tower have been found. However, the underwater search is still going on in the Seine. There is certainly a possibility that more bodies will show up downstream or in the wreckage of the Tower in the river. We have yet to determine how or when we can clear the remains of the Tower from the roadway and the river."

Looking around the table at his colleagues, he continued. "As you can imagine, the worst situations exist in the Metro. It appears, from everything we can tell, that it will be days before the rescue and recovery operations will be concluded. We are unclear as to the exact number of people who are trapped, injured, or dead from the Metro attacks. Bombs went off on every Metro line. On some lines, explosions brought the tunnels down on the trains. In those locations, we are trying to dig out the survivors. We are, at this time, limited by the shortage of equipment and the number of workers available. There is simply insufficient equipment and people to meet the needs at each of the explosion sites.

"Along certain routes, it is possible that people in the trains are alive, but their oxygen supply may be exhausted shortly. Due to lack of resources, I cannot assure you that we will reach them in time. For some of the stations, while suffering extensive damage, it is easier to reach and help those who are still alive."

Again referring to his phone, Foray continued his briefing, his low voice tense with emotion. "The scope of the damage is incredibly severe and may very well create economic havoc for years to come if we are not able to repair the damage in the near future. It will require a massive investment of funds to clear out and rebuild the Metro system. I cannot, at this time, even imagine how Parisians will be able to simply get to their places of employment. I would suggest that the president needs to create an agency that will have complete authority to rebuild the Metro system as soon as possible. We will need to commit equivalent resources to those invested in the Manhattan Project if we're going to have a chance at surviving the economic damage caused by these attacks."

Pierre Belcher listened carefully, as did the others around the table. He searched his mind for areas his team could offer assistance or support.

Pausing, Foray reached for a bottle of mineral water and after taking a long swallow, went on. "As to the assignment of police forces, we have obviously called in all officers who were not at work today. We have insufficient crime scene investigators to be effective at each attack site. We will request that other countries send investigators to help us in this work. I've given orders to my subordinates to prioritize the sites. Each site will be secured, but it will not be possible to investigate immediately. The prioritization of the sites will determine when each one is investigated.

"Mr. Minister, aside from rescue and recovery, the most urgent need now appears to be traffic control. It is 1330 now and many employees will begin their journey home, if they have not already left their workplaces. My guess is that most will have to walk. There simply are not enough buses and taxis to make up for the destruction of the Metro system. Frankly, if they are smart, they will stay at their places of employment through tomorrow.

"At this point, we're responding to calls of assistance in resolving traffic problems and other incidences. Any accidents that are occurring, we are simply sending the people on their way. In some areas, people are staying off the street. My officers have reported that there are places in Paris that resemble ghost towns."

Still listening carefully to the briefing, the minister stood up and walked to the tall windows that lined one wall of the conference room. Amazingly, bright sunlight shone through the glass, creating rays in which dust motes danced.

Foray riffled through his notes, and scrolled his phone to see if there were any updates. "Apparently, additional police officers from around the country are being transferred to Paris. As they arrive, investigation and control will improve. We are working on a plan for the assignment of all officers given their need to rest. The last thing I want to occur is to have mistakes happen because of exhaustion. We will be setting up centers to house and feed officers so they do not have to return home in the near future."

Looking directly at Dugand, Foray said, "I believe it would be very helpful if the general would assign his troops so they could be integrated into my police forces. That would result in an immediate influx of individuals who could help widen the scope of our work."

Dugand pondered the request for a moment and said, "I think that as soon as I have sufficient forces available to properly provide security for the locations that have been assigned to me, then I can assist the police by providing manpower. I suggest that a member of my staff coordinate this with a member of your staff. I cannot at this time tell you exactly when those troops will be available, but I would expect by no later than tomorrow evening."

Foray replied, "That will work for me. Thank you, General. Our staffs can coordinate the details. I think that concludes my report, gentlemen. Do you have questions for me?"

The minister turned from his place at the window, but Pierre interrupted him. "Gentlemen, I think we've forgotten something."

Then the minister looked at Belcher and sat down. "What's on your mind, Pierre?"

"All we have talked about this afternoon is what the current situation is and what we believe are the best ways to respond. What we have failed to discuss is what action these terrorists could take in addition to what they've done already. I am concerned that additional attacks may come. I'm not sure what form they would take or what the targets would be. However, perhaps we should think like terrorists to see if there is anything else they could do to create even more havoc."

"That's an interesting perspective, Pierre. General, are you prepared to think like a terrorist?"

The general nodded, as did Foray. "I agree that is exactly what we should do. But I'm not prepared to do it right now. I would like to assign members of my staff to work with Pierre. It would help if Jean Paul could assign some of his people to this task also. What do you think, Pierre?"

"This process should begin as soon as we can get everyone together. I'm not sure that time is on our side, and I would like to convene a meeting of members of your staff and my staff by, say 1700 this evening?"

The general looked at Jean-Paul Foray, who nodded at him. "We shall have our staff members at your office at that time."

"Thank you for your cooperation. Maybe we will get lucky and stop any further plans they may have."

With some effort, the minister straightened his somewhat stooped shoulders. Then he shook the hands of the other men in thanks and strode out of the room.

Chapter 32

Dr. Henry Smith was standing in the lobby of the Four Seasons Hotel, commonly known as the George V. He was speaking with the concierge, trying to decide the appropriate time for dinner for his colleagues and himself. They were planning to eat at the hotel. It had been a long flight from Seattle and he was feeling the effects of jet lag. Dr. Smith was a neurologist and had a thriving practice at the University of Washington Medical Center. He was scheduled to speak the following day at a conference for neurologists, who had arrived from around the world.

His thoughts were interrupted by the concierge, who began suggesting potential available times to dine. Dr. Smith intended to treat himself and his colleagues to an elegant meal. He expected that after a bottle of wine or two, it would be a fine start for their time in Paris.

Outside, a dark SUV approached the hotel. Inside the vehicle were five men, all dressed in black. Each man wore body armor and carried an AK-47. The pockets of the dark vests they wore were filled with extra ammunition and hand grenades. Each of the men had a radio connected by an earbud so that any communications would only be heard by them.

Their leader, Awadi, spoke softly as they approached the hotel. The men fixed their gazes on the handsome, dark-haired man. "Remember, follow the plan. We have practiced this over and over, but the time for practice is done. Now is the time to strike as hard and as viciously as we can. Do not waiver. Our time to please Allah is here." He looked at each one and saw the determination in their eyes. They were ready.

The vehicle came to an abrupt halt. The doors were opened and the men rushed into the George V. Dr. Smith heard the commotion and turned toward the door. Before his mind could comprehend what was occurring, he saw a rifle being pointed at him. His mouth opened to speak when he felt the impact of the slugs in his chest. His life turned into a slow-motion movie.

As Smith began to collapse, he saw the concierge's head explode into a red mist. He felt his body slam into the floor. His eyes could only see the ceiling and his ears only heard the screaming. Suddenly, he saw a man in black standing over him, the muzzle of his rifle pointing at the fallen man. The man with the gun had a twisted smile on his face. Dr. Smith only heard the words, "*Allahu Akbar*," before blackness engulfed him.

Awadi had killed everyone in the reception area. Then he headed for the restaurant. On the floors above, three of his men were going room to room, killing anyone they saw. As he walked into the restaurant, he could see that everyone was panicking. They were unsure of what was happening, but they had heard the firing and knew their lives were in danger.

People began running toward him. He stopped, raised the AK-47, and began firing on automatic. As if in a trance, he saw people begin to fall and the screaming rose to an even higher pitch. He had to change magazines several times. The people who initially rushed toward him were now either running away or lying on the floor. He walked into the restaurant and continued to fire. If he heard a sound from anyone lying on the floor, he shot them again.

As Awadi walked through the restaurant, he nearly slipped and fell in the blood that seemed to be everywhere on the floor. He next headed toward the outdoor patio. It seemed to be empty of people. However, he noticed several individuals attempting to hide. He walked toward them as they were screaming and pleading for the lives. Without mercy, he shot each one, including a baby in the arms of one of the woman.

He walked into the spa area and saw several men and women there. Perhaps they had not heard the commotion from the hotel. He began firing at various individuals. Soon, the screaming stopped. His eyes were drawn to the pool, where ever-expanding circles of blood were evident. One after another, the three men assigned to the guestrooms reported that they had completed their mission.

Through the radio, Awadi ordered them to meet in the lobby. His fourth man confirmed that he had cleared out the meeting rooms and other public areas.

As he returned to the lobby, he could hear the sound of shots being fired. When he arrived, he saw that his men were executing those who were wounded. He knew that many people had escaped, but it was not his plan to kill everyone. Someone had to be left to tell the story of what happened here this day. It would surely be on all the newscasts, which would send waves of fear rippling out across the world.

The tall man glanced at his watch; it read 1450. He looked at each of his men. "Well done. Now it is time for us to leave. We must go on to our next targets." As he walked out to the SUV, he saw panicked civilians fleeing Paris' most famous hotel.

As the SUV pulled away, Awadi called Samir. "It is done. We have struck a decisive blow against the French. I cannot tell you how many were killed, but it must be in the hundreds. We are heading towards our secondary target."

Samir smiled and replied, "Praise be to Allah. Continue as we planned."

He looked at Salah and Kamil. "This phase of our operation has begun with great success. Have we heard anything from our other units?"

Salah responded, "As you know, only three other high-end hotels were targeted. We've heard nothing from our people attacking the La Maison Favart or the Saint James Paris. The initial report from Le Bristol Paris is similar to Awadi's report. It seems that the success of this part of the mission is greater than I had hoped for."

Kamil looked at Samir. "I've heard nothing from our units attacking the various two- and three-star hotels we targeted. As you know, each of those units have fewer men and they are probably taking a longer time to complete their work. I'm confident we will have similar results."

Samir was standing in front of the television when the first reports of the attacks on the hotels were reported. Strobe-like flashes generated by the fleet of ambulances and police vehicles lit up the front of the George V. It appeared to be controlled chaos.

Suddenly, a man came on the screen. He was being interviewed by a reporter. You could see blood on the man's shirt and hands. The reporter had asked him to describe what he saw.

"It was terrible. There are bodies everywhere. There's blood everywhere. I don't know what to say."

The reporter appeared to show compassion while trying to interview this man. "Did you see any of the terrorists?"

"No, as soon as I heard the gunshots, I hid in the closet. It seemed like hours. After a while, there was no more firing. I opened the door and walked out. It was very quiet. For you see, the dead do not speak, and I was the only one alive in that area." The man stifled a sob, but tears gushed from his eyes and ran down his pallid, horrified face. He turned and walked away.

The reporter faced the camera. He started to speak but could not. He, too, turned away, his head down as his tears fell to the pavement below.

Chapter 33

Our hotel was a small one even by French standards. When you came through the front door, you entered the lobby. The receptionist's desk was to the left. Straight ahead was an elevator, and to the left of the elevator was a circular staircase that led to the first, second, third and fourth floors. The American first floor was the French ground floor. If you went down the stairs to the basement, you entered the breakfast room. Off the breakfast room was a small kitchen where only light breakfasts were prepared.

Mac, Ty and I were sitting in the lobby. It was an effort to watch TV now. There had been no new attacks for a while so the TV was running the same stories over and over; we turned the TV off. I looked out the windows of the hotel and saw that the streets were empty. It was deathly quiet out, as if noise could draw the attention of terrorists. I wondered if the attacks had finally come to an end.

Ty looked at me. "We need to figure out how these kids are going to eat. I know they're upset and frightened, but their stomachs will be talking to them shortly. Do you think we should see if there's a restaurant nearby? Mac, what do you think?"

"Well, I wouldn't mind getting a nice meal, but I'm not sure it's the safest thing to do. We would be sitting ducks in a restaurant with no place to hide. It's too bad that all the hotel staff has taken off. I don't know. Maybe we can bring some food back to the hotel. But definitely, these kids need to eat. Maybe we should just ask them what they feel comfortable doing."

Before I could respond, Natalie came running down the stairs. Her eyes were wide with fear and she had difficulty catching her breath. "They've done it! We have to leave now. Please! We have to leave now."

She was obviously in a panic and I placed my hands on her shoulders. "Natalie, calm down now. Calm down and tell me what you're talking about.

"You're not listening. We have to leave now. Don't you understand?"

"No, I don't understand. Tell me what you're talking about."

"It's on the TV. Haven't you been watching the TV? It's on the TV." Her voice was pitched much higher than normal, a sure indication of her panic.

"Calm down. What's on the TV?"

She took a deep breath before she continued. "The terrorists have attacked hotels. They are going into hotels and shooting anyone they can. It has happened at many hotels. Don't you understand! We have to leave! All of us want to leave now!"

"Ty, turn on the TV and let's see what's going on. Mac, go and see if anything is going on outside. Natalie, if this is true, where do you think we should go?"

Before she could respond, I continued. "First of all, they can't attack every hotel in Paris. There are thousands of them. Don't you think we'd be in more danger walking out in the open? So tell me, where do you think we should go?"

"We should go to the police station. We would be safe there. Anywhere but in the hotel."

"Do you know where a police station is? My guess is that the police are crazy busy trying to deal with all these attacks. Now is not the time to make poor decisions. Let's get everyone together and talk about it. Okay?"

"Yes, that's probably a good idea." She nodded, still trying to get herself under control.

"Good. I want you to go get everybody and bring them down to the lobby." Just then, Mac came back.

"There's nothing going on outside. In fact, there's nobody on the street. For now, I think we're safe."

Ty had been watching the TV as I talked with Natalie. "Apparently the attacks are taking a new direction. Several four-star hotels have been attacked. It appears that the terrorists are simply entering each hotel and killing anyone they can find. There were some unconfirmed reports that smaller hotels had been attacked also. This doesn't look good."

Mac sat down. "Well, that's an understatement. What the hell are we going to do?"

"I sent Natalie to round up the students and bring them here. She thinks we need to get out of the hotel and was on the verge of losing it. We need to keep these kids calm. I told her I thought it would be more dangerous walking out in the open than staying here. I don't think she bought it. What do you guys think?"

Mac spoke first, "Well, I'm not sure we have a lot of options. If we are outside and run into terrorists, we would be easy targets. Second of all, where would we go?"

"She wanted to go to the police station. I told her the authorities are probably a little busy now and I'm not sure where one is anyway. Ty, any thoughts?"

"Well, if we stay here, I think we have a better chance of defending ourselves. The terrorists would have to go room to room to find us and that would give us a chance to fight them. But to be honest, if they find us here, we might not make it. It's like the old adage—don't bring a knife to a gunfight."

"Are we agreed that we stay here?" Both Ty and Mac nodded at me. "What action should we take now?"

Ty stated, "We've got to make sure that we know what is happening outside the front door. Someone needs to be posted in an upstairs window looking up and down the street. If we are to have any chance, we need to have as much advance notice as we can."

Mac nodded to Ty. "You also need to decide who gets knives. We need to figure out what we're going to do if the terrorist should come to this hotel. We also need to decide in what rooms the students will be located. Frankly, I'm not sure we have a snowball's chance in hell if they come here."

Ty laughed. "We can do anything. We're Americans. Give us some time and we'll figure it out."

I looked at both. "Well, we had better figure it out. Our lives could depend on it."

Just then, we heard the students coming down the stairs. Some appeared very nervous, while others seemed calm.

"Okay, guys, come and sit down," I said as calmly as I could. "I'm sure you all know that some hotels have been attacked. Natalie brought this information to me and thought we should leave. This is how we view our situation. If we are out on the streets and run into terrorists, our chances of survival seem small. Think about it. They are armed with automatic weapons and we have knives. Their bullets shoot a lot farther than we can throw our knives. "

I looked around the room at their expectant faces. Ty motioned for me to continue.

"However, if we are in the hotel, they have to go room to room, and we will have a much better chance of defending ourselves. We believe that the chances of terrorists attacking this hotel out of the thousands of other hotels in Paris are quite small. But if that should happen, it seems to us that our ability to defend ourselves is better here than on the street. I can think of no place any safer than this hotel. "

They were all listening intently, some holding hands, others with arms crossed across their chests, defiant.

I went on. "Natalie suggested that we go to the police station, but my guess is they are swamped trying to respond to the attacks that are occurring. This is not a time for us to lose our heads. We must remain calm and make appropriate decisions about our safety."

Randy sat in one of the uncomfortable chairs, shaking his head. "This doesn't make any sense. If terrorists do come here, we're bottled up without a means of escape. At least on the street, we can hide in a house or we can run for it. But staying here means that we are just waiting to be shot. In my opinion, we simply need to get out of here. It's crazy to stay here now that we see what they're doing."

Becky spoke up immediately. "I agree with Randy. I just don't think we stand much of a chance if they walk in the front door. I mean, how are we going to get close enough to them to use our knives? I agree that this is the time for us to make appropriate decisions about our safety, but staying here simply is not right. I think you professors need to rethink this."

I nodded, acknowledging their input. "We will rethink this and get back to you. But for now, Mac and Ty have collected as many knives and other weapons that could be found in the hotel. We will be talking with each one of you to determine what role you will play should the terrorist come here. Guys, we begin the defense of this hotel now and will do so until we make the decision to leave. Do you have any questions?"

The room remained very quiet. "Okay, we need to get something to eat. Sheila, I want you and Sarah to go downstairs in the kitchen and see what you can find to eat. Mike, go with them and help them out. Derek and Jason, I want you to stay here for a moment. The rest of you go down to the breakfast room. Anyone else who wants to help with the food can do so. I know you're upset and nervous, but everyone needs to eat. There are no excuses. Okay?"

Slowly, everyone nodded. They all got up and filed down the stairs to the breakfast room.

"Okay, Derek and Jason, I have a job for you. You are going to be our first lookouts. Ty is going to take you upstairs, show you where he wants you to be and what he wants you to do. You'll be there probably for a couple of hours before someone takes your place. We'll bring you up some food."

Both kids followed Ty up the stairs.

"Mac, what do you think about what Randy had to say?" I asked.

"I can see where he and Becky are coming from, but that doesn't make their ideas any better than ours. In fact, I think they are acting out of fear rather than from a coolheaded review of the situation. Let's give them some time to think about it and then we can re-address it with everyone."

"When Ty gets back, we need to figure out what the hell we are going to do."

"Well, fearless leader, as I've said many times before, I'll follow you into hell."

His smile helped relieve my tension. "Yeah, as I've said many times before, you are a whole lot dumber than you look."

His smile never wavered. "I must be if I follow you."

Chapter 34

After walking downstairs to the breakfast room, Randy and Becky chose a table toward the back of the room. Becky was a tall and attractive young woman who wanted to be a lawyer. She majored in political science, but was also taking criminal justice classes. Randy, on the other hand, was majoring in forensics. His goal was to work in the lab of a large metropolitan police department. He was five foot ten and a little overweight for his size. Obviously, he spent too much time in the lab, and not enough time taking care of himself physically. Both were dressed casually, Becky in jeans and a pale pink sweater, Randy in casual slacks and a dark green polo shirt.

As they were waiting for whatever food was going to be prepared, Randy looked at her with a fierce determination in his eyes. "Becky, you know this is bullshit, right? I don't know why these professors think we're stupid. Staying here waiting for the attack to come is not very bright. It would seem to me that our only hope is heading for the embassy immediately. How do you feel about that?"

"I was thinking along the same lines. If we stay here and the terrorists target this hotel, I see no way we could survive. The profs evidently believe we can fight terrorists who have guns when we only have knives. That only happens in movies, not in real life. Do you think we are likely to run into terrorists if we head for the embassy?"

"I can't say for sure, but if we see any, we just run and hide until they're gone. You know there's gotta be other people walking the streets. Not everyone can be holed up in their homes, afraid of what might happen. If we run into any terrorists, I bet the French would help us hide also."

"Randy, do you think we should talk to some of the other students and see what they think? I mean, there may be others who are feeling the same way. Maybe if we get a lot of them to vote to go to the embassy, the professors will change their minds."

"I suppose it's possible, Becky. But what if they tell the professors what we're talking about? They could stop us from going."

"We're adults. They cannot tell us what to do, especially in this situation. I think we all should be able to choose. Now that I think about it, we should lay this option out for all the students. When should we do it?"

Randy stood up and looked at Becky. "Now." In a louder voice, he said, "Everybody listen up. Becky and I've been talking about what course of action we should take. We think that the professors' idea that we should stay here is simply wrong, and could lead to our being killed. It is our view that we should head for the embassy soon. We should not stay here and wait for the terrorists to come. It is up to us to protect ourselves. We do not have to give that right up to anybody, including the professors. I mean, think about it. If the terrorists target this hotel, we would be fighting rifles with knives. How does that make any sense at all? If they come to this hotel, the truth is, we will all die. I'm not taking that chance. Neither is Becky."

Randy had their full attention. "The profs said we might run into terrorists on the street if we tried to run for it. That might be true. However, when we see them, we should be able to run away. We will not be stuck in a hotel without a means of escape. We wanted to talk to you about this so that you can have the same option we're taking. We are adults and have the right to make the decisions that affect our lives. We are not sheep that can be led to our deaths. We have to be responsible for our own lives. Also, we are not going to go sneaking out of here. We will tell the professors of the choice we've made. How many of you would like to go with us?"

Randy's words started a heated conversation among all the students. Some flat-out wanted to stay with the professors. Others could see the merits of making for the embassy.

Randy and Becky watched the discussion go back and forth for 15 minutes. Finally, Randy stood up. "I think we've discussed this enough. Let's make a decision. Those of you who want to make for the embassy, please raise your hands. If there are enough of us who want to go, the professors may very well change their minds."

Melanie's hand rose tentatively. "I think I want to go with you."

Sitting next to her was Rochelle, her close friend. "Melanie, what the hell is wrong with you? You could be on the street and see a terrorist and run. But you can't outrun a bullet. It doesn't make any sense to go with Randy and Becky. We need to stick together. The professors certainly have more experience in these types of matters than those two. I don't want to have to tell your parents that you died because of this choice."

Tears were rolling down Rochelle's face. The passion with which she spoke stung Melanie.

"Okay, Rochelle, I won't go."

"Do you promise?"

"I promise."

Randy was still standing and gazed around the room. "Is anyone else going to join us?" No one responded. "Okay, I hope you make it."

He turned and looked at Becky. "Are you still with me?" Becky nodded. Randy smiled back at her. "I guess it's time to go talk to the professors." They both rose and headed for the stairs.

Ty was walking down the stairs after giving Derek and Jason their orders. "Hi, guys, what's up?" he asked the two students.

Randy responded, "We want to talk to you and the other professors."

"Okay, let's find them," Ty said agreeably.

Mac and I were sitting on the couch in the lobby. "Hey, Becky and Randy want to talk to us."

I pointed to the couch across from us. "What's on your mind?"

Randy looked at me and, without hesitation, said, "We do not think the best course of action is to remain here. We believe that if the terrorists target this hotel, we will all die. We intend to make for the embassy."

I looked at Mac and Ty and watched their eyebrows rise. "That's all well and good, but we feel that you're safer here. And it's important that we all stay together. As you know, you are our responsibility."

"I understand what you're saying, but I disagree. I have the right to be responsible for my own life. And I'm not going to wait here and get slaughtered."

"So, if I understand you, Randy, you're saying that you are adults and I have no right to control what you do during this current situation?" I said solemnly.

"That's exactly what we're saying," Randy said. Becky nodded.

Mac sat there, elbows on knees, chin in his hands. "Let's make sure you understand what you're facing. If you go out onto the streets of Paris with the many terrorist attacks that have taken place, you put your lives in a high degree of danger. When you're in the hotel, we have places to hide. We can fight them in close quarters if we have to. But when you're on the street and they come across you, you're sitting ducks for high-powered weapons. Do you really understand that?"

"Of course we do. We simply have a different view of where we are safest. If they come here, you'll be fighting guns with knives.

That doesn't make a lot of sense to me. If we see them on the street, we run and hide. I will simply not wait to be killed."

Mac looked at Becky. "Are you sure you've thought this completely through?" Becky nodded again, but did not say anything.

I looked at Ty, "Any words of wisdom?"

"How old are you, Randy?"

"I'm 21."

Ty shook his head and looked at both of them. "And you believe you have better judgment than the three of us?"

"I do when it concerns my life."

Ty looked at me and shrugged his shoulders. "Well, stupid is as stupid does. They are adults and they do have the right to decide what to do with their lives."

Being the attorney of the bunch, I addressed an important issue for me. "Before you leave, I'm going to draft a document that indicates that we have advised you of the dangers involved and urged you to remain with us. Also, it will indicate that you have chosen, as adults, to strike out on your own. I want you to sign it so that we can show it to the university and your parents if you don't make it. Any problems with that?"

Randy smiled. "None whatsoever."

Becky responded, "Me neither."

I paused to let them think about their decision. "Do you know why I am having you sign this?"

Randy grinned and said, "It's a cover-your-ass document."

"You're absolutely right. I want your parents and the school to understand, that if you die, it was your decision, and contrary to our recommendation."

"More importantly," Mac added. "It is our last attempt to convince you that your decision is simply wrong."

I walked to the reception desk, found some paper and drafted the document. I also added that each of them made this decision of their own free will and waived any rights against the university or ourselves. I handed them the document. They took a few moments reading it and then each of them signed. "We wish you the best of luck. I hope to see you at the university."

Randy reached out and shook my hand. "Thanks for under-standing. We're going to gather some of our belongings and then we'll be off."

With that, they left us standing there. Mac said, "I've got a bad feeling about this."

Ty and I sat down with troubled hearts. "All we can do is hope they make it."

Chapter 35

Wasi and Saad had checked into their hotel the previous afternoon. It was nearing 1400. Wasi was the leader of this unit. He was lying on his bed, just staring at the ceiling. He knew, that after all his training, the time had come to put it to use. He was a short man with a dark complexion and had the dark hair common in his country. His hands were large in comparison to his body. One could tell he had worked hard with those hands. He had lived in Paris for several years now. He not only spoke Arabic and French, but also English.

Wasi glanced over at Saad, who was sitting at the small desk. He had been writing something for some time.

"Saad, what are you writing? You've been at it for a long time. Is it important?"

"It is a letter to my family explaining why I have chosen to be a martyr. I intend to leave it here for someone to find. Perhaps I should just mail it. I want them to be proud of me, and they need to know that I've taken part in this glorious day."

Wasi studied Saad, taller than Wasi and very thin. He was also several years younger. Saad looked more like a store clerk than a terrorist. But Wasi knew that within Saad's breast beat the heart of a committed terrorist. He had been training with Saad for several months and was confident of Saad's skills and dedication.

Wasi was more concerned about himself than Saad. He had, in the last few months, noticed doubts creeping into his mind. He wondered if he could slaughter the innocent. He had been told that there are no truly innocent people—only the true disciples of Allah and everyone else. Still, he had awoken more than once with sweat running down his face, nagging thoughts pursuing his dreams. He was unsure if Allah would welcome him with open arms or decry the actions he was about to take. But he knew without question that he would do as he was trained. He would stay true to his teachings and trust that the imams were correct.

"Saad, I am sure your parents will be proud. They will hold your name up in joy and you will be remembered for all the days of their lives."

The two men had received their orders to proceed a few minutes earlier. "I think our time to go is upon us. Let's get ready."

With that, they pulled out their AK-47s from under the bed and put on their armored vests. They took as many magazines as they could, along with the two grenades they had been given, then checked each other to make sure that all was in good order. Saad smiled his determination once again. "Let us go and make the infidels pay. Allah will protect us until the time for martyrdom is upon us."

The hotel they were in was a small one with only 16 rooms. Saad's responsibility was to go from room to room and execute those inside. Wasi's responsibility was to go down to the lobby and shoot anyone there. Then, he would wait for Saad to join him. If anyone escaped Saad, Wasi would shoot them as they came down the stairs into the lobby.

Since he was on the second floor, it did not take but a few short seconds to traverse the stairs to the lobby. As he rounded the corner, he saw one man sitting in a chair watching TV and a young woman clerk seated behind the reception desk. As soon as he cleared the stairs, he fired one shot into the man and a second into the woman.

As Wasi watched the woman fall to the ground, he heard many shots coming from what he assumed was the fourth floor. Saad would work his way from the fourth to the lobby. He heard people's voices from above asking what was going on. More shots rang out and then the screaming started. He knew that people would be trying to escape from Saad and the firing from above.

Soon a man and woman came running down the stairs. He shot both in the chest and they fell without a word. Several more people ran down the stairs, trying to escape the bloodbath behind them. As they ran down the stairs with hope in their hearts that they were escaping death, a look of absolute shock crossed their faces right before Wasi ended their lives.

Saad came down the stairs, jumping over the bodies that blocked his way. Wasi could see that he was in a state of euphoria. "Wasi, we have been successful. Allah will be much pleased. Shall we continue as planned?" Both were relieved to be able to speak their native Arabic without fear of discovery.

"Yes, Saad, we shall fulfill our plan completely."

The two men walked out of the hotel and glanced up and down the street. Seeing nothing, they turned right. Their next target, a relatively small hotel, was ten blocks away. They had been told it catered to travelers who wanted economy over comfort.

As the men walked, their eyes were everywhere, searching for the military or police personnel who could interfere. There seemed to be no one around, however. As they approached the corner, Wasi thought he heard something. He held up his hand to Saad and put his fingers to his lips, indicating that he wanted quiet. He stood at the corner and then jumped around with his gun at the ready.

Not ten feet from the corner, walking toward him, were Randy and Becky. Wasi fired instantly, striking Randy in the chest. The force of the bullet knocked Randy backwards onto the ground. He never made a sound. Becky, however, began screaming. Wasi rushed up to her, grabbed her by the throat and told her to shut up. Becky was sobbing, and he slapped her across the face as hard as he could. He looked into her eyes and with evil in his voice said, "You make one more sound and you will die right here."

He turned to Saad. "Come, we will have some fun with her." They pulled her down a small alley and behind two dumpsters.

Still reeling from the blow, Becky was shaking uncontrollably, but she made no noise. Wasi raised his rifle and moved in toward her until his face was within six inches of hers. She could see the evil in his eyes and feel it radiate from his body.

"Do you want to die today?" the man growled in heavily accented English.

Becky shook her head back and forth, tears of terror streaming down her face. She understood that the next few moments would determine her fate.

"Good, I do not want to kill you. But you're going to have to earn your right to live today. Do you understand what I mean?"

Trembling and with her voice quavering, she answered, "No, I don't understand."

He touched the side of her soft face with his rough hand. "You will learn soon enough. Take off your clothes. This is not a request. You get to choose to live or die now."

He watched her begin to disrobe and then stop, sobs wracking her thin body.

"Everything!" The violence in his voice was visceral. He pointed to the ground and she lay down naked.

Saad touched his arm. "This is not what Allah would want."

"Perhaps not, but it is what I want. Leave and I will be with you shortly." He removed his pants and committed the rape Becky knew was coming. When he finished, he stood over her. She whimpered in fear and shock.

Wasi pulled up his pants, then raised his rifle.

A single thought ran through Becky's head. "Why did I go with Randy?" She did not hear the shot that took her life.

Wasi left the alley with a smile on his face.

Chapter 36

Samir was standing, looking at the TV. All normal broadcasting had been suspended as each station reported the newest attacks that were occurring all over Paris. As each one came through, he had to smile to himself, knowing that this was a glorious day. Several of the units had ended up in fights with local police and army troops as they attempted to carry out their attacks on the hotels.

Salah and Kamil were also in the room, monitoring reports of attacks being called in from their men. Salah walked up to Samir and stood next to him, watching the TV. A short break came and he interrupted Samir's focus on the television.

"I just heard from one of our units. They struck the hotel they were staying in and everything was successful. They are now on their way to the second hotel. Reports are coming in so fast that many end up leaving messages because I'm on the phone or radio with someone else. A few units have not reported in. I have tried to contact them without success. Clearly, we are losing some."

"That was to be expected. The real question is how many of their targets can they attack before they are killed? We'll just have to wait and see. How many units do we have left in reserve at this time?" Samir asked.

"As you know, we had five originally. So far, I have ordered three to take over for units that have not responded. Since each of the ones who had not responded had not reported in after the first attack, I assumed they were eliminated at that time. So I sent each of the three to the second target. At some point, it will be difficult to have these reserve units actually carry out their attacks, since the authorities will be concentrating on Middle Eastern men who are walking the streets."

Samir walked to the window and looked out. He saw nothing unusual and once again returned to the TV. He turned to Kamil. "What do you have to report on the units you've been monitoring?"

"Those are included in the report Salah gave you. I have kept him updated constantly on the reports I have received. We have accomplished a great feat today. Do you know if anyone has taken credit for our attacks?"

"Not yet, but it's only a matter of time. And as we have discussed, if the French follow those fools, it allows us to plan and execute our next attacks."

Samir sat down in the chair facing the TV. The coverage of the attacks was almost addictive; he found it difficult to divert his attention from the screen. Samir had worked so long and so hard planning for this day. Each reported success gave him a new high. Even when his units had been destroyed, they had been able to cause some, if not many, casualties. He now understood what addicts went through, because as he waited for additional news reports, he felt like he needed an additional hit to satisfy his cravings for the deaths he was causing.

Salah walked over to him. "As we planned previously, the phones have been switched over and ours have been destroyed. Our communication security plan is still operational."

"Good! How long do you think it will take for each unit to carry out its assigned five targets?"

"I anticipate about three hours, depending on the locations of the targets."

"As usual, keep me informed of our progress, Salah."

Samir's eyes returned to the TV for his next fix.

Chapter 37

Wasi and Saad walked slowly down the street. No people were visible. It was as if the town had been evacuated. They kept their eyes on each window and doorway waiting to see if anyone emerged. So far, all remained quiet. Their next target was only a block away. Wasi could see the hotel sign sticking out from the wall.

He had been by this hotel many times during his preparation for these attacks. Wasi had actually entered the hotel once, pretending to be a potential customer. The hotel clerk had even given him a key to an unoccupied room so he could look at it. He knew the hotel had four floors, with rooms on each side of the building, totaling 25 rooms. There was an elevator and a set of stairs that went up to the bedrooms and down to the breakfast room. He had briefly gone down to the basement, ostensibly to look at the breakfast room. Wasi had determined that this target would not present any great obstacles.

Still glowing inside from his encounter with the young American woman, he turned and looked at Saad. "I will go in and begin our attack. You stay outside and take care of anyone who comes running out. This should be easy." He looked back at the hotel, but could see no activity whatsoever either around or in the building.

* * * * *

Upstairs, Derek stood and ran to the door. "I think someone is coming!"

I quickly ran to his room and, while standing back from the window, looked out. Two men who looked Middle Eastern were about one block away, looking in our direction. Each carried an automatic rifle. I yelled to Ty, who was standing at the bottom of the circular stairway. "Looks like we have company. Get the students up to the top floors. Have Brandi come here."

Brandi, Mac and Ty approach me. Brandi was somewhat of a surprise. She stood about five foot eight and had long blonde hair that reached her waist. She was an attractive young woman, but extremely shy. Brandi had taken several of my classes, and I found her to be very bright. She could talk with other female students quite easily. But when she had conversations with the males, she routinely blushed over matters that did not require that type of reaction.

Previously, Mac, Ty and I had discussed what we should do if terrorists came to this hotel. We had expected that the terrorist would clear the reception area and then climb the stairs, going from room to room on the first floor before heading up to each floor above. We had decided we had to get into a position where we could attack them from behind, but our options were limited. We could lock the elevator door open and hide there, as it was right next to the stairs. However, if the terrorists looked into the open elevator, any surprise we had hoped for would be lost.

We decided that Ty, Derek and I would take our positions on the first floor, and Mac, Jared and Jason on the second. The top two floors had students assigned because we thought it was less likely the terrorists would start at the top floor. We told all the women we needed volunteers to be a distraction for the terrorists.

The idea we came up with was that the female student would stand outside the last door. As soon as she saw the terrorists, she would scream and bolt back into the room. We hoped that this would be an incentive for a terrorist to follow her. Each woman would lock herself in the bathroom, and the men assigned to that floor would wait for the terrorist to come to the room.

Ty and I would be inside the last room on the first floor. I would be by the door, and Ty would be against the wall to the side of the door. Derek would be in the room across from where we were. We had found some twine and had attached it to each wall of the hallway about 10 inches from the floor. If we were lucky, the terrorist would trip, which would give each of us a chance to jump him. We also understood that if more than one terrorist was on the floor, our chances of success dropped dramatically.

Because of Brandi's shyness, I was quite stunned that she volunteered to be on the first floor with us. She assured me that she could handle her role without any problem. I told her she had to be convincing and quick. She had to get the terrorist to come to her room and quickly get back should he fire his weapon. As Brandi and Ty approached, Ty walked to the window. Brandi stood beside me.

Ty looked out the window for a few moments. "They're just standing there, about a block away. They're either waiting for someone or deciding how to proceed. We might get lucky and they could just walk by."

"Let's hope so."

"Here they come. One crossed over to the other side of the street and they are holding their weapons at the ready."

I could see Brandi breathing heavily. "Take a deep breath. You need to calm down. This will work. Let's make it happen. Do you understand what you need to do?"

"Don't worry. I'm ready." She began taking her blouse off.

"What are you doing?"

"I'm going to make sure they come for me." In a moment, she was standing before me totally naked. She smiled at me. "Professor, you make sure your mind is where it needs to be."

Ty, who was still looking out the window, said, "One is across the street and the other just entered the hotel." He turned toward Brandi and me. "What the hell?"

Brandi, with her hands on her hips, stared at him, "Keep your mind on the plan."

* * * * *

When he reached the door to the hotel, Wasi looked at Saad and signaled he was going in. Saad nodded back at him. As he entered the reception area, he could see that it was empty. He wondered whether everyone had been evacuated. There was only one way to find out. Wasi headed toward the stairs. It was a circular staircase, too narrow for more than one person to use at a time. He slowly began his climb to the first floor.

We could hear one of the men on the steps from down the hall. I motioned Ty to the wall. In a few moments, we would learn whether we would live or die.

Wasi looked to the left and saw a long hallway. There were no rooms to the right. As he turned back to his left, he was stunned at what he saw. A slender, young blonde woman was coming out of the last room. She had absolutely no clothes on. She saw him and her hands went to cover her private parts. She screamed and ran back into the room.

Wasi smiled to himself. This was his lucky day. He could hear her crying, for she knew what was going to happen to her. Wasi ran quickly toward the room and as he approached the door, he suddenly seemed to be floating in air. He smashed hard into the hallway floor and lost his grip on his weapon. Wasi wondered if seeing this beautiful woman had taken away his ability to walk.

Before he could rise, he felt someone grab his hair and jerk his head back. Without understanding what was happening, he felt a sharp, slashing movement across his neck. His head dropped back to the floor. Wasi noticed something warm flowing around his face.

The moment before Wasi died, he realized that what he felt was his own blood. He tried to speak but no sound left his mouth. All he could hear was a gurgling noise and he wondered what that was. Wasi tried to get up, but a heavy boot rested between his shoulders, holding him down. No further thoughts entered his mind as his life oozed out onto the hallway floor.

Ty stood above the body, the bloody knife in his right hand. He knelt next to Wasi and felt for a pulse. "He's dead."

I saw Derek standing in the doorway. "Go bring Mac down here." He ran for the stairway. I walked to the window and stayed back in the shadows. I saw the second terrorist across the street. He seemed to be anxious. I'm sure he is wondering why there were no gunshots.

I looked back at Brandi. "Get your clothes on." She hurriedly did so. In the hallway, Derek had returned with Mac. Mac looked at the body before entering the room.

"Can you believe this shit? The plan worked! Ty, can you give me his rifle?" Mac said, amazement in his voice. Ty had already found the extra magazines and also a Glock on the body.

As Ty handed the AK-47 to Mac, I stated, "I expect the other guy is going to be coming here soon to find out what's going on. Ty, why don't you go to the elevator and wait for him? Mac, you can stand in the room across the hall. I'm going to have Brandi play like she's being raped. Hopefully, he will come down to investigate. Ty, you should be able to have a clear shot once he heads toward this room. If for some reason, Ty can't get him, Mac, you take him out. Any questions?"

Mac looked at Ty, "Makes sense to me." Ty nodded his agreement.

"Derek, put the body into one of the other rooms." Derek dragged the body into another room across the hall. When he returned, he pointed at the floor and asked, "What about the blood?"

"Get a towel and wipe it up as quickly as you can."

I walked over and gently put my hands on Brandi's now-clad shoulders. "How are you doing?"

"I'm okay. What do you want me to do now?"

"I'll be watching the other guy from the window. When he enters, I will nod at you. Then I want you to play as if you're being raped. Scream, yell, cry or whatever. You need to convince him to come and investigate. Do you think you can do that?" Her head nodded up and down.

I returned to the window and saw that the other terrorist was crossing the street. As soon as he entered the hotel, I nodded at Brandi.

Brandi let out a piercing scream. "Please don't do this. No. No. Just leave me alone. Please don't do this." She screamed again. Then she began to cry. Suddenly, she slapped her hands together. "Please don't hit me again, please don't hurt me." Then she began to moan very loudly.

Saad heard the first scream and stopped in his tracks. He listened for a moment and then headed up the stairs. When he reached the top, he could hear the woman crying. He started running down the hall.

Ty heard the terrorist begin to run. He stepped out from the elevator, raised the Glock and fired once. The round struck the terrorist between the shoulder blades.

Saad felt like he had been hit in the back with a 50-pound weight. His legs collapsed and he fell to the floor. He couldn't understand what was happening. He looked forward and saw two men approaching. He did not recognize either of them. One held an automatic weapon, which was pointed toward him. Before he could say anything, he heard the man say, "Asshole." He had no other sensation other than hearing the weapon fire.

I went back to the window and looked both ways. No one else was on the street. I came back to the hallway and motioned Derek over. "I want you to go upstairs and tell everyone it's over for the time being. Tell them that both terrorists who approached our hotel have been killed. I want them to stay where they are for a few minutes."

I turned to Mac and Ty. "We dodged a bullet there."

Mac shook his head. "We just carried out a plan that happened to work. What now?"

I nodded at Ty. "How are you doing?"

"I'm fine. I'm not going to lose any sleep over these shit bags. First of all, we need to get rid of these bodies."

"Any suggestions? I mean we don't want them hanging around here for the kids to see."

Mac interrupted. "There's a big waste bin out back. I'll get a couple of the guys to throw the bodies down from the window and dump them there." With that, he hurried upstairs.

Ty and I turned and saw Brandi sitting on the bed. We walked in. She didn't seem to be any worse for wear for what she had gone through. I smiled at her. "You did an awesome job back there. How are you doing now?"

"I'm good. Those guys got what they deserved." She got up and walked over to Ty, who had a half smile on his face. She poked him hard in the chest. "If you say anything about what I did down here or what you saw me do, I promise you I will kick you in the balls hard enough that they won't react the next time you see a naked woman. Do you understand?"

Ty lost his half smile very quickly. "Were you here during this? I didn't see a thing."

"Good. Don't make me have to remind you again." She walked out the door and headed for the stairs to rejoin the other students.

Ty shook his head. "I do believe she means that. But it was a sight I won't forget for a long time."

"I suggest you forget it now. You may wake up someday without any balls at all." I began laughing and felt the frustration and tension fall away.

Chapter 38

Pierre sat alone in his office. He had his eyes glued to the television, as did most of the people in France. His job was to prevent this type of attack. Obviously, he had failed to a degree no one had anticipated. What concerned him most was whether additional attacks were coming. Also, he couldn't shake the feeling that they had missed something from their previous intelligence. He had asked Mael and Claude to join him to review the information they had. Perhaps then, they could find some answers.

There was a knock on the door and Pierre looked up. "Enter." He saw both Mael and Claude come through the door. "Sit down. We have much to discuss."

Both men could see the stress etched in Pierre's face. They could only imagine the pressure he was getting from his superiors. They also knew that the innumerable casualties France had suffered weighed heavily on him. All three men realized that intelligence and counterterrorism could only prevent so much. A properly designed, secured and executed attack could not be stopped.

Pierre sighed and took a deep breath. "I think we need to go over the intelligence we have to see if we have missed anything. It is hard to imagine that these people could have planned and carried out this attack without our getting some wind of it. Let's take it step by step. We heard, as I recall, some information about the transfer of large amounts of weapons. I think these were small arms and RPGs. Is that correct?" Claude nodded his agreement. "Do we have any further information on that?"

Claude looked through his paperwork. "We have nothing more. It was just some information we received from various agents on the street. We had no dates, no times or ports indicating when these arms were supposed to arrive. What concerned us most was if the terrorists also had large quantities of explosives. We now know that was the case. How else could they do the damage they did to the Tower, the Metro and the bridges?"

Again, Claude referred to his notes. "There is another problem. Given the massive attacks, we would expect to find military-grade explosives potentially coming into the country, but as of now, we have found no trace of that. Which means, we probably need to check with the military to see if any of that has gone missing from their stores. If it's not military grade, then we're probably talking about something like fertilizer and oil. Oil is much too easy to obtain for us to try to track it. However, fertilizer may be something we should look at. I will have our people start checking out fertilizer purchases for at least a year back. Maybe something will come up there."

"Any other ideas?"

"Not on this issue."

"Mael, do you have anything to add?"

"It seemed to me that if military-grade explosives were used, we simply missed them. But if these attacks were in fact executed using fertilizer-based explosives, we could have missed a potentially obvious source that could be easily obtained within the country. I have asked all of my agents to contact their informants to see what they could find. Perhaps, with Claude checking with suppliers and delivery companies, and my people checking the information on the street, we may be able to develop some leads that we can follow. It may very well lead us to the perpetrators of these attacks. However, if we do find something, it probably will not stop current or future attacks."

Pierre nodded. "We cannot leave any stone unturned. If we do not have the information necessary to stop the attacks, we must find those who carried them out. So I want each of you to look into the fertilizer business as you've indicated."

He went on. "Let's review the information about the officer who stopped the semi. As I recall, he was killed. Is that correct?"

Mael nodded.

"Do you have anything else on that?"

Mael stood and walked around the office. "The only thing we found new was a likely type of tire the semi had. The officers were able to photograph and make casts of the tire marks they found in the mud. Unfortunately, the tread was common to many truck-trailer combinations. It seems that it was a popular tire for use in the transportation industry.

"The tire tracks we found at the beach had the same popular tread. It is possible that the same tires made both tracks. We can speculate that the semi carried explosives and/or small arms, but it would only be speculation. For all we know, the driver had some type of warrant out for his arrest and did not want to be caught. I'm not sure that it can point us in any direction that would be worth investing manpower to investigate."

"Have the local police officials come up with anything more?"

"Nothing whatsoever," Mael responded.

"Claude, any thoughts or ideas?"

"No, it seems like a dead-end to me."

"Mael, have you learned anything new about your missing agent?"

"Actually, his body was discovered this morning in a forest outside of Paris. A group of hikers happened to come upon it and called the local police. They were able to identify my man by his fingerprints, which led them to me. He is currently undergoing an autopsy. We have people at the scene to see what they can learn. It's too early to have anything concrete."

Changing the subject slightly, Mael looked at Pierre and Claude. "Speaking of bodies, we have people looking into the terrorists who were killed today. Hopefully, we will get something such as names or addresses. It will take some time to do so, however. I'm afraid that until the attacks end and things settle down, we may not make any progress in this area. As you know, Paris has become a complete nuthouse. When, and if, calm returns, we may be able to develop a coordinated approach to deciphering this information and seeing where it leads us."

Pierre stood and walked stiffly to his window. He gazed upon a scene he had never seen before. Below him, the streets were completely devoid of pedestrians and vehicular traffic. He guessed that was because of the government's request that people remain in their homes or businesses. It was a bit eerie to see his lively Paris become desperately quiet. He paced over to Claude. "Do you have any news from our friends overseas?"

"Nothing that is helpful. Everyone has offered any help they can give, but as far as additional information, we have nothing new. I cannot imagine how this could be pulled off without someone hearing of it. Furthermore, no group has, as of yet, claimed responsibility for these attacks, which is completely out of the ordinary. Usually, within an hour of such events, something is posted on the internet indicating who is claiming responsibility. I don't understand. This is not the common practice for the terrorist groups we have followed."

"What do you make of that?" Pierre asked.

"I don't know. All of our history with terrorist groups indicates that those groups want the publicity that accompanies these kinds of attacks. My best guess is that it is only a matter of time before someone claims responsibility. At least, when they do, we will know where to look. That's been one of the terrorists' downfalls. Trying to get credit seems to be an occupational requirement. If we have a new group that doesn't care about who gets credit, that will make our job harder."

"Mael, have you heard anything on the street about this?"

"Nothing at all. I would, however, be shocked if someone didn't take credit. If there is a new group in the game that doesn't want credit, I'm sure someone else will step forward to claim responsibility, whether it's true or not. I guess we'll just have to wait and see."

Pierre walked over to his colleagues, reached out and shook their hands. "Each of you have served your country well. I expect that I will be removed from my office in the not too distant future. The politicians will need someone to blame, and I'm probably the easiest target. After I'm gone, do not stop searching for these people. I truly appreciate the work you've done for me. In time, France also will appreciate the work you've done for your country."

He walked to the door and opened it. Mael and Claude walked out without a word.

Chapter 39

Ty and I were sitting on the couch in the reception area watching as Mac walked outside. He looked up and down the street once again. He came back into the hotel and sat down in front of us. "There's nothing out there. Maybe it's over."

Even though we had students acting as lookouts upstairs, we still felt the need to check for ourselves.

Ty stood up and stretched. "It might be over for us. I'm not sure we can count on that, though. We should prepare for another attack. What do you guys think?"

I stood and moved toward the window. Nothing moved on the street. "I agree. We are in a better place now than we were an hour ago. We have two rifles, two Glocks and four hand grenades." We had found the Glocks and grenades in the backpacks the terrorists were wearing. "We should divide these up somehow. How about I keep a Glock and a hand grenade. What do you prefer, Ty?"

"I'd like the other hand gun. Mac, you have a preference?"

"I'll take a grenade. I suggest we give the other rifle to Derek. He was in the Army and knows his way around weapons. We can probably give him a grenade too. Ty, I assume you want one, too."

"Yeah, I'll take one of those bad boys. I agree, let's give Derek one also."

I returned to the couch and sat down. I leaned forward, elbows on knees. "I'm concerned that if additional terrorists come, we could suffer some casualties. We have no medical supplies. The only thing I have is one of those first-aid kits I bought at Walmart. I think we need something more. My concern is that it might freak the students out if we get medical supplies."

Mac spoke up. "I understand where you're coming from, DJ, but the students have seen what is going on. I think they'll be okay."

Ty nodded to me. "I agree. Isn't there a pharmacy just a couple of stores down? Maybe we should go there and see what we can get."

Mac got up and slapped him on the back. "Great idea. Any suggestions on how we could do that? I mean, someone's going to have to walk to that store and back while terrorists may be out there."

"If we were targeted by those two terrorists, we are probably okay. If these attacks are simply random, then we run the risk of running into more terrorists. Still, I think it's a good idea and I'm willing to go down there and see what I can find."

I responded, "I agree that it is a good idea, Ty. But do you know what to look for?"

"Mac and I have had the same first-aid training. I guess I would just rely on that and see what I could find."

"Isn't Dana close to finishing the nursing program? Maybe she would be willing to go along. She probably knows more about what could be of use than any of us."

Mac stood up and walked toward the stairs. "I'll go up and bring her down. We'll see if she's willing to help."

Shortly thereafter, Mac returned with Dana. I pointed to the seat in front of me and she sat down. "I want to talk to you about something. We hope that there will be no further attacks on this hotel. But if there are, I'm concerned that we don't have sufficient medical supplies to treat anyone who might get injured. The three of us have been talking about how we could rectify that. There is a pharmacy down the street. Ty is willing to go there and see what he can find. However, he does not have the expertise to get everything we might need. We want to know, given your nursing background, whether you would be willing to go with him, see what they have and get what we need. You are under no obligation to do so, but it will be very helpful if you would."

She looked at all three of us with her big, blue eyes. "Isn't it dangerous to leave the hotel?"

"Maybe, but we don't think anything will happen. We wouldn't be leaving the hotel for good, but rather just for a few minutes. Frankly, it's worth the risk to get the supplies we need. "

Dana shook her blonde curls. "I'm really very afraid to do this. I mean, how will it happen?"

"Ty and you will run to the store. Ty will have a handgun for protection. Mac will be outside with his rifle and Derek will be upstairs with his rifle covering you from window. You go into the pharmacy and get what you need. And then you'll come back here as quickly as possible."

"Do you really think it's safe? It just scares me a lot." Dana's voice trembled.

"Yes, I think the way we've planned it, there will be no problem."

"Okay, I'll do it."

"Thank you, Dana. Now, please go upstairs and find a backpack you can put the supplies into. When you finish, come back here." She left and went upstairs, her slender shoulders somewhat slumped, but her back straight with resolve.

Mac walked up to me. "I think we need to change that plan a bit. I suggest that I go with Ty and Dana. While they are inside gathering supplies, I'll stand watch outside the door. I suggest you wait at the door here to provide additional cover."

"Not a problem with me. I'm going upstairs and tell Derek what's coming down."

After talking with Derek, I returned downstairs and found Dana waiting. "Well, are we ready?" Everyone nodded and we headed for the door. Ty went out first to check the street. He motioned for

Dana to follow him. They both ran at full speed to the pharmacy, which was about 50 yards away. Mac was close behind them. I knelt at the doorway, watching the street.

When Ty reached the pharmacy, he tried to open the door, but it was locked. With the butt of the Glock, he broke the glass door. He reached in and opened the door. "Come on, Dana. Let's make this quick." He watched as she entered the store, looked around and then headed to the shelves. He watched as she grabbed various items and put them into the backpack. "What are you getting?"

"I've got some bandages of different sizes, some antibacterial ointment and some aspirin so far. I'm looking for some stronger pain medication, but I'm having trouble with some of these French words." Within several minutes, Dana returned to the front of the store, carrying what appeared to be a fully loaded backpack. "I think I have everything we need."

They both moved to the front door. Mac was kneeling just outside with his weapon aimed up the street. He looked at both of them.

"Dana says she has everything we need. Let's get out of here."

Mac led the way back to the hotel, followed by Dana, with Ty bringing up the rear.

I saw them racing down the street. I opened the door for them. "Good job, guys. You did great, Dana. You are now the head of our medical department. I want you to go upstairs and find a couple of students who can assist you. Maybe you can give them a quick overview of first-aid."

She smiled at me, still breathing hard from the exertion and the uncertainty. "Thanks. I'll go find someone to help." She ran up the stairs on her new mission.

"So, guys, what do we do now?"

Mac walked to the window and peered out. "Now, we wait."

Chapter 40

André Grosjean, the top systems analyst for the Metro system, walked into the Gare du Nord train station. He stopped and looked around. As with most analysts, he was bland in appearance. His light brown hair was cut short, caramel-colored eyes hidden behind steel-rimmed glasses. His pale face lacked any indication that he ever spent time outdoors. Truth be told, he preferred pouring over documents in his office to any kind of social activity.

Like all Parisians, he had traveled across Europe from this station many times. It was usually bustling with thousands of people coming and going to various parts of France and beyond. At this point, however, no travelers were inside the building. The only people he could see were police and military personnel.

He walked up to an Army captain who appeared to be in charge of the troops here and handed the soldier his Metro identification. "I'm here to see what progress has been made and to determine what other steps we need to take to get the Metro operational."

The officer stared at the thin man in the white shirt and loosened tie. "Well, sir, I expect it's going to be some time. The explosion that occurred on the Metro station below means it may not be safe to operate the trains up here. I'm afraid this may take years to fix."

"Perhaps. However, that's what I'm here to determine. Maybe we'll get lucky." With that, André headed for the stairs that would take him down to the Metro station. As he entered the station, he looked around. He could see what appeared to be Metro employees, police officers, military and medical personnel scurrying about.

He walked up to the first Metro employee he could find. "I'm Grosjean. Who's in charge here?" The man pointed at another man standing near the opening to the Metro tunnel. André walked toward the man, who turned and saw him approaching.

The man held out his hand. Grosjean grasped his hand and felt a strong, firm grip. "I'm Jacques Segou." With a sweep of his beefy, calloused hand, he pointed to the activity going on around them. "I'm in charge of this location."

Jacques was clad in grease-stained coveralls, a good indication that he did not hesitate to fill in for a worker when the job needed to be done. His weathered face was etched with lines of concern.

"I'm Grosjean," André introduced himself.

"Yes, I know. I recognized you. Would you like a tour and explanation of what we found?"

"Yes, that would be a good start."

"Then follow me." With that, Jacques walked toward the tunnel. "Down there about 100 meters sits the train, or what's left of it. The explosion was in the first car and demolished it. The explosion also caused the ceiling to give way, covering that car and we think the car behind it. The people in the remaining cars were able to open the doors and walk to the next station."

André stared around at the destruction, a shudder of fear causing his stomach to clench.

Jacques continued with the tour. "We are attempting to dig out the first and second car. We do not expect to find survivors in the first car, but it is still possible. We have hope that there are survivors in the second car, but we won't know until we reach it. We also have people digging from the opposite side. It is a real mess due to the amount of material that collapsed."

"Monsieur Segou, do you have any idea what will be required for repairs, cost or the timeframe involved?" André asked.

"Not at this time. Until we have dug everything out, it will be impossible to answer those questions. I can tell you this, however. I expect the ceiling will have to be fixed, and, more than likely, the track and electrical systems will have to be repaired. The track and electrical systems should not take too long, but I've not been involved in repairing the ceiling previously. I'll have to get an expert in to make that call. Come with me and I will show you what concerns me the most." The two men, one tall and broad, the other slender and a head shorter, walked to the far wall, which had been blown out. "You see this wall?"

André examined the wall. It appeared that a sizable explosion had torn a large portion of the wall away. The damage was greater at floor level, but seemed to diminish toward the ceiling. "Tell me, what's your concern?"

"Well, Monsieur Grosjean, as you know, the train station is above us. Whoever planned this attack knew his business. This area is very near one of the supports that holds up the floor of the train station above us. We are going to have to determine whether that support has been damaged to any degree. Most likely, it has not, and the trains above can run normally. However, it is not impossible that this support could be damaged sufficiently enough that it might affect the stability of the floor above."

"Are you telling me that you have concerns that the floor holding the trains above could collapse?" André spoke in a hushed tone.

"It is certainly possible. Do I think that will happen? No. Could it happen? Absolutely. I believe that until we have made the determination that the support is safe, no train should be allowed to operate from this station. However, that call will have to be made by people above my pay grade. But, I will tell you this, if they decide to allow the continued operation of the trains and the floor collapses, someone's head will be on the chopping block."

"I understand, Monsieur Segou. How long will it take for you to determine whether or not the support is safe?"

"If we are able to get the appropriate equipment down here, probably not much more than a few days. My guess is that it will take some time to get that equipment, especially if the attacks are continuing. I've been down here most of the day. Are the attacks still going on?"

"Yes. We still have car bombs going off and groups of terrorists are attacking hotels. Who would've thought that someone could plan this type of attack and be so successful? What else do you have to show me?" André asked, gesturing around the rubble-strewn station.

For the next hour and a half, Jacques led him around the Gare du Nord. André took in everything. It seemed to him that a temporary fix could be made here within a reasonable timeframe. However, it would be a long time before this station was fully operational. He thanked Jacques for explaining the work that was required. He then took the steps two at a time and returned to the train station above.

André decided to inspect the train station also. As he walked around, he noticed cracks in one area of the floor. He wasn't sure if these had existed prior to the attack or had been caused by the explosion. He pulled out his cell phone and speed-dialed the director of the Metro system. After three rings, the Director's voice came on the line. "Hello."

"Sir, it is Grosjean. I've completed my inspection of the Gare du Nord." He explained to the Director everything he had learned. "There's one other matter I need to bring to your attention. I did a quick tour of the train station. In one area, there are many cracks in the floor. I do not know if they existed prior to today. I suggest that someone contact the appropriate train officials to have them examine that location. If these are new cracks, my guess is it will take a lot of work to make this station safe for operation."

"I'll take care of that," the Director growled.

"I'm heading for the Gare de L'Est. I will call you when I've completed my inspection of that station. Hopefully, it is in better shape than this one. Do you have any questions for me?"

"No, call me when you've completed your next inspection."

"I will." As he walked out the door of the Gare du Nord, it was clear to him that his country had suffered a severe blow. The economic impact at this station alone would be enormous. Maybe the next one would not be so bad.

Chapter 41

The president of the French Republic was alone in his office. Sitting at his massive mahogany desk, he rubbed his temples. He had a headache that seemed to originate in each temple and then expand through his head. The rubbing of his fingers did not ease the pain. He opened the top drawer of his desk and found the bottle of pain reliever. Opening the top, he shook out four pills and returned the bottle to the drawer. He picked up his coffee cup, washing the pills down with the bitter, cold brew and hoped this would give him some relief.

He sat back in his chair and closed his eyes. Why had this happened to his country? He knew the answer without even thinking about it. The Islamic radicals would attack whenever and whomever they could. Their ideology blinded them to the potential resolution of any issues they had with him, his country or other countries in the world. He wondered whether they would ever be able to coexist. They had in the past; so why was it so difficult now?

He expected that the French people would demand full-scale retaliation against those responsible for today's attacks. What concerned him most, however, was what if they could not determine who was behind these attacks? His people would want someone held responsible.

That was the difficulty he faced. In fact, that was the difficulty that faced any state that had ever been attacked by Islamic radicals.

If he ordered attacks just to attack, he would only drive more moderate Muslims into the hands of Islamic radicals.

In spite of the enormous stress, the president enjoyed the respite of being alone in his office. His day had consisted of one alarming report after another. He had conducted numerous meetings with various officials as they tried to determine the appropriate course of action his country should take.

At this moment, he was waiting for the heads of all the opposition political parties to come to his office. The president stood and carefully checked his reflection in the mirror behind the door. It would not do to have the leader of the country appear distraught or disheveled before his constituents. He saw a tall, slender, almost regal man with a full head of silver hair, not one of which was out of place. His face, though certainly not a young man's, still had a youthful glow. His trademark piercing green eyes were enhanced by the dark green tie and pocket square in the elegant, neatly pressed suit. The image he saw in the mirror was that of a man of power.

The president intended to lay out the facts as he knew them, so that in this time of crisis, everyone was on the same page. He hoped he would be able to gain unanimity of support for the actions he was going to propose.

His phone rang, startling him. He lifted the receiver to his ear and listened. It was his secretary informing him that everyone scheduled for this meeting had arrived. Pulling on his dark blue suit jacket, the president straightened his tie, went to the heavy wooden door, and pulled it open with a firm grip.

He walked into his secretary's office and greeted each of the various individuals present by name and with a handshake. For this emergency meeting, only eleven representatives from the various parties were able to attend. The four women and seven men, all leaders in their own right, were dressed somberly, as appropriate for the situation. "Come with me. We are going to the conference room." He led them down the hall.

Gesturing from the doorway, he said, "Please be seated wherever you would like."

The president took his place in the middle seat nearest the window. He waited for everyone to settle in.

"Thank you for joining me at this grave hour. We will not stand on ceremony here. It is time for us, as leaders of our parties, to determine the future course of our country. I understand, as head of the government, it is our party that has to make these difficult decisions. However, I want advice from all of you. We may have had our political disagreements in the past, but today, I think it is important for our country that we act in a unified fashion."

The president continued. "I have asked the prime minister to brief us on the situation as it exists right now. Following that, we will answer any questions you may have. I suggest that at that time, we take a short break. When we return, we need to discuss where we go from here."

In a somewhat less regal fashion than the president, the prime minister rose and looked at each of the individuals seated at the table. "Ladies and gentlemen, we are at a crossroads for this country. We have been struck an incredible blow. What I will lay out for you is as much as I know."

The gathered party leaders listened intently to the prime minister, though some were vaguely distracted by his dark, bronzed skin, likely the result of weeks at the ocean. The elegantly tailored suit hung well on his robust frame. He focused his steely gray eyes on each one of them as he spoke.

"First, two trucks breached security at the Eiffel Tower. These suicide bombers exploded their bombs almost simultaneously. The explosions weakened the two legs of the Tower closest to the river. The damage caused the Tower to collapse into the Seine. Most of the dead within the structure of the Tower have been recovered, but we're still searching for those who may have fallen into the river. The number of deaths as a result of this action is high. We are not able to give an exact number because the recovery work is still continuing."

He took a deep breath, looking around the large conference table. Stroking his thin mustache and letting the impact of his words sink in, he noticed one of the men dabbing at his eyes. "In addition, there have been numerous car bomb explosions through-out the city. It appears that these are not suicide bombers, but rather bombs placed strategically at these locations earlier. Evidently, they were set to go off at random intervals. Each one has caused considerable damage to the buildings around them. Some have caused deaths and injuries, while others have not. The problem with this type of attack is that there are cars parked all over Paris. We do not know, without checking each one of them, whether vehicles contain car bombs waiting to explode or not.

"The police are going street by street attempting to do just that. This is being done by contacting the owners and asking them to come down to open their cars. So far, we have found two cars whose owners did not respond. Bomb disposal units are checking each of those cars. They found explosives in both and disarmed them. Unfortunately, this will take an extended period of time, as I'm sure you can understand, to clear every car in Paris."

The assembled politicians listened attentively, some making notes on yellow pads, others simply listening.

The prime minister continued. "Most of you have seen or heard that several bridges were also attacked. Each of them has suffered sufficient damage and cannot be used until they are repaired. At this point, we have military personnel stationed at every bridge in Paris. Their orders are to stop all vehicles and determine whether they are safe to cross or not. As you can imagine, this has slowed traffic to a crawl. We have asked, through the media, that people not drive if at all possible."

The prime minister consulted his notes. "Next, there is an undetermined number of terrorists who are apparently targeting hotels and other businesses. One to six individuals attack each individual hotel, armed with automatic rifles, side arms and grenades. It appears their only aim is to cause chaos and terror. They have been very successful in doing that. We will be establishing roving military patrols throughout the city. Unless they run into the terrorists in the course of an attack, the terrorists may just fall back into the shadows until the military has passed by.

"Finally, the most destructive, have been the attacks on the Metro system. At least one bomb has exploded on every line. Several of the connecting stations have also been hit. Each of these has caused numerous casualties, including many fatalities. The damage is horrific. Collateral damage from the attacks on the Gare du Nord include potential damage to the train station above the Metro station. These stations are being inspected at this time.

"In summary, today, Paris has suffered an attack of enormous proportions. Many lives have been lost and many more people were wounded. At this time, the hospitals are struggling to keep up with the influx of casualties. Paris's infrastructure has received a stunning blow. One of our most treasured monuments has been taken from us. The cost to recover from this attack will be in the billions of Euros. Perhaps now is the time to take your questions."

The prime minister sat down and looked at the faces around the table. The silence was deafening. Finally, one party leader rose. "Sir, do you have any estimate of the total number of deaths?"

"That's difficult to say because we're getting different numbers from the hospitals. We have wounded going in and some of those are dying. We've not found all of the remains at the various attack sites. But I would guess that the number will easily exceed one thousand."

"Numbers of wounded?"

Referring once again to his notes, the prime minister said, "Well, as the recovery efforts continue, we are finding more dead and wounded. Again, I'm not sure the numbers we are getting from the hospitals are accurate. If I were to guess, I would say that ultimately, it will be two to three thousand. But we still have car bombs going off and terrorists attacking hotels and other targets."

Another leader rose. "Monsiueu Prime Minister, you've indicated you expect the cost of recovery to be in the billions of Euros. What do you base that on?"

"At this time, it is simply our best guess. We have not had the manpower to investigate all of the attacked sites. We are still in the rescue mode. As soon as possible, experts will be brought in to examine the damage and make estimates as to the cost of repair. But many of the attack locations within the Metro system need to be dug out before we can begin the process of estimating repairs. There are many decisions to be made. For example, do we replace the bridges with new modern structures or rebuild them as they were before the attacks? Also, the most looming question is whether or not to rebuild the Eiffel Tower? If the decision is made to do so, obviously, the cost will be enormous. All of these questions will need to be discussed in the National Assembly."

"What help do you need from each of us?"

The president responded, "What the prime minister and I have laid out for you are just a few of the difficult decisions we will face. We all have strong concerns, ideologies and constituencies. I think the most important thing we need to remember now is that we are people of France, not of individual parties. I hope that we can all join together in a nonpartisan attempt to help our country recover as quickly as possible."

The tall, elegant politician peered at his colleagues around the highly polished table. "There are going to be all sorts of issues to which we would normally take a partisan approach. As politicians, we might use these issues to our political advantage. But today, France is under attack. I hope that we can all act as one, as difficult as that may be. You have my promise that I will keep you apprised of what is happening. I also promise that we will bring you to the table before we embark on any strategy. In the end, you may disagree with course of action we choose. However, you have my word of honor that no decision will be taken on our future course of action without having first discussed it with all of you and having sought your ideas and opinions."

The first leader, a somewhat pudgy fellow in an ill-fitting suit, rose once again. "The course you suggest is fraught with difficulties. There is a question of trust, a question of ideology, and the question of what is best for France. But I agree with you—we have not before faced such an emergency as we face today. I, too, believe that we must act in unity on behalf of our country and our people. Therefore, I promise you today that we will step back from partisan politics and will work with you to assure the future of our country."

The president watched as each leader stood and made the same commitment. When they finished, he rose to address them. "Each of us in this room has had many difficult and sometimes personal disagreements with one another. But I must say, having heard each of you speak today, I have never been as proud of my countrymen and their service to France as I am right now. You've shown the true spirit of what it means to be French. I salute you. Please take note. Here are the direct telephone numbers to our offices and our cell phones. I invite you to contact us whenever necessary."

Nodding, a grim smile crossing his worried visage, the president of France once again looked at each person. "*Vive la France* and those who serve her."

More than one person present later reported they saw tears in the president's eyes.

Chapter 42

Melanie was sitting quietly on the bed in her fourth-floor room with her back tightly pressed into the corner. Her legs were drawn up to her chest, arms tightly wrapped around them, and her chin rested on one knee. She stared across the room.

As she watched, a small ant worked its way over the floor. While it was totally focused on its journey for food, Melanie's eyes never wavered from the small insect. *Is it afraid?* she wondered. *Is it as afraid as I am right now?*

She seemed to be having trouble breathing, her chest tight and constricted. While her eyes never left the ant, she realized how easily she could terminate its life. Melanie also understood how easily her own life could be ended. She had never thought about that before; she had always been supported by her father. She had never worried about where her next meal would come from or whether she would have a place to lay her head at night. Her only real concerns centered on the men in her life.

Occasionally, she worried about her classes and the grades she would receive, but now, as she watched the ant continue its journey, it struck her that she was a shallow individual. Now she was in a situation where she was not sure whether her life would continue beyond this day, and that realization caused a shudder to course through her body. Melanie tried to swallow but was unable to. She closed her eyes and felt the tears start to come.

There was a light knock at the door. She raised her head to see who was there, but the door had not opened. "Come in." She could see the knob turn and the door slowly opened. Soon, Derek appeared. She smiled as she recognized him. "Hi, what's up?"

"I was just checking to see how you're doing. How are you feeling?"

"Not so good." Her chin dropped back to her knees.

Derek walked in and closed the door behind him. He could see that she needed privacy. He walked over and sat down on the bed next to her. Derek reached over and placed his fingers under her chin and raised her face toward his. "I can see it's not so good. You've been crying."

She attempted to smile at him, but that act was a failure. She squeezed her eyes shut, but her tears started to flow once again. "I'm so scared. I think I'm about to go crazy."

"You're no different than the rest of us. We're all feeling the same thing."

She looked at him quizzically. "But you're not afraid. It's so easy to tell."

"Oh, how wrong you are. Sometimes my knees are shaking together. I mean, how can we not be afraid given everything that's happened? I think it's just because some people can handle emergency situations more easily. It's okay. Things will get better soon."

"How can you say that? We're here all by ourselves. There's no evidence of police officers nearby. I mean, we're just waiting for those terrorists to come back. And when that happens..." She sobbed once more. Derek reached over and pulled her close to him, holding her tightly. He rocked back and forth, trying to comfort her while she continued to cry. He stroked her short, dark brown in slow, gentle movements, as he would a young child.

"I know this is difficult, Melanie, but we'll get through it. All of us. In a day or so, you're going to look back and wonder why you felt so bad. Just wait and see."

"God, I hope you're right. But I have this feeling I can't shake that they're coming back for us. I just don't think we're going to make it."

Derek brushed the hair out of her eyes, and tilted her head so she was looking directly at him with her tear-reddened, yet amazing deep chocolate eyes. "Mel, have you thought about how different the situation is now compared to this morning? When this started, all we had to protect ourselves were knives. Now, we have two automatic rifles, two handguns and some hand grenades. That changes the equation completely. We are ready and able to defend ourselves as need be. Don't you think that makes a huge difference?"

She nodded at him. "But that doesn't help me shake this feeling. Who knows how many of them will come next time? There were two the first time. There could be many more the next time. What do we do if that happens?" She looked into his blue eyes and waited for a response that would make her feel better.

Derek smiled at her. "Ye of little faith. Why are you looking at it from the worst possible way? First of all, the chances are that no one will return. Then, all we have to do is wait until everything settles down. Second of all, you presume that they will want to come back here. Think about it. Why would they do that? We're not worth the hassle. I bet we could go to the restaurant down the street and have a nice meal without a problem."

"You know, Derek, you might be right."

"Now that's a first. I don't remember your ever thinking I was right. I like it better this way." His eyes twinkled as he looked at her.

Melanie started to laugh and punched him in the arm. "Don't let it go to your head. Everybody gets lucky once."

The door opened and Jackie walked in. "What the hell's going on in here? Or am I interrupting some special time between the two of you?"

Derek glanced at Jackie as he stood up from the bed. "You wouldn't know what a special time was even if it was standing right in front of you." His voice had a hardness to it that caused Jackie to step back. "Melanie was having a hard time, but is doing much better now."

Melanie stood up also. "He's right, but everything's okay."

Jackie walked over to Melanie and put her arms around her friend. "I'm sorry. I was just joking. I didn't mean anything by it. And you, Derek, lighten up, big guy. If you don't, I may have to take you outside and teach you a thing or two."

Derek looked at Jackie. She was not big or particularly threatening, but he wasn't quite sure he would want to take her up on her offer. "Okay. Seems like everybody's a little tense around here. What's going on downstairs, Jackie?"

"I haven't a clue. I've been in my room resting. Maybe I was just waiting for some big, strong guy like you, Derek, to walk in and give me a thrill."

All three started laughing.

"Be careful for what you ask, Jackie. It has crossed my mind." And with that, he winked at her.

"Derek, you're such a tease. You know, most of the girls here would give you the key to their room. Not me, of course, but maybe Melanie."

Melanie looked at both of them. "You're both so full of shit. I almost wish the terrorists would come back to save me from this. You know, now that I think about it, you two might just well deserve each other. I'm going to see what's going on downstairs." Melanie smiled at each of them and walked out the door.

As Jackie walked toward the door, Derek slapped her lightly on the butt. She turned on him with fire in her eyes. "You don't want to go there, trust me."

"Well, we went there last night. Why do you have an attitude now?"

"Because I can!" She slammed the door as she walked out.

Derek opened the door, and watched Jackie walk away. He smiled as he thought of their time together the night before. She was sassy, just like he liked his women.

Chapter 43

Samir had not left the TV since the attacks had started. He was like a moth being pulled to a light. He was holding a clipboard. It rested on his knee and he glanced at it occasionally. The papers on the clipboard had a step-by-step listing of the actions he had planned for this day. When a television reporter came on to describe the latest attack, he checked it off on his list.

With a fluid motion, Salah rose from his desk and walked to Samir. He stared at the television for a few moments. "It seems like we're near the completion of all our attacks. Is that how you see it?"

Samir thought for a moment and glanced at the clipboard. "Yes, I believe so. I think, but I'm not sure, that all but one or two car bombs have either exploded or have been found. But most of them went off. There's been nothing new reported on the television for some time now. Are you still getting reports from our people?"

"It's been quite interesting. Most of them have completed their tasks and are melting away to their respective safe houses. There is only one team that has not reported back. I've not sent back up units to them."

Samir looked at him. "Which unit hasn't reported?"

"Wasi and Saad. Since our attacks are nearly complete, do you want me to send a unit to their last reported target?"

"Which reserve units are still available?

"As I recall, we have a five-man and a ten-man unit remaining for assignment. Let me check." Salah walked to his desk and fumbled through some papers. He found the one he wanted and returned to Samir. "The last report we had from Wasi indicated they were heading toward their second target, a small hotel. I'm not sure it's worth sending a backup unit to that."

Samir rose and walked toward the window. He glanced out to see what was happening on the street, as he had done so many times that day. He saw nothing unusual and turned and faced Salah.

"I guess what needs to be answered is one, what happened to Wasi's unit and two, what do we do, if anything, about it? I'm inclined to let it go and keep our people in reserve for another day. But what bothers me is why would Wasi have any problem at a small hotel? Do we have anybody nearby who could simply check it out for us?"

Salah walked to his desk, sat down and started typing on his computer. In a moment, he stopped and looked at Samir with a smile. "We do. One of our supporters is right down the street. I could give him a call and ask him to walk down there and see what he can determine. I'm not sure it's worth his time."

"Humor me. Send him down as soon as he can go. We'll wait and see what he has to say." Samir strode back to the television. Everything being reported was merely a repeat of something that had been played earlier or an update on casualties. He could hear Salah talking with someone on the phone.

"He's on his way to the hotel. He said he can get back to us in five to ten minutes."

"Good." As he watched the TV, he could see that the French army was now in place in Paris. This was not unexpected and, in fact, he was surprised it had not occurred earlier. The talking heads on the screen were assuring everyone that all was well now that the army had arrived. He chuckled to himself. Since the attacks were almost completed, there was nothing for the army to protect them from. The damage had been, for the most part, completed. He was still surprised how well things had gone.

"Salah, do you think we should shut everything down now? Is there anything more that we can accomplish?"

"I think it's probably time we made our escape. There's no way to connect us to any of this. If we leave now, we can live to fight the next battle."

Just then, the phone rang. Salah picked it up and listened to the voice on the other end. The conversation went on for three or four minutes before Salah hung up. "Well, that's interesting."

"What was that about?"

"That was the man who checked out the hotel Wasi was supposed to attack. He said he went down there and there is evidence that a car bomb had gone off down the street. But there's no indication of any damage at the hotel itself. He saw no evidence of Wasi or Saad. It's like they did not reach the hotel. That in and of itself is very strange. What do you want to do?"

"It seems to me that either Wasi and Saad did not go to the hotel or something happened to them while they were there. In either event, the hotel remains undamaged. If they simply did not attack, we can deal with that at a later time. On the other hand, if the hotel shows no damage after their attack, we must do something about that. I think we should send our five-man reserve unit. What are your thoughts?"

Salah pondered that question for a few moments. "Well, we certainly can do that. However, I'm not sure what we gain."

"I don't like the idea of not succeeding in attacking a small hotel. Send the five-man unit to check it out. Have them report what they find before they go in."

Salah returned to the phone. He called the required number and gave the unit's leader his instructions. He looked back at Samir.

"What you have ordered has been done. We are lucky. They should be there within a half hour."

"Since we're talking about reserve units, Salah, do you have any suggestions on how we should use our ten-man unit? Or should we just hold them until a later time?"

"I suggest we wait until we learn what our five-man unit determines."

"Good idea. Let me know when we hear from them." Samir walked over to the TV, crossed his arms and continued to watch the reports of the day's attacks. It seemed that the government was slowly, but surely, responding to the attacks and preparing for additional confrontations. This did not concern him since his strikes were almost completed. "Salah, has anyone taken credit for today's actions?"

"Not yet. It seems that most of the speculation is coming from the news media about who might be responsible. There is nothing being reported that would relate to us in any way. I think we are okay."

"Good. Just as we planned. If nothing comes out in the next few hours, we may have to initiate something." Samir smiled to himself. "Is there a group we especially don't like on whom we can pin these attacks?"

"No one comes to mind, but it would be fun to come up with someone."

Chapter 44

walked up the stairs to the first floor and headed down the hallway. The door was open and Rick was seated at the window looking down the right side of the street. I stood there watching him for a few seconds before he noticed me.

"How's it going?"

He simply raised his right thumb to indicate that everything was good.

"See anything at all?"

"No, nothing. The streets are as empty as a church on Monday morning."

"Do you need someone to replace you?"

"No, not for a while. If you can, relieve me in an hour."

"Will do." I again started down the hallway. When I reached the end, the last room's door was also open. I looked in and saw Rochelle sitting at the window, looking to the left.

She heard me enter and swiveled her head at me. She was slouched down in the chair, the excitement of being a lookout had obviously worn off. "What's up, Professor?"

"Nothing. I just want to check and see how you were doing."

"I'm fine, don't worry."

"Do you want someone to take over for you?"

"Naw, I'm okay. Is Rick still down the hall looking the other way?"

"Yes, he is. I'm going to have someone take over for him in about an hour. I'll do the same for you."

She looked at me questioningly. "What is your best guess about what's going to happen?"

"I haven't a clue, Rochelle. Your guess is as good as mine. All we can do is be prepared. I'll see you in a bit."

Then I walked back down the hall to the stairs. Student voices drifted down the stairway. They all seemed to be doing fairly well, but that could change quickly if more terrorists showed up. I walked down the stairs to the lobby.

Both Mac and Ty were sitting in front of the TV. I stood there behind them watching the reporters describe the various attacks that had occurred. There was nothing new. I'd seen all these reports before.

Mac indicated the chair next to him and I sat down. He smiled once again and said, "How is our fearless leader doing now?" He saw me flip him off and started laughing. "What's the matter? Does the weight of authority weigh heavily upon you?" I flipped him off again, which merely made him laugh that much harder.

Ty gave a deep chuckle. "Well, fearless leader, I'm not sure that's an appropriate answer."

"Not you too? I had hope for you, Ty, but I guess your association with this guy has turned you toward the dark side. Such a waste."

"Mac, I think our fearless leader is having a bad day. Is there anything we can do to help him out?"

Mac patted the automatic rifle that lay across his legs. "I think we should stand him up against the wall and shoot him. That would put him out of his misery." Mac looked at me. "Just stand against the wall."

I slowly got up from the chair, and looked at both of them. "I think I'm going to go talk to a terrorist. It would have to be more meaningful than this conversation."

Mac pointed the gun over my head. "Shut the hell up and sit down or I will shoot you. How are the students doing?"

Ty answered first. "I talked to several of them and they seem to be okay. A couple of them have the shakes, which is understandable. They were talking about Becky and what's his name, wondering if they made it to safety. However, none of them seemed to want to take off on their own. They seem to have come to grips with the situation and are willing to wait it out."

Mac leaned his weapon against the wall. He crossed his arms and looked out the window. "I've been surprised at some of the students. Some I thought would be weak in this type of situation have shown me some real strength. A couple of the guys who usually talk pretty tough are not as tough as they think. Bottom line is that I think they'll follow our lead. Given what we walked into, that's probably as good as we could expect."

I spoke next. "Derek told me about a conversation he had with Melanie. He said she was very shaken up and crying. He said he tried to buck her up and she seemed better when they finished talking. Derek is one student I think we can count on if the going gets tough. But, let's hope we don't have to have that happen. Have they had anything to eat recently? I know I'm getting hungry."

Mac stood up and started for the stairs. "I'm not sure but I'm going to find out. I know there are people downstairs in the kitchen working on something. We might as well get everybody fed while we have some time."

Ty got up and headed for the stairs also. "I'll go upstairs and see if the kids are hungry. If they are, I'll send them down. You want me to get replacements for Rochelle and Rick?"

"Let's wait until everyone has eaten. Then they can come down and eat also," I said.

Ty nodded and I watched him head up the dark staircase. I got up from my seat and walked toward the receptionist desk, sat down and picked up the phone. There was no tone. The terrorists must have done something to cut off communications. It made sense to do that.

Then I took out my cell phone and attempted to make a call. The phone just told me all circuits were busy. I got up and headed back toward the sofa in front of the TV. I heard something from the stairway and turned to look. Mac emerged and was walking toward me, carrying a plate. He sat down and handed me the plate, which had a sandwich on it.

"It is important to keep our fearless leader energized. The students are making sandwiches for everyone."

"Thanks. By the way, how much food do we have? We should hopefully have enough to last us a couple of days," I said.

"That shouldn't be a problem. I checked out the food stores myself. There is sufficient ham and cheese for sandwiches for a few days. There is also plenty of fruit and water. I think we'll be okay in that department."

I heard some talking behind me and turned and saw the students heading toward the breakfast room. Their mood seemed subdued. A moment later, Ty appeared, walked over and sat down.

Ty jerked his finger toward the stairs. "I've got all the students going down to eat. Dumb shits, they were asking where they could get pizza. I also told Rochelle and Rick what the plan was. They're okay with it."

I looked at both men and stood up. "Can you think of anything else we should be doing? Sitting here and waiting is for the birds. I think we need to find something to keep the kids and ourselves busy."

Mac pointed at Ty. "I brought DJ a sandwich and I had one downstairs. You may want to go down to get something for yourself. DJ, I think you're right about keeping them busy. You know, all we have talked about is defending ourselves here. What happens if the bad guys come with more people?"

I nodded. "Any suggestions?"

Mac seemed deep in thought. "You know, I've been looking around this hotel, and there is no back door. I mean, how can you have a building without a second exit?"

I started laughing at him. "Well, dumb shit, you know these buildings were built in the 1700s. It's not like they had binding building regulations at that time. But I know how your mind thinks. You have a suggestion, don't you?" I waited for Mac to answer.

"How well you know me, DJ. You're just lucky you have someone who understands these details. If you go down into the kitchen, you'll find that there are windows about six feet off the floor. They lead to the alley behind this hotel. The windows are small, about two feet tall and three feet wide, and at the ground level of the alley. If we need to, we can exit through those windows. There are only two of them, so it will take a while for all of us to get out. So before we decide to make a break for it, let's be sure we have time to get everybody out."

"That's great work, smart ass, but where do we go once we get out?"

"Good question. I suggest one of us breaks a window, goes out and finds us an escape route. We should try to go into the building behind us. I'm not sure it would be very smart to go running down the alley, not knowing what's at the end."

"I agree," I nodded. "Why don't we go down and take a look? You're such an old fart I'm not sure you can climb out of the window. Why don't you stay here in case something happens and Ty and I will go check it out?"

Mac chuckled quietly. "That works for me, but if you get your fat ass stuck in the window, don't ask me for help."

Ty rose and headed toward the stairs. "You know, you guys sound like an old married couple. Is there something I don't know?" Both Mac and I flipped him off.

I followed him toward the stairs. "Who would want to marry that old fart anyway?"

Taking the worn steps down to the kitchen, I heard Mac's voice call us both assholes, followed by a belly laugh.

As we walked through the breakfast room, the students were eating their sandwiches and talking among themselves. We entered the kitchen and moved toward the back of the building until we saw the two windows Mac described. Ty found a chair and pushed it against the wall. He climbed up and looked out the window.

"I don't see anything out there. Hand me something so I can break the glass."

I searched through the kitchen until I found a wooden mallet. I handed it up to him. "Try not to make too much noise."

"Okay." He tapped the window a couple of times with the mallet until it broke. He cleared the glass away and eased himself out the window.

I climbed on the chair and followed him out. We looked up and down the alley and saw what appeared to be a typical Parisian alley. Small, smelly garbage dumpsters stood behind certain businesses. We wondered how the hotel got its garbage out since there was no door leading to the alley. Oh well, just another French mystery. I pointed toward a door about 100 feet away. "Maybe we should head for that?"

Ty saw where I was pointing. "I'm not sure I like that idea. I mean, we will be coming out of these windows fairly slowly and then have a bit of a run for safety. Not all of us may be able to make it that far."

He quickly crossed the alley to the back of the opposite building. He knelt down and looked into two windows, which were similar to the ones we had just exited. "Maybe we should go from our building to here and enter these windows?"

I saw the wisdom of his suggestion." Let's check out the building."

Ty kicked in the window and again removed the broken glass. "I'm going to go in and check it out. If I'm not back in a few minutes, send the cavalry." He smiled at me and dropped in through the window.

I waited there for what seemed like hours and was getting ready to go in through the window myself when Ty's head appeared.

"This seems to be a small store of some type. There is a basement and a ground floor. There's no way to go up. Access to the upper floors must be by way of an outside door. Do you want to come in and check it out? I think it will work fine."

"If you think it works, I don't need to see it. Let's break out the other window and get the glass cleared away so no one gets cut going in. And then let's get back to the hotel."

"I'll get the window here taken care of and then will be right back."

I returned to our hotel and slipped through the window that was just above ground level. Breathing hard from the exertion, I got the mallet and knocked the other window out. By the time I had cleaned up the glass, Ty was crawling through the window.

"Well, I think we have our escape route taken care of." He dusted off his hands and stood there, looking at our windows.

"We have one more thing to do. Unless we keep someone stationed here, a bad guy could slip in these windows. I saw some cardboard in the kitchen. Let's put it over each of the windows so it's not quite so obvious that someone could get in. Then we can pull those two shelving units over in front of the windows. Someone would have to knock those out of the way to get in and that would make one hell of a racket."

"Ty, I like the way you think." I grinned at my friend.

A few moments later, we had the cardboard over the windows and the shelving units moved in front of them. "Let's go tell Mac what we've come up with. I'm sure he'll give us shit about something."

When we got back up to the lobby, Mac was stretched out on the sofa with his eyes closed. "Great lookout you are."

"Shut up. I'm listening."

"Listening for what?"

"To the two assholes coming up the stairs. Don't forget, the lookouts are upstairs. I'm resting my trigger finger."

Ty was shaking his head. "Does he always have a quick comeback?"

"Always. And sometimes it's funny."

Once again, Mac flipped us off.

Chapter 45

When the phone rang in the small apartment, Nasser jolted upright. The two men sitting in the living room, one stocky, the other slender, looked at him questioningly. He got up and walked to the phone. He lifted the handset and said, "Yes?"

He heard Salah's gruff voice on the line. "You've been activated. One of our teams reported in after attacking its first target and indicated they were heading toward their second target. We have not heard from them since. I had one of our assets walk by the hotel. While there is indication of a car bomb explosion down the street, there is no sign of any attack on the hotel. It's our belief that either the unit fled before attacking their second target or they were somehow taken out. I want you to go down to the hotel and see what you can determine. Before you attack, I want you to call in and brief me on what you find."

He gave Nasser the address of the hotel. "Do you have any questions?"

"Do you have any idea what the situation is around that area? Are we going to run into the police or army units?"

"I don't believe so. It is a very small hotel, which should not garner protection from any of the government's people. How long do you think it will take you to get there?"

"From where we are, if there's not much traffic on the streets, maybe ten minutes."

"When will you be ready to leave?"

Nasser looked around and saw that his unit was already packing up. "Five minutes tops."

"Call me after you've looked around. Use your satellite phone."

Nasser walked into the bedroom and motioned for the two other men in his unit to come into the living room. "Okay, guys, we've been activated. We're going to take the van and head toward a small hotel. The unit assigned to attack it has gone missing. Salah doesn't know if the unit just left or whether something happened at the hotel. We're to see what's going on and report back. It's unclear whether we will attack or not. Let's get ready and head to the van."

A few minutes later, they were in a small, one-car garage. The four men got in the back of the van. Nasser opened the garage door, climbed into the driver seat, cranked the engine, and cautiously pulled the van out into the road. He was stunned to see how little traffic there was. It was clear to him that the people of Paris had become very frightened; this usually busy city was like a ghost town.

Nasser drove slowly toward the hotel. He parked on a side street approximately one block away. He turned and peered into the back of the van to check out his colleagues. Each man was armed with an AK-47 and carried a canvas bag of hand grenades. At their waists, each carried a Glock. They were also wearing vests that carried extra magazines for their weapons.

Nasser stated, "My friends, now is our time. For most of the day, others have been blessed by Allah. As you have seen on TV, their actions have pleased him greatly. We must also do our duty. It is not the time for the faint of heart but only those who will truly serve Allah. Does anyone have any doubts?"

Each man shook his head back and forth.

"Okay. Here's what we are going to do. I'm going to leave my rifle here. I'm going to go out and see what we face. I'll return shortly. You are to wait here until I return."

Nasser climbed slowly out of the van and looked up and down the street, but saw nothing of concern. Again, he was surprised at the lack of activity. He had never seen Paris so quiet. He walked to the side of the building and headed for the corner. When he reached it, he looked around carefully but again, saw nothing moving.

The entrance to the hotel was just down the street, opposite his location. He saw no movement in any of the windows of the hotel. When he examined the exterior of the hotel, he saw no damage of any kind. All of the windows seemed to be intact.

This is very strange, he thought. *The hotel has no damage, and there is no evidence of the team Salah mentioned.*

As he watched the hotel, it appeared to be deserted, like every other business on the street. Nasser walked back toward the van, pondering what he had seen. He opened the back doors of the van and leaned in to explain in a quiet voice what he had observed.

He pointed at Khalid. "I want you to go back to the corner and keep an eye on the hotel. Don't show yourself; just look around the corner. I'm going to check in and find out what we're supposed to do."

Khalid, a tall, slender man, opened the door, stepped gracefully out of the van and headed for the corner.

Nasser reached into his bag and pulled out his satellite phone. He dialed the number he had memorized long ago. After two rings, Salah answered. He gave Salah a brief description of what he'd seen. "How do you want us to proceed?"

"I will call you back shortly with instructions."

* * * * *

With a loud clunk, Salah hung up the phone. "Samir, that was our unit reporting in. Nasser described the situation in the same terms as the man we sent there previously. Do you want this five-man unit to go into the hotel or do you want them to return to their apartment?"

"This makes no sense, Salah. As I recall, Wasi and Saad were dedicated warriors. How do you think we should proceed?"

"I don't understand what could've happened. Let's send the unit in to do their job. If no one is there, no harm done. If there are people inside, our attack continues."

"I think you're right, Salah. Make the call and order the attack."

Salah dialed the phone number and relayed Samir's instructions. He finished with, "Make sure you report to me when you have completed the job."

"I will."

* * * * *

Nasser looked at the men who had become his friends. "We've been given the order to move forward. We're to check out the hotel. If no one is there, we're done. Now, here is the plan of attack. We will walk toward the hotel five abreast. When we enter the hotel, I will stay on the ground floor and each of you will clear a floor above. We should be done in five minutes. Any questions?"

One of his men raised his hand. "Do you expect any resistance?"

"No. What kind of resistance could these French people put up?"

The van door opened and the five men stepped out. Each adjusted their equipment as necessary. Nasser looked at each one of them. "Let's get this done." He led them to the corner and stepped out onto the street.

Chapter 46

Rick, who was on the first floor, had situated the chair to the side of the window. He was able to sit comfortably in the chair while looking down the street. Suddenly, his stomach growled. He was ready to get something to eat, and frankly, this lookout stuff was getting to be quite boring. He found it hard to keep focused on his responsibility. His mind played games with him as he passed the time.

Suddenly, he bolted upright. His eyes grew wide as he spotted the men in the street. Each of them carried an automatic rifle and had a very determined look about him. "Holy shit. Oh, holy shit."

He got up, ran to the head of the stairs and yelled down, "Oh, my God. They're coming. Oh, my God. There are five of them. What are we going to do? "

Mac, Ty and I jumped to our feet. We had talked about what we would do if this happened.

Ty spoke first. "Mac, let's get up there."

With rifles in hand, my ex-police friends ran for the stairs and disappeared from sight.

I ran down the stairs to the kitchen. "Derek, get up to the lobby. Listen up, everyone, five armed men are coming this way. Stay where you are." Several of the students began screaming.

"Shut up, now!" I said firmly. "We don't want them to know that we are here."

The screaming died away. In a moment, I followed Derek to the lobby. "We're going to do just as we planned. Mac and Ty are upstairs with rifles. They will fire first. We're going to remain here out of the way. If anyone comes in, we take them out. Understand?"

"Don't worry, I've got it." Derek went and hid behind the receptionist desk. I ran to the wall next to the window. If anyone came in the door, I would have a shot. If need be, Derek would pop up and fire at anyone in the lobby.

When Ty got to the first floor, he pointed at Rick. "Get down to the breakfast room." He then ran down to the room where Rochelle was stationed. She was standing there in shock. "Rochelle, get down to the breakfast room." She did not move. He walked up and grabbed her by the shoulders and shook her.

He looked in her eyes. "Listen to me, Rochelle. Get down to the breakfast room now!"

With that, he pushed her toward the door and she took off running. Ty went to the window and looked out. Approximately 200 feet away, he saw five men walking toward the hotel with their guns at the ready. He knelt down, back from the window, and made his rifle ready to fire.

Mac entered the room next to where Ty was. He too glanced out the window and saw the five men approaching. "Ty, can you hear me?"

"I hear you."

"When they're 50 feet away, let's fire at the same time. I'll count down from three."

"I'm with you. I have the one on the left."

"I'll take the guy on the right, and then we both work toward the middle."

"Okay."

In the lobby, I looked over to where Derek was hiding. "Are you okay?"

"Yes. Now we wait for Ty and Mac to fire, right?"

I nodded at him. It seemed like hours had passed.

On the street, Nasser held up his hand, stopping their advance. He didn't want to walk into a trap. "Keep an eye on all the windows and doorways. Let's make sure we're not surprised."

He heard one of his men respond that no one was around. "Maybe so, but let's keep alert. Let's move forward."

Mac watched the men coming toward the hotel. When they were about 60 feet away, he said "Okay Ty, get ready." As the terrorists continued to move forward, Mac found himself counting down from ten. When he reached four, he said loud enough for Ty to hear "Three ... two ... one."

Mac's rifle barrel rested on a chair, his sight squarely on the target's chest. He slowly squeezed the trigger until he felt the recoil. A fraction of a second before his weapon fired, Mac heard Ty's weapon fire. He watched as his target's face showed a stunned expression in slow motion. That was followed by a spurt of red coming from his chest as he flew backward. He saw Ty's target do the same.

As Mac moved his focus to the next man, the three remaining men fired wildly at the hotel. He heard the hotel windows in the reception area break. He had initially ducked, but when he realized the fire was not directed at him, he took aim at the second man. This man had turned and was running in the direction from which he had come.

Mac sighted on the man as he ran away. "Dumb shit, you can't outrun a bullet." With that, he pulled the trigger and watched the man sprawl forward on his face. Mac could see the blood coming from his back. As he turned toward the other targets, he saw that they had run toward the side of the street on which the hotel was located. He couldn't see them at all.

"I got two of them, Ty. I don't see the others."

"I got one, but the other two headed for this side of the road. I can't see them either. I don't think it would be a good idea to stick our heads out the window. You stay here and keep an eye out for them. I'm going to go downstairs to see if they need my help."

"Okay, let me know what's going on down there."

Ty backed carefully away from the window into the hall. He ran down to the stairs and looked down. "What's happening down there?"

I looked over at Derek. "Are you okay?"

"Yeah, I'm okay, but I may have to change my underwear."

I couldn't see Ty in the stairway, so I yelled, "We're okay down here. How are you guys? "

"We're okay, too. Mac took out two and I got one. The other two ran to our side of the street. We don't know whether they're still there or not. We can't see them and we're not gonna stick our heads out the window to find out. Can you see anything at all?"

"Nothing from here. Derek, can you see anything?" I saw him raise his head slightly over the desk counter and then shake his head no. "Ty, can you come down here and cover me? If you can, I think I can crawl to the other side of the room and look out the window there. It sticks out into the sidewalk just a bit."

"I'm on my way down. For God sake, don't shoot me." He ran over to where I was standing. "Now, where are you going to go?"

I pointed toward the bay window I wanted to reach. "Right there. I might be able to see what they're doing. Just make sure no one shoots me in the back as I'm crawling over there."

"I've got your back. Just be careful."

The windows had all been shot out. I crawled slowly in the direction I wanted to go. Someone would have to be relatively close to have a shot at me. It was the longest 30 seconds of my life. As I slowly made my way across the glass-covered floor, Derek called out.

"Here, I found this in the desk." He pushed a small, round make-up mirror to me. "That may help."

"Thanks, Derek, you may have just saved my life."

I finally reached the window that jutted slightly out into the sidewalk area. I could raise my head and look down the sidewalk to see if anybody was there. However, if they had a gun pointing toward me, it might be all over. I lay below the window, took the mirror with two fingers and slowly raised it to the window so I could look out. I was able to get it up just enough to see what was down the sidewalk. Two men were huddled with their backs against the building. They were moving slowly away.

"Ty, they're moving away from the hotel. Their guns are at the ready. Go tell Mac that in about 30 seconds I'm going to fire at them. I expect they'll fire back, which may give Mac a shot."

"I'm on my way."

I counted slowly to 30 as I continued to watch them back away. At the count, I raised my hand over the window sill and fired my Glock until it was empty. I didn't expect to hit anything since I wasn't looking where I was firing.

The terrorists opened up on full automatic. I could hear the bullets whizz by and hit the wall. I pressed myself so hard against the floor I was surprised I didn't leave an indentation. When their guns fell silent, I could hear the bang of Mac's rifle.

Then, the sound of the AK-47 reached my ears. I hoped Mac was okay. Suddenly, it was quiet. Deathly quiet. I slowly raised the mirror up to take a look and found that the sidewalk was empty except for one body sprawled there. I lay there for a few minutes waiting to see what would happen.

I crawled away from the window, stood and ran to the stairs.

"I think they're gone," I yelled. I heard no reply.

I looked at Derek "Stay here, I'll be right back."

I ran up the stairs and almost knocked Ty over as he was coming down. "Is Mac okay?"

"Of course I'm okay. These bastards can't hurt me." Mac came trotting down the hallway.

"What happened?" I asked.

"Your idea worked. As soon as they ran out of ammunition, I stuck my head out the window and took one shot at the closest one. I saw him fall. I also saw the guy behind him raise his weapon at me and pulled back inside the window. When I heard you yell that you thought they were gone, I poked my head out the window to find out. I saw the last guy go around the corner down the street. I think we're okay for the time being."

"Let's go see how Derek is doing."

We ran down the stairs to find Derek. He was now sitting in the receptionist's chair. He had his elbow on the desk, his gun pointing toward the window. He looked up. "Just in case, guys. You can't be too careful."

His smile seemed to wrap around his face. In fact, we were all pretty giddy that we were still alive.

From around the corner, I could hear tires squealing. I looked at Ty and Mac. "I think he took off."

Mac looked out and saw the four dead men lying in the street and on the sidewalk. "You think we should go out and get their weapons? They may come in handy. We'll have more people in the fight if they come back."

"Mac, you are certifiably, frigging nuts. Who the hell wants to go out there?"

"I'm serious, DJ. We may need those weapons. If the guy is gone, there's no problem."

"And if he's not gone?"

"There is a way to do this and here's how. Ty and I will stay here with our weapons aimed at the corner. Anybody sticks their head around, he's a dead man. All you have to do is run out there get the weapons and skedaddle back here as quickly as you can."

Ty looked at me. "You stay here with my rifle, and I'll go out and get the weapons."

"Ty, you are dumber than you look. I can't shoot worth shit. If I let you out there and get your ass shot off, I will feel guilty for the rest of my life."

Derek walked up to us. "Why don't we do it this way? Mac and Ty can cover you and me. I'll go get the weapons from the two guys on the right and you get the weapons from the guy on the left and the one by the building. I bet you we can be back here in under a minute."

"Derek, I thought you were smarter than that. I'm old enough to be your grandfather. It will take me two minutes just to reach the damn body."

"Do you want to live forever, Professor? Let's go," Derek blurted.

"Mac, if I'm killed, I will haunt you for the rest of your life. This is a bad idea." With that, Derek and I ducked and ran out the door. I was back within a minute and Derek was 15 seconds behind me. When I rushed through the door, both Mac and Ty were bent over with their hands on their knees laughing.

"What is so damn funny?" I panted.

Mac came up to me and slapped me on the back. "You haven't run so fast since your girlfriend's father found you in a rather compromising position."

I looked at Derek as he ran through the doorway. "What took you so long?"

"I can't run and laugh at the same time."

I looked at all three of them laughing. "If we get out of this alive, I may shoot each one of you myself."

Then I stalked off to let the students know what happened. Their laughter followed me all the way down the stairs.

Chapter 47

Gheneral Dugand was alone in his office. He stood in front of the window, ramrod straight, his hands behind his back. He was staring out over his Paris. Earlier in the day, Dugand had seen the smoke from the explosions rise above the buildings. But for some time now, it seemed the attacks had concluded. He knew that to presume would be an invitation to disaster. In his position, Dugand must act as if the terrorists had just begun their program of destruction.

As commander of the military district of Paris, it was his responsibility to protect the city from attack if the violence was of such a nature that local police agencies were incapable of protecting Paris. He had never had to step in previously, but today was the exception.

He heard a sharp knock on the door, glanced at his watch and saw that it was time for the staff meeting. "Enter."

Dugand turned and observed his staff walk in and head toward the oval conference table. They were still at attention as he walked to the table. He sat down and looked at each one of them. "Be seated. Let's begin. Colonel Legere, please provide us with your briefing?"

"Thank you, General. To make sure that we're all on the same page, I will give a brief overview of today's events. First, it goes without saying, we have suffered great damage from a well-coordinated attack by those who at this time are unknown. The number of casualties runs into the thousands. We have lost Paris' greatest monument. The Tower is completely destroyed. Our infrastructure has been severely damaged. The Metro has suffered attacks on every line and many stations. The destruction at Gare du Nord and Gare de L'Est Metro stations has also threatened the railway stations above them."

His face still tinged gray with shock, the man continued. "Several bridges across the Seine have also been destroyed. We've had random car bombs explode throughout the city and now it appears that various hotels and other public places have been struck by groups of terrorists. The only positive thing to note is that it appears these attacks have subsided for the most part."

Looking around the table, the uniformed man went on. "We have been directed to provide security for areas deemed critical to our city. We are doing this in conjunction with the local police authorities. The troops under our command are currently assigned to provide security for the following locations: the major monuments, all major churches, all major government buildings, all major museums, all train stations, the remaining bridges and many other areas designated important by the government. The number of soldiers we have assigned to each of these locations is substantially larger than the normal security forces we employ. Given that our security team at the Tower was overwhelmed in the initial attack, it was decided that we must increase the numbers so that they can repel a well-coordinated attack on any location."

He watched his colleagues nod, then took a sip of water and reviewed his notes.

"As you know, new military units are arriving in Paris as we speak. These units have been placed under the General's command. We are, at this time, trying to coordinate with the police on how these units, or portions of these units, will be deployed. Of course, these forces will supplement our current security forces as necessary. There also will be additional locations where security is needed and they will be assigned to those also. We have determined that as forces become available, we shall initiate roving patrols throughout the city. These units will be able to respond to new attacks, and hopefully, will act as a deterrent to any further attacks."

The man paused to take a sip of water from one of the glasses adorning the table.

"Monsieur General and colleagues, that is what is happening now. With the influx of new troops and the extended time on station for our own troops, we have certain issues we must deal with. First, where do these troops bed down? For today, the troops will simply remain at their stations. However, that cannot go on forever and we will need to determine where they will be when not on duty. Also, there is the issue of feeding them. Currently, they can eat prepared rations they carry with them, but if they're going to be stationed at these locations for very long, we'll have to make some alternative arrangements. None of these issues is insurmountable and the logistics can be figured out at the unit level. We may have to determine the parameters of those decisions, however."

He coughed and took another sip of water. "In summary, we have and continue to be in the process of determining the appropriate assignment of our current troop levels and those who continue to flow into the city. Ongoing planning should resolve any logistic issues we have."

Dugand leaned back in his chair. Once again, he looked around the room at the people seated at the conference table. "One issue we have not spoken at length on is the rules of engagement for the troops. My initial orders have been simple: they are to defend our people and property from any attacks by terrorists. During the height of the attacks, this order has not caused any problems. We need, I believe, to explore whether more in-depth rules should be adopted.

"Some of the questions I have are should the troops respond with deadly force when an attack may be in the works, as opposed to one being carried out? Also, what kind of weapons should we respond with? Can buildings be attacked if innocent civilians are present? These are just a few of my concerns. At the conclusion of this meeting, I want you to discuss these and many other questions you may have. Be prepared to present me with options for amended rules of engagement.

"Another issue we need to address concerns the type of military vehicles we should be using within the city. I assume at this time that tanks are certainly not required. However, do we need other types of armored vehicles? This question comes to mind less for our security forces protecting certain monuments and other stand-alone facilities, but rather for the roving patrols we will establish. What types of vehicles do they need? I want you to discuss this and have recommendations for me. It will not be long before more troops arrive in Paris. I need from you a well-thought-out plan on how we're going to use our roving patrols. For instance, how is the chain of command going to work for these roving patrols? Are we going to establish command authority by district? Anyway, you know what I'm getting at."

Dugand leaned forward, arms extended, palms flat on the table. "Finally, I want you to explore any and all options, ideas or concerns you may have. I want to have a plan ready for any issues that come up. In summary, gentlemen, I do not want to be surprised and have to pick a course of action on the run. Colonel Legere will coordinate all the information you develop. Let's make it happen."

Dugand stood and everyone came to attention. "Dismissed." The various staff officers headed for the conference room down the hall.

"Colonel Legere, would you stay behind for a moment?"

After everyone had left the general's quarters, Dugand sat down behind his desk. Colonel Legere took a seat in front of him.

"Colonel, I want you to light a fire under all of those officers. It is my intention that we make this city as safe as possible as quickly as possible." The general paused for a moment and pivoted on his chair to look out the window. "I'm sure that both you and I are going to be judged by what happens from this point on. We need to make sure that our actions are only viewed as positive. Frankly, our country needs us now more than ever to do the best job possible."

He turned and looked at the colonel once again. "Paris' safety is now in our hands. Let's show them that we were up to the task. Any questions?"

"None, sir. When we have completed our work here, I'm sure our people will say 'well done.' Now, if you don't mind, General, I need to go light the fires."

General Dugand laughed. "Keep me informed of your progress because I have people I need to keep informed. Good luck."

The colonel rose, came to attention, and saluted Dugand. He then turned and walked out of the office. He knew what the general meant. If they did not meet this challenge appropriately, their careers in the army were over.

Chapter 48

Nasser realized he was driving much too fast and had to talk himself into slowing down. To say that he was shaken was an understatement. He took one hand off the wheel and saw that it was trembling. He needed to get control of himself. Nasser pulled the van to the side of the road and stopped.

He started to replay in his mind the events that had just taken place. Nasser was still not sure exactly what had happened. He remembered that he and his unit were walking toward the hotel. He closed his eyes and watched the pictures of what he saw run through his mind. There had been absolutely no indication of anyone either in the hotel or in any of the other businesses on the street.

It was just so sudden. Shots rang out, and in his peripheral vision, he had seen two of his men fall to the ground. He had not seen where the shots had come from, nor had he seen any gunmen or gunfire. Stunned by the events, his training kicked in and he began firing at the hotel, which was the most likely location from which the gunfire originated.

Nasser did not recall running from the street to the sidewalk. He did remember pressing his back hard against the wall and the intense quiet surrounding him as he stood there. When he looked into the street, he saw the bodies of three of his men. He wondered how they could have been cut down so quickly.

His remaining man stood between him and the hotel. The frightened man had asked what happened and what they were going to do. Nasser remembered how hard he was breathing at that time and was unable to answer immediately. He made the decision to return to the van. However, he was not going to just turn his back and run. Nasser did not want to end up like the one man from his unit who lay on the street on his face, clearly shot in the back.

He and his remaining friend had moved backwards slowly with their guns at the ready, prepared to fire at any target that presented itself. Shortly after, they had started moving away from the hotel, when suddenly, shots were being fired at them once again.

It had taken Nasser a moment to see a handgun firing from the bottom of the front hotel window. Both he and the surviving member of his unit had opened fire in the direction of the gun. For a mad few seconds, the rapid fire from their automatic weapons filled his ears. He had emptied his magazine before the man in front of him. He was in the process of slamming a new magazine into his rifle when he had heard a shot and saw the man in front of him fall.

Nasser had seen a man in the high window of the hotel holding a rifle and assumed that he had fired the shot that struck his comrade. Immediately, Nasser had fired at that window. In that moment, he also realized he needed to leave quickly. He had turned and ran to the corner from where he'd come. Nasser had slipped around the corner without having heard another shot being fired.

Nasser had immediately run to the van, gotten in the driver's seat and taken off as quickly as he could. Now, as he sat there, he realized how close to death he had come. Once again, he looked at his hands and saw them shake. He clasped his hands, together trying to stop the quivering, but was unsuccessful.

Taking several deep breaths, Nasser tried to calm himself. Slowly, he succeeded. The question now was what he should do. Briefly, he considered returning to the hotel to continue his attack but quickly realized the folly of that notion. He dismissed that idea because he realized he did not have the resources for a successful attack. He knew there were at least two individuals in the hotel who were armed. There were probably more, given how quickly his men were cut down.

Nasser also realized he needed to report in, but feared the consequences of reporting his failure to complete the attack successfully. Momentarily, he thought of simply running away, but quickly dismissed that option. He was a dedicated soldier for Allah and would take responsibility for his actions. Nasser pondered what he should report to Salah. He determined that telling the truth was the best course of action, even though he feared the response he would receive.

After thinking for a few moments about how he would tell his story, he picked up his satellite phone and dialed Salah's number. His call was answered on the third ring. "This is Nasser."

"Hello, my friend. What news do you have for me?"

"I'm afraid, my friend, I bring you bad news."

Salah motioned for Samir to join him so he could hear the conversation. "What is the bad news?"

"We parked near the hotel in question. I briefed my men on our course of action. We spread out and walked toward the hotel. There appeared to be no evidence of anyone either at the hotel or in the surrounding businesses. It was very quiet. When we were within 20 meters of the hotel, many shots were fired. In the first few seconds, three of my men had fallen dead. We returned fire at the hotel and ran to the sidewalk, which would require anybody shooting at us to expose themselves from the hotel."

A grim silence could be heard on the other end of the line. Nasser took a deep breath and went on. "One man fired a pistol from a low window, and we immediately returned fire. While we were reloading, someone in an upper window fired at us. The remaining man in my unit was struck in the chest and fell to the ground. I immediately returned fire at the gunman. I then escaped to the van and drove off. When I got a safe distance away, I immediately pulled over and called you."

"Are all of your men dead?"

"Yes, I believe so. They did not move or make any sounds. Whoever fired the shots knew how to shoot. Each of them was hit in the chest or in the back. The weapon used appeared to be an automatic rifle like ours."

"Were you hit at all?"

"No."

Samir took the phone from Salah. "This is Samir. Are you telling me you were ambushed?"

"I really haven't thought about that, but the attack was a complete surprise. They seemed to be waiting for us. It just happened so quickly that we did not have time to avoid the initial onslaught. They must have known we were coming. But how could that be?" Nasser paused for a moment, clenching his fist to stop the trembling. "What do you want me to do now?"

Samir thought of the various options available to him. "I want you to go back and keep the hotel under observation. Don't expose yourself and don't let them know you're there. How far are you from that location?"

"I don't know. Maybe five minutes."

"Okay, head there now and call me when you have found a place to observe."

"All right, I'm on my way. You'll hear from me in a few moments." Nasser ended the phone call, started the van and drove off.

* * * * *

"Well, Salah, what should we do now?"

"This is troubling news. To be ambushed like that means someone knew we were coming. And where did they get automatic weapons?"

"Maybe those weapons came from Wasi and Saad. But I'm not sure it really matters. We know they're armed and hiding out in the hotel. But what we don't know is who is there. I suppose it could be the police or the army. But that doesn't make sense. Why would they be hiding out in a small hotel like that? This is all very strange."

The two men discussed the situation further and explored the various possible explanations. Suddenly the phone rang once again. Salah answered it. "Yes."

"It is Nasser. I have the hotel under surveillance. I'm located on the roof across the street from the hotel."

"Do you see any sign of anyone in the hotel?"

"No, nothing at all. In fact, there is no activity and no sound from anywhere around the neighborhood."

"Are the bodies of your men still there?"

"Yes, they do not appear to have been moved. Wait a minute. There is something."

"What are you talking about?"

"Their weapons are gone. When I escaped, their weapons were near their bodies. All four rifles are gone. Wait a minute. Their hand guns and bags of grenades are also missing. It's clear they've been stripped of their weapons."

"Are you sure?"

"Yes, they have no weapons on or near them. Someone has taken them."

"Okay, I understand. Stay there and keep watch until we get back to you. Report any movement or unusual activity immediately. Do you have any questions?"

"No, I understand, and I will inform you of anything that happens." Nasser took a deep breath. He felt better now since there were no accusations that he had failed in completing his job. Salah seemed to understand that it wasn't his fault. He would carry out his new responsibilities as best he could.

Salah laid the phone down and looked at Samir. "Well, it appears that we have some well-armed opponents in the hotel. What should we do now?"

"It also appears that we have armed our enemies. From the way this ambush was carried out, I would guess that these people are well-trained. Perhaps ex-military. But whose military? Is there any way we can determine who is staying at that hotel?"

"In fact, there might be. During the time we were planning this operation, I had our computer experts determine whether they could hack into the computers of the various police agencies and targets. They were not successful with the police agencies, and the firewalls for the large hotels were too difficult to penetrate. However, they were able to break into the computer systems of several of the smaller hotels. Let me see if this hotel was one of them." Salah sat at his computer and typed for a few minutes.

"Blessings to Allah. He shines his face upon us once again. I am into the computer system for that hotel." He continued to scan through the computer's database. After a few minutes, he rose and faced Samir. "The only people registered at this hotel now are a group of American college students and their professors. It looks like we are fighting the great Satan."

Samir walked pensively around the room. Soon he stopped, turned and faced Salah. "Well, this good fortune changes everything. We have the opportunity presented to us to kill these Americans, which will add fuel to the fires we started today. Allah provides us with the opportunity to serve him well."

"What do you have in mind, Samir?"

"We will send our ten-man reserve unit to destroy them. Doesn't that group also have RPGs available to them?"

"Yes, they do. What is your plan, Samir?"

"This opportunity requires the best. I want you to lead the unit and destroy these Americans. You will show no mercy at all; we must destroy them completely. What better way to send a message to the United States than to kill their children? Allah has provided us with the opportunity and the means to carry out this mission. Salah, I know you will not fail."

Salah looked surprised. In fact, he was shocked that Samir would send him into combat at this time. He felt he could do better helping Samir direct his operation. "Are you sure that it makes sense for me to lead this operation? I mean, I've not been in the field for some time. I believe we have a strong leader in that unit who is dedicated and very capable in this type of operation. I can serve you better by remaining here and helping you direct this and future operations."

Samir walked over and placed his hands on Salah's arms. "My friend, you have been with me for many years. We have fought many battles together. We have not always been successful, but we've always done our best to serve Allah. I think today that I should send only the best. And there is no doubt in my mind that you are the best one to lead this operation. When you are finished and have killed all of the Americans, you'll return here to me and we will begin planning for the future. You may have doubts that you are the best, but I know that you are the only one to lead this action. My faith in you is complete. Go and serve Allah well, my friend."

Salah looked at Samir. The men hugged, then Salah nodded, pulled himself even more erect than usual, and walked out of the room.

Chapter 49

Mac followed me down to the breakfast room while Ty stayed in the reception area to keep watch. As we walked into the room, all the students' conversations ended. I could feel the fear that permeated the room. They seemed to be waiting for me to open the conversation. I leaned against the wall and crossed my arms. Mac sat at one of the tables.

"Well, they came back. I know you heard the shooting, but I know you don't know what happened. So I'm going to be straight with you and explain exactly what occurred. After that, you can ask any questions. But I want you to hold them until I have finished. First, Rick spotted the terrorists coming down the street and warned us."

I looked toward Rick and nodded. "Good job, Rick. There were five of them standing abreast walking down the street. Each was armed with an automatic rifle, and later, we found that they had hand guns and some hand grenades. Mac, Ty and I had developed a plan should this occur. We followed the plan to the letter. Mac and Ty took the rifles upstairs. Derek and I were downstairs in the reception area. When the terrorists were within about 50 feet of us, Mac and Ty took over."

I looked at Mac. "Why don't you explain what happened from your perspective?"

Mac stood up and recounted the actions. He concluded by stating, "We now have quite a nice arsenal to protect ourselves, thanks to the bad guys."

I explained what had happened in the lobby and reception area, then looked around the room at the gathered students. "Well, I really have nothing further to add. Any questions?"

Rochelle looked at me. She was still visibly upset. "Do I understand that you guys killed four people?"

"Yes, that's exactly what we mean. Do you have a problem with that?" I responded.

"Well, I don't know. I mean, four people are dead because of us."

"No, that's not what happened. Those four individuals are dead because they came here to kill all of us. You've heard and watched what's happened in the city today. These people have literally killed thousands of individuals. It's our job to make sure that your name is not added to that list."

"I know. I know. It's just difficult to accept. But I understand what you're saying," Rochelle grasped her arms in front of her slender torso as if trying to get warm.

"Does anyone else have questions?"

Melanie stood up. "I don't care about the lives of those bastards. What I do care about is our lives and whether we're going to be able to get out of this alive. So the question I have is, what is the plan now?"

Mac answered that question. "At this point, we are continuing as planned. But as a practical matter, Ty, DJ and I've not had a chance to even discuss the situation as it stands right now. When we leave here, we will start talking about that."

"Well, it seems to me that staying here is out of the question. They know where we are and we need to get out of here. That's how I feel." Melanie turned and looked at the other students. "How do you guys feel?"

Rick spoke up. "I see no benefit in remaining in this hotel. We need to move. Before, I felt safer, but now that they know we're here, I think we need to move."

Seeing where this conversation was going, I decided we needed to end it right now. "Wait a minute. Let's stop right now. Give Mac, Ty and me a chance to discuss this. We will come back and tell you what we believe needs to happen."

A number of students started to talk at once. I held my hand up to quiet them down. "Give us a few minutes. All right? Is everyone okay with that?" Most of the students nodded. I looked at Melanie and Rick. "Are you willing to give us that time?"

Melanie nodded at us. "But don't take much more time than that, please."

I gestured. "Come on, Mac, let's go talk with Ty. We'll be back in a few minutes." Mac and I walked up the stairs to the lobby and over to where Ty was standing. "Well, we have an interesting situation brewing downstairs. Basically, the question is where do we go from here? Melanie and Rick raised the question that we should not stay here given what just happened. It seemed to me like there was some unanimity in the group to get out of this hotel. Mac, did you pick up on that?"

"Yeah, I think that's a fair reading of the sentiment."

"So what do you guys think? Should we move on or should we stay?"

Ty had a bit of a frown on his face as he pondered the question. "Well, it seems to me that it is a simple calculation of risk for either choice. Obviously, the terrorists know where we are. But we are not in any danger unless they choose to return. We know that at least one of them got away. Therefore, the call they make establishes the risk. If they don't come back, we're safe. If they do come back, they may bring more than five and we could be in a world of hurt."

Ty went on. "On the other hand, the same arguments for not leaving still exist. We could run into a group of terrorists and end up having to fight them in the open. That said, we may be able to slip through to a safer location. I'm not sure I know how to call this one."

Mac nodded as he listened to Ty's assessment of the situation. "I think your analysis is right on. We simply need to make a choice that puts us in less jeopardy. Perhaps, before we do anything, one of us should check out the alley behind us and see what it looks like out there."

I found myself nodding to that suggestion. "I think that's appropriate. Ty, do you want to check it out again?"

"Okay."

Mac nodded his agreement. "I think I'll check it out with you."

I watched them both walk down the stairs. I remained in the lobby, keeping watch in both directions to make sure no one snuck up on us. I stayed in that position for about five minutes before Mac and Ty returned.

"Well, what did you find?"

Ty said, "Mac and I both went into the building. We spent some time looking at the buildings across the street. We walked outside and checked in both directions. It seems quiet as a church. I think we can defend that location if we need to. We are at a disadvantage, however, since we have no access to the upper floors. I believe Mac agrees with my assessment." Mac nodded his agreement

"Let's go down and lay it out for the students." Mac and I headed downstairs to talk with them and left Ty standing lookout again. As we walked into the breakfast room, the students looked at us expectantly.

"Well, here's the deal." I laid out for them the assessment Ty had made of the risk involved. I also informed them that we had checked out the building on the other side of the alley and it appeared to be quiet. "Well, now you know what we know. What do you think we should do?"

In subdued tones, the students debated the various options for several minutes. At the conclusion of that discussion, there was a clear majority wanting to move out of our current hotel. I looked at their young faces.

"All right then, we'll move across the alley. I want all of you to go get your stuff together and be back down here as soon as possible. Put what you need for a day or so into a backpack, but no suitcases. You are not going to be able to carry a lot. Remember, we may have to run for it."

The students scurried off to get ready. Mac and I went back upstairs to let Ty know what the decision was.

It took less time than I expected for the students to complete their packing and return to the breakfast room. "Okay, this is how we're going to do it." I looked at all the students before making my next statement.

"There is going to be no discussion of how we're going to move. This is not a debating society. So listen up. Ty is going to go across first and make sure everything is still okay. He will come back and lead you, two at a time across the alley. You're going to be going up through small windows in the kitchen. You will immediately cross the alley and enter the two similarly sized windows in that building. Ty will show the first ones over where to stay. He will then return and make sure everybody gets over safely. "

The group was listening intently, hanging on every word.

"Mac and I will be the last across. As you cross the alley, make sure you look each way to see if anyone can see you. Any questions?"

No one raised a hand.

"Mac, please go up and relieve Ty. Send him down here," I said.

Mac nodded and headed upstairs. A moment later, Ty appeared. I explained to him how we were going to move everyone across. Derek and Rochelle were chosen as the first two students to cross the alley. They followed Ty and me to the windows.

Ty hopped up on the chair, looked out the window and hopped out. "I'll be back in a minute. I want to make sure it's still safe." I watched him cross the alley and enter the opposite window. He was gone much longer that he should have been. I was beginning to get worried and was going to follow him across when all of a sudden, he appeared at our window. He motioned us back and jumped down.

"We've got a problem. There are three men across the street from the building standing behind cars. They appear to be Middle Eastern. I'm not sure but I thought I could see that they were carrying AK-47s. They were watching this entire block. It was obvious that they were using the cars for protection. I don't think we can get a clean shot at them."

"Ty, get the cardboard back up on the windows and the shelves in place. Rochelle and Derek, come with me."

Everyone returned to the breakfast room. "Derek, go upstairs and stand watch for Mac. Have him come down here." A few moments later, Mac came walking down the stairs. I informed him and the students of what Ty had found.

Mac looked at Melanie and Rick. "That seems to be the end of our move. We are going to have to sit this out right here."

The students nodded their agreement.

We had previously given Jared one of the handguns. "Jared, I want you to go back into the kitchen and watch the windows. If anyone starts coming through the windows, shoot them. There's no one we know who will be entering this building that way. Any questions?"

"Nope. I'll take care of the windows." Jared said in a firm voice.

Mac, Ty and I previously discussed who should be armed within our group. We handed out the remaining weapons to those individuals. Mac spent some time making sure that each understood how to operate those weapons. I went up to talk with Ty and, shortly after that, Mac joined us. We spent the remaining half hour deciding how we would station the armed students within the building.

Mac spoke first. "One thing we didn't tell the students was that if they sent people to watch our escape route, that means the terrorists are coming back. This doesn't look good."

We all looked at each other and nodded our agreement. Now all we had to do was wait.

Chapter 50

Samir was in the apartment waiting for word from Salah. For the first time today, he could feel the empty pit in his stomach. This was not caused by lack of food, but rather an anxiety that had begun to form. Since he had sent Salah on his mission, Samir had begun to second-guess himself. What would be gained by sending more of his men to their potential destruction? While he had complete confidence in Salah's ability to complete the mission successfully, he worried about what could happen to his friend. They had been together for so long, and he relied on the other man so completely. These doubts continued to irritate his stomach.

If he lost Salah, he knew this mission would not have been worth the cost. The death of any of his other men would be acceptable. The loss of Salah would be catastrophic. Clearly, after hearing that Americans were in the hotel, he had reacted without thinking this mission through. It had occurred to him to simply recall Salah and pass the leadership to one of the unit's men. But that action, at this time, would raise additional problems. Sending Salah had signaled the unit's leader that Samir did not have faith in his ability to complete the mission. To choose someone other than the unit's leader meant that the unit would be going into battle led by someone of lesser abilities. So in the end, Samir had decided to leave Salah as the mission commander.

Samir's thoughts were interrupted by a sharp knocking on the door. He walked to the door, looked through the peep hole and saw

Ahmed standing there. He opened the door and Ahmed walked in. "Peace be to Allah. What brings you here, Ahmed?" The men hugged and Ahmed began speaking.

"Salah sent me to update you on his mission. Before he left, we had a brief conversation about this job. He told me he was concerned that he did not have enough men to attack the hotel. If the Americans had recovered all the weapons, they would have six men armed with AK-47s and six with handguns. If that was the case, Salah was not confident he could defeat the Americans."

Samir nodded, signaling Ahmed to continue.

"I was able to contact some of our men who participated in other attacks. As a result, he will not have ten men at his disposal, but rather, twenty. Salah took additional ammunition with him to make sure they were completely combat ready. Salah felt that with the addition of those men, he would be able to take the hotel and destroy any Americans within it. I also sent three men to block the escape of the Americans should they try to leave."

"Well done, Ahmed. But I have a question. I thought all of our men from the other attacks were supposed to be heading for their safe houses?" Samir said.

"That was the plan and most of them were on their way. I happened to reach these men as they were preparing to leave. I guess we were lucky that they were a little slower than the others."

Samir walked back to the sofa and sat down. He motioned for Ahmed to join him. "What other duties do you have to complete today?"

"None. I was preparing to leave when I spoke with Salah. Again, we were lucky in that respect. No one else would have been able to contact these people but me."

"When did you last speak with Salah?"

"I spoke with him just a few minutes ago by radio. Also, I brought one for you." With that, he reached into his pocket and pulled out a small, handheld radio. "This is set for the correct frequency. You can contact Salah at any time." He handed the radio to Samir, who examined it. It was not unlike any of the other radios that he had used previously.

Samir turned the radio on. "Hello, friend, are you there?"

A few seconds later, Salah answered. "I am here."

"What is your status?"

"I am waiting for the additional men. I expect they will be here within the next thirty minutes. Following that, we will head to the hotel. I've briefed the men who are here. They are excited about the possibility of killing Americans. They are very determined and thankful for this opportunity. Do you have any further instructions?"

"Yes. Salah, I want you to take care of yourself. I need you with me for future operations. Don't put yourself in a position where you do not come back. Do you understand?"

"Yes, I understand. However, there will obviously be personal risks in this attack. But I will do my best to follow your command."

"Very well. Report to me after you've reached the hotel and before you attack."

"Of course. I'll talk to you shortly." With that, the radio went silent.

Ahmed had listened to this conversation. He knew how important Salah was to Samir, and to the success of all their operations.

"Samir, you could send me to lead the mission if you wish. I have no doubt that I can successfully destroy the Americans. In that way, you do not have to run the risk of losing Salah in this battle."

Samir smiled at Ahmed. "I appreciate you offering yourself. However, the decision has been made. The longer we wait to initiate our attack, the more likely it is that the Americans will slip away. After the previous attack, they realize we know they're there.

They would be stupid to remain in the hotel, knowing we would be coming after them. I expect that once Salah gets there, the chances are he will find no one. If the Americans are present, it was a very smart move to place the men to block their escape. We also have Nasser watching the hotel from the front."

Ahmed nodded his understanding.

Samir went on. "Even if the Americans have recovered the weapons, that does not mean they know how to use them. It is one thing to have a weapon you might be able to fire and quite another thing to be an effective marksman. Our men have trained for combat. Many of them have fought in Afghanistan and elsewhere. We are dealing with soft American college students. They are not used to being in the heat of battle with bullets whizzing about them. I think we will be successful. In fact, we may not lose any men at all. The previous groups were surprised. No surprise exists at this time. Furthermore, we are prepared to die. Americans fear death and that is their weakness."

Ahmed listened to Samir quietly. Again, he nodded his agreement as Samir spoke. But he had deep reservations that he did not share with Samir. He had fought the Americans in Afghanistan. He knew that they were tough, disciplined warriors. If any of those warriors were among the students, this fight would not be as easy as Samir believed. Ahmed also knew that question would be answered soon enough.

Chapter 51

Ty, Mac and I joined one another in the lobby. Ty had indicated he had some concerns he wanted to bring up. As we sat down, he began. "I don't think we're ready."

Mac looked at me with surprise in his eyes. "What you talking about, Ty?"

"Well, we handed out the weapons, and we've told the students where we want them. I don't think that's enough. I've been thinking from the standpoint of the terrorists. I mean, if I was leading any group attacking us, I would not simply walk down the street like the previous group, and I think that's what we've been basing our decisions on."

My eyebrows rose and Mac simply nodded.

Ty continued. "Let me tell you what I would do. First of all, I would not walk down the street and let myself be shot. If the leader of the next attacking group has any sense at all, he will have a coordinated plan of attack. I would have people in the buildings across the street who could fire directly into the windows where we will be located. I would have people coming across the roof and attack down the stairs. I would try to find a way in from the rear of the building."

I trusted my friend's tactical thinking and listened carefully.

"If in fact they do that, having our people stationed at windows looking down the street means we will be defeated. In sum, I think we need to rethink how we are going to defend this hotel. And if we can't develop an appropriate plan, we need to fight our way out.

And we need to do that sooner than later. Who knows, they may attack any minute."

As Ty finished speaking, he watched Mac's and my faces for a reaction. I could feel the tension in the room.

Mac, who had been leaning forward, sat back in the sofa. "Damn, I think he's right. You know, DJ, he's smarter than he looks."

I stood and walked toward the window. I gazed out with my hands on my hips for a few minutes before turning around and looking directly at Mac. "I agree with Ty. And Mac, I also agree that Ty is smarter than he looks. However, you must be a whole lot older than you look since you missed what Ty figured out. It's so sad to see people lose their cognitive ability."

"The same goes for you, since you didn't see the issue either."

"I was just waiting to see if anyone would come up with it," I said with a wry grin.

"That doesn't even deserve a reply. Ty, do you want to be our leader?"

Ty looked at both of us once again. "You two are just an old married couple and need to can it so we can get down to business. That is, if either of you at your advanced age can remember what we were talking about to begin with."

Mac and I both started laughing, which released the tension. It was clear to all of us that our plan was insufficient to keep our students safe. I sat down again. "Okay, let's figure out what we need to do. Ty, what do you have in mind?"

"Well, first, by having students in various rooms facing the front of the hotel, I think we have that covered. We probably need to bring those students together and make sure they understand when and if they should fire."

I interrupted Ty. "Let's take these one at a time. What should their instructions be?"

Mac leaned forward again. On his hand, he ticked off on his fingers. "First of all, no weapon should be fired until the targets are fairly close. I'm not sure how well these kids can shoot, so we should make sure the targets are as near as possible. That should increase our number of hits."

He raised his index finger. "Second, we do not want to give away our positions until we have to. We will need to force the bad guys to come in through the front door. I expect they will be up against the buildings like those last two fellows. In that way, we have to expose ourselves to shoot them. We don't want our students doing anything of the kind. So it is possible that if the students are in the various rooms on the first floor, they may not even get a shot. We may want to think about repositioning them."

Mac went on. "Why don't you let me handle this, DJ? I'll make sure the students know what we expect of them, and if we need to reposition them, I'll let you know."

"Mac, you need to emphasize to them that there may be people either in the windows across the street or on the roof. If they are not careful, they could be killed."

Mac nodded his agreement. "I will. What next?"

Ty continued, "The next thing that really concerns me is what do we do if they come across the roofs. You know this whole street of buildings is connected. I was up on the roof and each building has a wall approximately four feet high to keep people from stepping over to the next building. These really are separate buildings though they share one wall. If they get on the roofs, they can move up and over each wall until they are on our roof. And all they have to do is come down the stairs and clear out room after room."

He continued, sketching his plan with his finger on the low coffee table in front of us. "It seems to me that we need one or more people up there to either fight them off or in the least to warn us that they're coming. The roof is going to be a dangerous place if they put a sniper on the roof across the street. I think that Derek and I should be positioned there."

I shifted uncomfortably on the sofa. "Ty, why do you think you'll be able to fight them off? If they send several people, you would be on the losing end of the stick."

"I've given that some thought. If they're coming across the roof, they won't have any cover. I'll have a clear shot at them and will be behind the wall. I will also have some grenades with me, which should make them think twice about coming across."

"And what if there are just simply too many?"

Ty smiled at me. "Well that's where we get a little tricky. We can use some grenades and set up booby-traps. For example, if it's too much, Derek and I will head down the stairs, but I can prepare a grenade that will go off if the door opens. If that happens, I think they'll be more careful about following us. Also, I can set up a few additional booby-traps to slow them down. It seems to me, that if they make it down from the roof, then we need to be vacating the hotel immediately. I don't think we want to get into a battle with them inside the hotel. If we do that, I'm afraid we'll suffer too many casualties."

"Ty, obviously you've put a lot of thought into this. Mac, should we let Ty handle the roof?"

"Yeah, that's probably the best course of action."

"Okay, Ty, what's next?"

"We need to figure out a way to watch our rear and keep our escape route open. They are one and the same. It seems to me that while this may be easier in some respect, it also presents its own challenges. The terrorists can only get to us through those two small windows. But if they can get to the windows, they can toss in a couple grenades and take out anybody who is in that area."

Ty continued explaining his strategy. "That being the case, I think we should station two people across the alley in the building that will be our escape route. Those students will have a direct line of fire against anybody coming up to those windows. The obvious concern would be once they've fired, their position would be known to the terrorists. When that happens, we need to have people in both sets of windows on either side of the alley so they can cover each other. They'll be shooting down the alley, so it's unlikely they'd be in danger of shooting one another. If we're lucky, the terrorists won't send many people through the alley. I can set that up before I head to the roof. Do you have any suggestions who we could put there?"

"Well, it has to be someone who can keep their cool. I don't think I would want a woman there unless she served in the service. My first choice would be Jared, and maybe Rick being the second. Mac, any suggestions on this point?"

"My only concern would be Rick. He was pretty jumpy just seeing the people coming down the street earlier. Ty, you've gotten to know him better than either of us. What do you think?"

"I think he'll be okay. Give me a chance to talk with him about what he needs to do. If I come to believe that he is not capable, I'll come back and we'll revisit the issue."

"That works for me." Mac stood up, walked over and stood in front of me. "Well, old man, that leaves the front of the hotel for you. You have any bright ideas?"

"Well, I tell you, after listening to Ty, I have all sorts of ideas. First, I'll need some mirrors to be able look down the sidewalks to see if we are under attack. I think we can probably fire down the sidewalk without exposing more than our weapons. But if too many of them are coming, we'll be in trouble. I think some hand grenades would help us down there also. One or more to toss down the sidewalk. We probably should put some booby-traps in the lobby also. I don't know how to do that, so I could use some help there."

Ty gave a thumbs up to me. "I'll show you how to do that."

"We are going to have to decide when it's time to evacuate. Our only escape route is through the breakfast room and into the kitchen. If they break through into the lobby, anybody above the ground floor will not be able to get out. So how do we handle that?"

Mac stood up and cautiously walked out the lobby door. He looked up and down the streets and also at the side of the building. With that completed, he returned to the lobby.

"One thing that would help repel an attack from the front would be if the students on the first floor were able to toss grenades down onto the sidewalk. Once the grenades go off, it will slow down the attack. But DJ, it's going to be your call if it appears they're going to break through in the front to get everyone down."

Ty went on. "Then we're going to need someone at the top of the stairs who can relay your orders. Now that I think about it, I'm not sure we should have anyone stationed in any room higher than the floor above us. If they don't break through from the roof, someone's going to have to notify Derek and me to get our asses downstairs. We can station a student at the top of every stairway who can relay those messages. Once they have been relayed and passed on, those people should head for the breakfast room immediately."

Ty leaned back in the sofa with his arms crossed behind his head. I could see how conflicted he was. "There's another thing we have to think about. We need to set up a first aid station. If someone gets hurt, we need to get that person to that location to do whatever we can. That should probably be in the breakfast room so any wounded can make their escape quickly. We will need to let our student nurse and anyone who is going to assist her get set up. DJ, I think you should talk with her about it."

"Okay, I will. Anything else?"

Mac looked at me. "Nothing else that I can think of."

We both looked at Ty.

He smiled at both of us. "Isn't that enough?"

"Let's get started," I said, rubbing my hands together. "Get Derek down here so he can keep watch. Mac, you go get the upstairs ready and brief everybody there. I'll go get our nurse and get her set up and then get organized down here. Ty, why don't you go get Jared and Rick established across the street? You know, before that, you may want to head to the roof and see what's up there. Any other ideas or suggestions?"

Hearing none, I went to find our nurse.

Chapter 52

I walked down into the breakfast room where most of the students were waiting.

"Where's Dana?" One of the students pointed toward the kitchen. I opened the door to the kitchen and looked in. I saw Dana cutting some cheese for the next round of sandwiches. I walked over to her. "Hey, Dana, I need to talk to you."

She put down the knife she was using and smiled at me. "What's up, Professor?"

"Well, we revised some of our plans and part of it involves you. We don't know what's going to happen, but we need to be prepared for anything. That includes injuries to any of us. So, you know that our escape route is through the windows over there." She nodded at me. "We need to have you set up, in essence, what would be an aid station. We want you to do it in the breakfast room so that when we need to make our escape, anybody who is injured is close to the windows. So I need to have you figure out the best way to help anybody who gets injured. By that I mean, you probably need to be there and set a bed up. You can put the tables together so people can lie down. You need to get your medical supplies here and set up. But you need to do that with the understanding that we may have to leave quickly. So be sure that they are easily packed and taken with you. Does that make sense?"

Concern clouded Dana's pretty face. What we had been talking about previously was a potentiality; she now realized it could actually happen. "Do you think that people are going to get injured?

I mean, you know, I'm only a nursing student, not a doctor. I'm not sure what I can do if someone is seriously injured."

"I totally understand that, Dana. All we're asking is that you do the best you can. We are not expecting any miracles from you. Do I think something will happen? I hope not but we need to be prepared if something does. Who would you like to have help you?"

"I think I would like to have Melanie. We've been talking about this and she seems willing to help. Would that be okay with you?"

"Because this is your responsibility, I think you should choose whomever you think would be the best person to assist you. If that's Melanie, so be it. You may want to have her assist you in setting this up so she knows what's going on. Also, I would give her a very quick run through on basic first aid if you haven't done so already. Does that work for you?"

"Would you come with me?" She walked back into the breakfast room and continued. "I think the best way to handle this would be to line up tables against the wall. They would be next to each other and could work as a gurney. We can put another table against this wall with all the medical supplies laid out." She paused a moment. "Yes, I think that's the best way to do it."

"Good, set it up that way. Have the students here help you get things moved as you want." The other students in the breakfast room had been listening to our conversation and it was clear they were wondering what was going on.

I went on. "Listen, guys, we need to be prepared for anything that might happen. That includes setting up an aid station for anybody who may be hurt or injured. We're going to do it here and Dana is in charge. She'll tell you what we need to have happen. Do what you can to help her. By the way, we have revised how we are going to defend ourselves. Either Mac, Ty or I will be talking to each of you shortly and explaining what your responsibility will be so that we can be prepared as soon as possible. Does anybody have any questions?" No one raised their hand. "As you can guess, we're getting down to crunch time. Here's how it's going to work." I hurriedly explained to them the plan that we developed.

"If one of us gives you any orders, you must carry them out immediately. Failing to do so, could result in someone being hurt. You've all done very well up to this time and I expect you will continue to do so." At that point, Mac walked into the room.

"Mike and Jason, I need you to follow me." We had decided that these two, based on their experience as hunters, would be the ones stationed in the windows on the first floor. They would be armed with AK-47s. Ty had previously gone over the weapons with them. It did not take long for them to be comfortable in handling this weapon.

They both followed Mac out the door and up one flight of stairs. Mac led them into one of the hotel bedrooms facing the street. "Okay, here's the deal. You guys will be stationed in rooms next to each other. Your responsibility is to keep the street clear of any terrorists. However, my guess is that they will be on the sidewalk against the building, which means you may not be able to shoot at them unless you stick your head out the window. If you do that, you'll be sitting ducks. So, do not, for any reason, take a shot while you're exposed.

Mac looked into their eyes and was met with grim determination rather than fear.

"If you do not have a shot while sitting back in the room, that's okay. Don't go playing hero and try to shoot by exposing yourself. Also, it is possible that they may have people on the roof or in windows of the buildings across the street. Remember, these terrorists are trained and will take you out unless you play this very smart. Understand?"

They both nodded.

"Okay, besides your AK, you're also going to have some hand grenades. They are to be used should anyone get close to the entrance to the hotel."

Mac took a grenade out of the pack on the floor.

"These have five-second fuses. What that means is once you pull the pin and release the lever, you have five seconds before the grenade goes off. Given the situation here, you should release the lever, count to two and get rid of it quickly. Once you throw it outside, use the wall to protect yourself from the blast.

Mike swallowed, his large Adam's apple bobbing. But he nodded his understanding.

Mac went on. "Next, we need to talk about escape. If we beat off the attack, no problem. But if at any time DJ, Ty or I determine that we must initiate our escape, this is how it will work. We're going to have people stationed in the stairwell on all floors. If, for example, DJ believes that he cannot stop the people from coming in the front of the hotel, he will yell out 'escape' or something to that effect. The person at the head of the stairwell on this floor will yell at the person on the floor above and then come and tell you both it is time to go. You will immediately pick up your hand grenades and weapons. Then head for the stairwell and make your way down to the breakfast room. Then you'll be told when to exit the kitchen through the windows and immediately get to the next building. Do you understand?"

Jason raised his hand. "What if for some reason, we don't get the announcement to leave?"

Mike immediately responded. "Yeah, that could easily happen. How do we know we won't be left behind?"

"There are two ways we are going to make sure that doesn't happen. First, before I go downstairs to the breakfast room, I will check these rooms to make sure you are not there. Second, before you escape through the kitchen windows, someone will be there to check every person off. If someone's name has not been checked off before I leave, I will find them. I promise you, no one will be left behind. Everybody in and out together, remember. No exceptions." Those comments appeared to ease their concern. Mac then took them to the rooms where they would be located.

Mac returned to the lobby and could see Derek standing guard. "Do you know where Ty is?

"He headed to the roof to check things out."

Mac decided to go up and have a look for himself.

While this was going on, Ty had reached the door opening onto the roof. The door resembled a trapdoor which opened upward. He opened it just enough to crawl out. Ty made his way to the corner of the building facing the street. He had taken the mirror that DJ had used to look down the sidewalk. With his back against the wall, he slowly brought the mirror up to look at the building across the street.

Immediately, he jerked the mirror down. He had seen someone across the street on the roof looking at the hotel. Ty recognized him as one of the five individuals who had attacked the hotel earlier, the only one who had gotten away. It appeared to Ty that the man was keeping an eye on what was happening at the hotel. This was not good news because it meant others were coming. Ty sat there for a moment, deliberating his options. He could go and report what he'd seen to the others, but he knew this man would have to be dealt with in some fashion.

Ty knew he was lucky the man had not seen him. The corner he had crawled to was only twenty feet to the left and across the street from where the man was situated. Slowly, Ty crawled all the way to the far corner. He checked his rifle and made sure it was ready to fire. He rose up slowly so as not to attract attention. He quickly sighted on the man. At just that moment, the man turned to look at him.

Ty pulled the trigger and saw a burst of pink as the man's head jerked backwards. He waited for a minute to see if anyone else appeared. Just then he heard some movement on the roof and turned quickly, pointing his rifle at the door.

What he saw was Mac's head peeking above the roof. Mac's eyes were as wide as they could be and his head dropped quickly.

The door opened slowly and Ty heard a voice say, "It's me, Mac. Don't shoot!" Ty started to crawl toward the door.

Once again, Mac's head rose slowly through the door. "You sonofabitch, you scared the hell out of me. I'm not sure, but I think I may have shit my pants." Ty put his head down and started laughing.

"I don't find anything funny about this!" Mac retorted.

"Next time, buddy, I suggest you knock before you come up. If you had any manners, that's what you would do." Ty had a difficult time stopping the chuckling. "I might have to write a book about this. I think your students would enjoy it." The chuckling continued.

"I can see why you might think that was funny. However, you may not want to turn your back on me if I'm carrying a weapon. And if you write a book, I will come looking for you. So what the hell happened?"

"One of the men who had attacked us last time was on the roof across the street. He seemed to be keeping watch on this hotel. I decided he could only be up to no good so I took him out from the corner over there. He won't be giving anyone any information on us, but the fact that he was there does not bode well. It's just another indication that they'll be back."

"Let's go tell DJ what happened."

"Why don't you go tell him? I need to get the guys set up across the alley. I think our time for preparation is running out." Both Mac and Ty ran down the stairs. Mac went to where DJ was in the lobby and informed him of what happened. Ty found Jared and Rick in the breakfast room. He walked over to them and had them sit down in the corner with him. "We've made some additional changes in our plans to defend ourselves. We need to make sure that our escape route is not blocked and that no one can enter the hotel through those two windows. I want you guys to be an important cog in that operation."

Jared looked at Mac. "What does that mean exactly?"

"I want the two of you to be stationed in the building across the alley. You will be armed with Glocks and a couple of grenades. Your responsibility is to stay out of sight but maintain surveillance on the alley. If I were going to attack our hotel, I would use a coordinated approach, going after each entrance. We have people covering the front, and Derek and I will be on the roof. Each of you will keep an eye out for people coming down from either direction."

Mac stared at the students. "Now this is important. If necessary, you are to take them out. But I want you to make sure that they are close to you so you will not miss. If there are more than one or two, fire and throw a grenade. Once you have given away your position, you will become more vulnerable. To support you, I'll have two people in the hotel windows across the alley similarly armed. The idea is that each of you can cover for the other."

Jared nodded. Rick nodded. Both students knew the critical nature of this situation.

"Next, if we decide, for some reason, that we are unable to continue defending the hotel, we will initiate our escape to that building. It is your job to cover everyone as they come across and help them through the window. Once everybody is across, we will decide on our next move. There is one complication however. There are three men that we think are terrorists across the street from that building. When we go over there, I'll show you. While I have no way to know for sure, I believe they are stationed there to stop an escape. I'm also going to position Sarah in that building. Her job will be to keep an eye on those men and to warn you if they come in your direction."

Sarah, who was sitting nearby, heard the conversation. Ty looked at her and motioned for her to come over. "Did you hear what I just said?" She nodded. "Are you good with that?"

"Do I have any choice?" She shrugged her slender shoulders, tossing her auburn hair back in a gesture of preparation.

"Yes. If you don't think you can do it, Sarah, I'll get someone else. However, when the time to escape comes, you will already be there and won't have to cross the alley with rest of us."

Jared could see the fear in her eyes. "It will be okay, Sarah. We'll make sure nothing happens to you. Besides, do you want to live forever?"

"Jared, you are such a smart ass." She smiled at him. "I guess that's why I like you. I'm okay with it."

Ty looked at all three and motioned toward the kitchen. "Let's get you set up then."

Ty led them into the kitchen and to the windows. They moved the shelves back and took the cardboard off of the windows. Ty moved the chair against the wall. He climbed up, stuck his head out the window and looked both ways. "It's all clear. Let's go."

Ty pulled himself through the window, which was at ground level, and he reached down to help Jared out. He pointed toward the window in the building across the alley. Jared scampered there and quickly went down through that window. Rick followed Jared into the building. Ty reached down and helped Sarah out and led her to the window. Jared helped Sarah into the building and Ty followed them. He led all three up to the ground floor, making sure they kept in the shadows. He pointed out the men across the street and showed Sarah where she could hide and still observe them.

Looking at each of them in turn, Ty said, "You are going to have to decide, should these men approach, what course of action you should take. Sarah, once you see them coming this way you need to go down and inform Jared and Rick. Guys, you should come up, evaluate the situation and do what you think is best. Your options are to defend this escape route if possible. If not, you can come back to the hotel. However, I must emphasize, that if you leave this building, our only option is to fight it out in the hotel. It's important to keep this escape route open if at all possible. Do any of you have any questions?"

Sarah raised her hand. "I feel like I'm out here all by myself. I have those guys out in front of me and Jared and Rick are downstairs. That doesn't exactly make me feel safe."

"I understand. Jared and Rick, I want one of you to come up and check on Sarah at least every 10 or 15 minutes. You think that will help, Sarah?"

"Yeah, that would be a big help."

Jared smiled at Sarah again. "We'll make sure to do that. We don't want you to feel like you're alone. Remember we're all in this together. In together and out together, right, Ty?"

"Absolutely!" Having said that, Ty gave Rick and Jared two grenades each and explained how to use them. Ty then headed for the window to the alley. The three of them watched him climb up and out into the alley and cross the street to the hotel.

Ty came up the stairs to the lobby and found Mac and me in a quiet conversation. He proceeded to tell us about the situation across the alley.

When Ty finished, I brought up an issue that was important to me. "What do you suggest for booby-traps down here? I think if we have to leave quickly that may be the only thing that allows us to get out."

Ty looked around the lobby. Previously, he had found some twine in the receptionist's desk. "I think we should leave the door open. Then we can attach twine to each side of the door about a foot high. I can rig the hand grenade in such a way that as the bad guys try to go through the twine, it will go off."

"What about the windows? They may very well just crawl through them since the glass is gone."

"Good point. If I put twine across the window, it would be high enough for them to see. Why don't we move the chairs so that they have to walk between them and we can rig the twine and grenades to be tripped that way? I'm also going to set a booby-trap for the door onto the roof and a series of booby-traps coming down the stairs. The only ones who have to worry about those are Derek and me. I will rig something in the kitchen that we can set up when we leave to catch them coming in there as well."

"How long will that take?"

"Not long if Mac will help me." He looked at Mac and smiled. "You're not afraid of helping me do that, are you?"

"Since when did you become such an asshole?"

"Since I met the two of you. Let me get Derek set up on the roof and then I'll come back down and we'll get this rigged up."

Ty signaled to Derek, who was standing near the door, to follow him. Then Ty headed toward the roof and returned a few minutes later. Ty and Mac went to work on the booby-traps and I was surprised at how little time it took them to complete their task.

When they returned to the lobby, I looked at both of them. "I guess we're as ready as we can be."

Mac walked to the stairs, turned and looked at the two of us. "As I said many times before, now we wait."

Chapter 53

Four vans entered the small square and pulled to the side of the road. Twenty men piled out of the vehicles and surrounded Salah, who quickly made sure that everyone was appropriately armed. As usual, each man had an AK-47 and a Glock. Two of the men also had RPGs.

Salah began, "We are soldiers of Allah and we have come to do his work. Let me explain to you what has happened. A unit of two men was assigned to destroy the hotel that is now our target. We never heard from them after they left their previous target. We had a five-man unit come here to determine what happened and, if necessary, to continue the attack. Four of those men were killed by Americans inside the hotel, who evidently had armed themselves with the first team's weapons."

He looked around to see that his words were hitting home. "The leader, and only survivor, of the second team is now on the roof of the building across the street from the hotel. We have three men on the next street over to make sure that the Americans do not try to escape that way. It is now our task to kill the Americans. The plan I have worked out requires us to coordinate our attacks. You all have radios so that we can be in constant contact.

"Here is what I've planned." He pointed at one of the men. "I want you to join Nasser on the roof. It will be your job to kill anyone you can see in the hotel. You're also to provide cover fire for the other attackers. Nasser doesn't have a radio, so I want you to give him this." Salah reached into his bag and pulled out a handheld radio.

The man nodded, took the radio and put it in his pocket. "When you're on the roof, make sure that Nasser calls me immediately so I can hear what is going on."

The other men surrounding Salah leaned in, eager to get their assignments.

"In planning this operation, I knew we would want to attack not only frontally, but also from the rooftop." Salah pointed to four men. "You four will conduct that attack. I do not expect that you will have any resistance on the roof. To avoid friendly fire, should you meet resistance, I want all four of you to attack from one side. You should be able to reach the roof from the last business on the street. I want you to leave now, and make your way to the roof. When you're on the roof, call me." The men nodded.

"Remember, the objective is to kill all of the Americans. You need to make sure that you are attacking only the Americans and not us. Many of us will be coming through the front door and up the stairs. So be careful. Get going."

The four men had already been briefed on the location of the hotel and the layout of the surrounding buildings. Soon they were out of sight.

Raising his hand, Salah pointed to three other men. "I want you to attack from the rear of the hotel. I have no idea where the door is. I want you to make your way down the alley until you can determine an entrance point. When you're there, call me and let me know what you see." The three nodded and took off.

"You two with RPGs will stay with me. The remaining men will be our frontal assault team. However, frontal assault is probably the wrong way of describing what I want you to do. The last team walked down the center of the street and were nearly annihilated. You are going to work down the side of the street that the hotel is on, keeping out of the direct line of fire from the hotel. When you get close to the front of the hotel, one of you will throw in two grenades and the rest will follow after the grenades go off. Once you're in the hotel, remember that these people have killed our friends. Show no mercy and kill everyone. Any questions?" Salah looked at the men but no one indicated they had a question.

He pointed at one of the men. "I want you to report to me when you're all ready to proceed. Go, get set up."

After the next team left, Salah looked at the remaining two and signaled for them to follow him. The three slowly made their way toward the hotel and entered the rear of a building situated across and down the street from the hotel. No one was in the business, a small real estate company. They worked their way to the front so they could observe the attack through the windows.

Salah pointed out the hotel to the two men. "You'll support the attack with your AKs from this location. If, and when, I decide to use the RPGs, I will tell you. Any questions?" Both men shook their heads. "Now we wait to hear from everyone else."

The man assigned to be with Nasser slowly worked his way to the rear of the building across the street from the hotel. While he knew that all the roofs were connected, he was not exactly sure on which roof Nasser was positioned.

He found a door to a small dry-cleaning establishment. He tried the handle and found it locked. He looked in the windows but saw no one. After glancing back and forth down the alley, he kicked in the door with his heavy boots. It slammed open noisily, and he stood there for a moment to see if anyone would respond. Hearing nothing, he entered the building and searched the rooms, but found no one. The man opened the inside door that led to the stairwell.

He stood for a moment, listening, but again heard nothing. He slowly walked up the stairwell, pausing at each landing to listen. After a few moments, he found the exit to the roof, which required him to push the door up. He stood there for a few seconds, wondering whether Nasser would fire at him. He opened the door just enough to peer out. Through the opening, he yelled out to Nasser.

"Nasser, I'm here to help. Don't shoot." He heard no response. After waiting a moment, he called once again. "Nasser, I'm here. I'm coming out to help you. Don't shoot." Again, there was no response.

He decided that Nasser must be far enough away not to hear him. Slowly, he opened the door a few more inches. As he stared out at the roof, he could see no one. He opened the door sufficiently to step onto the roof. He looked both ways, but no one was in sight. He decided that Nasser must be on one of the adjoining roofs.

Because he was a tall man, he stayed down on one knee so as not to be able to be seen from across the street. Then he moved quickly to the wall on his left. He thought that this was the direction Nasser would have taken to get the best view of the hotel. Then he crab-walked to the rear of the building and slowly and very carefully, raised his head to look over the wall.

He was stunned by what lay before him. Near the front of the roof facing the hotel was a body lying flat on its back with its feet toward the front of the building. He quickly jumped over the wall and crawled toward the body. Once he reached it, he could see that the man had been shot in the forehead. His eyes were wide open, staring in shock at nothing.

He sat down with his back against the wall next to the body. As instructed, he took out his handheld radio. "Salah, I'm on the roof."

"Good, let me talk to Nasser."

"I can't. Nasser is dead. He was shot in the head."

"What! Are you sure that it's him?"

"Yes, I met him once about two weeks ago. It's the same man."

Salah did not speak for a few moments as he considered this new information. "I want you to be very careful and look over the wall at the hotel. Check the roof first to see if anyone is there. If not, look down at each floor and see if you can see anything in the windows."

The man got to his knees and slowly, very slowly, looked over the top of the wall. He scanned the roof first, but saw nothing. He then slowly worked his gaze down the walls of the building, looking into each window. He made it all the way down to the ground floor without seeing anything.

Relaxing just a bit, he sat, leaning against the wall. "I have done what you asked. There is nobody on the opposite roof that I can see. All the windows are empty. It's as if no one had ever been there. What do you want me to do now?"

"Every once in a while, pop your head up and keep looking. If you see anything at all, let me know immediately. Understand?"

"Yes. If I see anything at all, I will call you."

"Good, I'll talk to you soon."

Salah knew that the death of Nasser was not a good sign. Somehow, the Americans had surprised him. He realized it could have been from the roof or one of the windows because Nasser would have had to show himself to be able to observe the hotel.

Salah immediately got on the radio to the man heading for the hotel roof. "Where are you now?"

A moment later, the man responded. "We are on the stairs heading up. We were going to call you once we were established on the roof."

"I have some information for you. Nasser, who was observing on the roof across from the hotel, has been found dead. He took a bullet to the head. We are not sure whether it came from the roof of the hotel, or from one of the windows below. Either could have happened. I'm telling you this just so you can be careful. Call me when you're on the roof and ready to attack."

"Yes, sir."

Salah kept looking out the window at the hotel. He could see no movement of any kind. Perhaps, he thought, the Americans have already fled. Just then, he heard some garbled words coming from his radio.

"Say that again. Your message is not clear," he barked.

It was from one of the men assigned to the alley behind the hotel. "We are at the alley. I see no movement of any kind nor do I see a door at the location where we believe the hotel is. There must be another way to enter. In any event, we are ready to attack when we find an entrance. Do you have orders for us at this time?"

"Not everyone is in position yet. Keep observing and if you see anything, call me."

"I understand." The radio clicked off.

Salah was once again concerned that the Americans may have escaped. He wished he could call the leader of the three men he had posted previously to stop an escape from behind the hotel. Unfortunately, they could not communicate, as they had been dispatched before radios were handed out.

Salah glanced out the window once again to observe the hotel. Again, he saw no movement or any indication of anyone within the hotel. He looked at the two men stationed with him. "Have you seen anything at all?"

"No, nothing. Maybe it's empty. If the Americans were smart, they would've left long ago."

"Yes, I think you're right." Then Salah saw the frontal attack unit walking slowly down the sidewalk toward the hotel. The lead man looked at him and waved.

"We are ready to go. Let us know when," he radioed.

"I will. It won't be long now."

Chapter 54

General Dugand walked into his office and sat down at his desk. The meetings he had been attending were as usual long and boring, which conflicted with his sense of urgency. The only thing worse than the meetings he was forced to attend was the amount of paperwork he had to complete.

Initially, he thought that the bureaucracy's normal work flow would lessen, given the current crisis. However, pile after pile of paperwork needing his review and signature lay on various parts of his desk.

Being a general brought with it many perks. And if he was totally honest, he would say he enjoyed them to a great extent. However, when he looked back on his career, Dugand knew that he most enjoyed the postings he received when he was a lieutenant or captain. During those times, he had direct command of his men. Now, he ordered men who ordered men who commanded men.

Suddenly, his phone rang. He picked it up. "Yes."

His secretary responded. "Your chief of staff is here to see you."

"Send him in, please." Shortly thereafter, Colonel Legere entered the office.

"Well, Colonel, I hope you have good news for me."

"Yes, sir, I do. Most of our units have arrived early and are being deployed."

"That's good to hear. Have you told the commanders what we expect from them?"

"Yes, sir. They all understand how you wish to proceed in this matter. I don't foresee any problems. May I bring you up to date on the tactics the staff agreed on?"

Dugand nodded his approval.

"First of all, we're using the men to supplement our security forces across the city. But the most important new development is that we have established the mobile fighting teams."

"Interesting. Please explain."

"The staff and I have been in a series of meetings and individual discussions trying to determine how best to respond to potentially widespread terrorist killing teams. Bomb disposal units are looking at the cars, as you know, but what has hurt us the most since the initial attacks are the groups of terrorists attacking hotels. It appears that those units contain between two and ten men."

Dugand nodded and the colonel went on. "Since we do not know where the terrorists are or where they will attack, we have set up a series of mobile fighting teams. They are roving throughout the city as we speak and will respond to any threats as we learn of them. So far, there has been no contact between any of these units and terrorists. Hopefully, there are no more attacks, but since this has been such a well-coordinated operation, we are preparing as if these attacks will continue."

The general responded. "We can do nothing else. The president and prime minister have made it quite clear that we should consider ourselves on a war footing and conduct ourselves accordingly. It is my expectation that we will be operating in this manner for several weeks. Who has control of these mobile fighting teams?"

"Our command structure is set up by districts within the city. In that way, we hope to be able to coordinate with the local officials since they know their district better than we do. Each mobile fighting team will have a city employee with them who knows the area they will be working in. So far, it seems to be working quite well. The reports I'm getting from those in command are that everybody wants to find these people and eliminate them. The usual petty quarrels over turf that one might expect are not taking place. I'm not sure how long that will last, but these attacks have brought everyone together."

General Dugand watched his chief of staff as he delivered his report. He knew the man was very competent and would be able to coordinate these actions appropriately. Still, he wanted to know more of the details. "These mobile fighting units you're talking about. What are they made up of?"

"When we decided to organize them, there were certain concerns and needs that we had to address. First, and foremost, we needed sufficient fighting ability to overcome and defeat any terrorist group we might encounter. For that purpose, we are employing the VBL light armored vehicle. Depending on the situation, any fighting unit may have one to three of those vehicles. The number depends simply on how large the areas are in any given district and the availability of those vehicles to the units assigned to each district. We have the capability, obviously, of backing one unit up with another if need be."

The colonel paused to ascertain the general's reaction. "Each unit will have transport vehicles to carry infantry men who may need to be deployed. To be safe, we've also assigned to each strike group a medical vehicle. Most of them are carrying medics, but some of the units have a doctor. Also, because the local hospitals are overwhelmed with casualties, we've established several mobile medical units within the city. Each of the mobile fighting units also has assigned to it a group of military policemen who can, if need be, set up a perimeter to keep traffic out of a certain area."

Dugand nodded thoughtfully as he leaned back in his chair, pondering the colonel's plan.

Legere continued. "These units may have an excess of people assigned to them. We will continue to feel out how this works as the day progresses, and, if necessary, make adjustments. Also, each district has at least one mobile fighting force being held in reserve. Therefore, if any unit is ambushed or in need of assistance, this reserve unit can be dispatched immediately."

"Colonel, you say that these units have not engaged any terrorists at this time. When was the last attack on hotels?"

The colonel glanced at some papers on the table in front of him. "It has been at least an hour, sir. That presumes, however, that such an attack has been reported. As you know, when the initial attacks began, the number of reports that flowed in to the police were simply too much to handle. Since then, the government has asked the public to be judicious regarding the frequency with which they make a report, and do so only when necessary. That creates a potential problem, however. There is the possibility that people will not report something worthy because they expect other people to do so, and they are trying to comply with the government's request. I can't say that that will happen, but it would not surprise me."

Dugand leaned back in his chair and stretched his arms over his head. He stood up and walked to the window. There was very little to see below. He turned and looked at the colonel. "Have you ever seen Paris so empty or so quiet?"

"No, but it seems we are in a new world now. We're not fighting an enemy along a front line. Rather, it seems more like Vietnam during the time the United States was there. You are not quite sure where the enemy is. They strike and they run, and if they don't run, they're not afraid to die. I think our people simply are afraid of being at the wrong place at the wrong time. No one wants to be the last person killed during a terrorist attack."

"That's a very interesting perspective, Colonel. It probably does explain the empty streets and lack of activity. That makes our job somewhat easier since we don't have to worry about civilian casualties. Well, please keep me updated. I have more of these damn meetings."

The colonel nodded, turned and walked out of the general's office. Dugand watched him leave and then looked at the various piles of paper on his desk. He picked up the phone and dialed the number.

His secretary answered. "Yes, General?"

"Would you please come into my office and take all of these stacks of paper out of here? You can bring them back when this emergency is over."

Chapter 55

Captain Marcel Forger had arrived in Paris a few hours earlier and was sitting in a large tent that was being used for this briefing. The colonel in charge of his battalion had just concluded his remarks. "Any questions gentlemen?" No one stood to raise a question. "Very well, dismissed."

Captain Forger and the other officers in attendance leapt up and stood at attention. The colonel walked out of the tent and was gone. Captain Forger turned to his best friend, Captain Bovée, who was standing next to him. "That seems relatively straight forward, wouldn't you say?"

"Yes, it is. But as with everything else, it's when you are on the streets that things can get complicated quickly."

"Do you think we'll run into something we can't handle?"

"I don't know, Marcel, but who would've guessed that the terrorists could pull off the type of attack they did today. I sure didn't. You know, I've heard that in some instances, they planned ambushes against first responders. I think we need to keep that in mind."

"Well, I'll tell you one thing; I wouldn't mind running into a group of terrorists and giving them everything the people of France would like to give them. I kind of hope they don't give up. It's time for a little revenge, if you ask me."

"I understand, Marcel. If you run into something that you can't handle, call me."

"There's nothing I won't be able to handle. However, I'll call you to come and see the results of our action."

They shook hands and left the tent, each returning to his own mobile fighting team. When Marcel reached his unit, he called his men together.

"Okay, the colonel's told us what our mission is. This mobile fighting team concept is new but I think it will work out fine. We will be assigned to a certain area in this district, which we will patrol. As you can see, we have three VBLs. These light armored vehicles will be our main strike force. I'll be in the command vehicle behind the VBLs. Following that will come the two trucks with the infantrymen who will be deployed as needed should we run into terrorists. Behind them will be our medical vehicle. The last in the formation will be the military police vehicles."

He looked at the military policeman. "Gentlemen, first of all, it will be your responsibility to provide rear security for our group. The second reason you have been added to this fighting team is that should we encounter terrorists, you may be required to form some kind of perimeter to keep other vehicles out. We don't want any stupid civilians getting killed while we engage the terrorists."

Forger looked at the lieutenant in charge of the military police. "Do you have any questions?"

"We will keep the rear cleared as we patrol. If you are engaged, we will dismount and provide continued rear security until we receive orders to set up a perimeter," responded the leader in a crisp, authoritative voice.

"That's exactly right. Also, if you run into any trouble as we move forward, radio me and I can send a VBL to assist. I'm not convinced we will find any terrorists today; it seems like the attacks have petered out. But I can tell you this, if we find any, we will make them regret the day they ever set foot in France."

Suddenly, his radioman ran up to him and handed him a headset.

"This is Captain Forger."

He listened for several minutes before handing the headset back to the radioman. He turned and faced his command. "We have received orders to move out. As you know, we have an area to patrol. Keep your eyes open and your mouth shut. I don't want any unnecessary radio traffic. Keep any radio reports short and to the point."

He watched as the men returned to their respective vehicles and loaded up. Forger strode to his command vehicle, boot heels clicking on the pavement, and got in. There were four men including him in his vehicle—the driver to his left, his radioman behind him and the machine gunner seated behind the driver.

Forger turned to his radioman and handed him a map. "Here is our assigned route. Radio the instructions for any turn to the lead VBL." The radioman took the map and nodded.

He reached back and asked the radioman for the headset. He spoke into the mouthpiece. "Okay, we're set to move out. My radioman will give you directions for our route. Make sure you keep a minimum of ten yards between each vehicle. Good luck. Let's move out."

Chapter 56

Salah had just finished asking each unit if the men were ready to go. Each had responded in the affirmative. Once again, he walked to the front windows. He had brought binoculars with him. He took them out of the case and raised them to his eyes. He started at the top of the hotel and worked down. He examined each window for any indication that someone was there. He saw nothing.

"Maybe it's true," he thought, "that the Americans have already made their escape." If they had, he would return to Samir, and they would leave the country as quickly as possible. If not, with the help of Allah, he would destroy these enemies of his people.

He looked up and down the street and saw nothing of concern. "All units, attack. Repeat, attack the hotel." With those few words, the battle began.

* * * * *

Ty and Derek had just slipped out onto the roof. Ty went to the wall to cover a rooftop attack. Derek went to the opposite corner to watch for an attack from the other side of the building. He was also at the front of the building and peered over the edge of the wall to look at the street. He saw someone looking down at the street from the building across from the hotel. He ducked back down quickly.

"Ty, there's someone on the roof across the street," Derek said in an urgent, low tone.

Staying low, Ty hurried from his location to the wall facing the street. He whispered, "Let's look at the same time. Whoever has a shot, takes it, okay?"

Derek gave him a thumbs up.

"On the count of three. One, two, three."

They both brought their guns up, ready to fire if someone looked over the wall. No one was there. Ty looked at Derek, shrugging his shoulders as if asking, "What's up?" As Ty turned back toward the building, he saw a man looking at him, eye to eye. The man's rifle was swinging toward him.

Ty dropped back down as fast as he could behind the wall as automatic fire zipped over his head. He heard one individual shot ring out. Then it was quiet. He looked over at Derek, who once again gave him a thumbs up, acknowledging that the student had taken out the terrorist.

"For an old man, Ty, you can move pretty fast," Derek said.

"Listen, asshole, an automatic rifle pointing at you is a good incentive." He took some deep breaths to calm himself down. He realized that if he had been a split-second slower, his life may have ended right then and there.

Suddenly, he heard Derek yell and point in the direction across the roofs. Ty looked in that direction and saw four men jump over a wall onto the roof. They were running slowly toward the next wall, the last one before they reached where Ty was kneeling. Ty looked in the opposite direction and saw no one coming over the roofs. He motioned for Derek to join him. Derek, keeping low, ran to him.

"I'm going to stay in this corner of the building, and I want you to go to the other corner. Get a grenade ready, and when all four of them cross the far wall, we'll each throw one. Get going."

Derek ran to the far corner. Ty took out his grenade from his belt and pulled the pin. He saw that Derek had done the same thing. He brought his head up and looked over the side of the wall. He saw no one. He knew it was only a matter of time before the terrorists would head for the wall he was hiding behind. He could only hope that he and Derek could catch them all in the open with the grenades.

Ty waited for what seemed like a lifetime. All of a sudden, two men leaped over the wall while the other two brought up their weapons to cover them. In short order, they saw both Derek and Ty peering over the wall. All four men seemed to see them at the same time. Suddenly, a firestorm of automatic fire came toward the two Americans. Both Ty and Derek ducked down, and tossed the grenades over the wall.

The explosions seemed deafening. Ty looked over the wall and saw one man writhing on the roof, screaming loudly. The other man was limping slightly and had just jumped back over the wall to safety. Ty raised his weapon and started firing in the direction of the terrorists. He could hear Derek doing the same. Both of them had fired on full automatic. They stopped and reloaded.

The terrorists continued firing, but neither Ty nor Derek had been hit. Both sides quickly saw the futility of continuing to fire while their opponents were hiding behind a solid wall, and soon ceased firing.

The only sound to be heard was the screaming of the man on the roof. Then the screaming stopped.

On the ground, Salah told the men with him to open fire. They fired into the lobby for several seconds. While they had heard the fighting on the roof initially, no other shots came from the hotel. He looked over at the main assault team on the sidewalk and motioned for them to go forward. They stopped when they were approximately seven meters from the hotel.

Mike was in the bedroom watching the street, well back from the window. He had broken the mirror in the bathroom, and had taken a small piece which he set it on the window sill, adjusting its placement until he had a good view of the sidewalk. Mike saw the men starting to move toward the hotel. He turned and looked at Mac, who was standing in the hallway. "Here they come from that direction." He was pointing in the direction from which the previous attack had come.

Mac ran to the stairway, and yelled to me. "Are you ready, DJ? Here they come."

He ran back to the bedroom where Mike was stationed and yelled at him and Jason. "All right, you guys, I want each of you to toss a grenade in that direction. Do it now!"

He saw Mike pull the pin on the grenade. Mike's back was against the wall as he stood near the window. He turned and swung his arm through the window and tossed the grenade. Mac heard two explosions.

Suddenly, automatic fire from across the street slammed into both rooms. He saw that Mike had knelt down by the window, but appeared okay. He ran to the next room and saw Jason was also crouched down. He also appeared fine.

Then Mac entered an empty bedroom and went up to the window. He peered out from the side to see if he could find where the automatic weapon fire was coming from. Suddenly, the firing started up once again. He heard it crash into the rooms where Mike and Jason were. The fire came from across the street through some ground-floor windows.

Mac leaned out and aimed his weapon at those windows. He fired at full automatic until the magazine was empty. Mac expected that would keep their heads down for a while. He glanced down the street where the grenades had been thrown. Two men were lying on the ground while the others still came forward. He took out a grenade, pulled the pin and tossed it out the window. It exploded and he heard the screams that followed.

I was lying on the stairs that led to the breakfast room. As uncomfortable as it was, I had placed myself in that position so I could duck down to avoid any bullets coming through the windows or door. My AK-47 was aimed at the windows closest to where the grenades had exploded. That was, I expected, the direction the attack would come from.

Even though I had yet to fire my weapon or to be in any real danger, I could feel an overwhelming fear in my heart. Except for two armed students in the breakfast room, I was the only one on the ground floor who stood between the students and any terrorists who came through the front of the hotel. If it appeared that I would be overrun, Mac would join me to carry on the fight. Our hope was the grenades I would throw and those thrown from up above would keep the terrorists from entering the lobby.

There seem to be a brief pause in the firing, which previously seemed to have no interruption. From the top of the stairs, I heard Mac's voice.

"What's going on down there?"

"I haven't seen a thing yet. Where are they?"

"They're coming from your left. We've thrown three grenades at them, which I think has hurt some and slowed them down. We're also getting some AK fire from across the street."

"Anything from the roof?"

"Nothing that I know of. I thought I heard some firing up there earlier. "

"Anything from the alley? I've heard nothing."

"Me neither."

Suddenly, I saw two hand grenades come through the window. They rolled to either side of the lobby. "Here they come!"

I ducked down as quickly as I could. After a few seconds that seemed like hours, two explosions rocked the room. I picked up one of my grenades, pulled the pin and threw it through the window. Just as I did that, a man leaped through the window firing his AK-47 in a wide sweeping motion.

Luckily, as he came through the window, the man tripped the booby-trap we had set up. It exploded with a deafening roar and was followed by a high-pitched scream. Within a second or two, the grenade I threw exploded as well.

I looked up over the stairs and saw a man on the floor screaming. He looked at me and I saw the pain in his eyes. He reached for his weapon, which had fallen to his side. I raised my rifle just as he looked at me again. His eyes were filled with anger and hate. He would give me no mercy, of that I was sure. I fired my weapon and saw a small hole appear above his left eye. He didn't move again. I waited for the next person to enter the lobby. But it was strangely quiet and no one appeared.

Mac ran back to the room where Mike was. He could see that Mike was again watching the sidewalk by using the mirror. "What's happening?"

He looked at me. "They've retreated back down the sidewalk."

"Good. Yell at me if they start coming back. Good job, guys."

In the basement of the building across the alley, Jared also had a mirror he was using to see if anybody was coming. "Holy shit, here they come." He uttered the words without the excitement of his previous observation. It was simply a statement of fact.

Rick walked over and looked at the mirror "Three of them. Are you ready? "

"Yes, I am. They're still fifty feet away. Why don't you let Sarah know what's happening." Rick ran upstairs and filled Sarah in; he could see her hands trembling. He ran back downstairs and positioned himself at the second window.

Rick watched as the three men slowly made their way down the alley. It was obvious they could hear the gunfire coming from the hotel; it was equally obvious they were confused by the fact that no door led into the hotel.

The men kept coming until they noticed the garbage container against the wall. One of them walked over to check it, as they had with the cans they passed previously. They did not want to be surprised by someone hiding there. The man opened the top cover and jerked back, dropping the lid. He motioned to one of the other men, who came over, opened the cover and shook his head. Both had seen the bodies of Saad and Wasi. Then the third man noticed the two lower windows, which were covered by cardboard.

Rick heard Jared say, "Now." They both opened fire with their Glocks. Two of the men fell and the third took off running down the alley. Their fire, for the most part, had been accurate. However, in the excitement, no one had fired at the third man.

Rick looked at Jared wide-eyed. "Wow, that was close. How did we miss that guy? Man, he is a fast SOB. He ran like hell."

"I'd run like hell too if somebody was shooting at me. Well, at least he knows that someone is waiting for him." Jared turned and ran up the stairs. He saw Sarah leaning against the wall, holding her hands over her ears. It was easy to tell that she was frightened. "It's okay, we took care of them. Anything new here?"

"The last time I looked, they had not moved. I haven't looked since the shooting started."

Jared stayed in the shadows and looked out the door. The three men were in the same position as they had been previously. He went over to Sarah and placed his arms around her shoulders. "Are you going to be okay?"

Even though she had tears in her eyes, Sarah nodded. "I think so. This is just so scary. Do you know what all that shooting across the alley was about? Are they okay? Not knowing is the worst, I think."

"I have no idea. We just need to be ready should they need to come to this building."

* * * * *

Across the street from the hotel, Salah realized that the initial attack had failed. It was clear that the Americans had been waiting for them. He needed to know what his casualties were. He took out his radio and called his men on the roof. There was no response. He called twice more before he concluded that the men had been killed.

Then Salah called the man in the alley. The man responded immediately. "They were waiting for us. The two others have been killed. I barely made it out alive."

"Do you think you can go back there and take care of them?"

"I doubt it. They were firing through small windows just above the alley itself. If I could get close, I might be able to get a hand grenade through one of the windows. However, given their ability to see me coming down the alley, I doubt I could get close enough."

"Okay, just keep an eye on the alley and if you see anything, call me immediately."

Salah cut the conversation and looked at the group of his men across the street. They had their backs against the wall to make it difficult to get a shot at them.

He again tried calling the men on the roof. The leader answered and Salah asked, "What is your situation?"

"One man is dead and one has minor injuries to his leg. When we went over the wall, someone was waiting for us. They threw two hand grenades."

"Are you able to complete a successful assault on their position?"

"Yes, I think so. We know where they are now. We could start by throwing hand grenades onto their portion of the roof. One of us can remain here and provide cover as the other two complete the assault. We can throw additional hand grenades as necessary. So yes, I think we can do it."

Salah then contacted each group individually again and told them they were going to stand down for about 15 minutes as he prepared the next assault.

Chapter 57

On the roof, Ty was sitting with Derek. They had not heard from anyone else for some time, but all was quiet and no one had fired in a while.

Tapping the younger man on the shoulder, Ty said, "Derek, you think you can handle this for a while? I need to go talk with Mac and DJ."

"Sure, I'm okay with that. But if you hear any firing, please get your ass back up here ASAP."

"Don't worry, I won't let you stay here by yourself if the terrorists attack again. I'll be back in just few minutes." Ty glanced over the wall once again and saw no one there. He hadn't heard anything from them for some time. He ran over to the door, lifted it up and went down the stairs.

When he reached the ground floor, he found Mac and me talking. "Well, guys, what do you think? We were able to hold them off this time. Did anybody get hurt?"

"Mac and I were just talking about that. It looks like we were lucky. Aside from a few scratches, everyone seems to be okay. How are you and Derek?"

"We're good. What is your take on the situation now?"

Mac spoke up first. "When the attack started, two men fired from across the street. Several men were coming along the sidewalk toward the front door. We tossed three grenades at them from above. Just a minute ago, I went down to the kitchen windows and yelled at Jared across the way. He said the three men came down the alley almost to the window. He and Rick fired, killing two. The other man got away. DJ, you tell him what happened down here."

"Not a lot happened at first. I was waiting on the stairs for the terrorists to come through the front door. Most of the action seemed to be upstairs. But a few moments later, a man came in the through the window and set off the booby-trap. Before he climbed in, he threw grenades into the lobby and they went off. Nobody got hurt or anything, but it was an incredible racket. I've never heard so much shooting and so many explosions as I have in the last half hour. I'm still trying to put it all together. How about you, Ty? What happened up there?"

"There were four guys on the roof. Two stayed beyond the far wall, providing cover for the two that came toward us. Derek and I each threw a grenade. Those took out one terrorist and the other one was limping while heading back to his two buddies. After that, not much happened. How are the troops down here holding up?"

I said, my heart still going a million miles a minute, "The girls on each floor of the stairwell are pretty shaken up. They didn't know what was going to happen and obviously were thinking the worst. You know, if they got me and the two students in the breakfast room, they would've gotten all the girls on the stairs and potentially everyone else in the breakfast room. We've got to change that. They came close to breaking through down here. Somehow we have to get more guns around here to allow the people upstairs to escape. The more I think about it, the more it seems that we were stupid in not having this access point better protected."

Mac walked up the stairs to the next floor and asked each girl in the stairwell how she was doing. All four girls responded with shaky voices; it was evident that someone had been crying.

He came back down and told us what he discovered. "I agree with you, DJ, something has to be changed. Maybe we should make our escape now."

Ty shook his head back and forth. "If we head to the building across the alley, we have people in front of us and behind us. We would be stuck there, caught between a rock and a hard place. We just need to restructure our group here. We have the protection of the physical layout of the hotel and the terrorists are out in the open while we're hidden."

Mac was standing near the stairway with his arms crossed. It was easy to see that he believed our decision could mean the difference between living and dying. Both Ty and I could see the stress in his face, the lines in his forehead becoming deeper as he pondered the question.

In his deep voice, he said, "There's no good answer to this question. If we choose wrong, it may be the end of all of us. I'm just not sure how long we can hold out here. We don't know how many men they have or might have coming. Staying here is a huge risk. If we do remain, I think we move the guys from upstairs down here to keep the bad guys from coming through the front. I have already moved the girls from the stairwell down into the breakfast room as well. That would give us a better chance for defending this location. What about you, Ty? We may have to abandon you, and you won't even know it."

"I think Derek and I should pull back to the door that goes to the roof. We can prop it open and have a clear field of fire at anybody coming over the wall. We would also be able to get downstairs if you need assistance. I have the booby-traps set up on the stairs. I just need to arm them. So if we have to leave and come downstairs, that should buy us enough time to get through to the next building. How's that sound to you?"

"I think that makes sense given our situation. DJ?" I nodded my agreement.

"Okay, I'll get my guys down here." Mac turned toward the stairs.

Suddenly, we heard a large explosion in the floor above, followed shortly thereafter by another one.

Mac hurried upstairs, followed by Ty. Ty continued to the top of the stairs. When he reached the door, he propped it open. He saw Derek firing wildly. "Derek! Get over here now!"

Derek looked at him with fear in his eyes. "Get over here now!" Derek set a speed record reaching the door and jumped in and down the stairs.

"Get back up here. We're going to defend the roof from right here."

Derek scrambled up and took a position beside Ty, breathing heavily.

"What happened?" Ty asked.

"I'm not sure. I was looking over the edge of the wall for a second just to make sure no one was coming. All of a sudden, there was firing. I had moved from my old location so the shots weren't even close. I glanced over the wall again, and saw two grenades had been thrown. I hit the ground. One grenade didn't make it over the wall, but the second one did. It was quite a ways away from me though. I wasn't hit."

"Think again. Look at your arm."

There was a dribble of blood coming from Derek's forearm. "I didn't even notice it."

"It's just a scratch. If things settle down, I'll send you down and let Dana look at it. You probably just need some ointment and a Band-Aid."

They had been talking to each other while facing the wall with their rifles at the ready. All of a sudden, two grenades came over the wall. "Duck, Derek." Ty pulled the heavy metal door closed. The explosions rocked the cover.

As soon as both grenades had exploded, Ty opened the door again. Two heads popped up from behind the wall and begin firing wildly. Both Ty and Derek returned fire. There was no evidence that either of them hit their targets. But as soon as they fired, the terrorists ducked back down behind the wall.

"Derek, I'm not sure how much longer we'll be able to sit here. They've seen where we are located. If they have more grenades, we could be in a world of hurt. You keep watching while I arm our booby-traps."

Ty returned a few moments later. "They're all set. When we head downstairs, you must be very careful. Make sure you stay right behind me and step where I step."

"Okay, when do you want to leave?"

"Soon. Let's try to hold them as long as we can."

* * * * *

While Ty and Derek were defending their roof position, Mac had run up the stairs to check on Mike and Jason. In the hallway, he found Mike standing outside of the bedroom he had been in, looking like he was in shock. Mac could smell cordite from the explosion. He glanced in; the room was in shambles, with plaster falling off the walls and debris scattered everywhere.

Mac looked at Mike and pointed toward the room. "Were you in there when it went off?"

"No, I had just gone to talk to Jason for a moment. After I left his room, that's when the explosions took place."

Mac quickly moved to Jason's room and looked in. Jason was crumpled on the floor in a pool of blood. Mac could tell by looking at him that he was dead. He walked over to the body and saw that his head had been split open. The rest of the room was also a mess. He knew that whatever had caused that explosion was something they could not survive. He guessed that it was probably an RPG.

The terrorists across the street were too far away to throw hand grenades and the ones next to the building simply would not have had a good angle to toss in a grenade.

His heart felt heavy with the weight of the responsibility he felt for this young man's death. Mac also knew that he couldn't stand around mourning for Jason because the battle was still on. He walked out into the hallway.

Mike looked up at him. "How's Jason?"

Mac nodded his head back and forth. "Jason didn't survive that. Come on, Mike, we're going downstairs."

As they were heading toward the stairs, Mike stopped and looked at his side, where blood was slowly seeping through his sweat-stained T-shirt. "Oh shit, I was hit."

Mac came over and looked at him. "There's a small entry wound here. You must've been hit by some shrapnel. Let's go downstairs. I want you to go see Dana to see what she can do."

Mike followed Mac down the stairs. While Mac stayed in the lobby, Mike continued down into the breakfast room. He walked up to Dana, and pointed at his side. "They got me. Mac said he thought it was a small piece of shrapnel."

Dana was examining the wound. "Does it hurt?"

"Not too much. What should I do?"

Dana was feeling around the entry wound. She stopped at one location and kept touching it. "I think I can feel something just under the skin. If that's the case, you should be fine. Let me put some antiseptic ointment on it and get it covered. You'll be fine until we find a doctor."

When she finished, she pointed back to the stairs. "You're good to go, Mike."

Mike headed back to the stairs and went up to the lobby. He found Mac and me lying on the stairs facing the front of the hotel. There was a tremendous amount of small arms fire coming into the lobby. It seemed to be coming from across the street. I kept watching it as it tore into the walls.

Mike yelled in my ear. "What do you want me to do now?"

When the firing stopped, I looked at Mike. "I want you to go up one flight of stairs and yell to Ty. Tell him I don't think we can hold this location if there is a concerted rush into the lobby. Tell him he probably should start making his way to the escape point."

Mike took the stairs three at a time. I heard Mike yelling my instructions to Ty. I also heard Ty reply that he understood. Mike returned and I sent him to the kitchen.

Mac ran down the stairs and around the corner to inform the students in the breakfast room to be prepared to exit through the windows. Ducking down, I moved toward the front windows to see if the attack had stopped.

Two men came into view. One was firing an AK-47 toward the hotel, but the other one was lifting an RPG into firing position. I fired as quickly as I could in their direction. No one fell or appeared to be hit by my shots. I ran back to the stairs for cover. I didn't see the RPG fire, but dropped onto the stairs instinctively.

I saw Mac come around the corner and look up at me. "Watch out!" I screamed.

Mac jumped back.

I felt more than heard the impact above me, and the most terrible scream I had ever experienced filled the air. The scream continued unabated. *Was I the one screaming?* And then I felt the pain. It seemed like my back was on fire, but the sharpest and worst pain came from my right leg. I didn't know why, but I was trying to pull myself up the stairs into the lobby. Then I heard more gunfire come from behind me.

Suddenly, Mac charged past me toward the front of the hotel. The automatic fire from his weapon was continuous and loud.

Someone else came pounding down the stairs from above. I heard a male voice yell that I had been hit. And then I did not hear anything.

Mac had hit both men across the street. He could see that one appeared to be dead and the other one was screaming, holding his stomach. Mac took out a grenade and tossed it toward the side of the building he expected the attack to come from. He peeked around the corner and saw several men glued to the wall of our building, as well as an older man running across the street to join them.

Ty ran up to Mac to provide additional fire power. Then, while Ty stood at the front of the lobby, Mac returned and found me conscious. After examining me, Mac went down the hallway, turned into the breakfast room and pointed at Dana.

"Dana, come with me. Hurry!"

She joined him and they both ran to where I lay. Mac tore off my shirt and could see multiple wounds in my back. "How are you doing?"

"My back hurts like hell, but it's not on fire anymore. What's it look like?" I asked through clenched teeth.

"You have a bunch of shrapnel wounds in your back. Can you get up?" I tried to but fell back down screaming. "My leg, my leg! Oh my God, that hurts."

Dana started feeling around my thigh. "Professor, I think you have a broken leg. Maybe in more than one place."

Mac grabbed me by the arm. "We need to get you downstairs."

As he tried to lift me, I screamed one more time. "Don't move me, please, just don't move me."

He set me back down.

"Mac, you have to get these kids out of here and into the other building. There's no way we can survive more RPG fire. You need to escape now."

I gritted my teeth as another wave of pain flowed over me.

"We'll get everyone out of here, including you. Just stay here for a moment. Ty, I'm going downstairs and get the kids moving to the building across the alley. Can you hold the bad guys off for a few more minutes?"

"I think so, but you better hurry. Our time in this building is done."

Mac darted down the stairs and into the breakfast room. "Mike, go up the stairs and stay with DJ. Okay, guys, we need to make our escape now. There is no time to waste!"

Mac ran into the kitchen, pushed the shelving units out of the way and tore off the cardboard. "Derek, I need you in here."

"Professor, they need me up here to help hold off the next attack."

"I don't give a shit. I need you now. Get over here!"

Derek came running into the kitchen.

Mac, voice tight with tension, said, "Prior to the last attack, three terrorists were coming down the alley to cut off our retreat. The guys over there killed two of them. There's one outside and up the alley. It is your job to make sure he does not get in the way as we move everyone to the next building. Do you understand? If you don't do this, we may not leave this building."

"Yeah, I got it," Derek replied.

With that, the young man pulled himself up through the window and into the alley. The garbage bin provided some cover. He looked around the side of the dumpster, but saw nothing. "I don't see anybody. I think we're clear to move."

Mac went back into the breakfast room. "Jackie, come here." She walked quickly to him. He took out a piece of paper from his pocket and handed it to her. "This is very important. We must be sure that we get everybody out and that no one is left behind. Do you understand me?" She nodded at him. "I want you to stay in here and as everybody goes through the windows, I want you to check their name off. This is the list of everyone on this trip. It's critically important for you to be accurate in this. If you don't, we could end up leaving someone behind."

"I understand. Don't worry, Professor, I'll take care of it."

"All right, everybody. Follow me into the kitchen so we can get you moving across the alley." Mac walked into the kitchen, then went up to the window and stood on the chair.

"Jared, can you hear me?" Mac said in a stage whisper. The young man's head popped up in the window and Mac saw him nod.

"We're beginning our escape. Two students are coming out of these windows. When they get to your windows, you and Rick help them down. We need to move very fast. Keep them in the basement. Don't let them go up the stairs yet. Understand?"

"We're ready. Send them over," Jared said, mimicking Mac's tone.

The students were very frightened, which made it difficult to get them through the windows and on their way. The first four made it over successfully before gun shots rang out from the alley. The next two students, who were halfway out the window, jumped back in. A single shot was fired next.

Derek's head appeared in the first window. "It's okay. I got him. You can start sending people over again."

Within five minutes, the only two students remaining in the hotel were Jackie and Mike.

Mac went back up the stairs. "Come on, Mike, you and Jackie are the only two left."

Suddenly, the lobby once again became the target of intense automatic rifle fire.

"Get going! Now!" Mac hollered above the deafening din.

Mike took off at a run, heading for the kitchen. Mac followed them into the kitchen. "Jackie, is everybody accounted for?"

"The only people who haven't left are Mike, Jason, me, and you three professors."

"Jason won't be here. He didn't make it. You guys get out of here now," Mac ordered, then turned to run back up the stairs. As impossible as it seemed, the level of firing had increased. The racket and noise were deafening. Without warning, a grenade exploded on the top floor.

Ty smiled. "I guess they didn't see the tripwire. We have two more set up. "

Mac reached for my shoulders. "Okay, let's get him out."

I knocked his hand away. "There's no time for that. You need to be on your way if you're going to make it at all."

"Bullshit on that. We're all going."

"Mac, I can't walk because of my leg. I'm deadweight, which will only slow you down. Your responsibility now is to these students and getting them to a safe place. If you take me, the chances are all three of us will be killed. Ty, they need you to take out those three men across the street watching our escape route. If you stay here, those kids are going to die. Get going now."

Ty looked at me, and in his eyes, I could see that he knew what I said was true. He took off for the kitchen.

I gritted my teeth and said, "Mac, you have to go. You have to take care of these kids. They are your responsibility now. Give me my rifle and an extra magazine." Mac did so. "Give me one more grenade."

"What do you want that for?"

I looked at him and smiled. "No one is going to cut my head off. Now get out of here before I shoot you myself."

Mac smiled. "I hate it when you're right. Good luck, DJ."

And then I was alone.

Chapter 58

With continuing doubt in his mind, Mac ran down the steps into the breakfast room and through the kitchen. He climbed onto the chair and looked out the window. Derek was still watching the alley. Mac pulled himself out of the window.

"All right, Derek, let's get going. We need to get the students moving."

With how closely they had been working with Derek, the professor-student relationship that existed before had been replaced with something else. They were now comrades in arms.

"What about DJ?" Derek asked.

"It's very difficult for him to move. He thinks he'll just hold us back. He's going to act as a rear guard. We tried to argue with him, but he would hear nothing of it. So, let's get moving."

Mac could see in Derek's eyes that he questioned that decision, but the younger man didn't argue any further. They crossed the alley and slipped into the building. Mac found all the students waiting downstairs, clearly nervous and frightened, but in control of themselves. Mac stopped to give them information.

"I want you to remain down here for a few minutes. As you know, three more terrorists are outside the front of this building. We're going to take care of them and then we'll move to a new location." Mac started for the stairs before Melanie interrupted him.

"Where's DJ?" she asked.

"He's acting as our rear guard in the other building so that we can make our escape."

"But he's badly hurt. How is he going to follow us?"

Mac decided it was time to be honest with them. "I don't have time to argue with you about this. DJ told us to go and make sure all of you were safe. He knows as well as we do that there is no way he can follow us. He has made it very clear to me that your safety comes first. So now let me continue with what he has asked me to do."

The students were silent as Mac and Derek hustled up the stairs and found Ty waiting for them. "What's the situation, Ty?"

"The three men are directly across from the door here. They are all behind one car. It doesn't appear that they have any intention of coming this way. They obviously heard the sounds of shooting and explosions, but they have made no movement of any kind. If you watch for a few minutes, you'll see that they keep checking both the street and this building. I think they are solely there to stop us from escaping. We need to figure out a way to take them out."

"Have you come up with a plan?"

"The only thing I can think of is that we place five of us here by the front door. The first two step out and toss grenades over so they land between the far building and the car. Once the grenades go off, four of us take off toward the car, two on each side. The remaining man fires at the car to keep the men down and act as cover for us. At that point we have four people converging on three. If they weren't killed by the grenades, then we kill them there. As soon as we verify that they are no longer a danger, I think we should move down toward the shop at the end of the street."

He walked over to the side of the window. He pointed the storefront out to Mac.

"Why do you think we should go there, Ty?"

"Because that is as far as we can get from this location without having to expose ourselves to what might be around the corner. Once we get there, we can determine what our next steps will be. If we get into the shop, anyone following us wouldn't know what direction we had taken or where we were."

"That makes sense to me. Let's get organized."

Mac chose Derek to go with him and Mike would go with Ty. Jared would remain in the doorway as the cover man and shooter.

Mac went back down the stairs to get Jared and Mike, bringing them upstairs. He explained to each one of them what the plan was and what their roles would be.

"Are you okay with that?" Mac asked, looking at each young man.

Derek stepped forward. "So how do Mike and I proceed? I mean, are we behind you, to the side or in front? I'm just not clear on how it's going to work."

"You'll be following me as I run toward the side of the car. I'll go past the car a couple of steps so you can be right behind me with a clear shot toward the three men. Just make sure you don't shoot Ty or Mike."

"But that's the problem, Mac. If we're firing at these guys who hopefully are on the ground, some of our shots may simply ricochet off the concrete and hit our guys. It's kind of like setting up an ambush on both sides of the road. What happens is you end up shooting each other. I think this is a tragedy waiting to happen."

"You know, I guess I never really thought this through. Smart thinking, Derek." Mac turned towards Ty. "What do you think?"

"Why take a chance? Why don't Mike and I go to the right side of the car and engage them if need be. You come out toward the car, and like Jared, fire to keep them down. How does that sound?"

Mac looked at Derek and saw him nod. Mac continued, "Okay, let's do it that way." Mac and the others moved as close as they could to the door without exposing themselves.

Mac and Derek would step out and throw the grenades and as soon as the explosives went off, Mike and Ty would head toward the car. "Wait a minute. I see another big problem here. If Derek and I step outside to toss the grenades, the men are going to turn toward us and began firing. It will be a few seconds before the grenades go off. During that time, the men are going to be firing like crazy at the doorway. That may delay your movement toward the car."

Ty nodded. "I understand what you're saying. Do you have any other suggestions?"

"I do. Why don't Derek and I each go over to the shop next to this one. Then we can step out that door to toss the grenades."

Derek stood there, shaking his head. "I don't think we have time to do that. We don't know when the rest of the terrorists will be coming across the alley. Let's just do this as originally planned. After we throw the grenades, we get back. They can shoot all they want until the grenades go off. Once that happens, they're not going to be looking here and the two of you can get going. The problem we have is time. Let's do it now."

Ty looked at Mac. "He's got a point. I think the risk is worth it because of the time concerns we have. Let's just do it." He waited for Mac's reply.

"All right, let's get this thing on the road."

Mac and Derek got to the side of the door, which would be opened. Jared was in position to pull the door back. When they were ready, Mac nodded to Jared and the door flew open. Derek stepped into the doorway, threw his grenade and jumped back. Mac did the same.

Just as Mac ran back into the room, automatic gunfire erupted from behind the car. It seemed to go on for a very long time before both grenades exploded.

As soon as the grenades went off, Mike and Ty started out the door, heading for the right side of the car. Following them, Derek and Mac stepped outside to each side of the door. Jared, per their plan, moved out into the center of the door. The three of them opened fire at the car on full automatic.

The sound of the gunfire was overwhelming. Holes appeared in the side of the car and the windows shattered. It reminded Mac of the movie *Bonnie and Clyde*. Mac, Derek and Jared fired until their magazines were emptied.

Mac saw Ty firing his rifle behind the car. Mac ran to Ty, "What happened?"

Breathing hard, Ty responded, "When I got to the car, two of these scumbags were not moving and the third was wounded. I fired two shots into each of them to make sure they wouldn't be a problem."

Then Ty continued. "Mike and I will head to the end of the street and check out that storefront. Why don't you get the students heading in that direction? We should be ready by the time they get there."

"All right. Get going and we'll be there in a few minutes." Mac watched Ty and Mike run down the street to the location they agreed upon. Then he and Derek hurried back toward where the students were waiting.

When they entered the building, Jared was waiting for them.

Mac said in a tight voice, "Jared, we're going to send the students up here. You point them immediately down the street to where Ty and Mike will be waiting."

Mac pointed out Ty and Mike running down the street. He and Derek then sped down the stairs. "Derek, I want you to wait at the window and be our rear guard. When everybody is out and in the new building, I'll let you know and we'll head down there."

"Okay, Mac, I'll be waiting for your signal."

When Mac reached the students, he had them gather around. "Okay, guys, the coast is clear to our new location. I want each of you to head up the stairs quickly, but don't knock anybody down. When you get upstairs, Jared will show you where to go. Once you get outside this building, I want you to run as fast as you can toward Ty and Mike, who will be waiting for you. Do you all understand?"

The students all nodded.

"Okay, follow me." Mac went up the stairs and stopped. He pointed toward Jared and the students walked in a hurried, but orderly, fashion to where Jared was standing. Jared pointed toward the building down the street.

It took only a few minutes for all the students to be on their way. Mac walked to the doorway and watched the students run down the street. When the last student had entered the shop, Mac walked back to the top of the stairs.

"Derek, let's go."

Derek came running up the stairs.

"Did you see anything across the alley?"

"No, nothing. It was very quiet, in fact," Derek responded.

"Okay, let's go."

Mac and Derek both took off running toward the end of the street. When they arrived, they found Ty and Mike looking through the side window. Mac walked forward to see what they were looking at. "What's up?"

"Mac, I think we should get farther away." Ty was pointing toward the end of the next street, which appeared to open into some kind of plaza. "I think we should head for the plaza. My guess is there would be more options available to us if we go there. There are probably several streets that intersect through the plaza."

"How do you suggest we check that out?"

"Why don't Mike and I go out this window and make our way there? We can do a quick reconnaissance and if it looks like it will work, I'll send Mike back to bring you guys there."

"Okay. But make sure it's safe before we leave. We probably need to do a real thorough check before the students leave this building."

Mac watched the two of them climb through the window and move off at a trot.

Chapter 59

Salah and his five remaining men went down the street away from the hotel. He needed to reassess their position and decide what to do next. There had been no firing of any kind for some time. Neither he nor the others had noticed any movement or indication that the hotel was still occupied. But that was no different than what they had seen when they initially arrived.

After the grenade exploded at the top of the stairs, his men on the roof had radioed him for instructions. He had told them to remain in position until further notice. He also radioed Samir to explain the current situation. Samir informed him that he simply needed to destroy the Americans. He left it up to Salah to determine the best course of action.

Salah finally decided that the only real thing they could do was to continue their coordinated attack. He would have the men on the roof slowly go down the stairs and check each floor to make sure no one was hiding. If they had not found anybody or detected any resistance when they reached the first floor, they would join him for the final attack on the hotel lobby. He gave them their instructions.

He told the men with him that they would slowly work their way back toward the hotel. If they reached it without running into any kind of resistance, they would toss grenades into the hotel lobby. If there was no firing, they would then enter the hotel. He decided to send one of his men across the street to their original location to provide cover fire. Salah chose one of his best marksmen, explained what he wanted him to do, and sent him across the street.

Salah did not like the position he was in. He did not know how many people were waiting in the hotel, nor did he know where they were located. The last thing he had heard from the remaining team member in the alley was that they had been surprised and two of his companions had been killed. He tried to contact the man again, but received no answer. Salah also did not know the status of the men covering any escape points from the building behind the hotel. That did not overly concern him since they had no radios. He was sure they had heard the fighting and would be on the alert for any escape attempt.

He had a queasy feeling in his stomach. This was really not the type of situation they typically encountered. Usually, they struck without warning against people who were unarmed. Now he was facing armed individuals who were just as intent on killing him as he was on killing them. He realized that he was afraid—not so much of dying as of failing to complete this mission successfully. Still, if he died doing Allah's work, he would be rewarded in Paradise.

Salah kept looking toward the hotel's entrance, wondering what was going on in there. If his men were in there, he knew that they too would be afraid. But those Americans who loved life would be afraid of dying. The time was approaching for him to lead his men and take those infidels' lives.

He turned around and faced his remaining men. "In five minutes, we go." He then radioed the men on the roof. "In five minutes, we begin the attack. Get ready."

Salah believed these would be the longest five minutes of his life.

Chapter 60

As they watched Ty and Mike leave, Derek turned to Mac. "How long do you think this will take?"

"Well, if they do it right, it will take several minutes. Why do you ask?"

Derek looked uneasy. "We've got everybody here and safe, except for DJ, and we've heard no firing from the hotel since we left. You know he always said, 'we are in together and out together.' I just think we should go and try to bring him out. If we can't get to him, then we can't. But what if we can? I'm not sure I'll ever forgive myself if we don't try."

Mac pondered that for a few seconds. He felt the same way as Derek, but would that endanger the remaining students? He and DJ were great friends, and he realized, as Derek had, that if he didn't try, he would not forgive himself. "All right. We'll try."

He called everybody together. "Derek and I are going to go back and see if we can get DJ. This is what I want you to do. Jared, you are now in charge. You stay here and figure out a defense for this location. You are not to leave until Ty or Mike returns and directs you to a new location. I want you to have someone watching to see us returning, and station someone to cover our retreat. Rick, you're going to come with us."

Mac saw that Rick was very uneasy with that. "Look, we need you at the window so you can help us get DJ through it. You won't be going into the hotel. If someone other than one of us comes through the hotel window, you can take off running back here. Understand? Can you do it?"

"Yes, I think so." Rick nodded, still uncertain.

"Good. Now, we're going to run down to the building we left. The three of us will go down the stairs to the windows. Derek and I will go out the window and cross the alley. If we hear nothing, we'll drop down into the kitchen and go get DJ. Rick, if you hear firing or anything else, you are not to leave until you see someone other than the three of us coming out the window. There may be people inside who we will need to fight off. If we are lucky, we will just pick up DJ and head back. Let's go."

Mac, Derek and Rick left the building and ran down the street. The door to the building was still open. All three of them ran down the stairs to the back window. Derek went out first. Mac gave Rick a thumbs up. "You know how much we're counting on you?"

"Yes, I do. Don't worry. I will be here."

Mac gave Rick a "good man" clap on the shoulder, then went through the window. Derek was waiting at the window for him. Mac started to go down when Derek grabbed his arm. "Let me go first. If something happens in there, I can get out faster than you can."

"What's the matter? Do you think I'm an old man and can't do the job?"

"I know you're an old man, and you know I should go first," Derek said with a half-grin.

"Well, shit, go ahead. They might as well shoot your ass off rather than mine."

"Okay, Grandpa, I'm on my way."

Mac watched Derek slip through the window and heard him go into the breakfast room. He was back in a few seconds. "Come on down. It looks like it's clear."

Mac worked his way through the window and followed Derek into the breakfast room. They made their way to the stairs and saw me lying where they left me. Mac worked his way up to my side. I did not move as he approached. He placed his hand on my shoulder; when I slowly turned to look at him, relief immediately crossed his face.

"What the hell are you doing here? I told you to get the students to safety," I said in a whisper.

"They're safe," Mac said, reassuring me. "We've already moved them out. Now if you stop acting like an asshole, we'll get you out, too. Has anything happened since we've left?"

"Nothing. If they had rushed in here, I wouldn't have lasted long."

"How are you feeling? Do you think we can move you?" he asked.

"What do you think? I hurt like hell. If I can, I'd rather get the hell out of here." I hadn't finished speaking before we heard the explosion go off up the stairs. "It sounds like they ran into one of Ty's surprises. But it also means they're coming into the hotel. We need to get out of here."

Suddenly, Mac spotted a grenade come through the front window. "Grenade! Duck!"

Derek, who was at the bottom of the stairs, jumped around the corner. Mac fell down next to me. The grenade exploded, rocking the room.

I lifted my head, and aimed my rifle toward the window. A man appeared and jumped through the window frame. He seemed to be older than the terrorists who had attacked the hotel previously. The man had his AK at the ready. I saw the shock on his face when he saw me with my weapon pointed at him. I didn't hesitate. I pulled the trigger and saw the blood explode from his chest. Immediately, the man crashed to the ground, dead.

As he fell, I saw his radio drop from his pocket and land a few feet away. Just then, the two grenades Mac had thrown through the window exploded. I heard shrill screams coming from outside.

The radio came to life. Arabic poured forth.

"*Salah, what is happening?*"

I looked at Mac when the radio crackled once again.

"*Salah, this is Samir. Have you destroyed the Americans?*"

While neither Mac nor I understood what had been said, the meaning seemed clear.

"Mac, give me that radio," I instructed my friend.

Mac gave me a funny look but jumped up, grabbed the radio and gave it to me. I spoke into the device. "Samir, you sonofabitch, I just killed Salah. I just wanted you to know what the situation was, asshole."

I threw the radio back toward Salah's body.

Mac started laughing and shook his head. "Well, I guess you told him what was going on, but now, I think we need to get going."

The rifle fire had died away.

Mac threw another grenade through the window and we waited for it to explode. He then jumped up and threw another grenade up the stairs where the man from the roof would be.

Then Mac hollered, "Derek, get over here! Pick DJ up and let's get the hell out of here!"

Derek turned me over onto my back, which brought forth my muffled scream.

"Oh, my God, that hurts. Please be careful. Oh, God," I moaned.

Derek then headed downstairs to the window that led to the alley. It was then that Mac noticed the large pool of blood that had been under my legs. He waited a moment to let Derek get me below.

I vaguely heard Mac fire a long burst toward where the terrorist had entered the room. He took out another grenade, and tossed it out the window, hoping it would keep anyone else out there away for a while.

Then Mac ran down to the kitchen window, where Derek and I were waiting for him. "Derek, I'll go out the window and you hand him up to me."

"Okay, once out, you drag him over to the other window. I'll fire some more rounds up the stairs to keep them back."

With a grunt, Derek lifted me up and through the window. Mac grabbed my shoulders and pulled me the rest of the way out. As they did this, I screamed and passed out.

* * * * *

I later learned that Mac dragged my limp body across the alley and helped Rick maneuver me through the window on the opposite side.

Mac ran back to the window and shouted, "Derek, come on! Now let's get out of here!" He heard Derek fire one last time. Derek ran toward the window, threw his rifle out and followed it. Both of them crossed the alley and dropped in through the opposite window in seconds.

I vaguely remember lying on the ground, drifting in and out of consciousness.

Rick stared down and through the agony, I heard him say in a hushed tone, "Look at his leg. Oh, my God, look at his leg."

Mac could see the bone had pierced the skin and blood was pumping out slowly, but surely.

"No time to worry about that now. We need to get him and our asses out of here. Derek, can you carry him?" Mac said urgently.

"Yes, just lift him up so I can get in position."

With some effort, Rick and Mac pulled me from the floor and hoisted me onto Derek's shoulder, fireman-style.

"I've got him. Let's go."

The three of them reached the top of the stairs and made it to the door. Mac grabbed Rick by the shoulder. "You lead the way, and I'll bring up the rear."

Rick bolted out the door and ran at full speed down the street. Derek followed him as fast as he could carrying my unconscious body.

As Mac left the doorway, he could see Jared kneeling and holding his rifle to cover them. A few moments later, they were back with the students.

As gently as he could, Derek laid me on the floor. "Dana, we need you over here."

The excruciating pain brought me to the surface again.

Dana came over and bent down beside me, examining my leg. She got up, ran into the bathroom and found a towel. With smooth motions, she began to wrap the towel around my leg. Then, to slow the bleeding, she tightened a leather belt to serve as a tourniquet. I did everything I could to keep from screaming.

Using some of her supplies, she then taped the towel as tightly as she could. She looked at Mac. "That's about all I can do. He needs a doctor quickly."

Mac motioned Jared over. "Have you heard anything from Ty or Mike?"

"Nothing since they left."

"Keep watch at the door. Let me know if you see anybody coming." Mac knew that I needed to get to a doctor as quickly as possible. I was woozy from loss of blood, and was sure that Dana's makeshift bandage was already turning red.

However, Mac knew if he left this relatively safe location and tried to follow Ty, he could put all the students in danger. Until he heard from Ty, they had to wait where they were.

Chapter 61

Ty and Mike worked their way slowly down the street toward the plaza. They peered through the windows of each of the shops fronting the street. Still, no one was visible. It felt like Paris had no population at all.

When they reached the end of the block, Ty motioned for Mike to stay pressed against the wall of the building. Ty then slowly made his way to the end of the building and looked around. What he saw was a small plaza. In its center was a statue of some long-forgotten individual. There was a small grassy area with benches around the edge. It was a perfect place for Parisians to come and enjoy an afternoon. Three streets converged on this plaza, the one on which Ty and Mike had come and two others, forming a Y.

Ty signaled for Mike to follow him. "We're going to check all the buildings around this Plaza. What I mean by that, is we're just simply going to look into the windows to see if we can see anything. If there isn't anything, we'll select one to hide out in. So follow me, but stay a few feet behind."

Ty led the way and they slowly made their way from shop to shop. As they reached the first leg of the Y, Ty signaled for them to stop.

He peered around the corner at the building down the street. Like the others, it was devoid of people or any activity at all. The two men quickly crossed the street and continued their inspection of the buildings. Again, each appeared to be empty of occupants.

When they reached the second leg of the Y, after cautiously glancing around the corner, Ty jerked back immediately. "Holy shit! Where did they get that kind of armor?"

It dawned on Ty that what he had actually seen was the tricolor of France flying from one of the vehicles. He handed his weapon to Mike. "Stay here while I check this out. I think we've run into a French patrol. If it doesn't go my way, run like hell and get out of here."

Ty took a deep breath and stepped around the corner with his hands raised in the air. He immediately saw a machine gun point at him. "Please don't shoot. I'm an American." He saw a man on the armored vehicle speak into his radio.

A man in uniform approached him from further back in the convoy. The man had a pistol drawn and pointed at Ty's chest. "Who are you and what are you doing here?"

Ty found his mouth dry and it was difficult to speak. "My name is Tyler Smith and I'm an American professor. Man, am I glad to see you. There are three of us professors and our students. We were attacked in our hotel by terrorists. We've been fighting them as best as we could and are now trying to escape. Thank God you're here."

The man did not lower his weapon. "If that's the case, where is everyone else?" he asked in accented, but excellent English.

Ty pointed in the direction from which had come. "Down that street."

"Explain to me what has happened," the man requested.

Ty gave the man a quick rundown of what they had been through. He explained how the fight began and how they ended up where they were. He also informed him about the casualties.

The man lowered his weapon and extended out his hand. "My name is Captain Marcel Forger. I command this unit. You're safe with us. Give me a moment to get our team organized and we will go get your friends."

Using his radio, he called the commanders of the three light armored vehicles and the infantry together. Forger instructed the lead VBL commander to mount three infantryman to accompany him. He would lead the way down the street to the place where the Americans were. The other two VBL commanders were also to mount three infantryman for support.

One VBL was directed to go down the alley and cut off any escaping terrorists. The third VBL was to make its way to the street fronting the hotel and to take care of any remaining terrorists. The infantry commander would take his remaining men and attack through the building from which the students had escaped. They would clear that building and proceed through the alley to clear the hotel.

Ty, who had retrieved Mike, walked up to the captain. "Can we ride your armored vehicle back to where the students are?"

"Yes, but you must get off at that location before they run into any terrorists."

With a roar, all three VBLs headed toward their assigned locations. Captain Forger followed the first VBL in his command vehicle. Ty and Mike dismounted when they reached the building. Captain Forger's vehicle also stopped at that location.

Mac had been looking out the window and saw the vehicles approach. Ty and Mike were on the first vehicle and knew things were getting better quickly. Mac walked outside and walked up to the captain.

Ty stood beside the captain. "Mac, this is Captain Forger. He is in command of this unit."

"Captain, am I glad to see you!"

"I'm glad that we are able to assist you. What do you need?"

"First of all, we have a man who needs to get to the hospital immediately. Following that, we would like to be taken somewhere safe."

"Take me to your injured man." Ty led the captain and his radioman into the building. They walked over to where I lay, still drifting in and out of consciousness.

Forger took one look at me and instructed his radioman to order the medical unit forward. Within minutes, the medics arrived. Two men carrying medical bags walked in and bent down over me. They did a cursory examination. They also removed the towel from around my leg. The medic looked up at the captain and spoke quickly in French.

Forger translated. "My medic agrees with you that this man needs to be taken to a hospital immediately. We're going to make arrangements for him and the rest of you to go to our field hospital. Because most of the French hospitals in Paris have been over-whelmed, the Army has set up field hospitals throughout the city."

The medics left the room and returned a few moments later with a stretcher. As gently as they could, they lifted me onto the stretcher, raised it on its wheels, and rolled me to their vehicle.

Captain Forger looked around at the remaining students. "Is anyone else hurt or injured?" He saw two hands go up. "You go with them in their vehicle. Your friends will be following you shortly."

Then Forger walked outside and watched the injured being loaded into the medical vehicle. The military police had followed the ambulance to this location. The captain ordered the MPs out of their vehicle and directed the remaining students to get in.

By then, the first VBL had returned. Its commander informed Forger that he had observed no terrorists. He also stated that the infantry men had cleared the building and were continuing on to the hotel.

The captain then ordered the VBL commander to lead the ambulance and the vehicles carrying the students to the field hospital. With that, they took off.

Forger heard some firing coming from the direction of the hotel. He got back into his command vehicle and headed for the alley. Once there, he could see the second VBL parked near what he thought was the back of the hotel. He radioed the commander of that VBL and requested a report of the situation. The commander informed him that the infantry had passed through his location into the hotel, but that he had not seen any terrorists. The commander further stated that no firing was going on, within or outside the hotel. The captain directed him to stay in his location and block any escape by the terrorists.

Captain Forger then headed to the street fronting the hotel. The firing had ceased. He drove down to the hotel, where he found the infantry commander who said his men had entered the hotel through the basement and came up the stairs to the ground floor. They found several terrorists there and a brief fight broke out. They had forced the terrorists back out onto the street, where the VBL had killed them. He also said two of his men had minor injuries.

Captain Forger then asked the infantry commander if all the bodies he saw here had been killed by his unit. The man responded in the negative. He said that many of these men have been dead for some time. Furthermore, he told the captain that whoever had fought these terrorists had put up an incredible battle. As he looked around at the devastation, Forger realized just how hard these Americans had fought for their lives. When he got back to the hospital, he wanted to hear the whole story from the American professors.

Chapter 62

Mac and Ty were seated outside the field hospital where they had been for nearly two hours while I was in surgery. However, no other information had been given to them. Ty was adamant that I would be fine, because, in his words, people didn't die from a broken leg. As the two friends talked about what had occurred that day, a French doctor approached them.

"Gentlemen, are you the two men awaiting word on the man we had in surgery?" The doctor spoke in low tones in good English.

"Yes. Please tell us how he is doing?"

"Only time will give us the answer to that question. When he was brought here, he had already lost a tremendous amount of blood. The loss of blood was caused by an artery in his leg that had been nicked by some shrapnel. We gave him several transfusions, repaired the artery and also fixed his fracture. We've also removed all the shrapnel from his back. Our biggest concern, once again, is the loss of blood. We're not sure if he has had a stroke or some other damage to his brain. We will be able to tell that once he comes out of the anesthetic he was given."

"Can we see him?"

"I prefer not. He will not come out of the anesthetic until early tomorrow morning. We will monitor him carefully throughout the night. Please return at 7 a.m. and we'll know more then."

"Thank you, Doctor, for your help. We'll be back tomorrow morning."

Somewhat relieved that I had made it through the surgery, Mac and Ty went back to where the students were staying in a series of Army tents that had been erected not far from the field hospital. The two professors provided them with an update on DJ's condition.

The doctor returned to the recovery room and looked at the man lying on the bed. He had been told about the Americans' battle with the terrorists. The doctor only hoped that his work on this man would be enough to have him survive. He looked at the man's eyes and saw the eyelids twitch. He wondered what was going on in there.

* * * * *

It was very dark; I could see nothing at all. Just barely, I could make out just a pinprick of light far away. I went toward it and the light slowly got larger. There was something in the light, an image of some kind. I kept walking toward the light, wondering what was at the end.

I saw the angel. She was dressed in white and seemed to be beckoning me toward her. I've never seen anything as beautiful as my angel. I knew I was in the right place. But then, slowly, everything went dark again.

* * * * *

Mac and Ty arrived at the hospital early the next morning. They asked to see the doctor and he soon appeared.

Ty spoke first. "How's he doing, doctor?"

"I can't tell you yet. He should have recovered from the anesthetic an hour ago. However, there's no indication that he is aware of what's going on. I'm afraid all we can do is wait."

Mac looked at Ty and shook his head, afraid of the news they were going to learn. "Doctor, can we go see him?"

"I don't see any reason why not. Follow me and I will take you to his room."

The doctor led them down the walkway of the large tent and into a small room. DJ lay there on his back. His arms were at his sides and they could see the IV lines that ran into his veins.

Mac and Ty walked over to the bed and looked at their friend. He seemed to be peaceful as he lay there. The doctor stood at the foot of the bed. Neither of them liked the look on the doctor's face as he observed DJ. The doctor left and they sat down on the folding chairs that had been brought in.

* * * * *

It was still dark, but the light I had seen previously was coming toward me again. It was still very small. I continued walking toward it. It was so bright and welcoming. The image was starting to form once again, and again I saw my angel. She seemed to beckon me toward her, and I felt great peace as I approached her. Her face was shining effervescently. Again, I'd never seen such beauty before. And then, as before, she faded away.

* * * * *

Mac stood up and walked toward the bed. "Ty, come here; I just saw his eyes move. He's in there, I know."

Ty joined Mac by the bed but could see nothing. Mac went and got the nurse. She stood at the foot of DJ's bed and watched him for a few moments, but she saw nothing either.

Suddenly, my eyes opened and I muttered, "My angel."

Mac looked at the nurse and pointed toward me. "What's that all about?"

The nurse smiled sweetly. "I have that effect on some of my patients. I think your friend is going to be fine. He just needs to sleep a little more. Why don't you come back in a couple of hours?"

Mac smiled at Ty. "Well, I'll be damned. We're all worried about how he's doing and he's thinking about that nurse. If that's so, he will never hear the end of this!"

Relief buoying their steps, the two men went to get some coffee and breakfast. When they returned, I was sitting up in my bed.

"Hey, guys, how are you doing?"

Mac just stared. "You seem to be much better since we left a couple hours ago."

"Yeah, I woke up feeling pretty good. I'm still a little groggy and my leg still hurts like hell, but they gave me some pain medicine that takes care of that. You know, they have some really nice people working here."

"We know that. Especially that angel of yours."

"What the hell are you talking about?"

"Ty, look at him. He's denying any knowledge of his angel." Mac leaned over me and looked me straight in the eye. "That angel of yours, you know, the nurse who just left here."

"Oh, you mean Bridget. Yes, she's great. Takes great care of me."

"Ty, you see what I mean. He really is an asshole."

Ty started laughing.

"I don't understand what you mean. What did I do to you?"

"You mean other than being an asshole? We'll explain later."

The doctor walked in the room and came to my bedside. "Well, I see you're doing much better. How are you feeling?"

"Pretty good. However, there's something wrong with these two guys. I suggest you check them out. I think the stress has gotten to them."

Puzzled, the doctor look at Mac and Ty. "Gentlemen, you're not feeling well?"

Ty answered first. "Listen, Doc, we left here this morning still worried about him. We get back here and he is sitting up, eating and enjoying your nurses. We promise you, his time will come."

The doctor started laughing. "Well it's better than other things that happen in this hospital." The doctor walked out of the room, still shaking his head at all of us.

I looked at Mac. "How are the students doing? Was anyone else hurt? Where are they staying?"

"No, no one else got hurt; they're all doing fine. They're worried about you, but when we go back, we will tell them you're doing fine."

"How long I've been here? Have you made any arrangements to get them back home?"

"No, that's actually being handled by the university. They initially made arrangements for the students to fly out today. But the students refused. They said we all came in together and we all go out together. Needless to say, the university wasn't too happy with them. Depending on when they're going to release you from the hospital, we'll all be heading home. Do you have any idea when that will happen?"

"Well I told them I don't mind staying for a while; I mean, the staff is very nice."

"Listen to me, asshole," Mac growled. "You don't want to go there."

I started laughing, but had to stop. "Don't make me laugh, it hurts." The shrapnel wounds on my back tugged and pulled.

"You deserve it and if you give us any more shit, I will start tickling you."

"Let me tell you. The doctor told me I could leave tomorrow if I needed to. I may need some help along the way, however," I lifted up the sheet to show my leg, which was encased in a full-length cast.

Ty walked over to the bed, and took out a pen. On the cast he wrote "Get well soon, dumb shit." We all started laughing at that.

"I think we should tell the university to get us out of here on the day after tomorrow," I said.

"Works for me," Mac said with a grin.

They left with promises to return the next day.

Chapter 63

On the day we were to return home, Ty and Mac showed up at the hospital at about 8 a.m. They told me that our plane was scheduled to depart from Charles de Gaulle airport at noon. The hospital had been informed and was ready to release me once Mac and Ty arrived.

The day before, they had brought me clothes that had survived the hotel attack. Today, I was dressed in tan slacks and a polo shirt. The nurse had cut the seam on one of the legs of my pants so that my cast would fit. It looked a little silly, but I didn't really care. I was just looking forward to going home.

The nurse brought a wheelchair to assist me outside the field hospital tent. She wheeled me to where a bus was waiting to take our group to the airport. We all said our goodbyes to the nurses and doctors who had helped us.

Captain Forger also showed up to say goodbye. He filled us in on what happened at the hotel after we left. We were saddened to learn from him that Randy and Becky's bodies had been discovered among the wounded and dead in the streets. He told us that there had been no progress in trying to find out who was behind the attacks in Paris. The name, Samir, had not been connected to any terrorist group. He also indicated that it would take years for Paris to recover. Forger shook each of our hands. As we drove away, he waved goodbye.

The drive to the airport took a little longer than it normally would have because of the crowded roadways. Upon arriving, we were met by security officials, who told us we were not going to have to go through the normal security procedures. They took us directly to the gate after we dropped off our luggage. We thanked them for their assistance and they left us there waiting to board.

An airline official approached us and asked us to wait until all the other passengers were on board. It seemed unusual but we really didn't mind. When our time came, we had our tickets checked and walked down the jetway to the plane.

As the first student entered the plane, the flight attendant asked her to wait. When it was clear that our students were not moving forward, Mac went up to see what was wrong. He approached the flight attendant. "Miss, do we have a problem?"

"No, sir, the pilot is merely going to make an announcement. We're just waiting for everybody to be seated."

At that point, the pilot's voice came over the intercom. "Ladies and gentlemen, this is your pilot speaking. You've all heard about the American university students who were involved in a desperate fight with the terrorists a few days ago. Well, those students and their professors are on our flight today and I wanted to acknowledge them to you. They will be entering the airplane at this time."

The flight attendant stepped back to let our group board the plane. As the students entered, the other passengers began to clap. When Mac, Ty and I entered the plane, the flight attendant stopped us. "Gentlemen, the airline would like to offer you first-class seats in recognition of what you've done."

Mac had a big smile on his face.

Ty just said, "Nice."

The thought of having some extra room for my leg was very appealing. However, I looked at Ty and Mac. "Yes, we appreciate that, but we all came in together and we're going out together. I would like to have a seat near my students."

Both Ty and Mac smiled their agreement. The flight attendant nodded and showed us to our seats.

The flight to Philadelphia did not seem to take as long as it normally did. I presume that it was because we were all just excited to get home. When we arrived at the airport, we exited the plane and waited for the whole group to gather.

A customs official met us as we deplaned. He indicated that he was going to be helping us through customs. As soon as they got me seated in a wheelchair, we headed toward customs. As the other passengers walked to the normal custom stations, the official led us through the VIP entryway. Once we retrieved our luggage, we were met by an official from the university. Red-carpet treatment is pretty wonderful!

"Welcome home. The president of the university has arranged for a private plane to bring you home. Follow me and we will be on our way."

It took about a half hour for the group to reach the private plane that awaited us. We all boarded and waited for it to take off.

Mac was sitting next to me. "Well, do you think they're going to fire us?"

"I'm sure we'll find out soon enough. But for now, let's just enjoy the flight."

We landed at the small airport in our hometown. As we left the plane and walked into the airport—or in my case, was wheeled—we were surprised not to see anyone we knew. There was some grumbling from the students. The president of the university walked out and shook our hands. "We have transportation ready for you. "

I didn't understand what was going on. "Where are we going?"

"Don't worry, you will see."

With that, we stowed our luggage, boarded the bus—again, this took me a bit longer than those with two functional legs—and it left the airport. We drove toward the university. The bus drove down the ramp to the basketball arena. We exited the bus and I found another wheelchair waiting for me.

The president walked over to me. "My assistant, Jeff, will bring you along shortly." He walked into the arena. As we waited there, the students and profs looked at each other with questions on our faces. Then Jeff asked us to follow him and walked toward the arena floor.

With a booming voice and a bit of feedback from the microphone, the president began to speak. "Ladies and gentlemen, thank you for coming to join us in this happy time. Our students have returned."

He was interrupted with applause and cheers. "Let me introduce you to the people who have represented us so well. He began reading each student's name, and Jeff guided the young men and women individually toward and onto the stage.

As each name was read, the applause became louder. When all the students were standing on the stage, the president continued. "And now, let me introduce to you the professors who kept our students safe."

Ty's name was read first, then Mac's, then mine.

As I came on the stage, I saw that it was occupied by more than just our students. I was surprise to see the governor and other officials. The president introduced the governor, who came to the podium. He spoke briefly but I really don't remember what he said.

Then the governor turned toward me and asked me to come forward and say a few words. He handed me a microphone as I sat in my wheelchair. I looked out at the crowd and saw the parents of our students sitting in the first row. The arena was nearly full.

I took a deep breath. "Ladies and gentlemen, we are surprised and pleased that you have come to see us. As you can imagine, this has been a trying and difficult time for all of us. I don't want to keep our students from greeting their families and friends. However, I do want to say a few things to you.

"First, we must never forget the three students who did not come home to share this moment with us. Our hearts and prayers go out to their families. Our biggest regret is that they are not here with us today." The arena was silent, and I could see tissues being removed from purses and pockets to wipe away tears.

"Second, these students, your children, have acted with incredible bravery. I'm not sure if I have ever seen such selfless behavior in their support of their fellow students. They are the future of our country, and I think—no, I know—our country is in fine hands. I am so proud of them and you should be also. I want to thank them for all they did to stand up for our country and each other in the face of such incredible odds." Applause rang through the arena.

"And finally, I want to thank my incredible colleagues for their bravery, their skill and their dedication in keeping your children safe."

I turned to face our students. "I think now is the time for you to go see your families." The students rose as one and ran down the stairs to the waiting arms of their families and friends. As I watched them embrace their loved ones, tears started to roll down my face. I couldn't help it.

Our job was now finished. I returned to where Mac and Ty were seated. They, too, had tears in their eyes.

Epilogue

My wife and I arrived at Mac's home at about 3 o'clock that afternoon. Mac greeted us at the door and led us into his family room. Ty and his wife were already seated. Ty had a beer in his hand and his wife had a glass of wine. Mac turned to me. "You want a beer or some wine?"

"Beer sounds good to me." Mac's wife had already handed my wife a glass of Merlot.

"Hey, guys, why don't we go out to the back porch?" Ty and I followed him out the door and we were soon seated on some rustic furniture looking over the valley. Our wives remained in the kitchen preparing dinner. It probably would take an hour or so, which meant we had some time to catch up.

It had been two months since we returned from Paris. Ty's and my classes would begin in a month. Mac, against our entreaties, had gone into blissful retirement. We discussed what we were teaching and whether we were ready. We had talked about what had occurred in Paris previously and felt no need to go over it again. We were simply three friends enjoying each other's company and looking forward to a meal with our wives.

Suddenly, my cell phone rang. I took it out of my pocket and looked at the screen. I didn't recognize the number and wasn't going to answer it.

Mac piped up. "Go ahead, DJ, we have plenty of time tonight."

I punched the answer key on my phone. "Hello?"

"Professor?"

I looked at Ty and Mac, raised my hand in a questioning fashion.

Mac signaled that I should put the phone on speaker, which I did. "Who's this?"

"Samir."

"Who?"

"You killed many of my men in Paris and my best friend, Salah. I just wanted to let you know that I'm coming for all of you now."

Acknowledgments

Many people are involved in the development and completion of a book such as this.

First, I want to thank Ron Flud and Dan Swanson for their thoughts and insights into police operations and the reactions of police officers. Their review and comments about Mac and Ty brought these characters to life.

Several individuals reviewed this manuscript and provided helpful advice in the development of the final product. Those individuals include Sharyl Admire, Beverly Flud, Madelyn Swanson, Doug Bennett, and Scott Wyatt. Pivotal to a good book are great editors. I had two of the best in Aimee Uchman and Katie Groves.

I also want to thank Ryan Allen of Big R Design for the exciting book cover he created.

Thanks to Sandi Lunt for the wonderful photographs.

I want to extend my gratitude to Kira Henschel and HenschelHAUS Publishing, Inc. for believing in this book and bringing it to you.

About the Author

Dave Admire received his law degree from the Catholic University of America. In his early career, he was both a prosecutor and defense attorney. At the age of 33, he was elected District Court Judge in the Seattle area. He served in this position for over 22 years. During his time on the bench, he developed a reputation for being creative and innovative in searching out alternatives to incarceration.

After retiring as a judge, Dave continued his work with young people by becoming a college professor. Before retiring, he was an adjunct professor at Seattle University for twenty years. He was chair of the Criminal Justice Department at Bethany College in Kansas. Subsequently, he became department chair of the Department of Political Science and Criminal Justice at Southern Utah University in Cedar City, Utah. In the summer of 2010, Dave served as a visiting professional at the International Criminal Court in The Hague, the Netherlands.

Dave is a well-known speaker at both national and international conferences. He has lectured at Oxford and Cambridge universities in England, Cergy Pontoise in France, and at Victoria University in New Zealand. Dave has also spoken at conferences in Bermuda and New Zealand. In the United States, he has spoken at conferences across the country.

For more information and to contact the author, please visit Dave's website, www.daveadmire.com.

Dave resides with his wife, Sharyl, in Cedar City, Utah, where he is working on his second novel, a sequel to *Terror in Paris*, entitled *Samir's Revenge—Terror in the United States*.